IN THE TOWN OF HAWKINS HOLLOW, IT'S CALLED THE SEVEN.

Every seven years, on the seventh day of the seventh month, strange things happen. It began when three young boys—Caleb, Fox, and Gage—went on a camping trip to the Pagan Stone. And twenty-one years later, it will end in a showdown between evil and the boys who have become men—and the women who love them…

FIRST IN A NEW TRILOGY FROM THE #1 *NEW YORK TIMES* BESTSELLING AUTHOR

It had been the Pagan Stone for hundreds of years, long before three boys stood around it and spilled their blood in a bond of brotherhood, unwittingly releasing a force bent on destruction . . .

Every seven years, there comes a week in July when the locals do unspeakable things—and then don't seem to remember them. The collective madness has made itself known beyond the town borders and has given Hawkins Hollow the reputation of a village possessed.

This modern-day legend draws reporter and author Quinn Black to Hawkins Hollow with the hope of making the eerie happening the subject of her new book. It is only February, but Caleb Hawkins, descendent of the town founders, has already seen and felt the stirrings of evil. Though he can never forget the beginning of the terror in the woods twenty-one years ago, the signs have never been this strong before. Cal will need the help of his best friends, Fox and Gage, but surprisingly he must rely on Quinn as well. She, too, can see the evil that the locals cannot, somehow connecting her to the town—and to Cal. As winter turns to spring, Cal and Quinn will shed their inhibitions, surrendering to a growing desire. They will form the cornerstone of a group of men and women bound by fate, passion, and the fight against what is to come from out of the darkness . . .

Turn the page for a complete list of titles by Nora Roberts and J. D. Robb from The Berkley Publishing Group . . .

Nora Roberts & J. D. Robb

REMEMBER WHEN

Nora Roberts

HOT ICE
SACRED SINS
BRAZEN VIRTUE
SWEET REVENGE
PUBLIC SECRETS
GENUINE LIES
CARNAL INNOCENCE
DIVINE EVIL
HONEST ILLUSIONS
PRIVATE SCANDALS
HIDDEN RICHES
TRUE BETRAYALS
MONTANA SKY
SANCTUARY
HOMEPORT
THE REEF
RIVER'S END
CAROLINA MOON
THE VILLA
MIDNIGHT BAYOU
THREE FATES
BIRTHRIGHT
NORTHERN LIGHTS
BLUE SMOKE
ANGELS FALL
HIGH NOON

Series

Born In Trilogy

BORN IN FIRE
BORN IN ICE
BORN IN SHAME

Dream Trilogy

DARING TO DREAM
HOLDING THE DREAM
FINDING THE DREAM

Chesapeake Bay Saga

SEA SWEPT
RISING TIDES
INNER HARBOR
CHESAPEAKE BLUE

Gallaghers of Ardmore Trilogy

JEWELS OF THE SUN
TEARS OF THE MOON
HEART OF THE SEA

Three Sisters Island Trilogy

DANCE UPON THE AIR
HEAVEN AND EARTH
FACE THE FIRE

Key Trilogy

KEY OF LIGHT
KEY OF KNOWLEDGE
KEY OF VALOR

In the Garden Trilogy

BLUE DAHLIA
BLACK ROSE
RED LILY

Circle Trilogy

MORRIGAN'S CROSS
DANCE OF THE GODS
VALLEY OF SILENCE

Sign of Seven Trilogy

BLOOD BROTHERS

Anthologies

FROM THE HEART
A LITTLE MAGIC
A LITTLE FATE

MOON SHADOWS
(with Jill Gregory, Ruth Ryan Langan, and Marianne Willman)

The Once Upon Series
(with Jill Gregory, Ruth Ryan Langan, and Marianne Willman)

ONCE UPON A CASTLE
ONCE UPON A STAR
ONCE UPON A DREAM
ONCE UPON A ROSE
ONCE UPON A KISS
ONCE UPON A MIDNIGHT

J. D. Robb

NAKED IN DEATH
GLORY IN DEATH
IMMORTAL IN DEATH
RAPTURE IN DEATH
CEREMONY IN DEATH
VENGEANCE IN DEATH
HOLIDAY IN DEATH
CONSPIRACY IN DEATH
LOYALTY IN DEATH
WITNESS IN DEATH
JUDGMENT IN DEATH
BETRAYAL IN DEATH
SEDUCTION IN DEATH
REUNION IN DEATH
PURITY IN DEATH
PORTRAIT IN DEATH
IMITATION IN DEATH
DIVIDED IN DEATH
VISIONS IN DEATH
SURVIVOR IN DEATH
ORIGIN IN DEATH
MEMORY IN DEATH
BORN IN DEATH
INNOCENT IN DEATH
CREATION IN DEATH

Anthologies

SILENT NIGHT
(with Susan Plunkett, Dee Holmes, and Claire Cross)

OUT OF THIS WORLD
(with Laurell K. Hamilton, Susan Krinard, and Maggie Shayne)

BUMP IN THE NIGHT
(with Mary Blayney, Ruth Ryan Langan, and Mary Kay McComas)

DEAD OF NIGHT
(with Mary Blayney, Ruth Ryan Langan, and Mary Kay McComas)

Also available . . .

THE OFFICIAL NORA ROBERTS COMPANION
(edited by Denise Little and Laura Hayden)

NORA ROBERTS

BLOOD BROTHERS

JOVE BOOKS, NEW YORK

THE BERKLEY PUBLISHING GROUP
Published by the Penguin Group
Penguin Group (USA) Inc.
375 Hudson Street, New York, New York 10014, USA
Penguin Group (Canada), 90 Eglinton Avenue East, Suite 700, Toronto, Ontario M4P 2Y3, Canada
(a division of Pearson Penguin Canada Inc.)
Penguin Books Ltd., 80 Strand, London WC2R 0RL, England
Penguin Group Ireland, 25 St. Stephen's Green, Dublin 2, Ireland (a division of Penguin Books Ltd.)
Penguin Group (Australia), 250 Camberwell Road, Camberwell, Victoria 3124, Australia
(a division of Pearson Australia Group Pty. Ltd.)
Penguin Books India Pvt. Ltd., 11 Community Centre, Panchsheel Park, New Delhi—110 017, India
Penguin Group (NZ), 67 Apollo Drive, Rosedale, North Shore 0632, New Zealand
(a division of Pearson New Zealand Ltd.)
Penguin Books (South Africa) (Pty.) Ltd., 24 Sturdee Avenue, Rosebank, Johannesburg 2196,
South Africa

Penguin Books Ltd., Registered Offices: 80 Strand, London WC2R 0RL, England

BLOOD BROTHERS

A Jove Book / published by arrangement with the author

PRINTING HISTORY
Jove mass-market edition / December 2007

ISBN: 978-0-515-14380-5

JOVE®
Jove Books are published by The Berkley Publishing Group,
a division of Penguin Group (USA) Inc.,
375 Hudson Street, New York, New York 10014.
JOVE® is a registered trademark of Penguin Group (USA) Inc.
The "J" design is a trademark belonging to Penguin Group (USA) Inc.

PRINTED IN THE UNITED STATES OF AMERICA

10 9 8 7 6 5 4 3 2

To my boys,
who roamed the woods,
even when they weren't supposed to.

Where God hath a temple,
the Devil will have a chapel.

—ROBERT BURTON

The childhood shows the man
As morning shows the day.

—JOHN MILTON

Prologue

Hawkins Hollow
Maryland Province
1652

IT CRAWLED ALONG THE AIR THAT HUNG HEAVY as wet wool over the glade. Through the snakes of fog that slid silent over the ground, its hate crept. It came for him through the heat-smothered night.

It wanted his death.

So he waited as it pushed its way through the woods, its torch raised toward the empty sky, as it waded across the streams, around the thickets where small animals huddled in fear of the scent it bore with it.

Hellsmoke.

He had sent Ann and the lives she carried in her womb away, to safety. She had not wept, he thought now as he sprinkled the herbs he'd selected over water. Not his Ann. But he had seen the grief on her face, in the deep, dark eyes he had loved through this lifetime, and all the others before.

The three would be born from her, raised by her, and taught by her. And from them, when the time came, there would be three more.

What power he had would be theirs, these sons, who

would loose their first cries long, long after this night's work was done. To leave them what tools they would need, the weapons they would wield, he risked all he had, all he was.

His legacy to them was in blood, in heart, in vision.

In this last hour he would do all he could to provide them with what was needed to carry the burden, to remain true, to see their destiny.

His voice was strong and clear as he called to wind and water, to earth and fire. In the hearth the flames snapped. In the bowl the water trembled.

He laid the bloodstone on the cloth. Its deep green was generously spotted with red. He had treasured this stone, as had those who'd come before him. He had honored it. And now he poured power into it as one would pour water into a cup.

So his body shook and sweat and weakened as light hovered in a halo around the stone.

"For you now," he murmured, "sons of sons. Three parts of one. In faith, in hope, in truth. One light, united, to strike back dark. And here, my vow. I will not rest until destiny is met."

With the athame, he scored his palm so his blood fell onto the stone, into the water, and into the flame.

"Blood of my blood. Here I will hold until you come for me, until you loose what must be loosed again on the world. May the gods keep you."

For a moment there was grief. Even through his purpose, there was grief. Not for his life, as the sands of it were dripping down the glass. He had no fear of death. No fear of what he would soon embrace that was not death. But he grieved that he would never lay his lips on Ann's again in this life. He would not see his children born, nor the children of his children. He grieved that he would not be able to stop the suffering to come, as he had been unable to stop the suffering that had come before, in so many other lifetimes.

He understood that he was not the instrument, but only the vessel to be filled and emptied at the needs of the gods.

So, weary from the work, saddened by the loss, he stood outside the little hut, beside the great stone, to meet his fate.

It came in the body of a man, but that was a shell. As his own body was a shell. It called itself Lazarus Twisse, an elder of "the godly." He and those who followed had settled in the wilderness of this province when they broke with the Puritans of New England.

He studied them now in their torchlight, these men and the one who was not a man. These, he thought, who had come to the New World for religious freedom, and then persecuted and destroyed any who did not follow their single, narrow path.

"You are Giles Dent."

"I am," he said, "in this time and this place."

Lazarus Twisse stepped forward. He wore the unrelieved formal black of an elder. His high-crowned, wide-brimmed hat shadowed his face. But Giles could see his eyes, and in his eyes, he saw the demon.

"Giles Dent, you and the female known as Ann Hawkins have been accused and found guilty of witchcraft and demonic practices."

"Who accuses?"

"Bring the girl forward!" Lazarus ordered.

They pulled her, a man on each arm. She was a slight girl, barely six and ten by Giles's calculation. Her face was wax white with fear, her eyes drenched with it. Her hair had been shorn.

"Hester Deale, is this the witch who seduced you?"

"He and the one he calls wife laid hands on me." She spoke as if in a trance. "They performed ungodly acts upon my body. They came to my window as ravens, flew into my room in the night. They stilled my throat so I could not speak or call for help."

"Child," Giles said gently, "what has been done to you?"

Those fear-swamped eyes stared through him. "They called to Satan as their god, and cut the throat of a cock in sacrifice. And drank its blood. They forced its blood on me. I could not stop them."

"Hester Deale, do you renounce Satan?"

"I do renounce him."

"Hester Deale, do you renounce Giles Dent and the woman Ann Hawkins as witches and heretics?"

"I do." Tears spilled down her cheeks. "I do renounce them, and pray to God to save me. Pray to God to forgive me."

"He will," Giles whispered. "You are not to blame."

"Where is the woman Ann Hawkins?" Lazarus demanded, and Giles turned his clear gray eyes to him.

"You will not find her."

"Stand aside. I will enter this house of the devil."

"You will not find her," Giles repeated. For a moment he looked beyond Lazarus to the men and the handful of women who stood in his glade.

He saw death in their eyes, and more, the hunger for it. This was the demon's power, and his work.

Only in Hester's did Giles see fear or sorrow. So he used what he had to give, pushed his mind toward hers. *Run!*

He saw her jolt, stumble back, then he turned to Lazarus.

"We know each other, you and I. Dispatch them, release them, and it will be between us alone."

For an instant he saw the gleam of red in Lazarus's eyes. "You are done. Burn the witch!" he shouted. "Burn the devil house and all within it!"

They came with torches, and with clubs. Giles felt the blows rain on him, and the fury of the hate that was the demon's sharpest weapon.

They drove him to his knees, and the wood of the hut began to flame and smoke. Screams rang in his head, the madness of them.

With the last of his power he reached out toward the demon inside the man, with red rimming its dark eyes as it fed on the hate, the fear, the violence. He felt it gloat, he felt it *rising*, so sure of its victory, and the feast to follow.

And he ripped it to him, through the smoking air. He heard it scream in fury and pain as the flames bit into flesh. And he held it to him, close as a lover as the fire consumed them.

And with that union the fire burst, spread, destroyed every living thing in the glade.

It burned for a day and a night, like the belly of hell.

One

Hawkins Hollow
Maryland
July 6, 1987

INSIDE THE PRETTY KITCHEN OF THE PRETTY house on Pleasant Avenue, Caleb Hawkins struggled not to squirm as his mother packed her version of campout provisions.

In his mother's world, ten-year-old boys required fresh fruit, homemade oatmeal cookies (they weren't so bad), half a dozen hard-boiled eggs, a bag of Ritz crackers made into sandwiches with Jif peanut butter for filling, some celery and carrot sticks (yuck!), and hearty ham-and-cheese sandwiches.

Then there was the thermos of lemonade, the stack of paper napkins, and the two boxes of Pop-Tarts she wedged into the basket for breakfast.

"Mom, we're not going to *starve* to death," he complained as she stood deliberating in front of an open cupboard. "We're going to be right in Fox's backyard."

Which was a lie, and kinda hurt his tongue. But she'd never let him go if he told her the truth. And, sheesh, he was ten. Or would be the very next day.

Frannie Hawkins put her hands on her hips. She was a pert, attractive blonde with summer blue eyes and a stylish curly perm. She was the mother of three, and Cal was her baby and only boy. "Now, let me check that backpack."

"Mom!"

"Honey, I just want to be sure you didn't forget anything." Ruthless in her own sunny way, Frannie unzipped Cal's navy blue pack. "Change of underwear, clean shirt, socks, good, good, shorts, toothbrush. Cal, where are the Band-Aids I told you to put in, and the Bactine, the bug repellant."

"Sheesh, we're not going to Africa."

"All the same," Frannie said, and did her signature finger wave to send him along to gather up the supplies. While he did, she slipped a card out of her pocket and tucked it into the pack.

He'd been born—after eight hours and twelve minutes of vicious labor—at one minute past midnight. Every year she stepped up to his bed at twelve, watched him sleep for that minute, then kissed him on the cheek.

Now he'd be ten, and she wouldn't be able to perform the ritual. Because it made her eyes sting, she turned away to wipe at her spotless counter as she heard his tromping footsteps.

"I got it all, okay?"

Smiling brightly, she turned back. "Okay." She stepped over to rub a hand over his short, soft hair. He'd been her towheaded baby boy, she mused, but his hair was darkening, and she suspected it would be a light brown eventually.

Just as hers would be without the aid of Born Blonde.

In a habitual gesture, Frannie tapped his dark-framed glasses back up his nose. "You make sure you thank Miss Barry and Mr. O'Dell when you get there."

"I will."

"*And* when you leave to come home tomorrow."

"Yes, ma'am."

She took his face in her hands, looked through the thick lenses into eyes the same color as his father's calm gray ones. “Behave,” she said and kissed his cheek. “Have fun.” Then the other. “Happy birthday, my baby.”

Usually it mortified him to be called her *baby*, but for some reason, just then, it made him feel sort of gooey and good.

“Thanks, Mom.”

He shrugged on the backpack, then hefted the loaded picnic basket. How the hell was he going to ride all the way out to Hawkins Wood with half the darn grocery store on his bike?

The guys were going to razz him something fierce.

Since he was stuck, he carted it into the garage where his bike hung tidily—by Mom decree—on a rack on the wall. Thinking it through, he borrowed two of his father’s bungee cords and secured the picnic basket to the wire basket of his bike.

Then he hopped on his bike and pedaled down the short drive.

FOX FINISHED WEEDING HIS SECTION OF THE vegetable garden before hefting the spray his mother mixed up weekly to discourage the deer and rabbits from invading for an all-you-can-eat buffet. The garlic, raw egg, and cayenne pepper combination stank so bad he held his breath as he squirted it on the rows of snap beans and limas, the potato greens, the carrot and radish tops.

He stepped back, took a clear breath, and studied his work. His mother was pretty damn strict about the gardening. It was all about respecting the earth, harmonizing with Nature, and that stuff.

It was also, Fox knew, about eating, and making enough food and money to feed a family of six—and whoever dropped by. Which was why his dad and his older sister, Sage, were down at their stand selling fresh eggs, goat’s milk, honey, and his mother’s homemade jams.

He glanced over to where his younger brother, Ridge,

was stretched out between the rows playing with the weeds instead of yanking them. And because his mother was inside putting their baby sister, Sparrow, down for her nap, he was on Ridge duty.

"Come on, Ridge, pull the stupid things. I wanna go."

Ridge lifted his face, turned his I'm-dreaming eyes on his brother. "Why can't I go with you?"

"Because you're eight and you can't even weed the dumb tomatoes." Annoyed, Fox stepped over the rows to Ridge's section and, crouching, began to yank.

"Can, too."

As Fox hoped, the insult had Ridge weeding with a vengeance. Fox straightened, rubbed his hands on his jeans. He was a tall boy with a skinny build, a mass of bark brown hair worn in a waving tangle around a sharp-boned face. His eyes were tawny and reflected his satisfaction now as he trooped over for the sprayer.

He dumped it beside Ridge. "Don't forget to spray this shit."

He crossed the yard, circling what was left—three short walls and part of a chimney—of the old stone hut on the edge of the vegetable garden. It was buried, as his mother liked it best, in honeysuckle and wild morning glory.

He skirted past the chicken coop and the cluckers that were pecking around, by the goat yard where the two nannies stood slack-hipped and bored, edged around his mother's herb garden. He headed toward the kitchen door of the house his parents had mostly built. The kitchen was big, and the counters loaded with projects—canning jars, lids, tubs of candle wax, bowls of wicks.

He knew most of the people in and around the Hollow thought of his family as the weird hippies. It didn't bother him. For the most part they got along, and people were happy to buy their eggs and produce, his mother's needlework and handmade candles and crafts, or hire his dad to build stuff.

Fox washed up at the sink before rooting through the

cupboards, poking in the big pantry searching for *something* that wasn't health food.

Fat chance.

He'd bike over to the market—the one right outside of town just in case—and use some of his savings to buy Little Debbies and Nutter Butters.

His mother came in, tossing her long brown braid off the shoulder bared by her cotton sundress. "Finished?"

"I am. Ridge is almost."

Joanne walked to the window, her hand automatically lifting to brush down Fox's hair, staying to rest on his neck as she studied her young son.

"There's some carob brownies and some veggie dogs, if you want to take any."

"Ah." Barf. "No, thanks. I'm good."

He knew that she knew he'd be chowing down on meat products and refined sugar. And he knew she knew he knew. But she wouldn't rag him about it. Choices were big with Mom.

"Have a good time."

"I will."

"Fox?" She stood where she was, by the sink with the light coming in the window and haloing her hair. "Happy birthday."

"Thanks, Mom." And with Little Debbies on his mind, he bolted out to grab his bike and start the adventure.

THE OLD MAN WAS STILL SLEEPING WHEN GAGE shoved some supplies into his pack. Gage could hear the snoring through the thin, crappy walls of the cramped, crappy apartment over the Bowl-a-Rama. The old man worked there cleaning the floors, the johns, and whatever else Cal's father found for him to do.

He might've been a day shy of his tenth birthday, but Gage knew why Mr. Hawkins kept the old man on, why they had the apartment rent-free with the old man supposedly being the maintenance guy for the building. Mr. Hawkins felt sorry for them—and mostly sorry for Gage because he was stuck as the motherless son of a mean drunk.

Other people felt sorry for him, too, and that put Gage's back up. Not Mr. Hawkins though. He never let the pity show. And whenever Gage did any chores for the bowling alley, Mr. Hawkins paid him in cash, on the side. And with a conspirator's wink.

He knew, hell, everybody knew, that Bill Turner knocked his kid around from time to time. But Mr. Hawkins was the *only* one who'd ever sat down with Gage and asked *him* what he wanted. Did he want the cops, Social Services, did he want to come stay with him and his family for a while?

He hadn't wanted the cops or the do-gooders. They only made it worse. And though he'd have given anything to live in that nice house with people who lived decent lives, he'd only asked if Mr. Hawkins would please, please, not fire his old man.

He got knocked around less whenever Mr. Hawkins kept his father busy and employed. Unless, of course, good old Bill went on a toot and decided to whale in.

If Mr. Hawkins knew how bad it could get during those times, he would call the cops.

So he didn't tell, and he learned to be very good at hiding beatings like the one he'd taken the night before.

Gage moved carefully as he snagged three cold ones out of his father's beer supply. The welts on his back and butt were still raw and angry and they stung like fire. He'd expected the beating. He always got one around his birthday. He always got another one around the date of his mother's death.

Those were the big, traditional two. Other times, the whippings came as a surprise. But mostly, when the old man was working steady, the hits were just a careless cuff or shove.

He didn't bother to be quiet when he turned toward his

father's bedroom. Nothing short of a raid by the A-Team would wake Bill Turner when he was in a drunken sleep.

The room stank of beer sweat and stale smoke, causing Gage to wrinkle his handsome face. He took the half pack of Marlboros off the dresser. The old man wouldn't remember if he'd had any, so no problem there.

Without a qualm, he opened his father's wallet and helped himself to three singles and a five.

He looked at his father as he stuffed the bills in his pocket. Bill sprawled on the bed, stripped down to his boxers, his mouth open as the snores pumped out.

The belt he'd used on his son the night before lay on the floor along with dirty shirts, socks, jeans.

For a moment, just a moment, it rippled through Gage with a kind of mad glee—the image of himself picking up that belt, swinging it high, laying it snapping hard over his father's bare, sagging belly.

See how you like it.

But there on the table with its overflowing ashtray, the empty bottle, was the picture of Gage's mother, smiling out.

People said he looked like her—the dark hair, the hazy green eyes, the strong mouth. It had embarrassed him once, being compared to a woman. But lately, since everything but that one photograph was so faded in his head, when he couldn't hear her voice in his head or remember how she'd smelled, it steadied him.

He looked like his mother.

Sometimes he imagined the man who drank himself into a stupor most nights wasn't his father.

His father was smart and brave and sort of reckless.

And then he'd look at the old man and know that was all bullshit.

He shot the old bastard the finger as he left the room. He had to carry his backpack. No way he could put it on with the welts riding his back.

He took the outside steps down, went around the back where he chained up his thirdhand bike.

Despite the pain, he grinned as he got on.

For the next twenty-four hours, he was free.

THEY'D AGREED TO MEET ON THE WEST EDGE OF town where the woods crept toward the curve of the road. The middle-class boy, the hippie kid, and the drunk's son.

They shared the same birthday, July seventh. Cal had let out his first shocked cry in the delivery room of Washington County Hospital while his mother panted and his father wept. Fox had shoved his way into the world and into his laughing father's waiting hands in the bedroom of the odd little farmhouse while Bob Dylan sang "Lay, Lady, Lay" on the record player, and lavender-scented candles burned. And Gage had struggled out of his terrified mother in an ambulance racing up Maryland Route 65.

Now, Gage arrived first, sliding off his bike to walk it into the trees where nobody cruising the road could spot it, or him.

Then he sat on the ground and lit his first cigarette of the afternoon. They always made him a little sick to his stomach, but the defiant act of lighting up made up for the queasiness.

He sat and smoked in the shady woods, and imagined himself on a mountain path in Colorado or in a steamy South American jungle.

Anywhere but here.

He'd taken his third puff, and his first cautious inhale, when he heard the bumps of tires over dirt and rock.

Fox pushed through the trees on Lightning, his bike so named because Fox's father had painted lightning bolts on the bars.

His dad was cool that way.

"Hey, Turner."

"O'Dell." Gage held out the cigarette.

They both knew Fox took it only because to do otherwise made him a dweeb. So he took a quick drag, passed it back. Gage nodded to the bag tied to Lightning's handlebars. "What'd you get?"

"Little Debbies, Nutter Butters, some TastyKake pies. Apple and cherry."

"Righteous. I got three cans of Bud for tonight."

Fox's eyes didn't pop out of his head, but they were close. "No shit?"

"No shit. Old man was trashed. He'll never know the difference. I got something else, too. Last month's *Penthouse* magazine."

"No way."

"He keeps them buried under a bunch of crap in the bathroom."

"Lemme see."

"Later. With the beer."

They both looked over as Cal dragged his bike down the rough path. "Hey, jerkwad," Fox greeted him.

"Hey, dickheads."

That said with the affection of brothers, they walked their bikes deeper into the trees, then off the narrow path.

Once the bikes were deemed secure, supplies were untied and divvied up.

"Jesus, Hawkins, what'd your mom put in here?"

"You won't complain when you're eating it." Cal's arms were already protesting the weight as he scowled at Gage. "Why don't you put your pack on, and give me a hand?"

"Because I'm carrying it." But he flipped the top on the basket and after hooting at the Tupperware, shoved a couple of the containers into his pack. "Put something in yours, O'Dell, or it'll take us all day just to get to Hester's Pool."

"Shit." Fox pulled out a thermos, wedged it in his pack. "Light enough now, Sally?"

"Screw you. I got the basket and my pack."

"I got the supplies from the market and my pack." Fox pulled his prized possession from his bike. "You carry the boom box, Turner."

Gage shrugged, took the radio. "Then I pick the tunes."

"No rap," Cal and Fox said together, but Gage only grinned as he walked and tuned until he found some Run-DMC.

With a lot of bitching and moaning, they started the hike.

The leaves, thick and green, cut the sun's glare and summer heat. Through the thick poplars and towering oaks, slices and dabs of milky blue sky peeked. They aimed for the wind of the creek while the rapper and Aerosmith urged them to walk this way.

"Gage has a *Penthouse*," Fox announced. "The skin magazine, numbnut," he said at Cal's blank stare.

"Uh-uh."

"Uh-huh. Come on, Turner, break it out."

"Not until we're camped and pop the beer."

"Beer!" Instinctively, Cal sent a look over his shoulder, just in case his mother had magically appeared. "You got beer?"

"Three cans of suds," Gage confirmed, strutting. "Smokes, too."

"Is this far-out or what?" Fox gave Cal a punch in the arm. "It's the best birthday ever."

"Ever," Cal agreed, secretly terrified. Beer, cigarettes, and pictures of naked women. If his mother ever found out, he'd be grounded until he was thirty. That didn't even count the fact he'd lied. Or that he was hiking his way through Hawkins Wood to camp out at the expressly forbidden Pagan Stone.

He'd be grounded until he died of old age.

"Stop worrying." Gage shifted his pack from one arm to the other, with a wicked glint of what-the-hell in his eyes. "It's all cool."

"I'm not worried." Still, Cal jolted when a fat jay zoomed out of the trees and let out an irritated call.

Two

HESTER'S POOL WAS ALSO FORBIDDEN IN CAL'S world, which was only one of the reasons it was irresistible.

The scoop of brown water, fed by the winding Antietam Creek and hidden in the thick woods, was supposed to be haunted by some weird Pilgrim girl who'd drowned in it way back whenever.

He'd heard his mother talk about a boy who'd drowned there when she'd been a kid, which in Mom Logic was the number one reason Cal was *never allowed* to swim there. The kid's ghost was supposed to be there, too, lurking under the water, just waiting to grab another kid's ankle and drag him down to the bottom so he'd have somebody to hang out with.

Cal had swum there twice that summer, giddy with fear and excitement. And both times he'd *sworn* he'd felt bony fingers brush over his ankle.

A dense army of cattails trooped along the edges, and around the slippery bank grew bunches of the wild orange lilies his mother liked. Fans of ferns climbed up the rocky slope, along with brambles of wild berries, which when ripe would stain the fingers a kind of reddish purple that looked a little like blood.

The last time they'd come, he'd seen a black snake slither its way up the slope, barely stirring the ferns.

Fox let out a shout, dumped his pack. In seconds he'd dragged off his shoes, his shirt, his jeans and was sailing over the water in a cannonball without a thought for snakes or ghosts or whatever else might be under that murky brown surface.

"Come on, you pussies!" After a slick surface dive, Fox bobbed around the pool like a seal.

Cal sat, untied his Converse All Stars, carefully tucked his socks inside them. While Fox continued to whoop and splash, he glanced over where Gage simply stood looking out over the water.

"You going in?"

"I dunno."

Cal pulled off his shirt, folded it out of habit. "It's on the agenda. We can't cross it off unless we all do it."

"Yeah, yeah." But Gage only stood as Cal stripped down to his Fruit of the Looms.

"We have to all go in, dare the gods and stuff."

With a shrug, Gage toed off his shoes. "Go on, what are you, a homo? Want to watch me take my clothes off?"

"Gross." And slipping his glasses inside his left shoe, Cal sucked in breath, gave thanks his vision blurred, and jumped.

The water was a quick, cold shock.

Fox immediately spewed water in his face, fully blinding him, then stroked off toward the cattails before retaliation. Just when he'd managed to clear his myopic eyes, Gage jumped in and blinded him all over again.

"Sheesh, you guys!"

Gage's choppy dog paddle worked up the water, so Cal swam clear of the storm. Of the three, he was the best swimmer. Fox was fast, but he ran out of steam. And Gage, well, Gage sort of attacked the water like he was in a fight with it.

Cal worried—even as part of him thrilled at the idea—that he'd one day have to use the lifesaving techniques his dad had taught him in their aboveground pool to save Gage from drowning.

He was picturing it, and how Gage and Fox would stare at him with gratitude and admiration, when a hand grabbed his ankle and yanked him underwater.

Even though he *knew* it was Fox who pulled him down, Cal's heart slammed into his throat as the water closed over his head. He floundered, forgetting all his training in that first instant of panic. Even as he managed to kick off the hold on his ankle and gather himself to push to the surface, he saw a movement to the left.

It—she—seemed to glide through the water toward him. Her hair streamed back from her white face, and her eyes were cave black. As her hand reached out, Cal opened his mouth to scream. Gulping in water, he clawed his way to the surface.

He could hear laughter all around him, tinny and echoing like the music out of the old transistor radio his father sometimes used. With terror biting inside his throat, he slapped and clawed his way to the edge of the pool.

"I saw her, I saw her, in the water, I saw her." He choked out the words while fighting to climb out.

She was coming for him, fast as a shark in his mind, and in his mind he saw her mouth open, and the teeth gleam sharp as knives.

"Get out! Get out of the water!" Panting, he crawled through the slippery weeds and rolling, saw his friends treading water. "She's in the water." He almost sobbed it, bellying over to fumble his glasses out of his shoe. "I *saw* her. Get out. Hurry up!"

"Oooh, the ghost! Help me, help me!" With a mock gurgle, Fox sank underwater.

Cal lurched to his feet, balled his hands into fists at his

sides. Fury tangled with terror to have his voice lashing through the still summer air. "Get the fuck out."

The grin on Gage's face faded. Eyes narrowed on Cal, he gripped Fox by the arm when Fox surfaced laughing.

"We're getting out."

"Come *on*. He's just being spaz because I dunked him."

"He's not bullshitting."

The tone got through, or when he bothered to look, the expression on Cal's face tripped a chord. Fox shot off toward the edge, spooked enough to send a couple of wary looks over his shoulder.

Gage followed, a careless dog paddle that made Cal think he was daring something to happen.

When his friends hauled themselves out, Cal sank back down to the ground. Drawing his knees up, he pressed his forehead to them and began to shake.

"Man." Dripping in his underwear, Fox shifted from foot to foot. "I just gave you a tug, and you freak out. We were just fooling around."

"I saw her."

Crouching, Fox shoved his sopping hair back from his face. "Dude, you can't see squat without those Coke bottles."

"Shut up, O'Dell." Gage squatted down. "What did you see, Cal?"

"*Her*. She had all this hair swimming around her, and her eyes, oh man, her eyes were black like the shark in *Jaws*. She had this long dress on, long sleeves and all, and she reached out like she was going to grab me—"

"With her bony fingers," Fox put in, falling well short of his target of disdain.

"They weren't bony." Cal lifted his head now, and behind the lenses his eyes were fierce and frightened. "I thought they would be, but she looked, all of her, looked just . . . real. Not like a ghost or a skeleton. Oh man, oh God, I saw her. I'm not making it up."

"Well Jee-sus." Fox crab-walked another foot away

from the pond, then cursed breathlessly when he tore his forearm on berry thorns. "Shit, now I'm bleeding." Fox yanked a handful of weedy grass, swiped at the blood seeping from the scratches.

"Don't even think about it." Cal saw the way Gage was studying the water—that thoughtful, wonder-what'll-happen gleam in his eye. "Nobody's going in there. You don't swim well enough to try it anyway."

"How come you're the only one who saw her?"

"I don't know and I don't care. I just want to get away from here."

Cal leaped up, grabbed his pants. Before he could wiggle into them, he saw Gage from behind. "Holy cow. Your back is messed up bad."

"The old man got wasted last night. It's no big deal."

"Dude." Fox walked around to get a look. "That's gotta hurt."

"The water cooled it off."

"I've got my first aid kit—" Cal began, but Gage cut him off.

"I said no big deal." He grabbed his shirt, pulled it on. "If you two don't have the balls to go back in and see what happens, we might as well move on."

"I don't have the balls," Cal said in such a deadpan, Gage snorted out a laugh.

"Then put your pants on so I don't have to wonder what that is hanging between your legs."

Fox broke out the Little Debbies, and one of the six-pack of Coke he'd bought at the market. Because the incident in the pond and the welts on Gage's back were too important, they didn't speak of them. Instead, hair still dripping, they resumed the hike, gobbling snack cakes and sharing a can of warm soda.

But with Bon Jovi claiming they were halfway there, Cal thought of what he'd seen. Why had he been the only one? How had her face been so clear in the murky water, and with his glasses tucked in his shoe? How could he have seen her? With every step he took away from the pond, it was easier to convince himself he'd just imagined it.

Not that he'd ever, *ever* admit that maybe he'd just freaked out.

The heat dried his damp skin and brought on the sweat. It made him wonder how Gage could stand having his shirt clinging to his sore back. Because, man, those marks were all red and bumpy, and really had to hurt. He'd seen Gage after Old Man Turner had gone after him before, and it hadn't ever, ever been as bad as this. He wished Gage had let him put some salve on his back.

What if it got infected? What if he got blood poisoning, got all delirious or something when they were all the way to the Pagan Stone?

He'd have to send Fox for help, yeah, that's what he'd do—send Fox for help while he stayed with Gage and treated the wounds, got him to drink something so he didn't—what was it?—dehydrate.

Of course, all their butts would be in the sling when his dad had to come get them, but Gage would get better.

Maybe they'd put Gage's father in jail. Then what would happen? Would Gage have to go to an orphanage?

It was almost as scary to think about as the woman in the pond.

They stopped to rest, then sat in the shade to share one of Gage's stolen Marlboros. They always made Cal dizzy, but it was kind of nice to sit there in the trees with the water sliding over rocks behind them and a bunch of crazy birds calling out to each other.

"We could camp right here," Cal said half to himself.

"No way." Fox punched his shoulder. "We're turning ten at the Pagan Stone. No changing the plan. We'll be there in under an hour. Right, Gage?"

Gage stared up through the trees. "Yeah. We'd be moving faster if you guys hadn't brought so much shit with you."

"Didn't see you turn down a Little Debbie," Fox reminded him.

"Nobody turns down Little Debbies. Well . . ." He crushed out the cigarette, then planted a rock over the butt. "Saddle up, troops."

Nobody came here. Cal knew it wasn't true, knew when deer was in season these woods were hunted.

But it *felt* like nobody came here. The two other times he'd been talked into hiking all the way to the Pagan Stone he'd felt exactly the same. And both those times they'd started out early in the morning instead of afternoon. They'd been back out before two.

Now, according to his Timex, it was nearly four. Despite the snack cake, his stomach wanted to rumble. He wanted to stop again, to dig into what his mother had packed in the stupid basket.

But Gage was pushing on, anxious to get to the Pagan Stone.

The earth in the clearing had a scorched look about it, as if a fire had blown through the trees there and turned them all to ash. It was almost a perfect circle, ringed by oaks and locus and the bramble of wild berries. In its center was a single rock that jutted two feet out of the burned earth and flattened at the top like a small table.

Some said altar.

People, when they spoke of it at all, said the Pagan Stone was just a big rock that pushed out of the ground. Ground so colored because of minerals, or an underground stream, or maybe caves.

But others, who were usually more happy to talk about it, pointed to the original settlement of Hawkins Hollow and the night thirteen people met their doom, burned alive in that very clearing.

Witchcraft, some said, and others devil worship.

Another theory was that an inhospitable band of Indians had killed them, then burned the bodies.

But whatever the theory, the pale gray stone rose out of the soot-colored earth like a monument.

"We made it!" Fox dumped his pack and his bag to dash forward and do a dancing run around the rock. "Is this cool? Is this cool? Nobody knows where we are. And we've got *all* night to do anything we want."

"Anything we want in the middle of the woods," Cal added. Without a TV, or a refrigerator.

Fox threw back his head and let out a shout that echoed away. "See that? Nobody can hear us. We could be attacked by mutants or ninjas or space aliens, and nobody would hear us."

That, Cal realized, didn't make his stomach feel any steadier. "We need to get wood for a campfire."

"The Boy Scout's right," Gage decided. "You guys find some wood. I'll go put the beer and the Coke in the stream. Cool off the cans."

In his tidy way, Cal organized the campsite first. Food in one area, clothes in another, tools in another still. With his Scout knife and compass in his pocket, he set off to gather twigs and small branches. The brambles nipped and scratched as he picked his way through them. With his arms loaded, he didn't notice a few drops of his blood drip onto the ground at the edge of the circle.

Or the way the blood sizzled, smoked, then was sucked into that scarred earth.

Fox set the boom box on the rock, so they set up camp with Madonna and U2 and the Boss. Following Cal's advice, they built the fire, but didn't set it to light while they had the sun.

Sweaty and filthy, they sat on the ground and tore into the picnic basket with grubby hands and huge appetites. As the food, the familiar flavors filled his belly and soothed his system, Cal decided it had been worth hauling the basket for a couple of hours.

Replete, they stretched out on their backs, faces to the sky.

"Do you really think all those people died right here?" Gage wondered.

"There are books about it in the library," Cal told him. "About a fire of, like, 'unknown origin' breaking out and these people burned up."

"Kind of a weird place for them to be."

"We're here."

Gage only grunted at that.

"My mom said how the first white people to settle here were Puritans." Fox blew a huge pink bubble with the Bazooka he'd bought at the market. "A sort of radical Puritan or something. How they came over here looking for religious freedom, but really only meant it was free if it was, you know, their way. Mom says lots of people are like that about religion. I don't get it."

Gage thought he knew, or knew part. "A lot of people are mean, and even if they're not, a lot more people think they're better than you." He saw it all the time, in the way people looked at him.

"But do you think they were witches, and the people from the Hollow back then burned them at the stake or something?" Fox rolled over on his belly. "My mom says that being a witch is like a religion, too."

"Your mom's whacked."

Because it was Gage, and because it was said jokingly, Fox grinned. "We're all whacked."

"I say this calls for a beer." Gage pushed up. "We'll share one, let the others get colder." As Gage walked off to the stream, Cal and Fox exchanged looks.

"You ever had beer before?" Cal wanted to know.

"No. You?"

"Are you kidding? I can only have Coke on special occasions. What if we get drunk and pass out or something?"

"My dad drinks beer sometimes. He doesn't, I don't think."

They went quiet when Gage walked back with the dripping can. "Okay. This is to, you know, celebrate that we're going to stop being kids at midnight."

"Maybe we shouldn't drink it until midnight," Cal supposed.

"We'll have the second one after. It's like . . . it's like a ritual."

The sound of the top popping was loud in the quiet

woods, a quick *crack*, almost as shocking to Cal as a gunshot might have been. He smelled the beer immediately, and it struck him as a sour smell. He wondered if it tasted the same.

Gage held the beer up in one hand, high, as if he gripped the hilt of a sword. Then he lowered it, took a long, deep gulp from the can.

He didn't quite mask the reaction, a closing in of his face as if he'd swallowed something strange and unpleasant. His cheeks flushed as he let out a short, gasping breath.

"It's still pretty warm but it . . ." He coughed once. "It hits the spot. Now you."

He passed the can to Fox. With a shrug, Fox took the can, mirrored Gage's move. Everyone knew if there was anything close to a dare, Fox would jump at it. "Ugh. It tastes like piss."

"You been drinking piss lately?"

Fox snorted at Gage's question and passed the can to Cal. "Your turn."

Cal studied the can. It wasn't like a sip of beer would kill him or anything. So he sucked in a breath and swallowed some down.

It made his stomach curl and his eyes water. He shoved the can back at Gage. "It does taste like piss."

"I guess people don't drink it for how it tastes. It's how it makes you feel." Gage took another sip, because he wanted to know how it made him feel.

They sat cross-legged in the circular clearing, knees bumping, passing the can from hand to hand.

Cal's stomach pitched, but it didn't feel sick, not exactly. His head pitched, too, but it felt sort of goofy and fun. And the beer made his bladder full. When he stood, the whole world pitched and made him laugh helplessly as he staggered toward a tree.

He unzipped, aimed toward the tree but the tree kept moving.

Fox was struggling to light one of the cigarettes when

Cal stumbled back. They passed that around the circle as well until Cal's almost ten-year-old stomach revolted. He crawled off to sick it all up, crawled back, and just lay flat, closing his eyes and willing the world to go still again.

He felt as if he were once again swimming in the pond, and being slowly pulled under.

When he surfaced again it was nearly dusk.

He eased up, hoping he wouldn't be sick again. He felt a little hollow inside—belly and head—but not like he was going to puke. He saw Fox curled against the stone, sleeping. He crawled over on all fours for the thermos and as he washed the sick and beer out of his throat, he was never so grateful for his mother and her lemonade.

Steadier, he rubbed his fingers on his eyes under his glasses, then spotted Gage sitting, staring at the tented wood of the campfire they'd yet to light.

"'Morning, Sally."

With a wan smile, Cal scooted over.

"I don't know how to light this thing. I figured it was about time to, but I needed a Boy Scout."

Cal took the book of matches Gage handed him, and set fire to several spots on the pile of dried leaves he'd arranged under the wood. "That should do it. Wind's pretty still, and there's nothing to catch in the clearing. We can keep feeding it when we need to, and just make sure we bury it before we go tomorrow."

"Smokey the Bear. You all right?"

"Yeah. I guess I threw most everything up."

"I shouldn't have brought the beer."

Cal lifted a shoulder, glanced toward Fox. "We're okay, and now we won't have to wonder what it tastes like. We know it tastes like piss."

Gage laughed a little. "It didn't make me feel mean." He picked up a stick, poked at the little flames. "I wanted to know if it would, and I figured I could try it with you and Fox. You're my best friends, so I could try it with you and see if it made me feel mean."

"How did it make you feel?"

"It made my head hurt. It still does a little. I didn't get sick like you, but I sorta wanted to. I went and got one of the Cokes and drank that. It felt better then. Why does he drink so goddamn much if it makes him feel like that?"

"I don't know."

Gage dropped his head on his knees. "He was crying when he went after me last night. Blubbering and crying the whole time he used the belt on me. Why would anybody want to feel like that?"

Careful to avoid the welts on Gage's back, Cal draped an arm over his shoulders. He wished he knew what to say.

"Soon as I'm old enough I'm getting out. Join the army maybe, or get a job on a freighter, maybe an oil rig."

Gage's eyes gleamed when he lifted his head, and Cal looked away because he knew the shine was tears. "You can come stay with us when you need to."

"It'd just be worse when I went back. But I'm going to be ten in a few hours. And in a few years I'll be as big as he is. Bigger maybe. I won't let him come after me then. I won't let him hit me. Screw it." Gage rubbed his face. "Let's wake Fox up. Nobody sleeps tonight."

Fox moaned and grumbled, and he got himself up to pee and fetch a cool Coke from the stream. They shared it with another round of Little Debbies. And, at last, the copy of *Penthouse*.

Cal had seen naked breasts before. You could see them in the *National Geographic* in the library, if you knew where to look.

But these were different.

"Hey guys, did you ever think about doing it?" Cal asked.

"Who doesn't?" they both replied.

"Whoever does it first has to tell the other two everything. All about how it feels," Cal continued. "And how you did it, and what she does. Everything. I call for an oath."

A call for an oath was sacred. Gage spat on the back of his hand, held it out. Fox slapped his palm on, spat on the back of his hand, and Cal completed the contact.

"And so we swear," they said together.

They sat around the fire as the stars came out, and deep in the woods an owl hooted its night call.

The long, sweaty hike, ghostly apparitions, and beer puke were forgotten.

"We should do this every year on our birthday," Cal decided. "Even when we're old. Like thirty or something. The three of us should come here."

"Drink beer and look at pictures of naked girls," Fox added. "I call for—"

"Don't." Gage spoke sharply. "I can't swear. I don't know where I'm going to go, but it'll be somewhere else. I don't know if I'll ever come back."

"Then we'll go where you are, when we can. We're always going to be best friends." Nothing would change that, Cal thought, and took his own, personal oath on it. Nothing ever could. He looked at his watch. "It's going to be midnight soon. I have an idea."

He took out his Boy Scout knife and, opening the blade, held it in the fire.

"What's up?" Fox demanded.

"I'm sterilizing it. Like, ah, purifying it." It got so hot he had to pull back, blow on his fingers. "It's like Gage said about ritual and stuff. Ten years is a decade. We've known each other almost the whole time. We were born on the same day. It makes us . . . different," he said, searching for words he wasn't quite sure of. "Like special, I guess. We're best friends. We're like brothers."

Gage looked at the knife, then into Cal's face. "Blood brothers."

"Yeah."

"Cool." Already committed, Fox held out his hand.

"At midnight," Cal said. "We should do it at midnight, and we should have some words to say."

"We'll swear an oath," Gage said. "That we mix our blood, um, three into one? Something like that. In loyalty."

"That's good. Write it down, Cal."

Cal dug pencil and paper out of his pack. "We'll write

words down, and say them together. Then we'll do the cut and put our wrists together. I've got Band-Aids for after if we need them."

Cal wrote the words with his Number Two pencil on the blue lined paper, crossing out when they changed their minds.

Fox added more wood to the fire so that the flames crackled as they stood by the Pagan Stone.

At moments to midnight, they stood, three young boys with faces lit by fire and starlight. At Gage's nod, they spoke together in voices solemn and achingly young.

"We were born ten years ago, on the same night, at the same time, in the same year. We are brothers. At the Pagan Stone we swear an oath of loyalty and truth and brotherhood. We mix our blood."

Cal sucked in a breath and geared up the courage to run the knife across his wrist first. "Ouch."

"We mix our blood." Fox gritted his teeth as Cal cut his wrist.

"We mix our blood." And Gage stood unflinching as the knife drew over his flesh.

"Three into one, and one for the three."

Cal held his arm out. Fox, then Gage pressed their scored wrists down to his. "Brothers in spirit, in mind. Brothers in blood for all time."

As they stood, clouds shivered over the fat moon, misted over the bright stars. Their mixed blood dripped and fell onto the burnt ground.

The wind exploded with a voice like a raging scream. The little campfire spewed up flame in a spearing tower. The three of them were lifted off their feet as if a hand gripped them, tossed them. Light burst as if the stars had shattered.

As he opened his mouth to shout, Cal felt something shove inside him, hot and strong, to smother his lungs, to squeeze his heart in a stunning agony of pain.

The light shut off. In the thick dark blew an icy cold that numbed his skin. The sound the wind made now was like an animal, like a monster that only lived inside books. Beneath him the ground shook, heaving him back as he tried to crawl away.

And something came out of that icy dark, out of that quaking ground. Something huge and horrible.

Eyes bloodred and full of . . . hunger. It looked at him. And when it smiled, its teeth glittered like silver swords.

He thought he died, and that it took him in, in one gulp.

But when he came to himself again, he could hear his own heart. He could hear the shouts and calls of his friends.

Blood brothers.

"Jesus, Jesus, what was that? Did you see?" Fox called out in a voice thin as a reed. "Gage, God, your nose is bleeding."

"So's yours. Something . . . Cal. God, Cal."

Cal lay where he was, flat on his back. He felt the wet warmth of blood on his face. He was too numb to be frightened by it. "I can't see." He croaked out a weak whisper. "I can't see."

"Your glasses are broken." Face filthy with soot and blood, Fox crawled to him. "One of the lenses is cracked. Dude, your mom's going to kill you."

"Broken." Shaking, Cal reached up to pull off his glasses.

"Something. Something was here." Gage gripped Cal's shoulder. "I felt something happen, after everything went crazy, I felt something happen inside me. Then . . . did you see it? Did you see that thing?"

"I saw its eyes," Fox said, and his teeth chattered. "We need to get out of here. We need to get out."

"Where?" Gage demanded. Though his breath still wheezed, he grabbed Cal's knife from the ground, gripped it. "We don't know where it went. Was it some kind of bear? Was it—"

"It wasn't a bear." Cal spoke calmly now. "It was what's been here, in this place, a long time. I can see . . . I can see it. It looked like a man once, when it wanted. But it wasn't."

"Man, you hit your head."

Cal turned his eyes on Fox, and the irises were nearly black. "I can see it, and the other." He opened the hand of the wrist he'd cut. In the palm was a chunk of a green stone spotted with red. "His."

Fox opened his hand, and Gage his. In each was an identical third of the stone. "What is it?" Gage whispered. "Where the hell did it come from?"

"I don't know, but it's ours now. Uh, one into three, three into one. I think we let something out. And something came with it. Something bad. I can see."

He closed his eyes a moment, then opened them to look at his friends. "I can see, but not with my glasses. I can see without them. It's not blurry. I can see without my glasses."

"Wait." Trembling, Gage pulled up his shirt, turned his back.

"Man, they're gone." Fox reached out to touch his fingers to Gage's unmarred back. "The welts. They're gone. And . . ." He held out his wrist where the shallow cut was already healing. "Holy cow, are we like superheroes now?"

"It's a demon," Cal said. "And we let it out."

"Shit." Gage stared off into the dark woods. "Happy goddamn birthday to us."

Three

Hawkins Hollow
February 2008

IT WAS COLDER IN HAWKINS HOLLOW, MARYLAND, than it was in Juno, Alaska. Cal liked to know little bits like that, even though at the moment he was in the Hollow where the damp, cold wind blew like a mother and froze his eyeballs.

His eyeballs were about the only things exposed as he zipped across Main Street from Coffee Talk, with a to-go cup of mochaccino in one gloved hand, to the Bowl-a-Rama.

Three days a week, he tried for a counter breakfast at Ma's Pantry a couple doors down, and at least once a week he hit Gino's for dinner.

His father believed in supporting the community, the other merchants. Now that his dad was semiretired and Cal oversaw most of the businesses, he tried to follow that Hawkins tradition.

He shopped the local market even though the chain supermarket a couple miles outside town was cheaper. If he wanted to send a woman flowers, he resisted doing so with a couple of clicks on his computer and hauled himself down to the Flower Pot.

He had relationships with the local plumber, electrician, painter, the area craftsmen. Whenever possible, he hired for the town from the town.

Except for his years away at college, he'd always lived in the Hollow. It was his place.

Every seven years since his tenth birthday, he lived through the nightmare that visited his place. And every seven years, he helped clean up the aftermath.

He unlocked the front door of the Bowl-a-Rama, relocked it behind him. People tended to walk right in, whatever the posted hours, if the door wasn't locked.

He'd once been a little more casual about that, until one fine night while he'd been enjoying some after-hours Strip Bowling with Allysa Kramer, three teenage boys had wandered in, hoping the video arcade was still open.

Lesson learned.

He walked by the front desk, the six lanes and ball returns, the shoe rental counter and the grill, turned and jogged up the stairs to the squat second floor that held his (or his father's if his father was in the mood) office, a closet-sized john, and a mammoth storage area.

He set the coffee on the desk, stripped off gloves, scarf, watch cap, coat, insulated vest.

He booted up his computer, put on the satellite radio, then sat down to fuel up on caffeine and get to work.

The bowling center Cal's grandfather had opened in the postwar forties had been a tiny, three-lane gathering spot with a couple of pinball machines and counter Cokes. It expanded in the sixties, and again, when Cal's father took the reins, in the early eighties.

Now, with its six lanes, its video arcade, and its private party room, it was *the* place to gather in the Hollow.

Credit to Grandpa, Cal thought as he looked over the party reservations for the next month. But the biggest chunk of credit went to Cal's father, who'd morphed the lanes into a family center, and had used its success to dip into other areas of business.

The town bears our name, Jim Hawkins liked to say. *Respect the name, respect the town.*

Cal did both. He'd have left long ago otherwise.

An hour into the work, Cal glanced up at the rap on his doorjamb.

"Sorry, Cal. Just wanted you to know I was here. Thought I'd go ahead and get that painting done in the rest rooms since you're not open this morning."

"Okay, Bill. Got everything you need?"

"Sure do." Bill Turner, five years, two months, and six days sober, cleared his throat. "Wonder if maybe you'd heard anything from Gage."

"Not in a couple months now."

Tender area, Cal thought when Bill just nodded. Boggy ground.

"I'll just get started then."

Cal watched as Bill moved away from the doorway. Nothing he could do about it, he told himself. Nothing he was sure he should do.

Did five years clean and sober make up for all those whacks with a belt, for all those shoves and slaps, all those curses? It wasn't for him to judge.

He glanced down at the thin scar that ran diagonally across his wrist. Odd how quickly that small wound had healed, and yet the mark of it remained—the only scar he carried. Odd how so small a thing had catapulted the town and people he knew into seven days of hell every seven years.

Would Gage come back this summer, as he had every seventh year? Cal couldn't see ahead, that wasn't his gift or his burden. But he knew when he, Gage, and Fox turned thirty-one, they would all be together in the Hollow.

They'd sworn an oath.

He finished up the morning's work, and because he couldn't get his mind off it, composed a quick e-mail to Gage.

Hey. Where the hell are you? Vegas? Mozambique? Duluth? Heading out to see Fox. There's a writer coming into the Hollow to do research on the history, the legend, and what they're calling the anomalies. Probably got it handled, but thought you should know.

It's twenty-two degrees with a windchill factor of fifteen. Wish you were here and I wasn't.

Cal

He'd answer eventually, Cal thought as he sent the e-mail, then shut down the computer. Could be in five minutes or in five weeks, but Gage would answer.

He began to layer on the outer gear again over a long and lanky frame passed down by his father. He'd gotten his outsized feet from dear old Dad, too.

The dark blond hair that tended to go as it chose was from his mother. He knew that only due to early photos of her, as she'd been a soft, sunny blonde, perfectly groomed, throughout his memory.

His eyes, a sharp, occasionally stormy gray, had been twenty-twenty since his tenth birthday.

Even as he zipped up his parka to head outside, he thought that the coat was for comfort only. He hadn't had so much as a sniffle in over twenty years. No flu, no virus, no hay fever.

He'd fallen out of an apple tree when he'd been twelve. He'd heard the bone in his arm snap, had felt the breathless pain.

And he'd felt it knit together again—with more pain—before he'd made it across the lawn to the house to tell his mother.

So he'd never told her, he thought as he stepped outside into the ugly slap of cold. Why upset her?

He covered the three blocks to Fox's office quickly, shooting out waves or calling back greetings to neighbors and friends. But he didn't stop for conversation. He might not get pneumonia or postnasal drip, but he was *freaking* tired of winter.

Gray, ice-crusted snow lay in a dirty ribbon along the curbs, and above, the sky mirrored the brooding color. Some of the houses or businesses had hearts and Valentine wreaths on doors and windows, but they didn't add a lot of cheer with the bare trees and winter-stripped gardens.

The Hollow didn't show to advantage, to Cal's way of thinking, in February.

He walked up the short steps to the little covered porch of the old stone townhouse. The plaque beside the door read: FOX B. O'DELL, ATTORNEY AT LAW.

It was something that always gave Cal a quick jolt and a quick flash of amusement. Even after nearly six years, he couldn't quite get used to it.

The long-haired hippie freak was a goddamn lawyer.

He stepped into the tidy reception area, and there was Alice Hawbaker at the desk. Trim, tidy in her navy suit with its bowed white blouse, her snowcap of hair and no-nonsense bifocals, Mrs. Hawbaker ran the office like a Border collie ran a herd.

She looked sweet and pretty, and she'd bite your ankle if you didn't fall in line.

"Hey, Mrs. Hawbaker. Boy, it is *cold* out there. Looks like we might get some more snow." He unwrapped his scarf. "Hope you and Mr. Hawbaker are keeping warm."

"Warm enough."

He heard something in her voice that had him looking more closely as he pulled off his gloves. When he realized she'd been crying he instinctively stepped to the desk. "Is everything okay? Is—"

"Everything's fine. Just fine. Fox is between appointments. He's in there sulking, so you go right on back."

"Yes, ma'am. Mrs. Hawbaker, if there's anything—"

"Just go right on back," she repeated, then made herself busy with her keyboard.

Beyond the reception area a hallway held a powder room on one side and a library on the other. Straight back,

Fox's office was closed off by a pair of pocket doors. Cal didn't bother to knock.

Fox looked up when the doors slid open. He did appear to be sulking as his gilded eyes were broody and his mouth was in full scowl.

He sat behind his desk, his feet, clad in hiking boots, propped on it. He wore jeans and a flannel shirt open over a white insulated tee. His hair, densely brown, waved around his sharp-featured face.

"What's going on?"

"I'll tell you what's going on. My administrative assistant just gave me her notice."

"What did you do?"

"Me?" Fox shoved back from the desk and opened the minifridge for a can of Coke. He'd never developed a taste for coffee. "Try *we*, brother. We camped out at the Pagan Stone one fateful night, and screwed the monkey."

Cal dropped into a chair. "She's quitting because—"

"Not just quitting. They're leaving the Hollow, she and Mr. Hawbaker. And yeah, because." He took a long, greedy drink the way some men might take a pull on a bottle of whiskey. "That's not the reason she gave me, but that's the reason. She said they decided to move to Minneapolis to be close to their daughter and grandchildren, and that's bogus. Why does a woman heading toward seventy, married to a guy older than dirt, pick up and move north? They've got another kid lives outside of D.C., and they've got strong ties here. I could tell it was bull."

"Because of what she said, or because you took a cruise through her head?"

"First the one, then the other. Don't start on me." Fox gestured with the Coke, then slammed it down on his desk. "I don't poke around for the fun of it. Son of a bitch."

"Maybe they'll change their minds."

"They don't want to go, but they're afraid to stay. They're afraid it'll happen again—which I could tell her it will—and they just don't want to go through it again. I offered her a raise—like I could afford it—offered her the whole month of July off, letting her know that I knew what was at the bottom of it. But they're going. She'll give me until April first. April frickin' Fools," he ranted. "To find somebody else, for her to show them the ropes. I don't know where the damn ropes are, Cal. I don't know half the stuff she does. She just does it. Anyway."

"You've got until April, maybe we'll think of something."

"We haven't thought of the solution to this in twenty years plus."

"I meant your office problem. But yeah, I've been thinking a lot about the other." Rising, he walked to Fox's window, looked out on the quiet side street. "We've got to end it. This time we've got to end it. Maybe talking to this writer will help. Laying it out to someone objective, someone not involved."

"Asking for trouble."

"Maybe it is, but trouble's coming anyway. Five months to go. We're supposed to meet her at the house." Cal glanced at his watch. "Forty minutes."

"We?" Fox looked blank for a moment. "That's today? See, see, I didn't tell Mrs. H, so it didn't get written down somewhere. I've got a deposition in an hour."

"Why don't you use your damn BlackBerry?"

"Because it doesn't follow my simple Earth logic. Reschedule the writer. I'm clear after four."

"It's okay, I can handle it. If she wants more, I'll see about setting up a dinner, so keep tonight open."

"Be careful what you say."

"Yeah, yeah, I'm going to. But I've been thinking. We've been careful about that for a long time. Maybe it's time to be a little reckless."

"You sound like Gage."

"Fox . . . I've already started having the dreams again."

Fox blew out a breath. "I was hoping that was just me."

"When we were seventeen they started about a week before our birthday, then when we were twenty-four, over a month. Now, five months out. Every time it gets stronger.

I'm afraid if we don't find the way, this time could be the last for us, and the town."

"Have you talked to Gage?"

"I just e-mailed him. I didn't tell him about the dreams. You do it. Find out if he's having them, too, wherever the hell he is. Get him home, Fox. I think we need him back. I don't think we can wait until summer this time. I gotta go."

"Watch your step with the writer," Fox called out as Cal started for the door. "Get more than you give."

"I can handle it," Cal repeated.

QUINN BLACK EASED HER MINI COOPER OFF THE exit ramp and hit the usual barrage at the interchange. Pancake House, Wendy's, McDonald's, KFC.

With great affection, she thought of a Quarter Pounder, with a side of really salty fries, and—natch—a Diet Coke to ease the guilt. But since that would be breaking her vow to eat fast food no more than once a month, she wasn't going to indulge.

"There now, don't you feel righteous?" she asked herself with only one wistful glance in the rearview at the lovely Golden Arches.

Her love of the quick and the greasy had sent her on an odyssey of fad diets, unsatisfying supplements, and miracle workout tapes through her late teens and early twenties. Until she'd finally slapped herself silly, tossed out all her diet books, her diet articles, her I LOST TWENTY POUNDS IN TWO WEEKS—AND YOU CAN, TOO! ads, and put herself on the path to sensible eating and exercising.

Lifestyle change, she reminded herself. She'd made a lifestyle change.

But boy, she missed those Quarter Pounders more than she missed her ex-fiancé.

Then again, who wouldn't?

She glanced at the GPS hooked to her dashboard, then

over at the directions she'd printed out from Caleb Hawkins's e-mail. So far, they were in tandem.

She reached down for the apple serving as her mid-morning snack. Apples were filling, Quinn thought as she bit in. They were good for you, and they were tasty.

And they were no Quarter Pounder.

In order to keep her mind off the devil, she considered what she hoped to accomplish on this first face-to-face interview with one of the main players in the odd little town of Hawkins Hollow.

No, not fair to call it odd, she reminded herself. Objectivity first. Maybe her research leaned her toward the odd label, but there would be no making up her mind until she'd seen for herself, done her interviews, taken her notes, scoped out the local library. And, maybe most important, seen the Pagan Stone in person.

She loved poking at all the corners and cobwebs of small towns, digging down under the floorboards for secrets and surprises, listening to the gossip, the local lore and legend.

She'd made a tiny name for herself doing a series of articles on quirky, off-the-mainstream towns for a small press magazine called *Detours*. And since her professional appetite was as well-developed as her bodily one, she'd taken a risky leap and written a book, following the same theme, but focusing on a single town in Maine reputed to be haunted by the ghosts of twin sisters who'd been murdered in a boardinghouse in 1843.

The critics had called the result "engaging" and "good, spooky fun," except for the ones who'd deemed it "preposterous" and "convoluted."

She'd followed it up with a book highlighting a small town in Louisiana where the descendent of a voodoo priestess served as mayor and faith healer. And, Quinn had discovered, had been running a very successful prostitution ring.

But Hawkins Hollow—she could just feel it—was going to be bigger, better, meatier.

She couldn't wait to sink her teeth in.

The fast-food joints, the businesses, the ass-to-elbow houses gave way to bigger lawns, bigger homes, and to fields sleeping under the dreary sky.

The road wound, dipped and lifted, then veered straight again. She saw a sign for the Antietam Battlefield, something else she meant to investigate and research firsthand. She'd found little snippets about incidents during the Civil War in and around Hawkins Hollow.

She wanted to know more.

When her GPS and Caleb's directions told her to turn, she turned, following the next road past a grove of naked trees, a scatter of houses, and the farms that always made her smile with their barns and silos and fenced paddocks.

She'd have to find a small town to explore in the Midwest next time. A haunted farm, or the weeping spirit of a milkmaid.

She nearly ignored the directions to turn when she saw the sign for Hawkins Hollow (est. 1648). As with the Quarter Pounder, her heart longed to indulge, to drive into town rather than turn off toward Caleb Hawkins's place. But she hated to be late, and if she got caught up exploring the streets, the corners, the *look* of the town, she certainly would be late for her first appointment.

"Soon," she promised, and turned to take the road winding by the woods she knew held the Pagan Stone at their heart.

It gave her a quick shiver, and that was strange. Strange to realize that shiver had been fear and not the anticipation she always felt with a new project.

As she followed the twists of the road, she glanced with some unease toward the dark and denuded trees. And hit the brakes hard when she shifted her eyes back to the road and saw something rush out in front of her.

She thought she saw a child—oh God, oh God—then thought it was a dog. And then . . . it was nothing. Nothing at all on the road, nothing rushing to the field beyond. Nothing there but herself and her wildly beating heart in the little red car.

"Trick of the eye," she told herself, and didn't believe it. "Just one of those things."

But she restarted the car that had stalled when she'd slammed the brakes, then eased to the strip of dirt that served as the shoulder of the road. She pulled out her notebook, noted the time, and wrote down exactly what she thought she'd seen.

Young boy, abt ten. Lng blck hair, red eyes. He LOOKED right at me. Did I blink? Shut my eyes? Opened, & saw lrg blck dog, not boy. Then poof. Nothing there.

Cars passed her without incident as she sat a few moments more, waited for the trembling to stop.

Intrepid writer balks at first possible phenom, she thought, turns around, and drives her adorable red car to the nearest Mickey D's for a fat-filled antidote to nerves.

She could do that, she considered. Nobody could charge her with a felony and throw her into prison. And if she did that, she wouldn't have her next book, or any self-respect.

"Man up, Quinn," she ordered. "You've seen spooks before."

Steadier, she swung back out on the road, and made the next turn. The road was narrow and twisty with trees looming on both sides. She imagined it would be lovely in the spring and summer, with the green dappling, or after a snowfall with all those trees ermine drenched. But under a dull gray sky the woods seemed to crowd the road, bare branches just waiting to reach out and strike, as if they and only they were allowed to live there.

As if to enforce the sensation, no other car passed, and when she turned off her radio as the music seemed too loud, the only sound was the keening curse of the wind.

Should've called it Spooky Hollow, she decided, and nearly missed the turn into the gravel lane.

Why, she wondered, would anyone *choose* to live here? Amid all those dense, thrusting trees where bleak pools of snow huddled to hide from the sun? Where the only sound was the warning growl of Nature. Everything was brown and gray and moody.

She bumped over a little bridge spanning a curve of a creek, followed the slight rise of the stingy lane.

There was the house, exactly as advertised.

It sat on what she would have termed a knoll rather than a hill, with the front slope tamed into step-down terraces decked with shrubs she imagined put on a hell of a show in the spring and summer.

There wasn't a lawn, so to speak, and she thought Hawkins had been smart to go with the thick mulch and shrubs and trees skirting the front instead of the traditional grass that would probably be a pain in the ass to mow and keep clear of weeds.

She approved of the deck that wrapped around the front and sides, and she'd bet the rear as well. She liked the earthy tones of the stone and the generous windows.

It sat like it belonged there, content and well-settled in the woods.

She pulled up beside an aging Chevy pickup, got out of her car to stand and take a long view.

And understood why someone would choose this spot. There was, unquestionably, an aura of spookiness, especially for one who was inclined to see and feel such things. But there was considerable charm as well, and a sense of solitude that was far from lonely. She could imagine very well sitting on that front deck some summer evening, drinking a cold one, and wallowing in the silence.

Before she could move toward the house, the front door opened.

The sense of déjà vu was vivid, almost dizzying. He stood there at the door of the cabin, the blood like red flowers on his shirt.

We can stay no longer.

The words sounded in her head, clear, and in a voice she somehow knew.

"Miss Black?"

She snapped back. There was no cabin, and the man standing on the lovely deck of his charming house had no blood blooming on him. There was no force of great love and great grief shining in his eyes.

And still, she had to lean back against her car for a minute and catch her breath. "Yeah, hi. I was just . . . admiring the house. Great spot."

"Thanks. Any trouble finding it?"

"No, no. Your directions were perfect." And, of course, it was ridiculous to be having this conversation outside in the freezing wind. From the quizzical look on his face, he obviously felt the same.

She pushed off the car, worked up what she hoped was a sane and pleasant expression as she walked to the trio of wooden steps.

And wasn't he a serious cutie? she realized as she finally focused on the reality. All that windblown hair and those strong gray eyes. Add the crooked smile, the long, lean body in jeans and flannel, and a woman might be tempted to hang a SOLD! sign around his neck.

She stepped up, held out a hand. "Quinn Black, thanks for meeting with me, Mr. Hawkins."

"Cal." He took her hand, shook it, then held it as he gestured to the door. "Let's get you out of the wind."

They stepped directly into a living room that managed to be cozy and male at the same time. The generous sofa faced the big front windows, and the chairs looked as though they'd allow an ass to sink right in. Tables and lamps probably weren't antiques, but looked to be something a grandmother might have passed down when she got the urge to redecorate her own place.

There was even a little stone fireplace with the requisite large mutt sprawled sleeping in front of it.

"Let me take your coat."

"Is your dog in a coma?" Quinn asked when the dog didn't move a muscle.

"No. Lump leads an active and demanding internal life that requires long periods of rest."

"I see."

"Want some coffee?"

"That'd be great. So would the bathroom. Long drive."

"First right."

"Thanks."

She closed herself into a small, spotlessly clean powder room as much to pull herself back together from a couple of psychic shocks as to pee.

"Okay, Quinn," she whispered. "Here we go."

Four

HE'D READ HER WORK; HE'D STUDIED HER AUthor photos and used Google to get some background, to read her interviews. Cal wasn't one to agree to talk to any sort of writer, journalist, reporter, Internet blogger about the Hollow, himself, or much of anything else without doing a thorough check.

He'd found her books and articles entertaining. He'd enjoyed her obvious affection for small towns, had been intrigued by her interest and treatment of lore, legend, and things that went bump in the night.

He liked the fact that she still wrote the occasional article for the magazine that had given her a break when she'd still been in college. It spoke of loyalty.

He hadn't been disappointed that her author photo had shown her to be a looker, with a sexy tumble of honey blond hair, bright blue eyes, and the hint of a fairly adorable overbite.

The photo hadn't come close.

She probably wasn't beautiful, he thought as he poured coffee. He'd have to get another look when, hopefully, his brain wouldn't go to fuzz, then decide about that.

What he did know, unquestionably, was she just plain radiated energy and—to his fuzzed brain—sex.

But maybe that was because she was built, another thing the photo hadn't gotten across. The lady had some truly excellent curves.

And it wasn't as if he hadn't seen curves on a woman before or, in fact, seen his share of naked female curves alive and in person. So why was he standing in his own kitchen frazzled because an attractive, fully dressed woman was in his house? For professional purposes.

"Jesus, grow up, Hawkins."

"Sorry?"

He actually jumped. She was in the kitchen, a few steps behind him, smiling that million-watt smile.

"Were you talking to yourself? I do that, too. Why do people think we're crazy?"

"Because they want to suck us into talking to them."

"You're probably right." Quinn shoved back that long spill of blond.

Cal saw he was right. She wasn't beautiful. The top-heavy mouth, the slightly crooked nose, the oversized eyes weren't elements of traditional beauty. He couldn't label her pretty, either. It was too simple and sweet a word. Cute didn't do it.

All he could think of was *hot*, but that might have been his brain blurring again.

"I didn't ask how you take your coffee."

"Oh. I don't suppose you have two percent milk."

"I often wonder why anybody does."

With an easy laugh that shot straight to his bloodstream, she wandered over to study the view outside the glass doors that led—as she'd suspected—to the rear portion of the circling deck. "Which also means you probably don't have any fake sugar. Those little pink, blue, or yellow packets?"

"Fresh out. I could offer you actual milk and actual sugar."

"You could." And hadn't she eaten an apple like a good girl? "And I could accept. Let me ask you something else, just to satisfy my curiosity. Is your house always so clean and tidy, or did you do all this just for me?"

He got out the milk. "*Tidy*'s a girlie word. I prefer the term *organized*. I like organization. Besides." He offered her a spoon for the sugar bowl. "My mother could—and does—drop by unexpectedly. If my house wasn't clean, she'd ground me."

"If I don't call my mother once a week, she assumes I've been hacked to death by an ax murderer." Quinn held herself to one scant spoon of sugar. "It's nice, isn't it? Those long and elastic family ties."

"I like them. Why don't we go sit in the living room by the fire?"

"Perfect. So, how long have you lived here? In this particular house," she added as they carried their mugs out of the kitchen.

"A couple of years."

"Not much for neighbors?"

"Neighbors are fine, and I spend a lot of time in town. I like the quiet now and then."

"People do. I do myself, now and again." She took one of the living room chairs, settled back. "I guess I'm surprised other people haven't had the same idea as you, and plugged in a few more houses around here."

"There was talk of it a couple of times. Never panned out."

He's being cagey, Quinn decided. "Because?"

"Didn't turn out to be financially attractive, I guess."

"Yet here you are."

"My grandfather owned the property, some acres of Hawkins Wood. He left it to me."

"So you had this house built."

"More or less. I'd liked the spot." Private when he needed to be private. Close to the woods where everything had changed. "I know some people in the trade, and we put the house up. How's the coffee?"

"It's terrific. You cook, too?"

"Coffee's my specialty. I read your books."

"How were they?"

"I liked them. You probably know you wouldn't be here if I hadn't."

"Which would've made it a lot tougher to write the book I want to write. You're a Hawkins, a descendent of the founder of the settlement that became the village that became the town. And one of the main players in the more recent unexplained incidents related to the town. I've done a lot of research on the history, the lore, the legends, and the various explanations," she said, and reached in the bag that served as her purse and her briefcase. Taking out a minirecorder, she switched it on, set it on the table between them.

Her smile was full of energy and interest when she set her notebook on her lap, flipped pages to a clear one. "So, tell me, Cal, about what happened the week of July seventh, nineteen eighty-seven, ninety-four, and two thousand one."

The tape recorder made him . . . itchy. "Dive right in, don't you?"

"I love knowing things. July seventh is your birthday. It's also the birthday of Fox O'Dell and Gage Turner—born the same year as you, who grew up in Hawkins Hollow with you. I read articles that reported you, O'Dell, and Turner were responsible for alerting the fire department on July eleventh, nineteen eighty-seven, when the elementary school was set on fire, and also responsible for saving the life of one Marian Lister who was inside the school at the time."

She continued to look straight into his eyes as she spoke. He found it interesting she didn't need to refer to notes, and that she didn't appear to need the little breaks from direct eye contact.

"Initial reports indicated the three of you were originally suspected of starting the fire, but it was proven Miss

Lister herself was responsible. She suffered second-degree burns on nearly thirty percent of her body as well as a concussion. You and your friends, three ten-year-old boys, dragged her out and called the fire department. Miss Lister was, at that time, a twenty-five-year-old fourth-grade teacher with no history of criminal behavior or mental illness. Is that all correct information?"

She got her facts in order, Cal noted. Such as the facts were known. They fell far short of the abject terror of entering that burning school, of finding the pretty Miss Lister cackling madly as she ran through the flames. Of how it felt to chase her through those hallways as her clothes burned.

"She had a breakdown."

"Obviously." Smile in place, Quinn lifted her eyebrows. "There were also over a dozen nine-one-one calls on domestic abuse during that single week, more than previously had been reported in Hawkins Hollow in the six preceding months. There were two suicides and four attempted suicides, numerous accounts of assault, three reported rapes, and a hit-and-run. Several homes and businesses were vandalized. None—virtually none—of the people involved in any of the reported crimes or incidents has a clear memory of the events. Some speculate the town suffered from mass hysteria or hallucinations or an unknown infection taken through food or water. What do you think?"

"I think I was ten years old and pretty much scared shitless."

She offered that brief, sunny smile. "I bet." Then it was gone. "You were seventeen in nineteen ninety-four when during the week of July seventh another—let's say outbreak—occurred. Three people were murdered, one of them apparently hanged in the town park, but no one came forward as a witness or to admit participation. There were more rapes, more beatings, more suicides, two houses burned to the ground. There were reports that you, O'Dell, and Turner were able to get some of the wounded and traumatized onto a school bus and transport them to the hospital. Is that accurate?"

"As far as it goes."

"I'm looking to go further. In two thousand one—"

"I know the pattern," Cal interrupted.

"Every seven years," Quinn said with a nod. "For seven nights. Days—according again to what I can ascertain—little happens. But from sundown to sunset, all hell breaks loose. It's hard to believe that it's a coincidence this anomaly happens every seven years, with its start on your birthday. Seven's considered a magickal number by those who profess to magicks, black and white. You were born on the seventh day of the seventh month of nineteen seventy-seven."

"If I knew the answers, I'd stop it from happening. If I knew the answers, I wouldn't be talking to you. I'm talking to you because maybe, just maybe, you'll find them, or help find them."

"Then tell me what happened, tell me what you *do* know, even what you think or sense."

Cal set his coffee aside, leaned forward to look deep into her eyes. "Not on a first date."

Smart-ass, she thought with considerable approval. "Fine. Next time I'll buy you dinner first. But now, how about playing guide and taking me to the Pagan Stone."

"It's too late in the day. It's a two-hour hike from here. We wouldn't make it there and back before dark."

"I'm not afraid of the dark."

His eyes went very cool. "You would be. I'll tell you this, there are places in these woods no one goes after dark, not any time of the year."

She felt the prick of ice at the base of her spine. "Have you ever seen a boy, about the age you'd have been in eighty-seven. A boy with dark hair. And red eyes." She saw by the way Cal paled she'd flicked a switch. "You have seen him."

"Why do you ask about that?"

"Because I saw him."

Now Cal pushed to his feet, paced to the window, stared

out at the woods. The light was dimmer, duller already than it had been an hour before.

They'd never told anyone about the boy—or the man—whatever form the thing chose to take. Yes, he'd seen him, and not only during that one hellish week every seven years.

He'd seen it in dreams. He'd seen it out of the corner of his eye, or loping through the woods. Or with its face pressed to the dark glass of his bedroom window . . . and its mouth grinning.

But no one, no one but he, Fox, and Gage had ever seen it in the between times.

Why had she?

"When and where did you see him?"

"Today, just before I turned off onto Pagan Road. He ran in front of my car. Came out of nowhere. That's what people always say, but this time it's true. A boy, then it wasn't a boy but a dog. Then it wasn't anything. There was nothing there."

He heard her rise, and when he turned was simply stunned to see that brilliant smile on her face. "And this kind of thing makes you happy?"

"It makes me thrilled. Excited. I'm saying wow! I had myself what we could call a close encounter with an unspecified phenomenon. Scary, I grant you, but again, wow. This sort of thing completely winds me up."

"I can see that."

"I knew there was something here, and I thought it was big. But to have it confirmed, the first day out, that's hitting the mother lode with the first whack of the pick."

"I haven't confirmed anything."

"Your face did." She picked up her recorder, turned it off. He wasn't going to tell her anything today. Cautious man, Caleb Hawkins. "I need to get into town, check into the hotel, get a lay of the land. Why don't I buy you that dinner tonight?"

She moved fast, and he made a habit of taking his time. "Why don't you take some time to settle in? We can talk about dinner and so on in a couple days."

"I love a man who's hard to get." She slipped her recorder, her notepad back in her bag. "I guess I'll need my coat."

After he'd brought it to her, she studied him as she shrugged it on. "You know, when you first came outside, I had the strangest sensation. I thought I recognized you, that I'd known you before. That you'd waited for me before. It was very strong. Did you feel anything like that?"

"No. But maybe I was too busy thinking, she looks better than her picture."

"Really? Nice, because I looked terrific in that picture. Thanks for the coffee." She glanced back to the dog who'd snored lightly the entire time they'd talked. "See you later, Lump. Don't work so hard."

He walked her out. "Quinn," he said as she started down the stairs. "Don't get any ideas about Lois Laning it and trying to find the Pagan Stone on your own. You don't know the woods. I'll take you there myself, sometime this week."

"Tomorrow?"

"I can't, I've got a full plate. Day after if you're in a hurry."

"I almost always am." She walked backward toward her car so she could keep him in view. "What time?"

"Let's say we'll meet here at nine, weather permitting."

"That's a date." She opened her car door. "The house suits you, by the way. Country boy with more style than pretention. I like it."

He watched her drive off—strange and sexy Quinn Black.

And he stood for a long time watching the light go dimmer in the woods where he'd made his home.

CAL HEADED FOX OFF WITH A PHONE CALL AND arranged to meet him at the bowling alley. Since the Pin Boys and the Alley Cats were having a league game on lanes one and two, he and Fox could have dinner and a show at the grill.

Added to it, there was little as noisy as a bowling alley, so their conversation would be covered by the crash of balls against pins, the hoots and hollers.

"First, let's backtrack into the land of logic for a minute." Fox took a swig of his beer. "She could've made it up to get a reaction."

"How did she know what to make up?"

"During the Seven, there are people who see it—who've said they did before it starts to fade on them. She got wind."

"I don't think so, Fox. Some talked about seeing something—boy, man, woman, dog, wolf—"

"The rat the size of a Doberman," Fox remembered.

"Thanks for bringing that one back. But no one ever claimed they'd seen it before or after the Seven. No one but us, and we've never told anyone." Cal arched his brow in question.

"No. You think I'm going to spread it around that I see red-eyed demons? I'd just rake in the clients that way."

"She's smart. I don't see why she'd claim to have seen it, outside the norm—ha-ha—if she hadn't. Plus she was psyched about it. Juiced up. So, let's accept she did and continue to dwell in the land of logic. One logical assumption is that the bastard's stronger, we know he will be. But strong enough to push out of the Seven into the between time."

Fox brooded over his beer. "I don't like that logic."

"Second option could be she's somehow connected. To one of us, the town, the incident at the Pagan Stone."

"I like that better. Everyone's connected. It's not just Kevin Bacon. If you work at it, you can put a handful of degrees between almost any two people." Thoughtful, Fox picked up his second slice of pizza. "Maybe she's a distant cousin. I've got cousins up the wazoo and so do you. Gage, not so much, but there's some out there."

"Possible. But why would a distant cousin see something none of our immediate family has? They'd tell us, Fox. They all know what's coming better and clearer than anyone else."

"Reincarnation. That's not off the Planet Logic, considering. Besides, reincarnation's big in the family O'Dell. Maybe she was there when it all happened. Another life."

"I don't discount anything. But more to the point, why is she here now? And will it help us put a goddamn end to this?"

"It's going to take more than an hour's chat in front of the fire to figure that out. I don't guess you heard from Gage."

"Not yet. He'll be in touch. I'm going to take her out to the stone day after tomorrow."

"Leaping forward fast, Cal."

Cal shook his head. "If I don't take her soon enough, she'll try it on her own. If something happened . . . We can't be responsible for that."

"We are responsible—isn't that the point? On some level it's on us." Frowning now, he watched Don Myers, of Myers Plumbing, make a seven-ten split to appropriate hoots and shouts. All three hundred twenty pounds of Myers did a flab-wriggling victory dance that was not a pretty sight.

"You go on," Fox said quietly, "day after day, doing what you do, living your life, making your life. Eating pizza, scratching your ass, getting laid if you're lucky. But you know, on some level you try to keep buried just to get through, that it's coming back. That some of the people you see on the street every day, maybe they won't make it through the next round. Maybe we won't. What the hell." He rapped his beer against Cal's. "We've got the now, plus five months to figure this out."

"I can try to go back again."

"Not unless Gage is here. We can't risk it unless we're together. It's not worth it, Cal. The other times you only got bits and pieces, and took a hell of a beating for it."

"Older and wiser now. And I'm thinking, if it's showing itself now—our dreams, what happened to Quinn—it's expending energy. I might get more than I have before."

"Not without Gage. That's . . . Hmm," he said as his attention wandered over his friend's shoulder. "Fresh flowers."

Glancing back, Cal saw Quinn standing behind lane one, her coat open and a bemused expression on her face as she watched Myers, graceful as a hippo in toe shoes, make his approach and release his lucky red ball.

"That's Quinn."

"Yeah, I recognized her. I read the books, too. She's hotter than her picture, and that was pretty hot."

"I saw her first."

Fox snorted, shifted his eyes to sneer at Cal. "Dude, it's not about who saw her first, it's who *she* sees. I pull out the full power of my sexual charm, and you'll be the Invisible Man."

"Shit. The full power of your sexual charm wouldn't light up a forty-watt bulb."

Cal pushed off the stool when Quinn walked toward him.

"So this is why I got the brush-off tonight," she said. "Pizza, beer, and bowling."

"The Hawkins Hollow hat trick. I'm on manager duty tonight. Quinn, this is Fox O'Dell."

"The second part of the triad." She shook Fox's hand. "Now I'm doubly glad I decided to check out what seems to be the town's hot spot. Mind if I join you?"

"Wouldn't have it any other way. Buy you a beer?" Fox asked.

"Boy, could you, but . . . make it a light one."

Cal stepped back to swing around the counter. "I'll take care of it. Anything to go with it? Pizza?"

"Oh." She looked at the pizza on the counter with eyes that went suddenly dewy. "Um, I don't suppose you have any with whole-wheat crust and low-fat mozzarella?"

"Health nut?" Fox asked.

"Just the opposite." Quinn bit her bottom lip. "I'm in a lifestyle change. Damn it, that really looks good. How about if we cut one of those slices in half." She sawed the side of her hand over the plate.

"No problem."

Cal got a pizza cutter and slid it down a slice.

"I love fat and sugar like a mother loves her child," Quinn told Fox. "I'm trying to eat more sensibly."

"My parents are vegetarians," Fox said as they each picked up a half slice. "I grew up on tofu and alfalfa."

"God. That's so sad."

"Which is why he ate at my house whenever he could manage it, and spent all his money on Little Debbies and Slim Jims."

"Little Debbies are food for the gods." She smiled at Cal when he set her beer on the counter. "I like your town. I took a walk up and down several blocks of Main Street. And since I was freezing my ass off, went back to the really charming Hotel Hollow, sat on my windowsill, and watched the world go by."

"Nice world," Cal said, "that moves a little slow this time of year."

"Umm," was her agreement as she took a minute bite of the point of her narrow triangle of pizza. She closed her eyes on a sigh. "It *is* good. I was hoping, being bowling-alley pizza, it wouldn't be."

"We do okay. Gino's across the street is better, and has more selections."

She opened her eyes to find him smiling at her. "That's a lousy thing to tell a woman in the middle of a lifestyle change."

Cal leaned on the counter, bringing that smile a little closer, and Quinn found herself losing her train of thought. He had the best quick and crooked grin, the kind a woman wanted to take a testing nibble of.

Before he could speak, someone hailed him, and those eyes of quiet gray glanced away from hers toward the end of the counter. "Be right back."

"Well." Jeez, her pulse had actually tripped. "Alone at last," she said to Fox. "So you and Cal and the as-yet-absent Gage Turner have been friends since you were kids."

"Babies, actually. In utero, technically. Cal's and Gage's mother got together with mine when my mother was teaching a Lamaze class. They had a kind of roundup with the class a couple months after everyone delivered the packages, and the deal about the three of us being born on the same day, same time came out."

"Instant mommy bonding."

"I don't know. They always got along, even though you could say they all came from different planets. They were friendly without being friends. My parents and Cal's still get along fine, and Cal's dad kept Gage's employed when nobody else in town would've hired him."

"Why wouldn't anyone have hired him?"

Fox debated for a minute, drank some of his beer. "It's no secret," he decided. "He drank. He's been sober for a while now. About five years, I guess. I always figured Mr. Hawkins gave him work because that's just the way he is, and, in a big part, he did it for Gage. Anyway, I don't remember the three of us not being friends."

"No 'you like him better than me,' major falling-outs or your basic and usual drifting apart?"

"We fought—fight still—now and then." Didn't all brothers? Fox thought. "Had your expected pissy periods, but no. We're connected. Nothing can snap that connection. And the 'you like him better than me'? Mostly a girl thing."

"But Gage doesn't live here anymore."

"Gage doesn't live anywhere, really. He's the original footloose guy."

"And you? The hometown boy."

"I thought about the bright lights, big city routine, even gave it a short try." He glanced over in the direction of the moans coming from one of the Alley Cats who had failed to pick up a spare. "I like the Hollow. I even like my family, most of the time. And I like, as it turns out, practicing small-town law."

Truth, Quinn decided, but not the whole truth of it. "Have you seen the kid with the red eyes?"

Off balance, Fox set down the beer he'd lifted to drink. "That's a hell of a segue."

"Maybe. But that wasn't an answer."

"I'm going to postpone my answer until further deliberation. Cal's taking point on this."

"And you're not sure you like the idea of him, or anyone, talking to me about what may or may not go on here."

"I'm not sure what purpose it serves. So I'm weighing the information as it comes in."

"Fair enough." She glanced over as Cal came back. "Well, boys, thanks for the beer and the slice. I should get back to my adorable room."

"You bowl?" Cal asked her, and she laughed.

"Absolutely not."

"Oh-oh," Fox said under his breath.

Cal walked around the counter, blocking Quinn before she could slide off the stool. He took a long, considering look at her boots. "Seven and a half, right?"

"Ah . . ." She looked down at her boots herself. "On the money. Good eye."

"Stay." He tapped her on the shoulder. "I'll be right back."

Quinn frowned after him, then looked at Fox. "He is *not* going to get me a pair of bowling shoes."

"Oh yeah, he is. You mocked the tradition, which—if you give him any tiny opening—he'll tell you started five thousand years ago. Then he'll explain its evolution and so on and so on."

"Well, Christ," was all Quinn could think to say.

Cal brought back a pair of maroon and cream bowling shoes, and another, larger pair of dark brown ones, which were obviously his. "Lane five's open. You want in, Fox?"

"Sadly, I have a brief to finish writing. I'll rain-check it. See you later, Quinn."

Cal tucked the shoes under his arm, then, taking Quinn's hand, pulled her off the stool. "When's the last time you bowled?" he asked as he led her across the alley to an open lane.

"I think I was fourteen. Group date, which didn't go well, as the object of my affection, Nathan Hobbs, only had eyes for the incessantly giggly and already well-developed Missy Dover."

"You can't let previous heartbreak spoil your enjoyment."

"But I didn't like the bowling part either."

"That was then." Cal sat her down on the smooth wooden bench, slid on beside her. "You'll have a better time with it tonight. Ever make a strike?"

"Still talking bowling? No."

"You will, and there's nothing much that beats the feeling of that first strike."

"How about sex with Hugh Jackman?"

He stopped tying his bowling shoe to stare over at her. "You had sex with Hugh Jackman?"

"No, but I'm willing to bet any amount of money that having sex with Hugh Jackman would, for me, beat out the feeling of knocking down ten pins with one ball."

"Okay. But I'm willing to bet—let's make it ten bucks—that when you throw a strike, you'll admit it's up there on the Thrill-O-Meter."

"First, it's highly unlikely I'll throw anything resembling a strike. Second, I could lie."

"You will. And you won't. Change your shoes, Blondie."

Five

IT WASN'T AS RIDICULOUS AS SHE'D ASSUMED IT would be. Silly, yes, but she had plenty of room for silly.

The balls were mottled black—the small ones without the three holes. The job was to heave it down the long polished alley toward the red-necked pins he called Duck Pins.

He watched as she walked up to the foul line, swung back, and did the heave.

The ball bounced a couple of times before it toppled into the gutter.

"Okay." She turned, tossed back her hair. "Your turn."

"You get two more balls per frame."

"Woo-hoo."

He shot her the quick grin. "Let's work on your delivery and follow-through, then we'll tackle approach." He walked toward her with another ball as he spoke. He handed her the ball. "Hold it with both hands," he instructed as he turned her around to face the pins. "Now you want to take a step forward with your left foot, bend your knees like you were doing a squat, but bend over from the waist."

He was snuggled up right behind her now, his front sort of bowing over her back. She tipped her face around to meet his eyes.

"You use this routine to hit on women, right?"

"Absolutely. Eighty-five percent success ratio. You're going to want to aim for the front pin. You can worry about the pockets and the sweet spot later. Now you're just going to bring your right arm back, then sweep it forward with your fingers aimed at the front pin. Let the ball go, following your fingers."

"Hmm." But she tried it. This time the ball didn't bounce straight into the gutter, but actually stayed on the lane long enough to bump down the two pins on the far right.

Since the woman in the next lane, who *had* to be sixty if she was a day, slid gracefully to the foul line, released, and knocked down seven pins, Quinn didn't feel like celebrating.

"Better."

"Two balls, two pins. I don't think that earns my bootie dance."

"Since I'm looking forward to your bootie dance, I'll help you do better yet. More from your shoulder down this time. Nice perfume," he added before he walked back to get her another ball.

"Thanks." Stride, bend, swing, release, she thought. And actually managed to knock down the end pin on the other side of the alley.

"Overcompensated." He hit the reset button. The grate came down, pins were swept off with a lot of clattering, and another full triangle thudded into place.

"She knocked them all down." Quinn gave a head nod toward the woman in the next lane who'd taken her seat. "She didn't seem all that excited."

"Mrs. Keefafer? Bowls twice a week, and has become

jaded. On the outside. Inside, believe me, she's doing her bootie dance."

"If you say so."

He adjusted Quinn's shoulders, shifted her hips. And yeah, she could see why he had such a high success rate with this routine. Eventually, after countless attempts, she was able to take down multiple pins that took odd bites out of the triangle.

There was a wall of noise, the low thunder of balls rolling, the sharp clatter of pins, hoots and cheers from bowlers and onlookers, the bright bells of a pinball machine.

She smelled beer and wax, and the gooey orange cheese—a personal favorite—from the nachos someone munched on in the next lane.

Timeless, all-American, she mused, absently drafting an article on the experience. Centuries-old sport—she'd need to research that part—to good, clean, family fun.

She thought she had the hang of it, more or less, though she was shallow enough to throw a deliberate gutter ball here and there so Cal would adjust her stance.

As he did, she considered changing the angle of the article from family fun to the sexiness of bowling. The idea made her grin as she took her position.

Then it happened. She released the ball and it rolled down the center of the alley. Surprised, she took a step back. Then another with her arms going up to clamp on the sides of her head.

Something tingled in her belly as her heartbeat sped up. "Oh. Oh. Look! It's going to—"

There was a satisfying *crack* and *crash* as ball slapped pins and pins tumbled in all directions. Bumping into each other, rolling, spinning, until the last fell with a slow, drunken sway.

"Well, my *God!*" She actually bounced on the toes of her rented shoes. "Did you see that? Did you—" And when she spun around, a look of stunned delight on her face, he was grinning at her.

"Son of a bitch," she muttered. "I owe you ten bucks."

"You learn fast. Want to try an approach?"

She wandered back toward him. "I believe I'm . . . spent. But I may come by some evening for lesson number two."

"Happy to oblige." Sitting hip-to-hip, they changed shoes. "I'll walk you back to the hotel."

"All right."

He got his coat, and on the way out shot a wave at the skinny young guy behind the shoe rental counter. "Back in ten."

"Quiet," she said the minute they stepped outside. "Just listen to all that quiet."

"The noise is part of the fun and the quiet after part of the reward."

"Did you ever want to do anything else, or did you grow up with a burning desire to manage a bowling alley?"

"Family fun center," he corrected. "We have an arcade—pinball, skee-ball, video games, and a section for kids under six. We do private parties—birthday parties, bachelor parties, wedding receptions—"

"Wedding receptions?"

"Sure. Bar mitzvahs, bat mitzvahs, anniversaries, corporate parties."

Definitely meat for an article, she realized. "A lot of arms on one body."

"You could say that."

"So why aren't you married and raising the next generation of Bowl-a-Rama kingpins, pun intended."

"Love has eluded me."

"Aw."

Despite the biting cold, it was pleasant to walk beside a man who naturally fit his stride to hers, to watch the clouds of their breath puff out, then merge together before the wind tore them to nothing.

He had an easy way about him and killer eyes, so there were worse things than feeling her toes go numb with cold in boots she knew were more stylish than practical.

"Are you going to be around if I think of some pertinent question to ask you tomorrow?"

" 'Round and about," he told her. "I can give you my cell phone number if—"

"Wait." She dug into her bag and came out with her own phone. Still walking, she punched a few keys. "Shoot."

He rattled it off. "I'm aroused by a woman who not only immediately finds what she's looking for in the mysterious depths of her purse, but who can skillfully operate electronic devices."

"Is that a sexist remark?"

"No. My mother always knows where everything is, but is still defeated by the universal remote. My sister Jen can operate anything from a six-speed to a wireless mouse, but can never find anything without a twenty-minute hunt, and my other sister, Marly, can't find anything, ever, and gets intimidated by her electric can opener. And here you are, stirring me up by being able to do both."

"I've always been a siren." She tucked her phone back in her bag as they turned to the steps leading to the long front porch of the hotel. "Thanks for the escort."

"No problem."

There was one of those beats; she recognized it. Both of them wondering, did they shake hands, just turn and go, or give in to curiosity and lean into a kiss.

"Let's stay to the safe road for now," she decided. "I admit, I like the look of your mouth, but moving on that's bound to tangle things up before I really get started on what brought me here."

"It's a damn shame you're right about that." He dipped his hands into his pockets. "So I'll just say good night. I'll wait, make sure you get inside."

"Good night." She walked up the steps to the door, eased it open. Then glanced back to see him standing, hands still in his pockets, with the old-fashioned streetlight spotlighting him.

Oh, yeah, she thought, it was a damn shame.

"See you soon."

He waited until the door shut behind her, then taking a couple of steps, studied the windows of the second and third floor. She'd said her window faced Main Street, but he wasn't sure what level she was on.

After a few moments, a light flashed on in a second-floor window, telling him Quinn was safe in her room.

He turned and had taken two steps when he saw the boy. He stood on the sidewalk half a block down. He wore no coat, no hat, no protection against the bite of wind. The long stream of his hair didn't stir in it.

His eyes gleamed, eerily red, as his lips peeled back in a snarl.

Cal heard the sound inside his head while ice balled in his belly.

Not real, he told himself. Not yet. A projection only, like in the dreams. But even in the dreams, it could hurt you or make you think you were hurt.

"Go back where you came from, you bastard." Cal spoke clearly, and as calmly as his shaken nerves would allow. "It's not your time yet."

When it is, I'll devour you, all of you, and everything you hold precious.

The lips didn't move with the words, but stayed frozen in that feral snarl.

"We'll see who feels the bite this round." Cal took another step forward.

And the fire erupted. It spewed out of the wide brick sidewalk, fumed across the street in a wall of wild red. Before he could register that there was no heat, no burn, Cal had already stumbled back, thrown up his hands.

The laughter rang in his head, as wild as the flames. Then both snapped off.

The street was quiet, the brick and buildings unmarred.

Tricks up his sleeve, Cal reminded himself. Lots of tricks up his sleeve.

He made himself stride forward, through where the false fire had run. There was a strong acrid odor that puffed then vanished like the vapor of his own breath. In that instant he recognized it.

Brimstone.

UPSTAIRS IN THE ROOM THAT MADE HER BLISSfully happy with its four-poster bed and fluffy white duvet, Quinn sat at the pretty desk with its curved legs and polished surface writing up the day's notes, data, and impressions on her laptop.

She loved that there were fresh flowers in the room, and a little blue bowl of artfully arranged fresh fruit. The bath held a deep and delightful claw-foot tub and a snowy white pedestal sink. There were thick, generous towels, two bars of soap, and rather stylish minibottles of shampoo, body cream, and bath gel.

Instead of boring, mass-produced posters, the art on the walls were original paintings and photos, which the discreet note on the desk identified as works by local artists available at Artful, a shop on South Main.

The room was full of homey welcoming touches, *and* provided high-speed Internet access. She made a note to reserve the same room after her initial week was up, for the return trips she planned in April, then again in July.

She'd accomplished quite a bit on her first day, which was a travel day on top of it. She'd met two of the three focal players, had an appointment to hike to the Pagan Stone. She'd gotten a feel for the town, on the surface in any case. And had, she believed, a personal experience with the manifestation of an unidentified (as yet) force.

And she had the bare bones for a bowling article that should work for her friends at *Detour*.

Not bad, especially when you added in she'd dined

sensibly on the grilled chicken salad in the hotel dining room, had *not* given in to temptation and inhaled an entire pizza but had limited herself to half a slice. And she'd bowled a strike.

On the personal downside, she supposed, as she shut down to prepare for bed, she'd also resisted the temptation to lock lips with the very appealing Caleb Hawkins.

Wasn't she all professional and unsatisfied?

Once she'd changed into her bedtime flannel pants and T-shirt, she nagged herself into doing fifteen minutes of pilates (okay, ten), then fifteen of yoga, before burrowing under the fabulous duvet with her small forest of down pillows.

She took her current book off the nightstand, burrowed into that as well until her eyes began to droop.

Just past midnight, she marked the novel, switched off the lamp, and snuggled into her happy nest.

As was her habit, she was asleep in a finger snap.

Quinn recognized the dream as a dream. Always, she enjoyed the sensation of the disjointed, carnival world of dreamscapes. It was, for her, like having some crazy adventure without any physical exertion. So when she found herself on a crooked path through a thick wood where the moonshine silvered the leaves and the curling fog rippled along the ground, a part of her mind thought: Oh boy! Here we go.

She thought she heard chanting, a kind of hoarse and desperate whisper, but the words themselves were indiscernible.

The air felt like silk, so soft, as she waded through the pools of fog. The chanting continued, drawing her toward it. A single word seemed to fly out of that moonstruck night, and the word was *bestia*.

She heard it over and over as she followed the crooked path through the silken air and the silver-laced trees. She felt a sexual pull, a heat and reaching in the belly toward whatever, whoever called out in the night.

Twice, then three times, the air seemed to whisper.

Beatus. The murmur of that warmed her skin. In the dream, she quickened her steps.

Out of the moon-drenched trees swam a black owl, its great wings stirring a storm in that soft air, chilling it until she shivered. And was, even in the dream, afraid.

With that cold wind stirring, she saw, stretched across the path, a golden fawn. The blood from its slit throat drenched the ground so it gleamed wet and black in the night.

Her heart squeezed with pity. So young, so sweet, she thought as she made herself approach it. Who could have done such a thing?

For a moment, the dead, staring eyes of the fawn cleared, shone as gold as its hind. It looked at her with such sorrow, such wisdom, tears gathered in her throat.

The voice came now, not through the whipped air, but in her mind. The single word: *devoveo*.

Then the trees were bare but for the ice that sheathed trunk and branch, and the silver moonlight turned gray. The path had turned, or she had, so now she faced a small pond. The water was black as ink, as if any light the sky pushed down was sucked into its depths and smothered there.

Beside the pond was a young woman in a long brown dress. Her hair was chopped short, with the strings and tufts of it sticking out wildly. Beside the black pond she bent to fill the pockets of her brown dress with stones.

Hello! Quinn called out. *What are you doing?*

The girl only continued to fill her pockets. As Quinn walked closer, she saw the girl's eyes were full of tears, and of madness.

Crap. You don't want to do that. You don't want to go Virginia Woolf. Wait. Just wait. Talk to me.

The girl turned her head, and for one shocked moment, Quinn saw the face as her own. *He doesn't know everything,* the mad girl said. *He didn't know you.*

She threw out her arms, and her slight body, weighed heavy with her cache of stones, tipped, tipped, tipped until it met the black water. The pond swallowed it like a waiting mouth.

Quinn leaped—what else could she do? Her body braced for the shock of cold as she filled her lungs with air.

There was a flash of light, a roar that might have been thunder or something alive and hungry. She was on her knees in a clearing where a stone rose out of the earth like an altar. Fire spewed around her, above her, through her, but she felt none of its heat.

Through the flames she saw two shapes, one black, one white, grappling like mad animals. With a terrible rending sound, the earth opened up, and like the waiting mouth of the pond, swallowed everything.

The scream ripped from her throat as that maw widened to take her. Clawing, she dragged herself toward the stone, fought to wrap her arms around it.

It broke into three equal parts, sending her tumbling, tumbling into that open, avid mouth.

She woke, huddled on the lovely bed, the linens tangled around her legs as she gripped one of the bedposts as if her life depended on it.

Her breath was an asthmatic's wheeze, and her heart beat so fast and hard it had her head spinning.

A dream, just a dream, she reminded herself, but couldn't force herself—not quite yet—to release her hold on the bedpost.

Clinging to it, she let her cheek rest on the wood, closed her eyes until the shaking had lessened to an occasional quiver.

"Hell of a ride," she mumbled.

The Pagan Stone. That's where she'd been at the end of the dream, she was certain of it. She recognized it from pictures she'd seen. Small wonder she'd have a scary dream about it, about the woods. And the pond . . . Wasn't there something in her research about a woman drowning in the pond? They'd named it after her. Hester's Pond. No, pool. Hester's Pool.

It all made sense, in dream logic.

Yeah, a hell of a ride, and she'd die happy if she never took another like it.

She glanced at her travel alarm, and saw by its luminous dial it was twenty after three. Three in the morning, she thought, was the dead time, the worst time to be wakeful. So she'd go back to sleep, like a sensible woman. She'd straighten the bed, get herself a nice cool drink of water, then tune out.

She'd had enough jolts and jumps for her first day.

She slid out of bed to tug the sheets and duvet back into some semblance of order, then turned, intending to go to the adjoining bath for a glass of water.

The scream wouldn't sound. It tore through her head like scrabbling claws, but nothing could tear its way out of the hot lock of her throat.

The boy grinned obscenely through the dark window. His face, his hands pressed against the glass bare inches away from her own. She saw its tongue flick out to roll across those sharp, white teeth, and those eyes, gleaming red, seemed as bottomless and hungry as the mouth of earth that had tried to swallow her in her dream.

Her knees wanted to buckle, but she feared if she dropped to the ground it would come crashing through the glass to latch those teeth on her throat like a wild dog.

Instead, she lifted her hand in the ancient sign against evil. "Get away from here," she whispered. "Stay away from me."

It laughed. She heard the horrible, giddy sound of it, saw its shoulders shake with mirth. Then it pushed off the glass into a slow, sinuous somersault. It hung suspended for a moment above the sleeping street. Then it . . . condensed, was all she could think. It shrank into itself, into a pinpoint of black, and vanished.

Quinn launched herself at the window, yanked the shade down to cover every inch of glass. And lowering to the floor at last, she leaned back against the wall, trembling.

When she thought she could stand, she used the wall as

a brace, quick-stepping to the other windows. She was out of breath again by the time all the shades were pulled, and tried to tell herself the room didn't feel like a closed box.

She got the water—she needed it—and gulped down two full glasses. Steadier, she stared at the covered windows.

"Okay, screw you, you little bastard."

Picking up her laptop, she went back to her position on the floor—it just felt safer under the line of the windowsills—and began to type up every detail she remembered from the dream, and from the thing that pressed itself to the night glass.

WHEN SHE WOKE, THE LIGHT WAS A HARD YELlow line around the cream linen of the shades. And the battery of her laptop was stone dead. Congratulating herself on remembering to back up before she'd curled onto the floor to sleep, she got her creaky self up.

Stupid, of course, she told herself as she tried to stretch out the worst of the stiffness. Stupid not to turn off her machine, then crawl back into that big, cozy bed. But she'd forgotten the first and hadn't even considered the second.

Now, she put the computer back on the pretty desk, plugged it in to recharge the batteries. With some caution—after all, it had been broad daylight when she'd seen the boy the first time—she approached the first window. Eased up the shade.

The sun was lancing down out of a boiled blue sky. On the pavement, on awnings and roofs, a fresh white carpet of snow shimmered.

She spotted a few merchants or their employees busily shoveling sidewalks or porches and steps. Cars putted along the plowed street. She wondered if school had been called or delayed due to the snow.

She wondered if the boy had demon classes that day.

For herself, Quinn decided she was going to treat her abused body to a long soak in the charming tub. Then she'd try Ma's Pantry for breakfast, and see who she could get to talk to her over her fruit and granola about the legends of Hawkins Hollow.

Six

CAL SAW HER COME IN WHILE HE CUT INTO HIS short stack at the counter. She had on those high, sharp-heeled boots, faded jeans, and a watch cap, bright as a cardinal, pulled over her hair.

She'd wound on a scarf that made him think of Joseph's coat of many colors, which added a jauntiness with her coat opened. Under it was a sweater the color of ripe blueberries.

There was something about her, he mused, that would have been bright and eye-catching even in mud brown.

He watched her eyes track around the diner area, and decided she was weighing where to sit, whom to approach. Already working, he concluded. Maybe she always was. He was damn sure, even on short acquaintance, that her mind was always working.

She spotted him. She aimed that sunbeam smile of hers, started over. He felt a little like the kid in the pickup game of ball, who got plucked from all the others waving their arms and shouting: Me! Me! Pick me!

"Morning, Caleb."

"Morning, Quinn. Buy you breakfast?"

"Absolutely." She leaned over his plate, took a long, dramatic sniff of his butter-and-syrup-loaded pancakes. "I bet those are fabulous."

"Best in town." He stabbed a thick bite with his fork, held it out. "Want a sample?"

"I can never stop at a taste. It's a sickness." She slid onto the stool, swiveled around to beam at the waitress as she unwound her scarf. "Morning. I'd love some coffee, and do you have any granola-type substance that could possibly be topped with any sort of fruit?"

"Well, we got Special K, and I could slice you up some bananas with it."

"Perfect." She reached over the counter. "I'm Quinn."

"The writer from up in PA." The waitress nodded, took Quinn's hand in a firm grip. "Meg Stanley. You watch this one here, Quinn," Meg said with a poke at Cal. "Some of those quiet types are sneaky."

"Some of us mouthy types are fast."

That got a laugh out of Meg as she poured Quinn's coffee. "Being quick on your feet's a strong advantage. I'll get that cereal for you."

"Why," Cal wondered aloud as he forked up another dripping bite of pancake, "would anyone willingly choose to eat trail mix for breakfast?"

"It's an acquired taste. I'm still acquiring it. But knowing myself, and I do, if I keep coming in here for breakfast, I'll eventually succumb to the allure of the pancake. Does the town have a gym, a health club, a burly guy who rents out his Bowflex?"

"There's a little gym down in the basement of the community center. You need a membership, but I can get you a pass on that."

"Really? You're a handy guy to know, Cal."

"I am. You want to change your order? Go for the gold, then the treadmill?"

"Not today, but thanks. So." After she'd doctored her

coffee, she picked up the cup with both hands, sipping as she studied him through the faint rise of steam. "Now that we're having our second date—"

"How'd I miss the first one?"

"You bought me pizza and a beer and took me bowling. In my dictionary, that falls under the definition of date. Now you're buying me breakfast."

"Cereal and bananas. I do appreciate a cheap date."

"Who doesn't? But since we're dating and all . . ." She took another sip as he laughed. "I'd like to share an experience with you."

She glanced over as Meg brought her a white stoneware bowl heaped with cereal and sliced bananas. "Figured you'd be going for the two percent milk with this."

"Perceptive and correct, thanks."

"Get you anything else?"

"We're good for now, Meg," Cal told her. "Thanks."

"Just give a holler."

"An experience," Cal prompted, as Meg moved down the counter.

"I had a dream."

His insides tensed even before she began to tell him, in a quiet voice and in careful detail of the dream she'd had during the night.

"I knew it was a dream," she concluded. "I always do, even during them. Usually I get a kick out of them, even the spooky ones. Because, you know, not really happening. I haven't actually grown a second head so I can argue with myself, nor am I jumping out of a plane with a handful of red balloons. But this . . . I can't say I got a charge out of it. I didn't just think I felt cold, for instance. I *was* cold. I didn't just think I felt myself hit and roll on the ground. I found bruises this morning that weren't there when I went to bed. Fresh bruises on my hip. How do you get hurt in a dream, if it's just a dream?"

You could, he thought, in Hawkins Hollow. "Did you fall out of bed, Quinn?"

"No, I didn't fall out of bed." For the first time, there

was a whiff of irritation in her voice. "I woke up with my arms locked around the bedpost like it was my long-lost lover. And all this was before I saw that red-eyed little bastard again."

"Where?"

She paused long enough to spoon up some cereal. He wasn't sure if the expression of displeasure that crossed her face was due to the taste, or her thoughts. "Did you ever read King's *Salem's Lot*?"

"Sure. Small town, vampires. Great stuff."

"Remember that scene? The little boys, brothers. One's been changed after they snatched him off the path in the woods. He comes to visit his brother one night."

"Nothing scarier than kiddie vampires."

"Not much, anyway. And the vampire kid's just *hanging* outside the window. Just floating out there, scratching on the glass. It was like that. He was pressed to the glass, and I'll point out I'm on the second floor. Then he did a stylish back flip in the air, and poofed."

He laid a hand over hers, found it cold, rubbed some warmth into it. "You have my home and cell numbers, Quinn. Why didn't you call me?"

She ate a little more, then, smiling at Meg, held up her cup for a top-off. "I realize we're dating, Cal, but I don't call all the guys I go bowling with at three thirty in the morning to go: eek! I slogged through swamps in Louisiana on the trail of the ghost of a voodoo queen—and don't think I don't know how that sounds. I spent the night, alone, in a reputedly haunted house on the coast of Maine, and interviewed a guy who was reported to be possessed by no less than thirteen demons. Then there was the family of werewolves in Tallahassee. But this kid . . ."

"You don't believe in werewolves and vampires, Quinn."

She turned on the stool to face him directly. "My mind's as open as a twenty-four-hour deli, and considering the circumstances, yours should be, too. But no, I don't think this thing is a vampire. I saw him in broad daylight, after all.

But he's not human, and just because he's not human doesn't make him less than real. He's part of the Pagan Stone. He's part of what happens here every seven years. And he's early, isn't he?"

Yeah, he thought, her mind was always working and it was sharp as a switchblade. "This isn't the best place to go into this any deeper."

"Say where."

"I said I'd take you to the stone tomorrow, and I will. We'll get into more detail then. Can't do it today," he said, anticipating her. "I've got a full plate, and tomorrow's better anyway. They're calling for sun and forties today and tomorrow." He hitched up a hip to take out his wallet. "Most of this last snow'll be melted." He glanced down at her boots as he laid bills on the counter to cover both their tabs. "If you don't have anything more suitable to hike in than those, you'd better buy something. You won't last a half mile otherwise."

"You'd be surprised how long I can last."

"Don't know as I would. I'll see you tomorrow if not before."

Quinn frowned at him as he walked out, then turned back as Meg slid her rag down the counter. "Sneaky. You were right about that."

"Known the boy since before he was born, haven't I?"

Amused, Quinn propped an elbow back on the bar as she toyed with the rest of her cereal. Apparently a serious scare in the night and mild irritation with a man in the morning was a more effective diet aid than any bathroom scale. Meg struck her as a comfortable woman, wide-hipped in her brown cords and flannel shirt, sleeves rolled up at the elbows. Her hair curled tight as a poodle's fur in a brown ball around a soft and lined face. And there was a quick spark in her hazel eyes that told Quinn she'd be inclined to talk.

"So, Meg, what else do you know? Say about the Pagan Stone."

"Buncha nonsense, you ask me."

"Really?"

"People just get a little"—she circled her finger at her ear—"now and again. Tip too much at the bottle, get all het up. One thing leads to another. Good for business though, the speculation, if you follow me. Get plenty of flatlanders in here wondering about it, asking about it, taking pictures, buying souvenirs."

"You never had any experiences?"

"Saw some people usually have good sense acting like fools, and some who got a mean streak in them acting meaner for a spell of time." She shrugged. "People are what people are, and sometimes they're more so."

"I guess that's true."

"If you want more about it, you should go on out to the library. There's some books there written about the town, the history and whatnot. And Sally Keefafer—"

"Bowling Sally?"

Meg snorted a laugh. "She does like to bowl. Library director. She'll bend your ear plenty if you ask her questions. She loves to talk, and never found a subject she couldn't expound on till you wanted to slap some duct tape over her mouth."

"I'll do that. You sell duct tape here?"

Meg hooted out another laugh, shook her head. "If you really want to talk, and get some sense out of it, you want Mrs. Abbott. She ran the old library, and she's at the new one for a spell most every day."

Then scooping up the bills Cal left, she went to refill waiting cups at the other end of the counter.

CAL HEADED STRAIGHT TO HIS OFFICE. HE HAD the usual morning's paperwork, phone calls, e-mails. And he had a morning meeting scheduled with his father and the arcade guy before the center opened for the afternoon leagues.

He thought of the wall of fire across Main Street the night before. Add that to two sightings by Quinn—an outsider—and it sure as hell seemed the *entity* that plagued the town was starting its jollies early.

Her dream troubled him as well. The details—he'd recognized where she'd been, what she'd seen. For her to have dreamed so lucidly about the pond, about the clearing, to have bruises from it, meant, in his opinion, she had to be connected in some way.

A distant relation wasn't out of the question, and there should be a way to do a search. But he had other relations, and none but his immediate family had ever spoken of any effects, even during the Seven.

As he passed through the bowling center, he sent a wave toward Bill Turner, who was buffing the lanes. The big, burly machine's throaty hum echoed through the empty building.

The first thing he checked in his office was his e-mail, and he let out a breath of relief when he saw one from Gage.

Prague. Got some business to clear up. Should be back in the U.S. of A. inside a couple weeks. Don't do anything stupider than usual without me.

No salutation, no signature. Very Gage, Cal thought. And it would have to do, for now.

Contact me as soon as you're Stateside, Cal wrote back. *Things are already rumbling. Will always wait for you to do the stupid, because you're better at it.*

After clicking Send, he dashed another off to Fox.

Need to talk. My place, six o'clock. Got beer. Bring food that's not pizza.

Best he could do, for now, Cal thought. Because life just had to keep rolling on.

QUINN WALKED BACK TO THE HOTEL TO RE-trieve her laptop. If she was going to the library, she might as well use it for a couple hours' work. And while she expected she had most, if not all, of the books tucked into the town's library already, maybe this Mrs. Abbott would prove to be a valuable source.

Caleb Hawkins, it appeared, was going to be a clam until the following day.

As she stepped into the hotel lobby she saw the pert blond clerk behind the desk—Mandy, Quinn thought after a quick scroll through her mental PDA—and a brunette in the curvy chair being checked in.

Quinn's quick once-over registered the brunette with the short, sassy do as mid to late twenties, with a travel-weary look about her that didn't do anything much to diminish the seriously pretty face. Jeans and a black sweater fit well over an athletic build. Pooled at her feet were a suitcase, a laptop case, a smaller bag probably for cosmetics and other female necessities, and an excellent and roomy hobo in slick red leather.

Quinn had a moment of purse envy as she aimed a smile.

"Welcome back, Miss Black. If you need anything, I'll be with you in just a minute."

"I'm fine, thanks."

Quinn turned to the stairs and, starting up, heard Mandy's cheerful, "You're all checked in, Miss Darnell. I'm just going to call Harry to help with your bags."

As was her way, Quinn speculated on Miss Gorgeous Red Bag Darnell as she climbed up to her room. Passing through on her way to New York. No, too odd a place to stop over, and too early in the day to stop a road trip.

Visiting relatives or friends, but why wouldn't she just bunk with said relatives or friends? Then again, she had some of both she'd rather not bunk with.

Maybe a business trip, Quinn mused as she let herself into her room.

Well, if Red Bag I Want for My Very Own stayed more than a few hours, Quinn would find out just who and what and why. It was, after all, what she was best at.

Quinn packed up her laptop, added a spare notebook and extra pencils in case she got lucky. Digging out her phone, she set it on vibrate. Little was more annoying, to her mind, than ringing cell phones in libraries and theaters.

She slipped a county map into her case in the event she decided to explore.

Armed, she headed down for the drive to the other end of town and the Hawkins Hollow Library.

From her own research, Quinn knew that the original stone building tucked on Main Street now housed the community center, and the gym she intended to make use of. At the turn of the current century the new library had been built on a pretty rise of land on the south end of town. It, too, was stone, though Quinn was pretty sure it was the facing used on concrete and such rather than quarried. It was two levels with short wings on either side and a portico-style entrance. The style, she thought, was attractively old-fashioned. One, she guessed, the local historic society had likely fought a war to win.

She admired the benches, and the trees she imagined made shady reading nooks in season as she pulled up to park in the side lot.

It smelled like a library, she thought. Of books and a little dust, of silence.

She saw a brightly lettered sign announcing a Story Hour in the Children's section at ten thirty.

She wound her way through. Computers, long tables, carts, a few people wandering the stacks, a couple of old men paging through newspapers. She heard the soft *hum-chuck* of a copier and the muted ringing of a phone from the Information Desk.

Reminding herself to focus because if she wandered she'd be entranced by the spell she believed all libraries wove, she aimed straight for Information. And in the hushed tone reserved for libraries and churches, addressed the stringy man on duty. "Good morning, I'm looking for books on local history."

"That would be on the second floor, west wing. Steps over to the left, elevator straight back. Anything in particular you're after?"

"Thanks, but I'm just going to poke. Is Mrs. Abbott in today?"

"Mrs. Abbott is retired, but she's in most every day by eleven. In a volunteer capacity."

"Thanks again."

Quinn used the stairs. They had a nice curve to them, she thought, almost a *Gone With the Wind* sort of swish. She put on mental blinders so as not to be tempted by stacks and reading areas until she found herself in Local Interest.

It was more a room—a mini-library—than a section. Nice cozy chairs, tables, amber-shaded lamps, even footrests. And it was larger than she'd expected.

Then again, she should have accounted for the fact that there had been battles fought in and around the Hollow in both the Revolutionary and Civil Wars.

Books pertaining to those were arranged in separate areas, as were books on the county, the state, and the town.

In addition there was a very healthy section for local authors.

She tried that section first and saw she'd hit a treasure trove. There had to be more than a dozen she hadn't come across on her own hunt before coming to town. They were self-published, vanity-pressed, small local publishers.

Titles like *Nightmare Hollow* and *The Hollow, The Truth* had her giddy with anticipation. She set up her laptop, her notebook, her recorder, then pulled out five books. It was then she noticed the discreet bronze plaque.

The Hawkins Hollow Library
gratefully acknowledges the generosity of
the Franklin and Maybelle Hawkins Family

Franklin and Maybelle. Very probably Cal's ancestors. It struck Quinn as both suitable and generous that they would have donated the funds to sponsor this room. This particular room.

She settled at the table, chose one of the books at random, then began to read.

She'd covered pages of her notebook with names, locations, dates, reputed incidents, and any number of theories when she scented lavender and baby powder.

Surfacing, she saw a trim and tidy old woman standing in black, sensible shoes with her hands folded neatly at the waist of her purple suit.

Her hair was a thinning snowball; her clear framed glasses so thickly lensed Quinn wondered how the tiny nose and ears supported their weight.

She wore pearls around her neck, a gold wedding band on her finger, and a leather-banded watch with a huge face that looked to be as practical as her thick-soled shoes.

"I'm Estelle Abbott," she said in her creaky voice. "Young Dennis said you asked after me."

As Quinn had gauged Dennis at Information as tumbling down the back end of his sixties, she imagined the woman who termed him young must have him by a good two decades.

"Yes." Quinn got to her feet, crossed over to offer her hand. "I'm Quinn Black, Mrs. Abbott. I'm—"

"Yes, I know. The writer. I've enjoyed your books."

"Thank you very much."

"No need. If I hadn't liked them I'd've told you straight-out. You're researching for a book on the Hollow."

"Yes, ma'am, I am."

"You'll find quite a bit of information here. Some of it useful." She peered at the books on the table. "Some of it nonsense."

"Then in the interest of separating the wheat from the chaff, maybe you could find some time to talk to me at some point. I'd be happy to take you to lunch or dinner whenever you—"

"That's very nice of you, but unnecessary. Why don't we sit down for a while, and we'll see how things go?"

"That would be great."

Estelle crossed to a chair, sat, then with her back ruler-straight and her knees glued together, folded her hands in her lap. "I was born in the Hollow," she began, "lived here all of my ninety-seven years."

"Ninety-seven?" Quinn didn't have to feign the surprise. "I'm usually pretty good at gauging age, and I'd put you a solid decade under that."

"Good bones," Estelle said with an easy smile. "I lost my husband, John, also born and raised here, eight years back come the fifth of next month. We were married seventy-one years."

"What was your secret?"

That brought on another smile. "Learn to laugh, otherwise, you'll beat them to death with a hammer first chance."

"Just let me write that down."

"We had six children—four boys, two girls—and all of them living still and not in jail, thank the Lord. Out of them, we had ourselves nineteen grandchildren, and out of them got ourselves twenty-eight greats—last count, and five of the next generation with two on the way."

Quinn simply goggled. "Christmas must be insane in a good way."

"We're scattered all over, but we've managed to get most everybody in one place at one time a few times."

"Dennis said you were retired. You were a librarian?"

"I started working in the library when my youngest started school. That would be the old library on Main Street. I worked there more than fifty years. Went back to school myself and got my degree. Johnnie and I traveled, saw a lot of the world together. For a time we thought about moving on down to Florida. But our roots here were too deep for that. I went to part-time work, then I retired when my Johnnie got sick. When he passed, I came back—still the old one while this was being built—as a volunteer or as an artifact, however you look at it. I tell you this so you'll have some idea about me."

"You love your husband and your children, and the children who've come from them. You love books, and you're proud of the work you've done. You love this town, and respect the life you've lived here."

Estelle gave her a look of approval. "You have an efficient and insightful way of summing up. You didn't say I loved my husband, but used the present tense. That tells me you're an observant and sensitive young woman. I sensed from your books that you have an open and seeking mind. Tell me, Miss Black, do you also have courage?"

Quinn thought of the thing outside the window, the way its tongue had flicked over its teeth. She'd been afraid, but she hadn't run. "I like to think so. Please call me Quinn."

"Quinn. A family name."

"Yes, my mother's maiden."

"Irish Gaelic. I believe it means 'counselor.' "

"It does, yes."

"I have a well of trivial information," Estelle said with a tap of her finger to her temple. "But I wonder if your name isn't relevant. You'll need to have the objectivity, and the sensitivity of a counselor to write the book that should be written on Hawkins Hollow."

"Why haven't you written it?"

"Not everyone who loves music can play the tune. Let me tell you a few things, some of which you may already know. There is a place in the woods that borders the west of this town, and that place was sacred ground, sacred and volatile ground long before Lazarus Twisse sought it out."

"Lazarus Twisse, the leader of the Puritan sect—the radical sect—which broke off or, more accurately, was cut off, from the godly in Massachusetts."

"According to the history of the time, yes. The Native Americans held that ground as sacred. And before them, it's said, powers battled for that circle of ground, both—the dark and the light, good and evil, whatever terms you prefer—left some seeds of that power there. They lay dormant, century by century, with only the stone to mark what had passed there. Over time the memories of the battle were forgotten or bastardized in folklore, and only the sense many felt that this ground and its stone were not ordinary dirt and rock remained."

Estelle paused, fell into silence so that Quinn heard the click and hum of the heater, and the light slap of leather shoes on the floor as someone passed by the room toward other business.

"Twisse came to the Hollow, already named for Richard Hawkins, who, with his wife and children, had carved a small settlement in 1648. You should remark that Richard's eldest daughter was Ann. When Twisse came, Hawkins, his family, and a handful of others—some who'd fled Europe as criminals, political or otherwise—had made their life here. As had a man calling himself Giles Dent. And Dent built a cabin in the woods where the stone rose out of the ground."

"What's called the Pagan Stone."

"Yes. He troubled no one, and as he had some skill and knowledge of healing, was often sought out for sickness or injury. There are some accounts that claim he was known as the Pagan, and that this was the basis of the name the Pagan Stone."

"You're not convinced those accounts are accurate."

"It may be that the term stuck, entered the language and the lexicon at that time. But it was the Pagan Stone long before the arrival of Giles Dent or Lazarus Twisse. There are other accounts that claim Dent dabbled in witchcraft, that he enspelled Ann Hawkins, seduced and impregnated her. Others state that Ann and Dent were indeed lovers, but that she went to his bed of her own free will, and left her family home to live with him in the little cabin with the Pagan Stone."

"It would've been difficult for her—for Ann Hawkins—either way," Quinn speculated. "Enspelled or free will, to live with a man, unmarried. If it was free will, if it was love, she must have been very strong."

"The Hawkinses have always been strong. Ann had to be strong to go to Dent, to stay with him. Then she had to be strong enough to leave him."

"There are a lot of conflicting stories," Quinn began. "Why do you believe Ann Hawkins left Giles Dent?"

"I believe she left to protect the lives growing inside her."

"From?"

"Lazarus Twisse. Twisse and those who followed him came to Hawkins Hollow in sixteen fifty-one. He was a powerful force, and soon the settlement was under his rule. His rule decreed there would be no dancing, no singing, no music, no books but the Bible. No church but his church, no god but his god."

"So much for freedom of religion."

"Freedom was never Twisse's goal. In the way of those thirsty for power above all else, he intimidated, terrorized, punished, banished, and used as his visible weapon, the wrath of his chosen god. As Twisse's power grew, so did his punishments and penalties. Stocks, lashings, the shearing of a woman's hair if she was deemed ungodly, the branding of a man should he be accused of a crime. And finally, the burning of those he judged to be witches. On the night of July the seventh, sixteen fifty-two, on the accusation of a young woman, Hester Deale, Twisse led a mob from the settlement to the Pagan Stone, and to Giles Dent. What happened there . . ."

Quinn leaned forward. But Estelle sighed and shook her head. "Well, there are many accounts. As there were many deaths. Seeds planted long before stirred in the ground. Some may have sprouted, only to die in the blaze that scorched the clearing.

"There are . . . fewer reports of what immediately followed, or followed over the next days and weeks. But in time, Ann Hawkins returned to the settlement with her three sons. And Hester Deale gave birth to a daughter eight months after the killing blaze at the Pagan Stone. Shortly, very shortly after her child, whom she claimed was sired by the devil, was born, Hester drowned herself in a small pond in Hawkins Wood."

Loading her pockets with stones, Quinn thought with a

suppressed shudder. "Do you know what happened to her child? Or the children of Ann Hawkins?"

"There are some letters, some journals, family Bibles. But most concrete information has been lost, or has never come to light. It will take considerable time and effort to dig out the truth. I can tell you this, those seeds stayed dormant until a night twenty-one years ago this July. They were awakened, and what sowed them awakened. They bloom for seven nights every seven years, and they strangle Hawkins Hollow. I'm sorry, I tire so quickly these days. It's irritating."

"Can I get you something? Or drive you home?"

"You're a good girl. My grandson will be coming along to pick me up. You'll have spoken, I imagine, to his son by now. To Caleb."

Something in the smile turned a switch in Quinn's brain. "Caleb would be your—"

"Great-grandson. Honorary, you could say. My brother Franklin and his wife, my dearest friend, Maybelle, were killed in an accident just before Jim—Caleb's father was born. My Johnnie and I stood as grandparents to my brother's grandchildren. I'd have counted them and theirs in that long list of progeny before."

"You're a Hawkins by birth then."

"I am, and our line goes back, in the Hollow, to Richard Hawkins, the founder—and through him to Ann." She paused a moment as if to let Quinn absorb, analyze. "He's a good boy, my Caleb, and he carries more than his share of weight on his shoulders."

"From what I've seen, he carries it well."

"He's a good boy," Estelle repeated, then rose. "We'll talk again, soon."

"I'll walk you downstairs."

"Don't trouble. They'll have tea and cookies for me in the staff lounge. I'm a pet here—in the nicest sense of the word. Tell Caleb we spoke, and that I'd like to speak with you again. Don't spend all this pretty day inside a book. As much as I love them, there's life to be lived."

"Mrs. Abbott?"

"Yes?"

"Who do you think planted the seeds at the Pagan Stone?"

"Gods and demons." Estelle's eyes were tired, but clear. "Gods and demons, and there's such a thin line between the two, isn't there?"

Alone, Quinn sat again. Gods and demons. Those were a big, giant step up from ghosts and spirits, and other bump-in-the-night residents. But didn't it fit, didn't it click right together with the words she remembered from her dreams?

Words she'd looked up that morning.

Bestia, Latin for beast.

Beatus, Latin for blessed.

Devoveo, Latin for sacrifice.

Okay, okay, she thought, if we're heading down that track, it might be a good time to call in the reserves.

She pulled out her phone. When she was greeted by voice mail, Quinn pushed down impatience and waited for her cue to leave a message.

"Cyb, it's Q. I'm in Hawkins Hollow, Maryland. And, wow, I've hooked a big one. Can you come? Let me know if you can come. Let me know if you can't come so I can talk you into it."

She closed the phone, and for the moment she ignored the stack of books she'd selected. Instead, she began to busily type up notes from Estelle Hawkins Abbott's recitation.

Seven

CAL DID WHAT HE THOUGHT OF AS THE PASS-OFF to his father. Since the meetings and the morning and afternoon league games were over and there was no party or event scheduled, the lanes were empty but for a couple of old-timers having a practice game on lane one.

The arcade was buzzing, as it tended to between the last school bell and the dinner hour. But Cy Hudson was running herd there, and Holly Lappins manned the front desk. Jake and Sara worked the grill and fountain, which would start hopping in another hour.

Everything, everyone was in its place, so Cal could sit with his father at the end of the counter over a cup of coffee before he headed for home, and his dad took over the center for the night.

They could sit quietly for a while, too. Quiet was his father's way. Not that Jim Hawkins didn't like to socialize. He seemed to like crowds as much as his alone time, remembered names, faces, and could and would converse on any subject, including politics and religion. The fact that he could do so without pissing anyone off was, in Cal's opinion, one of his finest skills.

His sandy-colored hair had gone a pure and bright silver over the last few years, and was trimmed every two weeks at the local barbershop. He rarely altered his uniform of khakis, Rockports, and oxford shirts on workdays.

Some would have called Jim Hawkins habitual, even boring. Cal called him reliable.

"Having a good month so far," Jim said in his take-your-time drawl. He took his coffee sweet and light, and by his wife's decree, cut off the caffeine at six p.m. sharp. "Kind of weather we've been having, you never know if people are going to burrow in, or get cabin fever so bad they want to be anywhere but home."

"It was a good idea, running the three-game special for February."

"I get one now and again." Jim smiled, lines fanning out and deepening around his eyes. "So do you. Your mom's wishing you'd come by, have dinner some night soon."

"Sure. I'll give her a call."

"Heard from Jen yesterday."

"How's she doing?"

"Fine enough to flaunt that it was seventy-four in San Diego. Rosie's learning to write her letters, and the baby's getting another tooth. Jen said she'd send us pictures."

Cal heard the wistfulness. "You and Mom should take another trip out there."

"Maybe, maybe in a month or two. We're heading to Baltimore on Sunday to see Marly and her brood. I saw your great-gran today. She told me she had a nice chat with that writer who's in town."

"Gran talked with Quinn?"

"In the library. She liked the girl. Likes the idea of this book, too."

"And how about you?"

Jim shook his head, contemplated as Sara drew off Cokes for a couple of teenagers taking a break from the arcade. "I don't know what I think, Cal, that's the plain truth.

I ask myself what good's it going to do to have somebody—and an outsider at that—write all this down so people can read about it. I tell myself that what happened before won't happen again—"

"Dad."

"I know that's not true, or most likely not true."

For a moment Jim just listened to the voices from the boys at the other end of the counter, the way they joked and poked at each other. He knew those boys, he thought. He knew their parents. If life worked as it ought to work, he'd know their wives and kids one day.

Hadn't he joked and poked at his own friends here once upon a time, over fountain Cokes and fries? Hadn't his own children run tame through this place? Now his girls were married and gone, with families of their own. And his boy was a man, sitting with worry in his eyes over problems too big to be understood.

"You have to prepare for it to happen again," Jim continued. "But for most of us, it all hazes up, it just hazes up so you can barely remember what did happen. Not you, I know. It's clear for you, and I wish that wasn't so. I guess if you believe this writer can help find the answers, I'm behind you on that."

"I don't know what I believe. I haven't worked it out yet."

"You will. Well. I'm going to go check on Cy. Some of the evening rollers'll be coming in before long, wanting a bite before they suit up."

He pushed away from the counter, took a long look around. He heard the echoes of his boyhood, and the shouts of his children. He saw his son, gangly with youth, sitting at the counter with the two boys Jim knew were the same as brothers to him.

"We've got a good place here, Cal. It's worth working for. Worth fighting to hold it steady."

Jim gave Cal a pat on the shoulder, then strolled away.

Not just the center, Cal thought. His father had meant the town. And Cal was afraid that holding it steady this time was going to be one hell of a battle.

He went straight home where most of the snow had melted off the shrubs and stones. Part of him had wanted to hunt Quinn down, pump out of her what she and his great-grandmother had talked about. Better to wait, he thought as he jingled his keys, better to wait then ease it out of her the next day. When they went to the Pagan Stone.

He glanced toward the woods where trees and shadows held pockets and rivers of snow, where he knew the path would be muddy from the melt.

Was it in there now, gathering itself? Had it somehow found a way to strike outside the Seven? Maybe, maybe, but not tonight. He didn't feel it tonight. And he always did.

Still, he couldn't deny he felt less exposed when he was inside the house, after he'd put on lights to push away the gloom.

He went through to the back door, opened it, and gave a whistle.

Lump took his time as Lump was wont to do. But the dog eased his way out of the doghouse and even stirred up the energy for a couple of tail wags before he moseyed across the backyard to the bottom of the deck stairs.

He gave a doggie sigh before clumping up the short flight. Then he leaned his whole body against Cal.

And that, Cal thought, was love. That was welcome home, how ya doing, in Lump's world.

He crouched down to stroke and ruffle the fur, to scratch between the floppy ears while Lump gazed at him soulfully. "How's it going? Get all your work done? What do you say we have a beer?"

They went inside together. Cal filled the dog bowl from the bin of chow while Lump sat politely, though Cal assumed a large portion of his dog's manners was sheer laziness. When the bowl was set in front of him, Lump ate slowly, and with absolute focus on the task at hand.

Cal pulled a beer out of the fridge and popped the top. Leaning back on the counter he took that first long swallow that signaled the end of the workday.

"Got some serious shit on my mind, Lump. Don't know what to do about it, think about it. Should I have found a way to stop Quinn from coming here? Not sure that would've worked since she seems to go where the hell she wants, but I could've played it different. Laughed it off, or pushed it higher, so the whole thing came off as bogus. Played it straight, so far, and I don't know where that's going to lead."

He heard the front door open, then Fox shouted, "Yo!" Fox came in carrying a bucket of chicken and a large white takeout bag. "Got tub-o-cluck, got fries. Want beer."

After dumping the food on the table, Fox pulled out a beer. "Your summons was pretty abrupt, son. I might've had a hot date tonight."

"You haven't had a hot date in two months."

"I'm storing it up." After the first swig, Fox shrugged off his coat, tossed it over a chair. "What's the deal?"

"Tell you while we eat."

As he'd been too brainwashed by his mother to fall back on the single-man's friend of paper plates, Cal set out two of stoneware in dull blue. They sat down to fried chicken and potatoes with Lump—as the only thing that lured the dog from food was more food—caging fries by leaning against Cal's knee or Fox's.

He told Fox everything, from the wall of fire, through Quinn's dream, and up to the conversation she'd had with his great-grandmother.

"Seeing an awful lot of the fucker for February," Fox mused. "That's never happened before. Did you dream last night?"

"Yeah."

"Me, too. Mine was a replay of the first time, the first summer. Only we didn't get to the school in time, and it wasn't just Miss Lister inside. It was everybody." He scrubbed a hand over his face before taking a long pull of beer. "Everybody in town, my family, yours, all inside. Trapped, beating on the windows, screaming, their faces at the windows while the place burned." He offered Lump another fry, and his eyes were as dark and soulful as the dog's. "Didn't happen that way, thank Christ. But it felt like it did. You know how that goes."

"Yeah." Cal let out a breath. "Yeah, I know how that goes. Mine was from that same summer, and we were all riding our bikes through town the way we did. Buildings were burned out, windows broken, cars wrecked and smoking. Bodies everywhere."

"It didn't happen that way," Fox repeated. "We're not ten anymore, and we're not going to let it happen that way."

"I've been asking myself how long we can do this, Fox. How long can we hold it back as much as we do? This time, the next. Three more times? How many more times are we going to watch people we know, people we see most every day turn? Go crazy, go mean. Hurt each other, hurt themselves?"

"As long as it takes."

Cal shoved his plate aside. "Not good enough."

"It's all we've got, for now."

"It's like a virus, an infection, passing from one person to another. Where's the goddamn antidote?"

"Not everyone's affected," Fox reminded him. "There has to be a reason for that."

"We've never found it."

"No, so maybe you were right. Maybe we do need fresh eyes, an outsider, objectivity we just don't have. Are you still planning to take Quinn to the stone tomorrow?"

"If I don't, she'll go anyway. So yeah, it's better I'm there."

"You want me? I can cancel some stuff."

"I can handle it." Had to handle it.

QUINN STUDIED THE MENU IN THE HOTEL'S ALmost empty dining room. She'd considered getting some takeout and eating in her room over her laptop, but she fell too easily into that habit, she knew. And to write about a town, she had to experience the town, and couldn't do that closed up in her pretty room eating a cold-cut sub.

She wanted a glass of wine, something chilly with a subtle zip. The hotel's cellar was more extensive than she'd expected, but she didn't want a whole bottle. She was frowning over the selections offered by the glass when Miss Fabulous Red Bag stepped in.

She'd changed into black pants, Quinn noted, and a cashmere sweater in two tissue-thin layers of deep blue under pale. The hair was great, she decided, pin straight with those jagged ends just past chin length. What Quinn knew would look messy on her came off fresh and stylish on the brunette.

Quinn debated catching her eye, trying a wave. She could ask Red Purse to join her for dinner. After all, who didn't hate to eat alone? Then she could pump her dinner companion for the really important details. Like where she got that bag.

Even as she charged up her smile, Quinn saw it.

It *slithered* across the glossy planks of the oak floor, leaving a hideous trail of bloody ooze behind it. At first she thought snake, then slug, then could barely think at all as she watched it slide up the legs of a table where an attractive young couple were enjoying cocktails by candlelight.

Its body, thick as a truck tire, mottled red over black, wound its way over the table, leaving that ugly smear on the snowy linen while the couple laughed and flirted.

A waitress walked briskly in, stepped in and through the sludge on the floor, to serve the couple their appetizers.

Quinn swore she could hear the table creak under its weight.

And its eyes when they met hers were the eyes of the boy, the red gleam in them bright and somehow *amused.* Then it began to wiggle wetly down the skirt of the tablecloth, and toward the brunette.

The woman stood frozen in place, her face bone white. Quinn pushed to her feet and, ignoring the surprised look from the waitress, leaped over the ugly path. She gripped the brunette's arm, pulled her out of the dining room.

"You saw it, too," Quinn said in a whisper. "You saw that thing. Let's get out of here."

"What? What?" The brunette cast shocked glances over her shoulder as she and Quinn stumbled for the door. "You saw it?"

"Sluggy, red-eyed, very nasty wake. Jesus. Jesus." She gulped in the raw February air on the hotel's porch. "They didn't see it, but you did. I did. Why is that? Fuck if I know, but I have an idea who might. That's my car right there. Let's go. Let's just go."

The brunette didn't say another word until they were in the car and Quinn was squealing away from the curb. "Who the hell are you?"

"Quinn. Quinn Black. I'm a writer, mostly on the spooky. Of which there is a surplus in this town. Who are you?"

"Layla Darnell. What *is* this place?"

"That's what I want to find out. I don't know if it's nice to meet you or not, Layla, under the circumstances."

"Same here. Where are we going?"

"To the source, or one of them." Quinn glanced over, saw Layla was still pale, still shaky. Who could blame her? "What are you doing in Hawkins Hollow?"

"I'm damned if I know, but I think I've decided to cut my visit short."

"Understandable. Nice bag, by the way."

Layla worked up a wan smile. "Thanks."

"Nearly there. Okay, you don't know why you're here, so where did you come from?"

"New York."

"I knew it. It's the polish. Do you love it?"

"Ah." Layla combed her fingers through her hair as she swiveled to look back. "Most of the time. I manage a boutique in SoHo. Did. Do. I don't know that anymore either."

Nearly there, Quinn thought again. *Let's keep calm.* "I bet you get great discounts."

"Yeah, part of the perks. Have you seen anything like that before. Like that *thing*?"

"Yeah. Have you?"

"Not when I was awake. I'm not crazy," Layla stated. "Or I am, and so are you."

"We're not crazy, which is what crazy people tend to say, so you'll just have to take my word." She swung onto Cal's lane, and aimed the car over the little bridge toward the house where lights—thank God—glowed in the windows.

"Whose house is this?" Layla gripped the front edge of her seat. "Who lives here?"

"Caleb Hawkins. His ancestors founded the town. He's okay. He knows about what we saw."

"How?"

"It's a long story, with a lot of holes in it. And now you're thinking, what am I doing in this car with a complete stranger who's telling me to go into this house pretty much in the middle of nowhere."

Layla took firm hold on the short strap of her bag, as if she might use it as a weapon. "The thought's crossed."

"Your instinct put you in the car with me, Layla. Maybe you could follow along with that for the next step. Plus, it's cold. We didn't bring our coats."

"All right. Yes, all right." With a bracing breath, Layla opened the door, and with Quinn walked toward the house. "Nice place. If you like isolated houses in the woods."

"Culture shock for the New Yorker."

"I grew up in Altoona, Pennsylvania."

"No kidding. Philadelphia. We're practically neighbors." Quinn knocked briskly on the door, then just opened the door and called in, "Cal!"

She was halfway across the living room when he hurried in. "Quinn? What?" Spotted Layla. "Hello. What?"

"Who's here?" Quinn demanded. "I saw another car in the drive."

"Fox. What's going on?"

"The bonus-round question." She sniffed. "Do I smell

fried chicken? Is there food? Layla—this is Layla Darnell; Layla, Cal Hawkins—Layla and I haven't had dinner."

She moved right by him, and walked toward the kitchen.

"I'm sorry, I think, to bust in on you," Layla began. It passed through her mind that he didn't look like a serial killer. But then again, how would she know? "I don't know what's happening, or why I'm here. I've had a confusing few days."

"Okay. Well, come on back."

Quinn already had a drumstick in her hand, and was taking a swig of Cal's beer. "Layla Darnell, Fox O'Dell. I'm not really in the mood for beer," she said to Cal. "I was about to order some wine when Layla and I were disgustingly interrupted. Got any?"

"Yeah. Yeah."

"Is it decent? If you run to jug or twist caps, I'll stick with beer."

"I've got some damn decent wine." He yanked a plate out, pushed it at her. "Use a plate."

"He's completely Sally about things like that," Fox told her. He'd risen, and pulled out a chair. "You look a little shaken up—Layla, right? Why don't you sit down?"

She just couldn't believe psycho killers sat around a pretty kitchen eating bucket chicken and debating wine over beer. "Why don't I? I'm probably not really here." She sat, dropped her head in her hands. "I'm probably in some padded room imagining all this."

"Imagining all what?" Fox asked.

"Why don't I take it?" Quinn glanced at Layla as Cal got out wineglasses. "Then you can fill in as much of your own backstory as you want."

"Fine. That's fine."

"Layla checked into the hotel this morning. She's from New York. Just a bit ago, I was in the hotel dining room, considering ordering the green salad and the haddock, along with a nice glass of white. Layla was just coming in, I assume, to have her own dinner. I was going to ask you to join me, by the way."

"Oh. Ah, that's nice."

"Before I could issue the invite, what I'd describe as a sluglike creature thicker than my aunt Christine's thigh and about four feet in length oozed its way across the dining room, up over the table where a couple happily continued their dining foreplay, then oozed down again, leaving a revolting smear of God-knows-what behind it. She saw it."

"It looked at me. It looked right at me," Layla whispered.

"Don't be stingy with the wine, Cal." Quinn stepped over to rub a hand on Layla's shoulder. "We were the only ones who saw it, and no longer wishing to dine at the hotel, and believing Layla felt the same, we booked. And I'm now screwing my caloric intake for the day with this drumstick."

"You're awfully . . . blithe. Thanks." Layla accepted the wineglass Cal offered, then drank half the contents at one go.

"Not really. Defense mechanism. So here we are, and I want to know if either of you have ever seen anything like I just described."

There was a moment of silence, then Cal picked up his beer, drank. "We've seen a lot of things. The bigger question for me is, why are you seeing them, and part two, why are you seeing them now?"

"Got a theory."

Cal turned to Fox. "Such as?"

"Connections. You said yourself there had to be some connection for Quinn to see it, to have the dream—"

"Dreams." Layla's head came up. "You've had dreams?"

"And so, apparently, have you," Fox continued. "So we'll connect Layla. Figuring out how they're connected may take a while, but let's just go with the hypothesis that they are, and say, what if. What if, due to this connection, due to Quinn, then Layla being in the Hollow, particularly during the seventh year, gives it some kind of psychic boost? Gives it the juice to manifest?"

"That's not bad," Cal replied.

"I'd say it's damn good." Quinn cocked her head as she considered. "Energy. Most paranormal activity stems from energy. The energy the . . . well, entity or entities, the actions, the emotions thereof, leave behind, and the energy of the people within its sphere, let's say. And we could speculate that this psychic energy has built over time, strengthened, so that now, with the addition of other connected energies, it's able to push out into our reality, to some extent, outside of its traditional time frame."

"What in God's name are you people talking about?" Layla demanded.

"We'll get to that, I promise." Quinn offered her a bolstering smile. "Why don't you eat something, settle the nerves?"

"I think it's going to be a while before food holds any appeal for me."

"Mr. Slug slimed right over the bread bowl," Quinn explained. "It was pretty damn gross. Sadly, nothing puts me off food." She snagged a couple of cold fries. "So, if we run with Fox's theory, where is its counterpoint? The good to its bad, the white to its dark. All my research on this points to both sides."

"Maybe it can't pull out yet, or it's hanging back."

"Or the two of you connect to the dark, and not the light," Cal added.

Quinn narrowed her eyes at him, with something glinting between her lashes. Then she shrugged. "Insulting, but unarguable at this time. Except for the fact that, logically, if we were more a weight on the bad side, why is said bad side trying to scare the living daylights out of us?"

"Good point," Cal conceded.

"I want some answers."

Quinn nodded at Layla. "I bet you do."

"I want some serious, sensible answers."

"Thumbnail: The town includes an area in the woods known as the Pagan Stone. Bad stuff happened there. Gods, demons, blood, death, fire. I'm going to lend you a couple of books on the subject. Centuries pass, then something opened it up again. Since nineteen eighty-seven, for seven nights in July, every seventh year, it comes out to play. It's mean, it's ugly, and it's powerful. We're getting a preview."

Gratefully, Layla held out her glass for more wine as she studied Quinn. "Why haven't I ever heard of this? Or this place?"

"There have been some books, some articles, some reports—but most of them hit somewhere between alien abductions and sightings of Bigfoot," Quinn explained. "There's never been a serious, thorough, fully researched account published. That's going to be my job."

"All right. Say I believe all this, and I'm not sure I'm not just having the mother of all hallucinations, why you, and you?" she said to Fox and Cal. "Where do you come in?"

"Because we're the ones who opened it," Fox told her. "Cal, me, and a friend who's currently absent. Twenty-one years ago this July."

"But you'd have been kids. You'd have had to have been—"

"Ten," Cal confirmed. "We share a birthday. It was our tenth birthday. Now, we showed some of ours. How about seeing some of yours. Why did you come here?"

"Fair enough." Layla took another slow sip of her wine. Whether it was that or the brightly lit kitchen with a dog snoring under the table or just having a group of strangers who were likely to believe what she was about to tell them, her nerves were steadier.

"I've been having dreams for the last several nights. Nightmares or night terrors. Sometimes I'd wake up in my bed, sometimes I'd wake up trying to get out the door of my apartment. You said blood and fire. There was both in the dreams, and a kind of altar in a clearing in the woods. I think it was stone. And there was water, too. Black water. I was drowning in it. I was captain of the swim team in high school, and I was drowning."

She shuddered, took another breath. "I was afraid to sleep. I thought I heard voices even when I wasn't asleep. I couldn't understand them, but I'd be at work, doing my job, or stopping by the dry cleaners on the way home, and these voices would just *fill* my head. I thought I was having a breakdown. But why? Then I thought maybe I had a brain tumor. I even thought about making an appointment with a neurologist. Then last night, I took a sleeping pill. Maybe I could just drug my way out of it. But it came, and in the dream something was in bed with me."

Her breath trembled out this time. "Not my bed, but somewhere else. A small room, a small hot room with a tiny window. I was someone else. I can't explain it, really."

"You're doing fine," Quinn assured her.

"It was happening to me, but I wasn't me. I had long hair, and the shape of my body, it was different. I was wearing a long nightgown. I know because it . . . it pulled it up. It was touching me. It was cold, it was so cold. I couldn't scream, I couldn't fight, even when it raped me. It was inside me, but I couldn't see, I couldn't move. I felt it, all of it, as if it were happening, but I couldn't stop it."

She wasn't aware of the tears until Fox pressed a napkin into her hand. "Thanks. When it was over, when it was gone, there was a voice in my head. Just one voice this time, and it calmed me, it made me warm again and took away the pain. It said: 'Hawkins Hollow.' "

"Layla, were you raped?" Fox spoke very quietly. "When you came out of the dream, was there any sign you'd been raped?"

"No." She pressed her lips together, kept her gaze on his face. His eyes were golden brown, and full of compassion. "I woke up in my own bed, and I made myself go . . . check. There was nothing. It hurt me, so there would've been bruises, there would've been marks, but there was nothing. It was early in the morning, not quite four in the morning, and I kept thinking Hawkins Hollow. So I packed, and I took a cab out to the airport to rent a car. Then I drove here. I've never been here."

She paused to look at Quinn now, at Cal. "I've never heard of Hawkins Hollow that I can remember, but I *knew* what roads to take. I knew how to get here, and how to get to the hotel. I checked in this morning, went up to the room they gave me, and I slept like the dead until nearly six. When I walked into the dining room and saw that thing, I thought I was still asleep. Dreaming again."

"It's a wonder you didn't bolt," Quinn commented.

Layla sent her an exhausted look. "To where?"

"There's that." Quinn put a hand on Layla's shoulder, rubbing gently as she spoke. "I think we all need as much information as there is to be had, from every source there is. I think, from this point, it's share and share alike, one for goddamn all and all for goddamn one. You don't like that," she said with a nod toward Cal, "but I think you're going to have to get used to it."

"You've been in this for days. Fox and I have lived with it for years. Lived *in* it. So, don't put on your badge and call yourself captain yet, Blondie."

"Living in it for twenty-one years gives you certain advantages. But you haven't figured it out, you haven't stopped it or even identified it, as far as I can tell, in your twenty-one-year experience. So loosen up."

"You poked at my ninety-seven-year-old great-grandmother today."

"Oh, bull. Your remarkable and fascinating ninety-seven-year-old great-grandmother came up to where I was researching in the library, sat down, and had a conversation with me of her own free will. There was no poking. My keen observation skills tell me you didn't inherit your tight-ass tendencies from her."

"Kids, kids." Fox held up a hand. "Tense situation, agreed, but we're all on the same side, or are on the same side potentially. So chill. Cal, Quinn makes a good point, and it bears consideration. At the same time, Quinn, you've been in the Hollow a couple of days, and Layla less than that. You're going to have to be patient, and accept the fact that some areas of information are more sensitive than others, and may take time to be offered. Even if we start with what can and has been corroborated or documented—"

"What are you, a lawyer?" Layla asked.

"Yeah."

"Figures," she said under her breath.

"Let's just table this," Cal suggested. "Let's let it sit, so we can all think about it for the night. I said I'd take you to the Pagan Stone tomorrow, and I will. Let's see how it goes."

"Accepted."

"Are you two all right at the hotel? You can stay here if you're not easy about going back."

The fact that he'd offered had Quinn's hackles smoothing down again. "We're not wimps, are we, Layla?"

"I wouldn't have said I was a few days ago. Now, I'm not so sure. But I'll be all right at the hotel." In fact, she wanted to go back, crawl into that big, soft bed and pull the covers over her head. "I slept better there than I have all week, so that's something."

Quinn decided she'd wait until they were back before she advised Layla to lower all the shades, and maybe leave a light burning.

Eight

IN THE MORNING, QUINN PRESSED AN EAR AGAINST the door to Layla's room. Since she heard the muted sounds of the *Today* show, she gave the door a knuckle rap. "It's Quinn," she added, in case Layla was still jumpy.

Layla opened the door in a pretty damn cute pair of purple-and-white-striped pajama pants and a purple sleep tank. There was color in her cheeks, and her quiet green eyes had the clarity that told Quinn she'd been awake awhile.

"I'm about to head out to Cal's. Mind if I come in a minute?"

"No." She stepped back. "I was trying to figure out what I'm supposed to do with myself today."

"You can come with me if you want."

"Into the woods? Not quite ready for that, thanks. You know . . ." Layla switched off the TV before dropping into a chair. "I was thinking about the wimp statement you made last night. I've never been a wimp, but it occurred to me as I was huddled in bed with the shades drawn and this stupid chair under the doorknob that I've never had anything happen that tested that before. My life's been pretty normal."

"You came here, and you're still here. So I'm thinking that puts you pretty low on the wimp scale. How'd you sleep?"

"Good. Once I got there, good. No dreams, no visitations, no bumps in the night. So, of course, now I'm wondering why."

"No dreams for me either." Quinn glanced around the room. Layla's bed was a sleigh style and the color scheme was muted greens and creams. "We could theorize that your room here's a safe zone, but that's off because mine isn't, and it's two doors down. It could be that whatever it is just took the night off. Maybe needed to recharge some expended energy."

"Happy thought."

"You've got my cell number, Cal's, Fox's. We've got yours. We're—connected. I wanted to let you know that the diner across the street, figuring you're not going to try the dining room here again, has a nice breakfast."

"I'm thinking I might try room service, and start on the books that you gave me last night. I didn't want to try them for bedtime reading."

"Wise. Okay. If you head out, it's a nice town. Some cute little shops, a little museum I haven't had time to explore so can't give you a rating, and there's always the Bowl-a-Rama."

A hint of a smile appeared around Layla's mouth. "Is there?"

"It's Cal's family's place. Interesting, and it feels like the hub of the town. So, I'll look you up when I get back?"

"Okay. Quinn?" Layla added as Quinn reached for the door. "Wimp scale or not, I'm not sure I'd still be here if I hadn't run into you."

"I know how you feel. I'll see you later."

CAL WAS WAITING FOR HER WHEN SHE DROVE UP. He stepped out, started down the steps, the dog wandering behind him, as she got out of the car. He took a scan, starting with her feet. Good, sturdy hiking boots that showed some scars and wear, faded jeans, tough jacket in I'm-Not-a-Deer red, and a multistriped scarf that matched the cloche-style cap on her head. Silly hat, he mused, that was unaccountably appealing on her.

In any case, he decided she knew what to wear on a hike through the winter woods.

"Do I pass muster, Sergeant?"

"Yeah." He came down the rest of the steps. "Let's start this off with me saying I was off base by a couple inches last night. I haven't completely resolved dealing with you, and now there's another person in the mix, another unknown. When you live with this as long as I have, part of you gets used to it, and other parts just get edgier. Especially when you're into the seventh year. So, I'll apologize, if you need it."

"Well. Wind, sails sucked out. Okay, I can't be pissed off after that or it's just bitchy instead of righteous. So let me say this. Before I came here, this was an idea for a book, a job I enjoy on a level some might consider twisted, and that I consider vastly fascinating. Now, it's more personal. While I can appreciate you being somewhat edgy, and somewhat proprietary, I'm bringing something important to the table. Experience and objectivity. And guts. I've got some impressive guts."

"I've noticed."

"So, we're going to do this thing?"

"Yeah, we're going to do it."

She gave the dog who came over to lean on her a rub. "Is Lump seeing us off on our adventure?"

"He's coming. He likes to walk in the woods when the mood strikes. And if he's had enough, he'll just lie down and sleep until he's in the mood to walk back home again."

"Strikes me as a sensible attitude." She picked up a small pack, hitched it on, then drew her tape recorder out of her pocket. It was attached to the pocket with a small clamp. "I'm going to want to record observations, and whatever you tell me. Okay with that?"

"Yeah." He'd given it a lot of thought overnight. "I'm okay with that."

"Then I'm ready when you are, Tonto."

"Trail's going to be sloppy," he said as they started toward the woods. "Given that, from this point it'll take about two hours—a little more depending—to reach the clearing."

"I'm in no hurry."

Cal glanced up at the sky. "You will be if the weather turns, or anything holds us up after sundown."

She clicked on her recorder, and hoped she'd been generous enough with her cache of extra tapes and batteries. "Why?"

"Years back people hiked or hunted in this section of the woods routinely. Now they don't. People got lost, turned around, spooked. Some reported hearing what they thought were bear or wolves. We don't have wolves and it's rare for bear to come this far down the mountains. Kids, teens mostly, used to sneak in to swim in Hester's Pool in the summer, or to screw around. Now they don't. People used to say the pool was haunted, it was kind of a local legend. Now, people don't like to talk about it."

"Do you think it's haunted?"

"I know there's something in it. I saw it myself. We'll talk about that once we get to the pool. No point in going into it now."

"All right. Is this the way the three of you came in on your birthday twenty-one years ago?"

"We came in from the east." He gestured. "Track closest to town. This way's shorter, but it would've been a longer ride around for us from town. There wasn't anything . . . off about it, until we got to the pool."

"Have the three of you been back together since that night?"

"Yeah, we went back. More than once." He glanced toward her. "I can tell you that going back anytime near the Seven isn't an experience I look forward to repeating."

"The Seven?"

"That's what we call the week in July."

"Tell me more about what happens during the Seven."

It was time to do just that, he thought. To say it straight-out to someone who wanted to know. To someone, maybe, who was part of the answer.

"People in the Hollow get mean, violent, even murderous. They do things they'd never do at any other time. Destroy property, beat the hell out of each other, start fires. Worse."

"Murders, suicides."

"Yeah. After the week's up, they don't remember clearly. It's like watching someone come out of a trance, or a long illness. Some of them are never the same. Some of them leave town. And some fix up their shop or their house, and just go on. It doesn't hit everyone, and it doesn't hit those it does all in the same way. The best I can explain is it's like a mass psychotic episode, and it gets stronger each time."

"What about the police?"

Out of habit, Cal reached down, picked up a stick. There was no point in tossing it for Lump, that would only embarrass them both. So he held it down so Lump could take it into his mouth and plod contentedly along.

"Chief Larson was in charge last time. He was a good man, went to school with my father. They were friends. The third night, he locked himself in his office. I think he, some part of him anyway, knew what was happening to him, and didn't want to risk going home to his wife and kids. One of the deputies, guy named Wayne Hawbaker, nephew to Fox's secretary, came in looking for him, needed help. He heard Larson crying in the office. Couldn't get him to come out. By the time Wayne knocked down the door, Larson had shot himself. Wayne's chief of police now. He's a good man, too."

How much loss had he seen? Quinn wondered. How many losses had he suffered since his tenth birthday? And yet he was walking back into these woods, back where it all began for him. She didn't think she'd ever known a braver stand.

"What about the county cops, the state cops?"

"It's like we're cut off for that week." A cardinal winged by, boldly red, carelessly free. "Sometimes people get out, sometimes they get in, but by and large, we're on our own. It's like . . ." He groped for words. "It's like this veil comes down, and nobody sees, not clearly. Help doesn't come, and after, nobody questions it too closely. Nobody looks straight on at what happened, or why. So it ends up being lore, or *Blair Witch* stuff. Then it fades off until it happens again."

"You stay, and you look at it straight on."

"It's my town," he said simply.

No, Quinn thought, *that* was the bravest stand she'd ever known.

"How'd you sleep last night?" he asked her.

"Dreamlessly. So did Layla. You?"

"The same. Always before, once it started, it didn't stop. But then, things are different this time around."

"Because I saw something, and so did Layla."

"That's the big one. And it's never started this early, or this strong." As they walked, he studied her face. "Have you ever had a genealogy done?"

"No. You think we're related back when, or I'm related to someone who was involved in whatever happened at the Pagan Stone way back when?"

"I think, we've always thought, this was about blood." Absently, he glanced at the scar on his wrist. "So far, knowing or sensing that hasn't done any good. Where are your ancestors from?"

"England primarily, some Irish tossed in."

"Mine, too. But then a lot of Americans have English ancestry."

"Maybe I should start researching and find out if there are any Dents or Twisses in my lineage?" She shrugged when he frowned at her. "Your great-grandmother sent me down that path. Have you tried to trace them? Giles Dent and Lazarus Twisse?"

"Yeah. Dent may be an ancestor, if he did indeed father the three sons of Ann Hawkins. There's no record of him. And other than accounts from the time, some old family letters and diaries, no Giles Dent on anything we've dug up. No record of birth, death. Same for Twisse. They could've dropped down from Pluto as far as we've been able to prove."

"I have a friend who's a whiz on research. I sent her a heads-up. And don't get that look on your face again. I've known her for years, and we've worked together on other projects. I don't know as yet if she can or will come in on this, but trust me, if she does, you'll be grateful. She's brilliant."

Rather than respond, he chewed on it. How much of his resistance was due to this feeling of losing control over the situation? And had he ever had any control to begin with? Some, he knew, was due to the fact that the more people who became involved, the more people he felt responsible for.

And maybe most of all, how much was all this exposure going to affect the town?

"The Hollow's gotten some publicity over the years, focused on this whole thing. That's how you found out about us to begin with. But it's been mild, and for the most part, hasn't done much more than bring interested tourists through. With your involvement, and now potentially two others, it could turn the Hollow into some sort of lurid or ridiculous caption in the tourist guides."

"You knew that was a risk when you agreed to talk to me."

She was keeping pace with him, stride-by-stride on the sloppy ground. And, she was striding into the unknown without a quake or a quiver. "You'd have come whether or not I agreed."

"So part of your cooperation is damage control." She nodded. "Can't blame you. But maybe you should be thinking bigger picture, Cal. More people invested means more brains and more chance of figuring out how to stop what's been happening. Do you want to stop it?"

"More than I can possibly tell you."

"I want a story. There's no point in bullshitting you about that. But I want to stop it, too. Because despite my famous guts, this thing scares me. Better shot at that, it seems to me, if we work together and utilize all our resources. Cybil's one of mine, and she's a damn good one."

"I'll think about it." For now, he thought, he'd given her enough. "Why don't you tell me what made you head down the woo-woo trail, writing-wise."

"That's easy. I always liked spooky stuff. When I was a kid and had a choice between, say, *Sweet Valley High* or Stephen King, King was always going to win. I used to write my own horror stories and give my friends nightmares. Good times," she said and made him laugh. "Then, the turning point, I suppose, was when I went into this reputed haunted house with a group of friends. Halloween. I was twelve. Big dare. Place was falling down and due to be demolished. We were probably lucky we didn't fall through floorboards. So we poked around, squealed, scared ourselves, and had some laughs. Then I saw her."

"Who?"

"The ghost, of course." She gave him a friendly elbow poke. "Keep up. None of the others did. But I saw her, walking down the stairs. There was blood all over her. She looked at me," Quinn said quietly now. "It seemed like she looked right at me, and walked right by. I felt the cold she carried with her."

"What did you do? And if I get a guess, I'm guessing you followed her."

"Of course, I followed her. My friends were running around, making spooky noises, but I followed her into the falling-down kitchen, down the broken steps to the basement by the beam of my Princess Leia flashlight. No cracks."

"How can I crack when I had a Luke Skywalker flashlight?"

"Good. What I found were a lot of spiderwebs, mouse droppings, dead bugs, and a filthy floor of concrete. Then the concrete was gone and it was just a dirt floor with a hole—a grave—dug in it. A black-handled shovel beside it. She went to it, looked at me again, then slid down, hell, like a woman might slide into a nice bubble bath. Then I was standing on the concrete floor again."

"What did you do?"

"Your guess?"

"I'd guess you and Leia got the hell out of there."

"Right again. I came out of the basement like a rocket. I told my friends, who didn't believe me. Just trying to spook them out as usual. I didn't tell anyone else, because if I had, our parents would have known we were in the house and we'd have been grounded till our Social Security kicked in. But when they demolished the house, started jackhammering the concrete floor, they found her. She'd been in there since the thirties. The wife of the guy who'd owned the house had claimed she'd run off. He was dead by then, so nobody could ask him how or why he'd done it. But I knew. From the time I saw her until they found her bones, I dreamed about her murder, I saw it happen.

"I didn't tell anyone. I was too afraid. Ever since, I've told what I find, confirming or debunking. Maybe partly to make it up to Mary Bines—that was her name. And partly because I'm not twelve anymore, and nobody's going to ground me."

He said nothing for a long time. "Do you always see what happened?"

"I don't know if it's seeing or just intuiting, or just my imagination, which is even more far-famed than my guts. But I've learned to trust what I feel, and go with it."

He stopped, gestured. "This is where the tracks cross.

We came in from that direction, picked up the cross trail here. We were loaded down. My mother had packed a picnic basket, thinking we were camping out on Fox's family farm. We had his boom box, his load from the market, our backpacks full of the stuff we figured we couldn't live without. We were still nine years old. Kids, pretty much fearless. That all changed before we came out of the woods again."

When he started to walk once more, she put a hand on his arm, squeezed. "Is that tree bleeding, or do you just have really strange sap in this part of the world?"

He turned, looked. Blood seeped from the bark of the old oak, and seeped into the soggy ground at its trunk.

"That kind of thing happens now and again. It puts off the hikers."

"I bet." She watched Lump plod by the tree after only a cursory sniff. "Why doesn't he care?"

"Old hat to him."

She started to give the tree a wide berth, then stopped. "Wait, wait. This is the spot. This is the spot where I saw the deer across the path. I'm sure of it."

"He called it, with magick. The innocent and pure."

She started to speak, then looking at Cal's face, held her tongue. His eyes had darkened; his cheeks had paled.

"Its blood for the binding. Its blood, his blood, the blood of the dark thing. He grieved when he drew the blade across its neck, and its life poured onto his hands and into the cup."

As his head swam, Cal bent over from the waist. Prayed he wouldn't be sick. "Need a second to get my breath."

"Take it easy." Quickly, Quinn pulled off her pack and pulled out her water bottle. "Drink a little."

Most of the queasiness passed when she took his hand, pressed the bottle into it. "I could see it, *feel* it. I've gone by this tree before, even when it's bled, and I never saw that. Or felt that."

"Two of us this time. Maybe that's what opened it up."

He drank slowly. Not just two, he thought. He'd walked this path with Fox and Gage. We two, he decided. Something about being here with her. "The deer was a sacrifice."

"I get that. *Devoveo*. He said it in Latin. Blood sacrifice. White witchery doesn't ascribe to that. He had to cross over the line, smear on some of the black to do what he felt he needed to do. Was it Dent? Or someone who came long before him?"

"I don't know."

Because she could see his color was eking back, her own heart rate settled. "Do you see what came before?"

"Bits, pieces, flashes. Not all of it. I generally come back a little sick. If I push for more, it's a hell of a lot worse."

"Let's not push then. Are you okay to go on?"

"Yeah. Yeah." His stomach was still mildly uneasy, but the light-headedness had passed. "We'll be coming to Hester's Pool soon."

"I know. I'm going to tell you what it looks like before we get there. I'm telling you I've never been there before, not in reality, but I've seen it, and I stood there night before last. There are cattails and wild grass. It's off the path, through some brush and thorny stuff. It was night, so the water looked black. Opaque. Its shape isn't quite round, not really oval. It's more of a fat crescent. There were a lot of rocks. Some more like boulders, some no more than pebbles. She filled her pockets with them—they looked to be about hand-sized or smaller—until her pockets were sagging with the weight. Her hair was cut short, like it'd been hacked at, and her eyes looked mad."

"Her body didn't stay down, not according to reports."

"I've read them," Quinn acknowledged. "She was found floating in the pool, which came to bear her name, and because it was suicide, they buried her in unconsecrated ground. Records I've dug up so far don't indicate what happened to the infant daughter she left behind."

Before replacing the pack, she took out a bag of trail mix. Opened it, offered. Cal shook his head. "There's plenty of bark and twigs around if I get that desperate."

"This isn't bad. What did your mother pack for you that day?"

"Ham-and-cheese sandwiches, hard-boiled eggs, apple slices, celery and carrot sticks, oatmeal cookies, lemonade." Remembering made him smile. "Pop-Tarts, snack pack cereal for breakfast."

"Uppercase *M* Mom."

"Yeah, always has been."

"How long do we date before I meet the parents?"

He considered. "They want me to come for dinner some night soon if you want in."

"A home-cooked meal by Mom? I'm there. How does she feel about all this?"

"It's hard for them, all of this is hard. And they've never let me down in my life."

"You're a lucky man, Cal."

He broke trail, skirting the tangles of blackberry bushes, and following the more narrow and less-trod path. Lump moved on ahead, as if he understood where they were headed. The first glint of the pool brought a chill down his spine. But then, it always did.

Birds still called, and Lump—more by accident than design, flushed a rabbit that ran across the path and into another thicket. Sunlight streamed through the empty branches onto the leaf-carpeted ground. And glinted dully on the brown water of Hester's Pool.

"It looks different during the day," Quinn noted. "Not nearly as ominous. But I'd have to be very young and very hot to want to go splashing around in that."

"We were both. Fox went in first. We'd snuck out here before to swim, but I'd never much liked it. Who knew what was swimming under there? I always thought Hester's bony hand was going to grab my ankle and pull me under. Then it did."

Quinn's eyebrows shot up, and when he didn't continue, she sat on one of the rocks. "I'm listening."

"Fox was messing with me. I was a better swimmer, but he was sneaky. Gage couldn't swim for crap, but he was game. I thought it was Fox again, dunking me, but it was her. I saw her when I went under. Her hair wasn't short the way you saw her. I remember how her hair streamed out. She didn't look like a ghost. She looked like a woman. Girl," he corrected. "I realized when I got older she was just a girl. I couldn't get out fast enough, and I made Fox and Gage get out. They hadn't seen anything."

"But they believed you."

"That's what friends do."

"Did you ever go back in?"

"Twice. But I never saw her again."

Quinn gave Lump, who wasn't as particular as his master, a handful of trail mix. "It's too damn cold to try now, but come June, I'd like to take a dip and see what happens." She munched some mix as she looked around. "It's a nice spot, considering. Primitive, but still picturesque. Seems like a great place for three boys to run a little wild."

She cocked her head. "So do you usually bring your women here on dates?"

"You'd be the first."

"Really? Is that because they haven't been interested, or you haven't wanted to answer questions pertaining."

"Both."

"So I'm breaking molds here, which is one of my favorite hobbies." Quinn stared out over the water. "She must've been so sad, so horribly sad to believe there was no other way for her. Crazy's a factor, too, but I think she must've been weighed down by sadness and despair before she weighed herself down with rocks. That's what I felt in the dream, and it's what I feel now, sitting here. Her horrible, heavy sadness. Even more than the fear when it raped her."

She shuddered, rose. "Can we move on? It's too much, sitting here. It's too much."

It would be worse, he thought. If she felt already, sensed or understood this already, it would be worse. He took her hand to lead her back to the path. Since, at least for the moment, it was wide enough to walk abreast, he kept ahold of her hand. It almost seemed as if they were taking a simple walk in the winter woods.

"Tell me something surprising about you. Something I'd never guess."

He cocked his head. "Why would I tell you something about me you'd never guess?"

"It doesn't have to be some dark secret." She bumped her hip against his. "Just something unexpected."

"I lettered in track and field."

Quinn shook her head. "Impressive, but not surprising. I might've guessed that. You've got a yard or so of leg."

"All right, all right." He thought it over. "I grew a pumpkin that broke the county record for weight."

"The fattest pumpkin in the history of the county?"

"It missed the state record by ounces. It got written up in the paper."

"Well, that is surprising. I was hoping for something a bit more salacious, but am forced to admit, I'd never have guessed you held the county record for fattest pumpkin."

"How about you?"

"I'm afraid I've never grown a pumpkin of any size or weight."

"Surprise me."

"I can walk on my hands. I'd demonstrate, but the ground's not conducive to hand-walking. Come on. You wouldn't have guessed that."

"You're right. I will, however, insist on a demo later. I, after all, have documentation of the pumpkin."

"Fair enough."

She kept up the chatter, light and silly enough to make him laugh. He wasn't sure he'd laughed along this path since that fateful hike with his friends. But it seemed natural enough now, with the sun beaming down through the trees, the birds singing.

Until he heard the growl.

She'd heard it, too. He couldn't think of another reason her voice would have stopped so short, or her hand would have gripped his arm like a vise. "Cal—"

"Yeah, I hear it. We're nearly there. Sometimes it makes noise, sometimes it makes an appearance." Never this time of year, he thought, as he hitched up the back of his jacket. But these, apparently, were different times. "Just stay close."

"Believe me, I . . ." Her voice trailed off this time as he drew the large, jagged-edged hunting knife. "Okay. Okay. Now *that* would have been one of those unexpected things about you. That you, ah, carry a Crocodile Dundee around."

"I don't come here unarmed."

She moistened her lips. "And you probably know how to use it, if necessary."

He shot her a look. "I probably do. Do you want to keep going, or do you want to turn around and go back?"

"I'm not turning tail."

He could hear it rustling in the brush, could hear the slide of mud underfoot. Stalking them, he thought. He imagined the knife was as useless as a few harsh words if the thing meant business, but he felt better with it in his hand.

"Lump doesn't hear it," Quinn murmured, lifting her chin to where the dog slopped along the path a few feet ahead. "Even he can't be that lazy. If he heard it, scented it, he'd show some concern. So it's not real." She took a slow breath. "It's just show."

"Not real to him, anyway."

When the thing howled, Cal took her firmly by the arm and pulled her through the edge of the trees into the clearing where the Pagan Stone speared up out of the muddy earth.

"I guess, all things considered, I was half expecting something along the lines of the king stone from Stonehenge." Quinn stepped away from Cal to circle the stone.

"It's amazing enough though, when you take a good look, the way it forms a table, or altar. How flat and smooth the top is." She laid her hand on it. "It's warm," she added. "Warmer than stone should be in a February wood."

He put his hand beside hers. "Sometimes it's cold." He fit the knife back into its sheath. "Nothing to worry about when it's warm. So far." He shoved his sleeve back, examined the scar on his wrist. "So far," he repeated.

Without thinking, he laid his hand over hers. "As long as—"

"It's heating up! Feel that? Do you feel that?"

She shifted, started to place her other hand on the stone. He moved, felt himself move as he might have through that wall of fire. Madly.

He gripped her shoulders, spinning her around until her back was pressed to the stone. Then sated the sudden, desperate appetite by taking her mouth.

For an instant, he was someone else, as was she, and the moment was full of grieving desperation. Her taste, her skin, the beat of her heart.

Then he was himself, feeling Quinn's lips heat under his as the stone had heated under their hands. It was her body quivering against his, and her fingers digging into his hips.

He wanted more, wanted to shove her onto the table of rock, to cover her with his body, to surround himself with all she was.

Not him, he thought dimly, or not entirely him. And so he made himself pull back, forced himself to break that connection.

The air wavered a moment. "Sorry," he managed. "Not altogether sorry, but—"

"Surprised." Her voice was hoarse. "Me, too. That was definitely unexpected. Made me dizzy," she whispered. "That's not a complaint. It wasn't us, then it was." She took another steadying breath. "Call me a slut, but I liked it both ways." With her eyes on his, she placed her hand on the stone again. "Want to try it again?"

"I think I'm still a man, so damn right I do. But I don't think it'd be smart, or particularly safe. Plus, I don't care for someone—something—else yanking on my hormones. Next time I kiss you, it's just you and me."

"All right. Connections." She nodded. "I'm more in favor than ever about the theory regarding connections. Could be blood, could be a reincarnation thing. It's worth exploring."

She sidestepped away from the stone, and him. "So, no more contact with each other and that thing for the time being. And let's take it back to the purpose at hand."

"Are you okay?"

"Stirred me up, I'll admit. But no harm, no foul." She took out her water bottle, and this time drank deep.

"I wanted you. Both ways."

Lowering the bottle, she met those calm gray eyes. She'd just gulped down water, she thought, but now her throat was dry again. "I know. What I don't know is if that's going to be a problem."

"It's going to be a problem. I'm not going to care about that."

Her pulse gave a couple of quick jumps. "Ah . . . This probably isn't the place to—"

"No, it's not." He took a step forward, but didn't touch her. And still her skin went hot. "There's going to be another place."

"Okay." She cleared her throat. "All right. To work."

She did another circle while he watched her. He'd made her a little jumpy. He didn't mind that. In fact, he considered it a point for his side. Something might have pushed him to kiss her that way, but he knew what he'd felt as that *something* released its grip. He knew what he'd been feeling since she'd stepped out of her car at the top of his lane.

Plain and simple lust. Caleb Hawkins for Quinn Black.

"You camped here, the three of you, that night." Apparently taking Cal at his word about the safety of the area,

Quinn moved easily around the clearing. "You—if I have any understanding of young boys—ate junk food, ragged on each other, maybe told ghost stories."

"Some. We also drank the beer Gage stole from his father, and looked at the skin mags he'd swiped."

"Of course, though I'd have pegged those activities for more like twelve-year-olds."

"Precocious." He ordered himself to stop thinking about her, to take himself back. "We built a fire. We had the boom box on. It was a pretty night, still hot, but not oppressive. And it was our night. It was, we thought, our place. Sacred ground."

"So your great-grandmother said."

"It called for ritual." He waited for her to turn to him. "We wrote down words. Words we made. We swore an oath, and at midnight, I used my Boy Scout knife to cut our wrists. We said the words we'd made and pressed our wrists together to mix the blood. To make us blood brothers. And hell opened up."

"What happened?"

"I don't know, not exactly. None of us do, not that we can remember. There was a kind of explosion. It seemed like one. The light was blinding, and the force of it knocked me back. Lifted me right off my feet. Screams, but I've never known if they were mine, Fox's, Gage's, or something else. The fire shot straight up, there seemed to be fire everywhere, but we weren't burned. Something *pushed* out, pushed into me. Pain, I remember pain. Then I saw some kind of dark mass rising out, and felt the cold it brought with it. Then it was over, and we were alone, scared, and the ground was scorched black."

Ten years old, she thought. Just a little boy. "How did you get out?"

"We hiked out the next morning pretty much as we'd hiked in. Except for a few changes. I came into this clearing when I was nine. I was wearing glasses. I was nearsighted."

Her brows rose. "Was?"

"Twenty–one hundred in my left eye, twenty-ninety in my right. I walked out ten, and twenty-twenty. None of us had a mark on him when we left, though Gage especially had some wounds he brought in with him. Not one of us has been sick a day since that night. If we're injured, it heals on its own."

There was no doubt on her face, only interest with a touch, he thought, of fascination. It struck him that other than his family she was the only one who knew. Who believed.

"You were given some sort of immunity."

"You could call it that."

"Do you feel pain?"

"Damn right. I came out with perfect vision, not X-ray. And the healing can hurt like a mother, but it's pretty quick. I can see things that happened before, like out on the trail. Not all the time, not every time, but I can see events of the past."

"A reverse clairvoyance."

"When it's on. I've seen what happened here on July seventh, sixteen fifty-two."

"What happened here, Cal?"

"The demon was bound under the stone. And Fox, Gage, and I, we cut the bastard loose."

She moved to him. She wanted to touch him, to soothe that worry from his face, but was afraid to. "If you did, you weren't to blame."

"Blame and responsibility aren't much different."

The hell with it. She laid her hands on his cheeks even when he flinched. Then touched her lips gently to his. "That was normal. You're responsible because, to my mind, you're willing to take responsibility. You've stayed when a lot of other men would've walked, if not run, away from here. So I say there's a way to beat it back where it belongs. And I'm going to do whatever I can to help you do just that."

She opened her pack. "I'm going to take photos, some measurements, some notes, and ask a lot of annoying questions."

She'd shaken him. The touch, the words, the faith. He wanted to draw her in, hold on to her. Just hold on. Normal, she'd said, and looking at her now, he craved the bliss of normality.

Not the place, he reminded himself, and stepped back. "You've got an hour. We start back in an hour. We're going to be well out of the woods before twilight."

"No argument." This time, she thought, and went to work.

Nine

SHE SPENT A LOT OF TIME, TO CAL'S MIND, WANdering around, taking what appeared to be copious notes and a mammoth number of photographs with her tiny little digital, and muttering to herself.

He didn't see how any of that was particularly helpful, but since she seemed to be absorbed in it all, he sat under a tree with the snoring Lump and let her work.

There was no more howling, no more sense of anything stalking the clearing, or them. Maybe the demon had something else to do, Cal thought. Or maybe it was just hanging back, watching. Waiting.

Well, he was doing the same, he supposed. He didn't mind waiting, especially when the view was good.

It was interesting to watch her, to watch the way she moved. Brisk and direct one minute, slow and wandering the next. As if she couldn't quite make up her mind which approach to take.

"Have you ever had this analyzed?" she called out. "The stone itself? A scientific analysis?"

"Yeah. We took scrapings when we were teenagers, and took them to the geology teacher at the high school. It's limestone. Common limestone. And," he continued, anticipating her, "we took another sample a few years later, that Gage took to a lab in New York. Same results."

"Okay. Any objection if I take a sample, send it to a lab I've used, just for one more confirmation?"

"Help yourself." He started to hitch up a hip for his knife, but she was already taking a Swiss Army out of her pocket. He should've figured her for it. Still, it made him smile.

Most of the women he knew might have lipstick in their pocket, but wouldn't consider a Swiss Army. He was betting Quinn had both.

He watched her hands as she scraped stone dust into a Baggie she pulled out of her pack. A trio of rings circled two fingers and the thumb of her right hand to catch quick glints of the sun with the movement.

The glints brightened, beamed into his eyes.

The light changed, softened like a summer morning even as the air warmed and took on a weight of humidity. Leaves budded, unfurled, then burst into thick green on the trees, casting shade and light in patterns on the ground, on the stone.

On the woman.

Her hair was long and loose, the color of raw honey. Her face was sharp-featured with eyes long and tipped up slightly. She wore a long dress of dusky blue under a white apron. She moved with care, and still with grace, though her body was heavily pregnant. And she carried two pails across the clearing toward a little shed behind the stone.

As she walked she sang in a voice clear and bright as the summer morning.

All in a garden green where late I laid me down upon a bank of chamomile where I saw upon a style sitting, a country clown . . .

Hearing her, seeing her, Cal was filled with love so urgent, so ripe, he thought his heart might burst from it.

The man stepped through the door of the shed, and that love was illuminated on his face. The woman stopped, gave a knowing, flirtatious toss of her head, and sang as the man walked toward her.

. . . holding in his arms a comely country maid. Courting her with all his skill, working her unto his will. Thus to her he said, Kiss me in kindness, sweetheart.

She lifted her face, offered her lips. The man brushed them with his, and as her laugh burst like a shooting star, he took the pails from her, setting them on the ground before wrapping her in an embrace.

Have I not told you, you are not to carry water or wood? You carry enough.

His hands stroked over the mound of her belly, held there when hers covered them. *Our sons are strong and well. I will give you sons, my love, as bright and brave as their father. My love, my heart.* Now Cal saw the tears glimmer in those almond-shaped eyes. *Must I leave you?*

You will never leave me, not truly, nor I you. No tears. He kissed them away, and Cal felt the wrench of his own heart. *No tears.*

No. I swore an oath against them. So she smiled. *There is time yet. Soft mornings and long summer days. It is not death. You swear to me?*

It is not death. Come now. I will carry the water.

When they faded, he saw Quinn crouched in front of him, heard her saying his name sharply, repeatedly.

"You're back. You went somewhere. Your eyes . . . Your eyes go black and . . . *deep* is the only word I can think of when you go somewhere else. Where did you go, Cal?"

"She's not you."

"Okay." She'd been afraid to touch him before, afraid if she did she'd push them both into that somewhere else, or yank him back before he was done. Now she reached out to rest her hand on his knee. "I'm not who?"

"Whoever I was kissing. Started to, then it was you, but before, at first . . . Jesus." He clamped the heels of his hands at his temple. "Headache. Bitch of a headache."

"Lean back, close your eyes. I'll—"

"It'll pass in a minute. They always do. We're not them. It's not a reincarnation deal. It doesn't feel right. Sporadic possession maybe, which is bad enough."

"Who?"

"How the hell do I know?" His head screamed until he had to lower his head between his knees to fight off the sudden, acute nausea. "I'd draw you a damn picture if I could draw. Give me a minute."

Rising, Quinn went behind him and, kneeling, began to massage his neck, his shoulders.

"Okay, all right. Sorry. Christ. It's like having an electric drill inside my head, biting its way out through my temples. It's better. I don't know who they were. They didn't call each other by name. But best guess is Giles Dent and Ann Hawkins. They were obviously living here, and she was really, really pregnant. She was singing," he said and told her what he'd seen.

Quinn continued to rub his shoulders while she listened. "So they knew it was coming, and from what you say, he was sending her away before it did. 'Not death.' That's interesting, and something to look into. But for now, I think you've had enough of this place. And so have I."

She sat on the ground then, hissed a breath out, sucked one in. "While you were out, let's say, it came back."

"Jesus Christ." He started to spring up, but she gripped his arm.

"It's gone. Let's just sit here until we both get our legs back under us. I heard it growling, and I spun around. You were taking a trip, and I quashed my first instinct to grab you, shake you out of it, in case doing that pulled me in with you."

"And we'd both be defenseless," he said in disgust.

"And now Mr. Responsibility is beating himself up because he didn't somehow see this coming, fight off the magickal forces so he could stay in the here and now and protect the girl."

Even with the headache, he could manage a cool, steely stare. "Something like that."

"Something like that is appreciated, even if it is annoying. I had my handy Swiss Army knife, which, while it isn't up to Jim Bowie standards, does include a nice corkscrew and tweezers, both of which you never know when you may need."

"Is that spunk? Are you being spunky?"

"I'm babbling until I level out and I'm nearly there. The thing is, it just circled, making its nasty 'I'll eat you, my pretty and your big, lazy dog, too.' Rustling, growling, snarling. But it didn't show itself. Then it stopped, and you came back."

"How long?"

"I don't know. I think just a couple minutes, though it seemed longer at the time. However long, I'm so ready to get gone. I hope to hell you can walk back, Cal, because strong and resilient as I am, there's no way I can carry you piggyback."

"I can walk."

"Good, then let's get the hell out of here, and when we get to civilization, Hawkins, you're buying me a really big drink."

They gathered their packs; Cal whistled Lump awake. As they started back he wondered why he hadn't told her of the bloodstone—the three pieces he, Fox, and Gage held. The three pieces that he now knew formed the stone in the amulet Giles Dent had worn when he'd lived at the Pagan Stone.

WHILE CAL AND QUINN WERE HIKING OUT OF Hawkins Wood, Layla was taking herself out for an aimless walk around town. It was odd to just let her feet choose any direction. During her years in New York she'd always had a specific destination, always had a specific task, or several specific tasks to accomplish within a particular time frame.

Now, she'd let the morning stretch out, and had accomplished no more than reading sections of a few of the odd books Quinn had left with her. She might have stayed right there, inside her lovely room, inside that safe zone as Quinn had termed it.

But she'd needed to get away from the books. In any case, it gave the housekeeper an opportunity to set the room to rights, she supposed. And gave herself an opportunity to take a real look at the town she'd been compelled to visit.

She didn't have the urge to wander into any of the shops, though she thought Quinn's assessment was on the mark. There were some very interesting possibilities.

But even window shopping made her feel guilty for leaving the staff of the boutique in the lurch. Taking off the way she had, barely taking the time to call in from the road to tell the owner she'd had a personal emergency and wouldn't be in for the next several days.

Personal emergency covered it, Layla decided.

And it could very well get her fired. Still, even knowing that, she couldn't go back, pick things up, forget what had happened.

She'd get another job if she had to. When and if, she'd find another. She had some savings, she had a cushion. If her boss couldn't cut her some slack, she didn't want that stupid job anyway.

And, oh God, she was already justifying being unemployed.

Don't think about it, she ordered herself. Don't think about that right this minute.

She didn't think about it, and didn't think twice when her feet decided to continue on beyond the shops. She couldn't have said why they wanted to stop at the base of the building. LIBRARY was carved into the stone lintel over the door, but the glossy sign read HAWKINS HOLLOW COMMUNITY CENTER.

Innocuous enough, she told herself. But when a chill danced over her skin she ordered her feet to keep traveling.

She considered going into the museum, but couldn't work up the interest. She thought about crossing the street to Salon A and whiling away some time with a manicure, but simply didn't care about the state of her nails.

Tired and annoyed with herself, she nearly turned around and headed back. But the sign that caught her eye this time drew her forward.

FOX O'DELL, ATTORNEY AT LAW.

At least he was someone she knew—more or less. The hot lawyer with the compassionate eyes. He was probably busy with a client or out of the office, but she didn't care. Going in was something to do other than wander around feeling sorry for herself.

She stepped into the attractive, homespun reception area. The woman behind the gorgeous old desk offered a polite smile.

"Good morning—well, afternoon now. Can I help you?"

"I'm actually . . ." What? Layla wondered. What exactly was she? "I was hoping to speak to Mr. O'Dell for a minute if he's free."

"Actually, he's with a client, but they shouldn't be much longer if you'd like to . . ."

A woman in tight jeans, a snug pink sweater, and an explosion of hair in an improbable shade of red marched out on heeled boots. She dragged on a short leather jacket. "I want him skinned, Fox, you hear? I gave that son of a bitch the best two years and three months of my life, and I want him skinned like a rabbit."

"So noted, Shelley."

"How could he do that to me?" On a wail she collapsed into Fox's arms.

He wore jeans as well, and an untucked pinstriped shirt, along with an expression of resignation as he glanced over at Layla. "There, there," he said, patting the sobbing Shelley's back. "There, there."

"I just bought him new tires for his truck! I'm going to go slash every one of them."

"Don't." Fox took a good hold of her before Shelley, tears streaming away in fresh rage, started to yank back. "I don't want you to do that. You don't go near his truck, and for now, honey, try to stay away from him, too. And Sami."

"That turncoat slut of a bitch."

"That's the one. Leave this to me for now, okay? You go on back to work and let me handle this. That's why you hired me, right?"

"I guess. But you skin him raw, Fox. You crack that bastard's nuts like pecans."

"I'm going to get right on that," he assured her as he led her to the door. "You just stay above it all, that's the way. I'll be in touch."

After he'd closed the door, leaned back on it, he heaved out a breath. "Holy Mother of God."

"You should've referred that one," Alice told him.

"You can't refer off the first girl you got to second base with when she's filing for divorce. It's against the laws of God and Man. Hello, Layla, need a lawyer?"

"I hope not." He was better looking than she remembered, which just went to show the shape she'd been in the night before. Plus he didn't look anything like a lawyer. "No offense."

"None taken. Layla . . . It's Darnell, right?"

"Yes."

"Layla Darnell, Alice Hawbaker. Mrs. H, I'm clear for a while?"

"You are."

"Come on back, Layla." He gestured. "We don't usually put a show on this early in the day, but my old pal Shelley walked into the back room over at the diner to visit her twin sister, Sami, and found her husband—that would be Shelley's husband, Block—holding Sami's tip money."

"I'm sorry, she's filing for divorce because her husband was holding her sister's tip money?"

"It was in Sami's Victoria's Secret Miracle Bra at the time."

"Oh. Well."

"That's not privileged information as Shelley chased them both out of the back room and straight out onto Main

Street—with Sami's miraculous bra in full view—with a rag mop. Want a Coke?"

"No, I really don't. I don't think I need anything to give me an edge."

Since she looked inclined to pace, he didn't offer her a chair. Instead, he leaned back against his desk. "Rough night?"

"No, the opposite. I just can't figure out what I'm doing here. I don't understand any of this, and I certainly don't understand my place in it. A couple hours ago I told myself I was going to pack and drive back to New York like a sane person. But I didn't." She turned to him. "I couldn't. And I don't understand that either."

"You're where you're supposed to be. That's the simplest answer."

"Are you afraid?"

"A lot of the time."

"I don't think I've ever been really afraid. I wonder if I'd be so damned edgy if I had something to *do*. An assignment, a task."

"Listen, I've got to drive to a client a few miles out of town, take her some papers."

"Oh, sorry. I'm in the way."

"No, and when I start thinking beautiful women are in my way, please notify my next of kin so they can gather to say their final good-byes before my death. I was going to suggest you ride out with me, which is something to do. And you can have chamomile tea and stale lemon snaps with Mrs. Oldinger, which is a task. She likes company, which is the real reason she had me draw up the fifteenth codicil to her will."

He kept talking, knowing that was one way to help calm someone down when she looked ready to bolt. "By the time that's done, I can swing by another client who's not far out of the way and save him a trip into town. By my way of thinking, Cal and Quinn should be just about back home by the time we're done with all that. We'll go by, see what's what."

"Can you be out of the office all that time?"

"Believe me." He grabbed his coat, his briefcase. "Mrs. H will holler me back if I'm needed here. But unless you've got something better to do, I'll have her pull out the files I need and we'll take a drive."

It was better than brooding, Layla decided. Maybe she thought it was odd for a lawyer, even a small-town lawyer to drive an old Dodge pickup with a couple of Ring Ding wrappers littering the floorboards.

"What are you doing for the second client?"

"That's Charlie Deen. Charlie got clipped by a DUI when he was driving home from work. Insurance company's trying to dance around some of the medical bills. Not going to happen."

"Divorce, wills, personal injury. So you don't specialize?"

"All law, all the time," he said and sent her a smile that was a combination of sweet and cocky. "Well, except for tax law if I can avoid it. I leave that to my sister. She's tax and business law."

"But you don't have a practice together."

"That'd be tough. Sage went to Seattle to be a lesbian."

"I beg your pardon?"

"Sorry." He boosted the gas as they passed the town limits. "Family joke. What I mean is my sister Sage is gay, and she lives in Seattle. She's an activist, and she and her partner of, hmm, I guess about eight years now run a firm they call Girl on Girl. Seriously," he added when Layla said nothing, "They specialize in tax and business law for gays."

"Your family doesn't approve?"

"Are you kidding? My parents eat it up like tofu. When Sage and Paula—that's her partner—got married. Or had their life-partner affirmation, whatever—we all went out there and celebrated like mental patients. She's happy and that's what counts. The alternate lifestyle choice is just kind of a bonus for my parents. Speaking of family, that's my little brother's place."

Layla saw a log house all but buried in the trees, with a sign near the curve of the road reading HAWKINS CREEK POTTERY.

"Your brother's a potter."

"Yeah, a good one. So's my mother when she's in the mood. Want to stop in?"

"Oh, I . . ."

"Better not," he decided. "Ridge'll get going and Mrs. H has called Mrs. Oldinger by now to tell her to expect us. Another time."

"Okay." Conversation, she thought. Small talk. Relative sanity. "So you have a brother and sister."

"Two sisters. My baby sister owns the little vegetarian restaurant in town. It's pretty good, considering. Of the four of us I veered the farthest off the flower-strewn path my counterculture parents forged. But they love me anyway. That's about it for me. How about you?"

"Well . . . I don't have any relatives nearly as interesting as yours sound, but I'm pretty sure my mother has some old Joan Baez albums."

"There, that strange and fateful crossroads again."

She started to laugh, then gasped with pleasure as she spotted the deer. "Look! Oh, look. Aren't they gorgeous, just grazing there along the edge of the trees?"

To accommodate her, Fox pulled over to the narrow shoulder so she could watch. "You're used to seeing deer, I suppose," she said.

"Doesn't mean I don't get a kick out of it. We had to run herds off the farm when I was a kid."

"You grew up on a farm."

There was that urban-dweller wistfulness in her voice. The kind that said she saw the pretty deer, the bunnies, the sunflowers, and happy chickens. And not the plowing, the hoeing, weeding, harvesting. "Small, family farm. We grew our own vegetables, kept chickens and goats, bees. Sold some of the surplus, some of my mother's crafts, my father's woodwork."

"Do they still have it?"

"Yeah."

"My parents owned a little dress shop when I was a kid. They sold out about fifteen years ago. I always wished—Oh God, oh my God!"

Her hand whipped over to clamp on his arm.

The wolf leaped out of the trees, onto the back of a young deer. It bucked, it screamed—she could hear its high-pitched screams of fear and pain—it bled while the others in the small herd continued to crop at grass.

"It's not real."

His voice sounded tinny and distant. In front of her horrified eyes the wolf took the deer down, then began to tear and rip.

"It's not real," he repeated. He put his hands on her shoulders, and she felt something click. Something inside her pushed toward him and away from the horror at the edge of the trees. "Look at it, straight on," he told her. "Look at it and *know* it's not real."

The blood was so red, so wet. It flew in ugly rain, smearing the winter grass of the narrow field. "It's not real."

"Don't just say it. Know it. It lies, Layla. It lives in lies. It's not real."

She breathed in, breathed out. "It's not real. It's a lie. It's an ugly lie. A small, cruel lie. It's not real."

The field was empty; the winter grass ragged and unstained.

"How do you live with this?" Shoving around in her seat, Layla stared at him. "How do you stand this?"

"By knowing—the way I knew that was a lie—that some day, some way, we're going to kick its ass."

Her throat burned dry. "You did something to me. When you took my shoulders, when you were talking to me, you did something to me."

"No." He denied it without a qualm. He'd done something *for* her, Fox told himself. "I just helped you remember it wasn't real. We're going on to Mrs. Oldinger. I bet you could use that chamomile tea about now."

"Does she have any whiskey to go with it?"
"Wouldn't surprise me."

QUINN COULD SEE CAL'S HOUSE THROUGH THE trees when her phone signaled a waiting text-message. "Crap, why didn't she just call me?"

"Might've tried. There are lots of pockets in the woods where calls drop out."

"Color me virtually unsurprised." She brought up the message, smiling a little as she recognized Cybil's shorthand.

Bzy, but intrig'd. Tell u more when. Cn B there in a wk, 2 latest. Tlk whn cn. Q? B-ware. Serious. C.

"All right." Quinn replaced the phone and made the decision she'd been weighing during the hike back. "I guess we'll call Fox and Layla when I'm having that really big drink by the fire you're going to build."

"I can live with that."

"Then, seeing as you're a town honcho, you'd be the one to ask about finding a nice, attractive, convenient, and somewhat roomy house to rent for the next, oh, six months."

"And the tenant would be?"

"Tenants. They would be me, my delightful friend Cybil, whom I will talk into digging in, and most likely Layla, whom—I believe—will take a bit more convincing. But I'm very persuasive."

"What happened to staying a week for initial research, then coming back in April for a follow-up?"

"Plans change," she said airily, and smiled at him as they stepped onto the gravel of his driveway. "Don't you just love when that happens?"

"Not really." But he walked with her onto the deck and opened the door so she could breeze into his quiet home ahead of him.

Ten

THE HOUSE WHERE CAL HAD GROWN UP WAS, IN his opinion, in a constant state of evolution. Every few years his mother would decide the walls needed "freshening," which meant painting—or often in his mother's vocabulary a new "paint treatment."

There was ragging, there was sponging, there was combing, and a variety of other terms he did his best to tune out.

Naturally, new paint led to new upholstery or window treatments, certainly to new bed linens when she worked her way to bedrooms. Which invariably led to new "arrangements."

He couldn't count the number of times he'd hauled furniture around to match the grafts his mother routinely generated.

His father liked to say that as soon as Frannie had the house the way she wanted, it was time for her to shake it all up again.

At one time, Cal had assumed his mother had fiddled, fooled, painted, sewed, arranged, and re-arranged out of boredom. Although she volunteered, served on various committees, or stuck her oar in countless organizations, she'd never worked outside the home. He'd gone through a period in his late teens and early twenties where he'd imagined her (pitied her) as an unfulfilled, semidesperate housewife.

At one point he, in his worldliness of two college semesters, got her alone and explained his understanding of her sense of repression. She'd laughed so hard she'd had to set down her upholstery tacks and wipe her eyes.

"Honey," she'd said, "there's not a single bone of repression in my entire body. I love color and texture and patterns and flavors. And oh, just all sorts of things. I get to use this house as my studio, my science project, my laboratory, and my showroom. I get to be the director, the designer, the set builder, and the star of the whole show. Now, why would I want to go out and get a job or a career—since we don't need the money—and have somebody else tell me what to do and when to do it?"

She'd crooked her finger so he leaned down to her. And she'd laid a hand on his cheek. "You're such a sweetheart, Caleb. You're going to find out that not everybody wants what society—in whatever its current mood or mode might be—tells them they should want. I consider myself lucky, even privileged, that I was able to make the choice to stay home and raise my children. And I'm lucky to be able to be married to a man who doesn't mind if I use my talents—and I'm damned talented—to disrupt his quiet home with paint samples and fabric swatches every time he turns around. I'm happy. And I love knowing you worried I might not be."

He'd come to see she was exactly right. She did just as she liked, and was terrific at what she did. And, he'd come to see that when it came down to the core, she was the power in the house. His father brought in the money, but his mother handled the finances. His father ran his business, his mother ran the home.

And that was exactly the way they liked it.

So he didn't bother telling her not to fuss over Sunday dinner—just as he hadn't attempted to talk her out of extending the invitation to Quinn, Layla, and Fox. She lived to fuss, and enjoyed putting on elaborate meals for people, even if she didn't know them.

Since Fox volunteered to swing into town and pick up the women, Cal went directly to his parents' house, and went early. It seemed wise to give them some sort of groundwork—and hopefully a few basic tips on how to deal with a woman who intended to write a book on the Hollow, since the town included people, and those people included his family.

Frannie stood at the stove, checking the temperature of her pork tenderloin. Obviously satisfied with that, she crossed to the counter to continue the layers of her famous antipasto squares.

"So, Mom," Cal began as he opened the refrigerator.

"I'm serving wine with dinner, so don't go hunting up any beer."

Chastised, he shut the refrigerator door. "Okay. I just wanted to mention that you shouldn't forget that Quinn's writing a book."

"Have you noticed me forgetting things?"

"No." The woman forgot nothing, which could be a little daunting. "What I mean is, we should all be aware that things we say and do may end up in a book."

"Hmm." Frannie layered pepperoni over provolone. "Do you expect me or your father to say or do something embarrassing over appetizers? Or maybe we'll wait until dessert. Which is apple pie, by the way."

"No, I— You made apple pie?"

She spared him a glance, and a knowing smile. "It's your favorite, isn't it, my baby?"

"Yeah, but maybe you've lost your knack. I should sample a piece before company gets here. Save you any embarrassment if it's lousy pie."

"That didn't work when you were twelve."

"I know, but you always pounded the whole if-you-don't-succeed chestnut into my head."

"You just keep trying, sweetie. Now, why are you worried about this girl, who I'm told you've been seen out and about with a few times, coming around for dinner?"

"It's not like that." He wasn't sure what it was like. "It's about why she's here at all. We can't forget that, that's all I'm saying."

"I never forget. How could I? We have to live our lives, peel potatoes, get the mail, sneeze, buy new shoes, in spite of it all, maybe because of it all." There was a hint of fierceness in her voice he recognized as sorrow. "And that living includes being able to have a nice company meal on a Sunday."

"I wish it were different."

"I know you do, but it's not." She kept layering, but her eyes lifted to his. "And, Cal, my handsome boy, you can't do more than you do. If anything, there are times I wish you could do less. But . . . Tell me, do you like this girl? Quinn Black?"

"Sure." Like to get a taste of that top-heavy mouth again, he mused. Then broke off that train of thought quickly since he knew his mother's skill at reading her children's minds.

"Then I intend to give her and the others a comfortable evening and an excellent meal. And, Cal, if you didn't want her here, didn't want her to speak with me or your dad, you wouldn't let her in the door. I wouldn't be able, though my powers are fierce, to shove you aside and open it myself."

He looked at her. Sometimes when he did, it surprised him that this pretty woman with her short, streaked blond hair, her slim build and creative mind could have given birth to him, could have raised him to be a man. He could look and think she was delicate, and then remember she was almost terrifyingly strong.

"I'm not going to let anything hurt you."

"Back at you, doubled. Now get out of my kitchen. I need to finish up the appetizers."

He'd have offered to lend her a hand, but would have earned one of her pitying stares. Not that she didn't allow kitchen help. His father was not only allowed to grill, but encouraged to. And any and all could and were called in as line chefs from time to time.

But when his mother was in full-out company-coming mode, she wanted the kitchen to herself.

He passed through the dining room where, naturally, the table was already set. She'd used festive plates, which meant she wasn't going for elegant or drop-in casual. Tented linen napkins, tea lights in cobalt rounds, inside a centerpiece of winter berries.

Even during the worst time, even during the Seven, he could come here and there would be fresh flowers artfully arranged, furniture free of dust and gleaming with polish, and intriguing little soaps in the dish in the downstairs powder room.

Even hell didn't cause Frannie Hawkins to break stride.

Maybe, Cal thought as he wandered into the living room, that was part of the reason—even the most important reason—he got through it himself. Because whatever else happened, his mother would be maintaining her own brand of order and sanity.

Just as his father would be. They'd given him that, Cal thought. That rock-solid foundation. Nothing, not even a demon from hell had ever shaken it.

He started to go upstairs, hunt down his father who, he suspected, would be in his home office. But saw Fox's truck pull in when he glanced out the window.

He stood where he was, watched Quinn jump out first, cradling a bouquet wrapped in green florist paper. Layla slid out next, holding what looked to be a wine gift bag. His mother, Cal thought, would approve of the offerings. She herself had shelves and bins in her ruthlessly organized workroom that held carefully selected emergency hostess gifts, gift bags, colored tissue paper, and an assortment of bows and ribbons.

When Cal opened the door, Quinn strode straight in. "Hi. I love the house and the yard! Shows where you came by your eye for landscaping. What a great space. Layla, look at these walls. Like an Italian villa."

"It's their latest incarnation," Cal commented.

"It looks like home, but with a kick of style. Like you could curl up on that fabulous sofa and take a snooze, but you'd probably read *Southern Homes* first."

"Thank you." Frannie stepped out. "That's a lovely compliment. Cal, take everyone's coats, will you? I'm Frannie Hawkins."

"It's so nice to meet you. I'm Quinn. Thanks so much for having us. I hope you like mixed bouquets. I have a hard time deciding on one type of mostly anything."

"They're wonderful, thank you." Frannie accepted the flowers, smiled expectantly at Layla.

"I'm Layla Darnell, thank you for having us in your home. I hope the wine's appropriate."

"I'm sure it is." Frannie took a peek inside the gift bag. "Jim's favorite cabernet. Aren't you clever girls? Cal, go up and tell your father we have company. Hello, Fox."

"I brought you something, too." He grabbed her, lowered her into a stylish dip, and kissed both her cheeks. "What's cooking, sweetheart?"

As she had since he'd been a boy, Frannie ruffled his hair. "You won't have long to wait to find out. Quinn and Layla, you make yourselves comfortable. Fox, you come with me. I want to put these flowers in water."

"Is there anything we can do to help?"

"Not a thing."

When Cal came down with his father, Fox was doing his version of snooty French waiter as he served appetizers. The women were laughing, candles were lit, and his mother carried in her grandmother's best crystal vase with Quinn's flowers a colorful filling.

Sometimes, Cal mused, all really was right with the world.

HALFWAY THROUGH THE MEAL, WHERE THE CONversation stayed in what Cal considered safe territories, Quinn set down her fork, shook her head. "Mrs. Hawkins, this is the most amazing meal, and I have to ask. Did you study? Did you have a career as a gourmet chef at some point or did we just hit you on a really lucky day?"

"I took a few classes."

"Frannie's taken a lot of 'a few classes,'" Jim said. "In all kinds of things. But she's just got a natural talent for cooking and gardening and decorating. What you see around here, it's all her doing. Painted the walls, made the curtains—sorry, window treatments," he corrected with a twinkle at his wife.

"Get out. You did all the faux and fancy paintwork? Yourself?"

"I enjoy it."

"Found that sideboard there years back at some flea market, had me haul it home." Jim gestured toward the gleaming mahogany sideboard. "A few weeks later, she has me haul it in here. Thought she was pulling a fast one, had snuck out and bought something from an antique store."

"Martha Stewart eats your dust," Quinn decided. "I mean that as a compliment."

"I'll take it."

"I'm useless at all of that. I can barely paint my own nails. How about you?" Quinn asked Layla.

"I can't sew, but I like to paint. Walls. I've done some ragging that turned out pretty well."

"The only ragging I've done successfully was on my ex-fiancé."

"You were engaged?" Frannie asked.

"I thought I was. But our definition of same differed widely."

"It can be difficult to blend careers and personal lives."

"Oh, I don't know. People do it all the time—with varying degrees of success, sure, but they do. I think it just has to be the right people. The trick, or the first of probably many tricks, is recognizing the right person. Wasn't it like that for you? Didn't you have to recognize each other?"

"I knew the first time I saw Frannie. There she is." Jim beamed down the table at his wife. "Frannie now, she was a little more shortsighted."

"A little more practical," Frannie corrected, "seeing as we were eight and ten at the time. Plus I enjoyed having you moon over and chase after me. Yes, you're right." Frannie looked back at Quinn. "You have to see each other, and see in each other something that makes you want to take the chance, that makes you believe you can dig down for the long haul."

"And sometimes you think you see something," Quinn commented, "but it was just a—let's say—trompe l'oeil."

ONE THING QUINN KNEW HOW TO DO WAS FINAGLE. Frannie Hawkins wasn't an easy mark, but Quinn managed to charm her way into the kitchen to help put together dessert and coffee.

"I love kitchens. I'm kind of a pathetic cook, but I love all the gadgets and tools, all the shiny surfaces."

"I imagine with your work, you eat out a lot."

"Actually, I eat in most of the time or call for takeout. I implemented a lifestyle change—nutrition-wise—a couple of years ago. Determined to eat healthier, depend less on fast or nuke-it-out-of-a-box food. I make a really good salad these days. That's a start. Oh God, oh God, that's apple pie. Homemade apple pie. I'm going to have to do double duty in the gym as penance for the huge piece I'm going to ask for."

Her enjoyment obvious, Frannie shot her a wicked smile. "À la mode, with vanilla bean ice cream?"

"Yes, but only to show my impeccable manners." Quinn hesitated a moment, then jumped in. "I'm going to ask you, and if you want this off-limits while I'm enjoying your hospitality, just tell me to back off. Is it hard for you to nurture this normal life, to hold your family, yourself, your home together when you know all of it will be threatened?"

"It's very hard." Frannie turned to her pies while the coffee brewed. "Just as it's very necessary. I wanted Cal to go, and if he had I would have convinced Jim to leave. I could do that, I could turn my back on it all. But Cal couldn't. And I'm so proud of him for staying, for not giving up."

"Will you tell me what happened when he came home that morning, the morning of his tenth birthday?"

"I was in the yard." Frannie walked over to the window that faced the back. She could see it all, every detail. How green the grass was, how blue the sky. Her hydrangeas were headed up and beginning to pop, her delphiniums towering spears of exotic blue.

Deadheading her roses, and some of the coreopsis that had bloomed off. She could even hear the busy *snip*, *snip* of her shears, and the hum of the neighbor's—it had been the Petersons, Jack and Lois, then—lawn mower. She remembered, too, she'd been thinking about Cal, and his birthday party. She'd had his cake in the oven.

A double-chocolate sour cream cake, she remembered. She'd intended to do a white frosting to simulate the ice planet from one of the *Star Wars* movies. Cal had loved *Star Wars* for years and years. She'd had the little action figures to arrange on it, the ten candles all ready in the kitchen.

Had she heard him or sensed him—probably some of both—but she'd looked around as he'd come barreling up on his bike, pale, filthy, sweaty. Her first thought had been accident, there'd been an accident. And she'd been on her feet and rushing to him before she'd noticed he wasn't wearing his glasses.

"The part of me that registered that was ready to give him a good tongue-lashing. But the rest of me was still running when he climbed off his bike, and ran to me. He ran to me and he grabbed on so tight. He was shaking—my little boy—shaking like a leaf. I went down on my knees, pulling him back so I could check for blood or broken bones."

What is it, what happened, are you hurt? All of that, Frannie remembered had flooded out of her, so fast it was like one word. *In the woods,* he'd said. *Mom. Mom. In the woods.*

"There was that part of me again, the part that thought what were you doing in the woods, Caleb Hawkins? It all came pouring out of him, how he and Fox and Gage planned this adventure, what they'd done, where they'd gone. And that same part was coldly devising the punishment to fit the crime, even while the rest of me was terrified, and relieved, so pitifully relieved I was holding my dirty, sweaty boy. Then he told me the rest."

"You believed him?"

"I didn't want to. I wanted to believe he'd had a nightmare, which he richly deserved, that he'd stuffed himself on sweets and junk food and had a nightmare. Even, that someone had gone after them in the woods. But I couldn't look at his face and believe that. I couldn't believe the easy that, the fixable that. And then, of course, there were his eyes. He could see a bee hovering over the delphiniums across the yard. And under the dirt and sweat, there wasn't a bruise on him. The nine-year-old I'd sent off the day before had scraped knees and bruised shins. The one who came back to me hadn't a mark on him, but for the thin white scar across his wrist he hadn't had when he left."

"Even with that, a lot of adults, even mothers, wouldn't have believed a kid who came home with a story like that."

"I won't say Cal never lied to me, because obviously he did. He had. But I knew he wasn't lying. I knew he was telling me the truth, all the truth he knew."

"What did you do?"

"I took him inside, told him to clean up, change his clothes. I called his father, and got his sisters home. I burned his birthday cake—completely forgot about it, never heard the timer. Might've burned the house down if Cal himself hadn't smelled the burning. So he never got his ice planet or his ten candles. I hate remembering that. I burned his cake and he never got to blow out his birthday candles. Isn't that silly?"

"No, ma'am. No," Quinn said with feeling when Frannie looked at her, "it's not."

"He was never really, not wholly, a little boy again." Frannie sighed. "We went straight over to the O'Dells, because Fox and Gage were already there. We had what I guess you could call our first summit meeting."

"What did—"

"We need to take in the dessert and coffee. Can you handle that tray?"

Understanding the subject was closed for now, Quinn stepped over. "Sure. It looks terrific, Mrs. Hawkins."

In between moans and tears of joy over the pie, Quinn aimed her charm at Jim Hawkins. Cal, she was sure, had been dodging and weaving, avoiding and evading her since their hike to the Pagan Stone.

"Mr. Hawkins, you've lived in the Hollow all your life."

"Born and raised. Hawkinses have been here since the town was a couple of stone cabins."

"I met your grandmother, and she seems to know town history."

"Nobody knows more."

"People say you're the one who knows real estate, business, local politics."

"I guess I do."

"Then you may be able to point me in the right direction." She slid a look at Cal, then beamed back at his father. "I'm looking to rent a house, something in town or close to it. Nothing fancy, but I'd like room. I have a friend coming in soon, and I've nearly talked Layla into staying longer. I think we'd be more comfortable, and it would be more efficient, for the three of us to have a house instead of using the hotel."

"How long are you looking for?"

"Six months." She saw it register on his face, just as she noticed the frown form on Cal's. "I'm going to stay through July, Mr. Hawkins, and I'm hoping to find a house that would accommodate three women—potentially three—" she said with a glance at Layla.

"I guess you've thought that over."

"I have. I'm going to write this book, and part of the angle I'm after is the fact that the town remains, the people—a lot of them—stay. They stay and they make apple pie and have people over to Sunday dinner. They bowl, and they shop. They fight and they make love. They live. If I'm going to do this right, I want to be here, before, during, and after. So I'd like to rent a house."

Jim scooped up some pie, chased it with coffee. "It happens I know a place on High Street, just a block off Main. It's old, main part went up before the Civil War. It's got four bedrooms, three baths. Nice porches, front and back. Had a new roof on her two years ago. Kitchen's eat-in size, though there's a little dining room off it. Appliances aren't fancy, but they've only got five years on them. Just been painted. Tenants moved out just a month ago."

"It sounds perfect. You seem to know it well."

"Should. We own it. Cal, you should take Quinn by. Maybe run her and Layla over there on the way home. You know where the keys are."

"Yeah," he said when Quinn gave him a big, bright smile. "I know where the keys are."

AS IT MADE THE MOST SENSE, QUINN HITCHED A ride with Cal, and left Fox and Layla to follow. She stretched out her legs, let out a sigh.

"Let me start off by saying your parents are terrific, and you're lucky to have grown up in such a warm, inviting home."

"I agree."

"Your dad's got that Ward Cleaver meets Jimmy Stewart thing going. I could've eaten him up like your mother's—Martha Stewart meets Grace Kelly by way of Julia Child—apple pie."

His lips twitched. "They'd both like those descriptions."

"You knew about the High Street house."

"Yeah, I did."

"You knew about the High Street house, and avoided telling me about it."

"That's right. You found out about it, too, before dinner, which is why you did the end-run around me to my father."

"Correct." She tapped her finger on his shoulder. "I figured he'd point me there. He likes me. Did you avoid telling me because you're not comfortable with what I might write about Hawkins Hollow?"

"Some of that. More, I was hoping you'd change your mind and leave. Because I like you, too."

"You like me, so you want me gone?"

"I like you, Quinn, so I want you safe." He looked at her again, longer. "But some of the things you said about the Hollow over apple pie echoed pretty closely some of the things my mother said to me today. It all but eliminates any discomfort with what you may decide to write. But it makes me like you more, and that's a problem."

"You had to know, after what happened to us in the woods, I wouldn't be leaving."

"I guess I did." He pulled off into a short, steep driveway.

"Is this the house? It *is* perfect! Look at the stonework, and the big porch, the windows have shutters."

They were painted a deep blue that stood out well against the gray stone. The little front yard was bisected by a trio of concrete steps and the narrow walkway. A trim tree Quinn thought might be a dogwood highlighted the left square of front yard.

As Fox's truck pulled in behind, Quinn popped out to stand, hands on hips. "Pretty damned adorable. Don't you think, Layla?"

"Yes, but—"

"No buts, not yet. Let's take a look inside." She cocked her head at Cal. "Okay, landlord?"

As they trooped up to the porch, Cal took out the keys he'd grabbed off their hook from his father's home office. The ring was clearly labeled with the High Street address.

The fact that the door opened without a creak told Quinn the landlords were vigilant in the maintenance department.

The door opened straight into the living area that stood twice as long as it was wide, with the steps to the second floor a couple of strides in on the left. The wood floors showed wear, but were spotlessly clean. The air was chilly and carried the light sting of fresh paint.

The small brick fireplace delighted her.

"Could use your mother's eye in the paint department," Quinn commented.

"Rental properties get eggshell, through and through. It's the Hawkins's way. Tenants want to play around with that, it's their deal."

"Reasonable. I want to start at the top, work down. Layla, do you want to go up and fight over who gets which bedroom?"

"No." Cal thought there was mutiny, as well as frustration on her face. "I *have* a bedroom. In New York."

"You're not in New York," Quinn said simply, then dashed up the steps.

"She's not listening to me," Layla muttered. "I don't seem to be listening to me either about going back."

"We're here." Fox gave a shrug. "Might as well poke around. I really dig empty houses."

"I'll be up." Cal started up the stairs.

He found her in one of the bedrooms, one that faced the tiny backyard. She stood at the long, narrow window, the fingertips of her right hand pressed to the glass. "I thought I'd go for one of the rooms facing the street, catch the who's going where when and with who. I usually go for that. Just have to know what's going on. But this is the one for me. I bet, in the daylight, you can stand here, see backyards, other houses, and wow, right on to the mountains."

"Do you always make up your mind so fast?"

"Yeah, usually. Even when I surprise myself like now. Bathroom's nice, too." She turned enough to gesture to the door on the side of the room. "And since it's girls, if any of us share that one, it won't be too weird having it link up the two bedrooms on this side."

"You're sure everyone will fall in line."

Now she turned to him, fully. "Confidence is the first step to getting what you want, or need. But we'll say I'm hoping Layla and Cyb will agree it's efficient, practical, and would be more comfortable to share the house for a few months than to bunk at the hotel. Especially considering the fact that both Layla and I are pretty well put off of the dining room there after Slugfest."

"You don't have any furniture."

"Flea markets. We'll pick up the essentials. Cal, I've stayed in less stellar accommodations and done it for one thing. A story. This is more. Somehow or other I'm connected to this story, this place. I can't turn that off and walk away."

He wished she could, and knew if she could his feelings for her wouldn't be as strong or as complex. "Okay, but let's agree, here and now, that if you change your mind and do just that, no explanations needed."

"That's a deal. Now, let's talk rent. What's this place going to run us?"

"You pay the utilities—heat, electric, phone, cable."

"Naturally. And?"

"That's it."

"What do you mean, that's it?"

"I'm not going to charge you rent, not when you're staying here, at least in part, because of me. My family, my friends, my town. We're not going to make a profit off that."

"Straight arrow, aren't you, Caleb?"

"About most."

"I'll make a profit—she says optimistically—from the book I intend to write."

"If we get through July and you write a book, you'll have earned it."

"Well, you drive a hard bargain, but it looks like we have a deal." She stepped forward, offered a hand.

He took it, then cupped his other at the back of her neck. Surprise danced in her eyes, but she didn't resist as he eased her toward him.

He moved slow, the closing together of bodies, the meeting of lips, the testing slide of tongues. There was no explosion of need as there had been in that moment in the clearing. No sudden, almost painful shock of desire. Instead, it was a long and gradual glide from interest to pleasure to ache while her head went light and her blood warmed. It seemed everything inside her went quiet so that she heard, very clearly, the low hum in her own throat as he changed the angle of the kiss.

He felt her give, degree by degree, even as he felt the hand he held in his go lax. The tension that had dogged him throughout the day drained away, so there was only the moment, the quiet, endless moment.

Even when he drew back, that inner stillness held. And she opened her eyes, met his.

"That was just you and me."

"Yeah." He stroked his fingers over the back of her neck. "Just you and me."

"I want to say that I have a policy against becoming romantically, intimately, or sexually—just to cover all my bases—involved with anyone directly associated with a story I'm researching."

"That's probably smart."

"I am smart. I also want to say I'm going to negate that policy in this particular case."

He smiled. "Damn right you are."

"Cocky. Well, mixed with the straight arrow, I have to like it. Unfortunately, I should get back to the hotel. I have a lot of . . . things. Details to see to before I can move in here."

"Sure. I can wait."

He kept her hand in his, switching off the light as he led her out.

Eleven

CAL SENT A DOZEN PINK ROSES TO HIS MOTHER. She liked the traditional flower for Valentine's Day, and he knew his father always went for the red. If he hadn't known, Amy Yost in the flower shop would have reminded him, as she did every blessed year.

"Your dad ordered a dozen red last week, for delivery today, potted geranium to his grandma, *and* he sent the Valentine's Day Sweetheart Special to your sisters."

"That suck-up," Cal said, knowing it would make Amy gasp and giggle. "How about a dozen yellow for my gran. In a vase, Amy. I don't want her to have to fool with them."

"Aw, that's sweet. I've got Essie's address on file, you just fill out the card."

He picked one out of the slot, gave it a minute's thought before writing: *Hearts are red, these roses are yellow. Happy Valentine's Day from your best fellow.*

Corny, sure, he decided, but Gran would love it.

He reached for his wallet to pay when he noticed the

red-and-white-striped tulips behind the glass doors of the refrigerated display. "Ah, those tulips are . . . interesting."

"Aren't they pretty? And they just make me feel like spring. It's no problem if you want to change either of the roses for them. I can just—"

"No, no, maybe . . . I'll take a dozen of them, too. Another delivery in a vase, Amy."

"Sure." Her cheerful round face lit up with curiosity and the anticipation of good gossip. "Who's your valentine, Cal?"

"It's more a housewarming kind of thing." He couldn't think of any reason why *not* to send Quinn flowers. Women liked flowers, he thought as he filled out the delivery form. It was Valentine's Day, and she was moving into the High Street house. It wasn't like he was buying her a ring and picking out a band for the wedding.

It was just a nice gesture.

"Quinn Black." Amy wiggled her eyebrows as she read the name on the form. "Meg Stanley ran into her at the flea market yesterday, along with that friend of hers from New York. They bought a bunch of stuff, according to Meg. I heard you were going around with her."

"We're not . . ." Were they? Either way, it was best to leave it alone. "Well, what's the damage, Amy?"

With his credit card still humming, he stepped outside, hunched his shoulders against the cold. There might be candy-striped tulips, but it didn't feel as if Mother Nature was giving so much as a passing thought to spring. The sky spat out a thin and bitter sleet that lay slick as grease on the streets and sidewalks.

He'd walked down from the bowling center as was his habit, timing his arrival at the florist to their ten o'clock opening. It was the best way to avoid the panicked rush of others who had waited until the last minute to do the Valentine's thing.

It didn't appear he'd needed to worry. Not only had no other customers come in while he'd been buying his roses and impulsive tulips, but there was no one on the sidewalks, no cars creeping cautiously toward the curb in front of the Flower Pot.

"Strange." His voice sounded hollow against the sizzle of sleet striking asphalt. Even on the crappiest day, he'd pass any number of people on his walks around town. He shoved his gloveless hands into his pockets and cursed himself for not breaking his routine and driving.

"Creatures of habit freeze their asses off," he muttered. He wanted to be inside in his office, drinking a cup of coffee, even preparing to start the cancellation process on the evening's scheduled Sweetheart Dance if the sleet worsened. If he'd just taken the damn truck, he'd already be there.

So thinking, he looked up toward the center, and saw the stoplight at the Town Square was out.

Power down, Cal thought, and that was a problem. He quickened his steps. He knew Bill Turner would make certain the generator kicked on for the emergency power, but he needed to be there. School was out, and that meant kids were bound to be scattered around in the arcade.

The hissing of the sleet increased until it sounded like the forced march of an army of giant insects. Despite the slick sidewalk, Cal found himself breaking into a jog when it struck him.

Why weren't there any cars at the Square, or parked at the curbs? Why weren't there any cars anywhere?

He stopped, and so did the hiss of the sleet. In the ensuing silence, he heard his own heart thumping like a fist against steel.

She stood so close he might have reached out to touch her, and knew if he tried, his hand would pass through her as it would through water.

Her hair was deep blond, worn long and loose as it had been when she'd carried the pails toward the little cabin in Hawkins Wood. When she'd sung about a garden green. But her body was slim and straight in a long gray dress.

He had the ridiculous thought that if he had to see a ghost, at least it wasn't a pregnant one.

As if she heard his thoughts, she smiled. "I am not your fear, but you are my hope. You and those who make up the whole of you. What makes you, Caleb Hawkins, is of the past, the now, and the yet to come."

"Who are you? Are you Ann?"

"I am what came before you, and you are formed through love. Know that, know that long, long before you came into the world, you were loved."

"Love isn't enough."

"No, but it is the rock on which all else stands. You have to look; you have to see. This is the time, Caleb. This was always to be the time."

"The time for what?"

"The end of it. Seven times three. Death or life. He holds it, prevents it. Without his endless struggle, his sacrifice, his courage, all this . . ." She held out her arms. "All would be destroyed. Now it is for you."

"Just tell me what I need to do. Goddamn it."

"If I could. If I could spare you." She lifted a hand, let it fall again. "There must be struggle, and sacrifice, and great courage. There must be faith. There must be love. It is courage, faith, love that holds it so long, that prevents it from taking all who live and breathe within this place. Now it is for you."

"We don't know *how*. We've tried."

"This is the time," she repeated. "It is stronger, but so are you, and so are we. Use what you were given, take what it sowed but could never own. You cannot fail."

"Easy for you to say. You're dead."

"But you are not. They are not. Remember that."

When she started to fade, he did reach out, uselessly. "Wait, damn it. Wait. Who are you?"

"Yours," she said. "Yours as I am and always will be his."

She was gone, and the sleet sizzled on the pavement again. Cars rumbled by as the traffic light on the Square glowed green.

"Not the spot for daydreaming." Meg Stanley skidded by, giving him a wink as she pulled open the door of Ma's Pantry.

"No," Cal muttered. "It's not."

He started toward the center again, then veered off to take a detour to High Street.

Quinn's car was in the drive, and through the windows he could see the lights she must've turned on to chase back the gloom. He knocked, heard a muffled call to come in.

When he did, he saw Quinn and Layla trying to muscle something that resembled a desk up the stairs.

"What are you doing? Jesus." He stepped over to grip the side of the desk beside Quinn. "You're going to hurt yourselves."

In an annoyed move, she tossed her head to flip the hair away from her face. "We're managing."

"You'll be managing a trip to the ER. Go on up, take that end with Layla."

"Then we'll both be walking backward. Why don't you take that end?"

"Because I'm going to be taking the bulk of the weight this way."

"Oh." She let go, squeezed between the wall and the desk.

He didn't bother to ask why it had to go up. He'd lived with his mother too long to waste his breath. Instead he grunted out orders to prevent the edge of the desk from bashing into the wall as they angled left at the top of the stairs. Then followed Quinn as she directed the process to the window in the smallest bedroom.

"See, we were right." Quinn panted, and tugged down a Penn State sweatshirt. "This is the spot for it."

There was a seventies chair that had seen better days, a pole lamp with a rosy glass shade that dripped long crystals, and a low bookshelf varnished black over decades that wobbled when he set a hand on it.

"I know, I know." Quinn waved away his baleful look.

"But it just needs a little hammering or something, and it's really just to fill things out. We were thinking about making it a little sitting room, then decided it would be better as a little office. Hence the desk we originally thought should be in the dining room."

"Okay."

"The lamp looks like something out of *The Best Little Whorehouse in Texas*." Layla gave one of the crystals a flick with her fingers. "But that's what we like about it. The chair is hideous."

"But comfortable," Quinn inserted.

"But comfortable, and that's what throws are for."

Cal waited a beat as both of them looked at him expectantly. "Okay," he repeated, which was generally how he handled his mother's decorating explanations.

"We've been busy. We turned in Layla's rental car, then hit the flea market just out of town. Bonanza. Plus we agreed no secondhand mattresses. The ones we ordered should be here this afternoon. Anyway, come see what we've got going so far."

Quinn grabbed his hand, pulled him across the hall to the room she'd chosen. There was a long bureau desperately in need of refinishing, topped by a spotted mirror. Across the room was a boxy chest someone had painted a murderous and shiny red. On it stood a Wonder Woman lamp.

"Homey."

"It'll be very livable when we're done."

"Yeah. You know I think that lamp might've been my sister Jen's twenty, twenty-five years ago."

"It's classic," Quinn claimed. "It's kitschy."

He fell back on the standard. "Okay."

"I think I have Danish modern," Layla commented from the doorway. "Or possibly Flemish. It's absolutely horrible. I have no idea why I bought it."

"Did you two haul this stuff up here?"

"Please." Quinn tossed her head.

"We opted for brain over brawn."

"Every time. That and a small investment. Do you know how much a couple of teenage boys will cart and carry for twenty bucks each and the opportunity to ogle a couple of hot chicks such as we?" Quinn fisted a hand on her hip, struck a pose.

"I'd've done it for ten. You could have called."

"Which was our intention, actually. But the boys were handy. Why don't we go down and sit on our new third- or fourthhand sofa?"

"We did splurge," Layla added. "We have an actual new coffeemaker and a very eclectic selection of coffee mugs."

"Coffee'd be good."

"I'll get it started."

Cal glanced after Layla. "She seems to have done a one-eighty on all this."

"I'm persuasive. And you're generous. I think I should plant one on you for that."

"Go ahead. I can take it."

Laughing, she braced her hands on his shoulders, gave him a firm, noisy kiss.

"Does that mean I don't get ten bucks?"

Her smile beamed as she poked him in the belly. "You'll take the kiss and like it. Anyway, part of the reason for Layla hanging back was the money. The idea of staying was—is—difficult for her. But the idea of taking a long leave, unpaid, from her job, coming up with rent money here, keeping her place in New York, that was pretty much off the table."

She stepped up to the bright red chest to turn her Wonder Woman lamp on and off. From the look on her face, Cal could see the act pleased her.

"So, the rent-free aspect checked one problem off her list," Quinn went on. "She hasn't completely committed. Right now, it's a day at a time for her."

"I've got something to tell you, both of you, that may make this her last day."

"Something happened." She dropped her hand, turned. "What happened?"

"I'll tell you both. I want to call Fox first, see if he can swing by. Then I can tell it once."

HE HAD TO DO IT WITHOUT FOX, WHO, ACCORDing to Mrs. Hawbaker, was at the courthouse being a lawyer. So he sat in the oddly furnished living room on a couch so soft and saggy he was already wishing for the opportunity to get Quinn naked on it, and told them about the visitation on Main Street.

"An OOB," Quinn decided.

"An oob?"

"No, no. Initials, like CYA. Out of body—experience. It sounds like that might be what you had, or maybe there was a slight shift in dimensions and you were in an alternate Hawkins Hollow."

He might have spent two-thirds of his life caught up in something beyond rational belief, but he'd never heard another woman talk like Quinn Black. "I was not in an alternate anything, and I was right inside my body where I belong."

"I've been studying, researching, and writing about the paranormal for some time now." Quinn drank some coffee and brooded over it.

"It could be he was talking to a ghost who caused the illusion that they were alone on the street, and caused everyone else out there to—I don't know—blip out for a few minutes." Layla shrugged at Quinn's narrowed look. "I'm new at this, and I'm still working really hard not to hide under the covers until somebody wakes me up and tells me this was all a dream."

"For the new kid, your theory's pretty good," Quinn told her.

"How about mine? Which is what she said is a hell of a lot more important right now than how she said it."

"Point taken." Quinn nodded at Cal. "This is the time, she said. Three times seven. That one's easy enough to figure."

"Twenty-one years." Cal pushed up to pace. "This July makes twenty-one years."

"Three, like seven, is considered a magickal number. It sounds like she was telling you it was always going to come now, this July, this year. It's stronger, you're stronger, they're stronger." Quinn squeezed her eyes shut.

"So, it and this woman—this spirit—have both been able to . . ."

"Manifest." Quinn finished Layla's thought. "That follows the logic."

"Nothing about this is logical."

"It is, really." Opening her eyes again, Quinn gave Layla a sympathetic look. "Inside this sphere, there's logic. It's just not the kind we deal with, or most of us deal with, every day. The past, the now, the yet to be. Things that happened, that are happening, and that will or may are all part of the solution, the way to end it."

"I think there's more to that part." Cal turned back from the window. "After that night in the clearing, the three of us were different."

"You don't get sick, and you heal almost as soon as you're hurt. Quinn told me."

"Yeah. And I could see."

"Without your glasses."

"I could also see before. I started—right there minutes afterward—to have flashes of the past."

"The way you did—both of us did," Quinn corrected, "when we touched the stone together. And later, when we—"

"Like that, not always that clear, not always so intense. Sometimes awake, sometimes like a dream. Sometimes completely irrelevant. And Fox . . . It took him a while to understand. Jesus, we were ten. He can see now." Annoyed with himself, Cal shook his head. "He can see, or sense what you're thinking, or feeling."

"Fox is psychic?" Layla demanded.

"Psychic lawyer. He's so hired."

Despite everything, Quinn's announcement made Cal's lips twitch. "Not like that, not exactly. It's never been something we can completely control. Fox has to deliberately push it, and it doesn't always work then. But since then he has an instinct about people. And Gage—"

"He sees what could happen," Quinn added. "He's the soothsayer."

"It's hardest for him. That's why—one of the reasons why—he doesn't spend much time here. It's harder here. He's had some pretty damn vicious dreams, visions, nightmares, whatever the hell you want to call them."

And it hurts you when he hurts, Quinn thought. "But he hasn't seen what you're meant to do?"

"No. That would be too easy, wouldn't it?" Cal said bitterly. "Has to be more fun to mess up the lives of three kids, to let innocent people die or kill and maim each other. Stretch that out for a couple of decades, then say: Okay, boys, now's the time."

"Maybe there was no choice." Quinn held up a hand when Cal's eyes fired. "I'm not saying it's fair. In fact, it sucks. Inside and out, it sucks. I'm saying maybe it couldn't be another way. Whether it was something Giles Dent did, or something set in motion centuries before that, there may have been no other choice. She said he was holding it, that he was preventing it from destroying the Hollow. If it was Ann, and she meant Giles Dent, does that mean he trapped this thing, this *bestia*, and in some form—*beatus*—has been trapped with it, battling it, all this time? Three hundred and fifty years and change. That sucks, too."

Layla jumped at the brisk knock on the door, then popped up. "I'll get it. Maybe it's the delivery."

"You're not wrong," Cal said quietly. "But it doesn't make it easier to live through it. It doesn't make it easier to know, in my gut, that we're coming up to our last chance."

Quinn got to her feet. "I wish—"

"It's flowers!" Layla's voice was giddy with delight as she came in carrying the vase of tulips. "For you, Quinn."

"Jesus, talk about weird timing," Cal muttered.

"For me? Oh God, they look like lollipop cups. They're gorgeous!" Quinn set them on the ancient coffee table. "Must be a bribe from my editor so I'll finish that article on—" She broke off as she ripped open the card. Her face was blank with shock as she lifted her eyes to Cal. "You sent me flowers?"

"I was in the florist before—"

"You sent me flowers on Valentine's Day."

"I hear my mother calling," Layla announced. "Coming, Mom!" She made a fast exit.

"You sent me tulips that look like blooming candy canes on Valentine's Day."

"They looked like fun."

"That's what you wrote on the card. 'These look like fun.' Wow." She scooped a hand through her hair. "I have to say that I'm a sensible woman, who knows very well Valentine's Day is a commercially generated holiday designed to sell greeting cards, flowers, and candy."

"Yeah, well." He slid his hands into his pockets. "Works."

"And I'm not the type of woman who goes all mushy and gooey over flowers, or sees them as an apology for an argument, a prelude to sex, or any of the other oft-perceived uses."

"I just saw them, thought you'd get a kick out of them. Period. I've got to get to work."

"But," she continued and moved toward him, "strangely, I find none of that applies in the least in this particular case. They are fun." She rose up on her toes, kissed his cheek. "And they're beautiful." Then his other cheek. "And thoughtful." Now his lips. "Thank you."

"You're welcome."

"I'd like to add that . . ." She trailed her hands down his shirt, up again. "If you'll tell me what time you finish up tonight, I'll have a bottle of wine waiting in my bedroom upstairs, where I can promise you, you're going to get really, really lucky."

"Eleven," he said immediately. "I can be here at eleven-oh-five. I— Oh shit. Sweetheart Dance, that's midnight. Special event. No problem. You'll come."

"That's my plan." When he grinned, she rolled her eyes. "You mean to this dance. At the Bowl-a-Rama. A Sweetheart Dance at the Bowl-a-Rama. God, I'd *love* that. But, I can't leave Layla here, not at night. Not alone."

"She can come, too—to the dance."

Now her eyeroll was absolutely sincere. "Cal, no woman wants to tag along with a couple to a dance on Valentine's Day. It paints a big *L* for loser in the middle of her forehead, and they're so damn hard to wash off."

"Fox can take her. Probably. I'll check."

"That's a possibility, especially if we make it all for fun. You check, then I'll check, then we'll see. But either way." She grabbed a fistful of his shirt, and this time brought him to her for a long, long kiss. "My bedroom, twelve-oh-five."

LAYLA SAT ON HER BRAND-NEW DISCOUNT MATtress while Quinn busily checked out the clothes she'd recently hung in her closet.

"Quinn, I appreciate the thought, I really do, but put yourself in my place. The third-wheel position."

"It's perfectly acceptable to be the third wheel when there're four wheels altogether. Fox is going."

"Because Cal asked him to take pity on the poor dateless V-Day loser. Probably told him or bribed him or—"

"You're right. Fox certainly had to have his arm twisted to go out with such an ugly hag like yourself. I admit every time I look at you, I'm tempted to go: woof, woof, what a dog. Besides . . . Oh, I love this jacket! You have the best clothes. But this jacket is seriously awesome. Mmm." Quinn stroked it like a cat. "Cashmere."

"I don't know why I packed it. I don't know why I packed half the stuff I did. I just started grabbing things. And you're trying to distract me."

"Not really, but it's a nice side benefit. What was I saying? Oh, yeah. Besides, it's not a date. It's a gang bang," she said and made Layla laugh. "It's just the four of us going to a bowling alley, for God's sake, to hear some local band play and dance a little."

"Sure. After which, you'll be hanging a scarf over the doorknob of your bedroom. I went to college, Quinn. I had a roommate. Actually, I had a nympho of a roommate who had an endless supply of scarves."

"Is it a problem?" Quinn stopped poking in the closet long enough to look over her shoulder. "Cal and me, across the hall?"

"No. No." And now didn't she feel stupid and petty? "I think it's great. Really, I do. Anybody can tell the two of you rev like engines when you're within three feet of each other."

"They can?" Quinn turned all the way around now. "We do."

"*Vroom, vroom.* He's great, it's great. I just feel . . ." Layla rolled her shoulders broadly. "In the way."

"You're not. I couldn't stay here without you. I'm pretty steady, but I couldn't stay in this house alone. The dance isn't a big deal. We don't have to go, but I think it'd be fun, for all of us. And a chance to do something absolutely normal to take our minds off everything that isn't."

"That's a good point."

"So get dressed. Put on something fun, maybe a little sexy, and let's hit the Bowl-a-Rama."

THE BAND, A LOCAL GROUP NAMED HOLLOWED Out, was into its first set. They were popular at weddings and corporate functions, and regularly booked at the center's events because their playlist ran the gamut from old standards to hip-hop. The something-for-everybody kept the dance floor lively while those sitting one out could chat at one of the tables circling the room, sip drinks, or nibble from the light buffet set up along one of the side walls.

Cal figured it was one of the center's most popular annual events for good reason. His mother headed up the decorating committee, so there were flowers and candles, red and white streamers, glittering red hearts. It gave people a chance to get a little dressed up in the dullness that was

February, get out and socialize, hear some music, show off their moves if they had them. Or like Cy Hudson, even if they didn't.

It was a little bright spot toward the end of a long winter, and they never failed to have a full house.

Cal danced with Essie to "Fly Me to the Moon."

"Your mother was right to make you take those dance lessons."

"I was humiliated among my peers," Cal said. "But light on my feet."

"Women tend to lose their heads over a good dancer."

"A fact I've exploited whenever possible." He smiled down at her. "You look so pretty, Gran."

"I look dignified. Now, there was a day when I turned plenty of heads."

"You still turn mine."

"And you're still the sweetest of my sweethearts. When are you going to bring that pretty writer to see me?"

"Soon, if that's what you want."

"It feels like time. I don't know why. And speaking of—" She nodded toward the open double doors. "Those two turn heads."

He looked. He noticed Layla, in that she was there. But his focus was all for Quinn. She'd wound that mass of blond hair up, a touch of elegance, and wore an open black jacket over some kind of lacey top—camisole, he remembered. They called them camisoles, and God bless whoever invented them.

Things glittered at her ears, at her wrists, but all he could think was she had the sexiest collarbone in the history of collarbones, and he couldn't wait to get his mouth on it.

"You're about to drool, Caleb."

"What?" He blinked his attention back to Essie. "Oh. Jeez."

"She does look a picture. You take me on back to my table now and go get her. Bring her and her friend around to say hello before I leave."

By the time he got to them, Fox had already scooped them up to one of the portable bars and sprung for champagne. Quinn turned to Cal, glass in hand, and pitched her voice over the music. "This is great! The band's hot, the bubbly's cold, and the room looks like a love affair."

"You were expecting a couple of toothless guys with a washboard and a jug, some hard cider, and a few plastic hearts."

"No." She laughed, jabbed him with her finger. "But something between that and this. It's my first bowling alley dance, and I'm impressed. And look! Isn't that His Honor, the mayor, getting down?"

"With his wife's cousin, who is the choir director for the First Methodist Church."

"Isn't that your assistant, Fox?" Layla gestured to a table.

"Yeah. Fortunately, the guy she's kissing is her husband."

"They look completely in love."

"Guess they are. I don't know what I'm going to do without her. They're moving to Minneapolis in a couple months. I wish they'd just take off for a few weeks in July instead of—" He caught himself. "No shop talk tonight. Do you want to scare up a table?"

"Perfect for people-watching," Quinn agreed, then spun toward the band. " 'In the Mood'!"

"Signature piece for them. Do you swing?" Cal asked her.

"Damn right." She glanced at him, considered. "Do you?"

"Let's go see what you've got, Blondie." He grabbed her hand, pulled her out to the dance floor.

Fox watched the spins and footwork. "I absolutely can't do that."

"Neither can I. Wow." Layla's eyes widened. "They're really good."

On the dance floor, Cal set Quinn up for a double spin, whipped her back. "Lessons?"

"Four years. You?"

"Three." When the song ended and bled into a slow number, he fit Quinn's body to his and blessed his mother. "I'm glad you're here."

"Me, too." She nuzzled her cheek to his. "Everything feels good tonight. Sweet and shiny. And mmm," she murmured when he led her into a stylish turn. "Sexy." Tipping back her head, she smiled at him. "I've completely reversed my cynical take on Valentine's Day. I now consider it the perfect holiday."

He brushed his lips over hers. "After this dance, why don't we sneak off to the storeroom upstairs and neck?"

"Why wait?"

With a laugh, he started to bring her close again. And froze.

The hearts bled. The glittery art board dripped, and splattered red on the dance floor, plopped on tables, slid down the hair and faces of people while they laughed, or chatted, strolled or swayed.

"Quinn."

"I see it. Oh God."

The vocalist continued to sing of love and longing as the red and silver balloons overhead popped like gunshots. And from them rained spiders.

Twelve

QUINN BARELY MANAGED TO MUFFLE A SCREAM, and would have danced back as the spiders skittered over the floor if Cal hadn't gripped her.

"Not real." He said it with absolute and icy calm. "It's not real."

Someone laughed, and the sound spiked wildly. There were shouts of approval as the music changed tempo to hip-grinding rock.

"Great party, Cal!" Amy from the flower shop danced by with a wide, blood-splattered grin.

With his arm still tight around Quinn, Cal began to back off the floor. He needed to see his family, needed to see . . . And there was Fox, gripping Layla's hand as he wound his way through the oblivious crowd.

"We need to go," Fox shouted.

"My parents—"

Fox shook his head. "It's only happening because we're here. I think it only can happen because we're here. Let's move out. Let's move."

As they pushed between tables, the tiny tea lights in the centerpieces flashed like torches, belching a volcanic spew of smoke. Cal felt it in his throat, stinging, even as his foot crunched down on a fist-sized spider. On the little stage, the drummer swung into a wild solo with bloodied sticks. When they reached the doors, Cal glanced back.

He saw the boy floating above the dancers. Laughing.

"Straight out." Following Fox's line of thought, Cal pulled Quinn toward the exit. "Straight out of the building. Then we'll see. Then we'll damn well see."

"They didn't see." Out of breath, Layla stumbled outside. "Or feel. It wasn't happening for them."

"It's outside the box, okay, it's pushed outside the lines. But only for us." Fox stripped off his jacket and tossed it over Layla's shaking shoulders. "Giving us a preview of coming attractions. Arrogant bastard."

"Yes." Quinn nodded, even as her stomach rolled. "I think you're right, because every time it puts on a show, it costs energy. So we get that lull between production numbers."

"I have to go back." He'd left his family. Even if retreat was to defend, Cal couldn't stand and do nothing while his family was inside. "I need to be in there, need to close down when the event's over."

"We'll all go back," Quinn linked her cold fingers with Cal's. "These performances are always of pretty short duration. It lost its audience, and unless it's got enough for a second act, it's done for tonight. Let's go back. It's freezing out here."

Inside, the tea lights glimmered softly, and the hearts glittered. The polished dance floor was unstained. Cal saw his parents dancing, his mother's head resting on his father's shoulder. When she caught his eye and smiled at him, Cal felt the fist twisting in his belly relax.

"I don't know about you, but I'd really like another glass of champagne." Quinn blew out a breath, as her eyes went sharp and hard. "Then you know what? Let's dance."

FOX WAS SPRAWLED ON THE COUCH WATCHING some drowsy black-and-white movie on TV when Cal and Quinn came into the rental house after midnight. "Layla went up," he said as he shoved himself to sitting. "She was beat."

The subtext, that she'd wanted to be well tucked away before her housemate and Cal came up, was perfectly clear.

"Is she all right?" Quinn asked.

"Yeah. Yeah, she handles herself. Anything else happen after we left?"

Cal shook his head as his gaze tracked over to the window, and the dark. "Just a big, happy party momentarily interrupted for some of us by supernatural blood and spiders. Everything okay here?"

"Yeah, except for the fact these women buy Diet Pepsi. Classic Coke," he said to Quinn. "A guy has to have some standards."

"We'll look right into that. Thanks, Fox." She stepped up and kissed his cheek. "For hanging out until we got back."

"No big. It got me out of cleanup duty and let me watch . . ." He looked back at the little TV screen. "I have no idea. You ought to think about getting cable. ESPN."

"I don't know how I've lived without it these last few days."

He grinned as he pulled on his coat. "Humankind shouldn't live by network alone. Call me if you need anything," he added as he headed for the door.

"Fox." Cal trailed behind him. After a murmured conversation, Fox sent Quinn a quick wave and left.

"What was that?"

"I asked if he'd bunk at my place tonight, check on Lump. It's no problem. I've got Coke and ESPN."

"You've got worry all over you, Cal."

"I'm having a hard time taking it off."

"It can't hurt us, not yet. It's all head games. Mean, disgusting, but just psychological warfare."

"It means something, Quinn." He gave her arms a quick, almost absent rub before turning to check the dark, again. "That it can do it now, with us. That I had that episode with Ann. It means something."

"And you have to think about it. You think a lot, have all sorts of stores up here." She tapped her temple. "The fact that you do is, well, it's comforting to me and oddly attractive. But you know what? After this really long, strange day, it might be good for us not to think at all."

"That's a good idea." Take a break, he told himself. Take some normal. Walking back to her, he skimmed his fingers over her cheek, then let them trail down her arm until they linked with hers. "Why don't we try that?"

He drew her toward the steps, started up. There were a few homey creaks, the click and hum of the furnace, and nothing else.

"Do you—"

He cut her off by cupping a hand on her cheek, then laying his lips on hers. Soft and easy as a sigh. "No questions either. Then we'd have to think of the answers."

"Good point."

Just the room, the dark, the woman. That was all there would be, all he wanted for the night. Her scent, her skin, the fall of her hair, the sounds two people made when they discovered each other.

It was enough. It was more than enough.

He closed the door behind him.

"I like candles." She drew away to pick up a long, slim lighter to set the candles she'd scattered around the room to flame.

In their light she looked delicate, more delicate than she was. He enjoyed the contrast of reality and illusion. The mattress and box spring sat on the floor, covered by sheets that looked crisp and pearly against a blanket of deep, rich purple. His tulips sat like a cheerful carnival on the scarred wood of her flea market dresser.

She'd hung fabric in a blurry blend of colors over the windows to close out the night. And when she turned from them, she smiled.

It was, for him, perfect.

"Maybe I should tell you—"

He shook his head, stepped toward her.

"Later." He did the first thing that came to mind, lifting his hands to her hair. He drew the pins out, let them fall. When the weight of it tumbled free, over her shoulders, down her back, he combed his fingers through it. With his eyes on hers, he wrapped her hair around his fist like a rope, gave a tug.

"There's still a lot of later," he said, and took her mouth with his.

Her lips, for him, were perfect. Soft and full, warm and generous. He felt a quick tremble from her as her arms wound around him, as she pressed her body to his. She didn't yield, didn't soften—not yet. Instead she met his slow, patient assault with one of her own.

He slid the jacket from her shoulders, let it fall like the pins so his hands, his fingertips could explore silk and lace and flesh. While their lips brushed, rubbed, pressed, her hands came to his shoulders, then shoved at his jacket until it dropped away.

He tasted her throat, heard her purr of approval. As he eased back, he danced his fingers over the alluring line of her collarbone. Her eyes were vivid, alight with anticipation. He wanted to see them heavy. He wanted to see them go blind. Watching them, watching her, he let his fingers trail down to the swell of her breast where the lace flirted. And watching her still, glided them over the lace, over the silk to cup her while his thumb lightly rubbed, rubbed to tease her nipple.

He heard her breath catch, release, felt her shiver even

as she reached to him to unbutton his shirt. Her hands slid up his torso, spread. He knew his heartbeat skipped, but his own hand made the journey almost lazily to the waistband of her pants. The flesh there was warm, and her muscles quivered as his fingers did a testing sweep. Then with a flick and a tug, her pants floated down her legs.

The move was so sudden, so unexpected, she couldn't anticipate or prepare. Everything had been so slow, so dreamy, then his hands hooked under her arms, lifted her straight off her feet. The quick, careless show of strength shocked her system, made her head swim. Even when he set her back down, her knees stayed weak.

His gaze skimmed down, over the camisole, over the frothy underwear she'd donned with the idea of making him crazy. His lips curved as his eyes came back to hers.

"Nice."

It was all he said, and her mouth went dry. It was ridiculous. She'd had other men look at her, touch her, want her. But he did, and her throat went dry. She tried to find something clever and careless to say back, but could barely find the wit to breathe.

Then he hooked his finger in the waist of her panties, gave one easy tug. She stepped toward him like a woman under a spell.

"Let's see what's under here," he murmured, and lifted the camisole over her head. "Very nice," was his comment as he traced his fingertip along the edge of her bra.

She couldn't remember her moves, had to remind herself she was *good* at this—actively good, not just the type who went limp and let a guy do all the work. She reached for the hook of his trousers, fumbled.

"You're shaking."

"Shut up. I feel like an idiot."

He took her hands, brought them both to his lips and she knew she was as sunk as the *Titanic*. "Sexy," he corrected. "What you are is stupendously sexy."

"Cal." She had to concentrate to form the words. "I really need to lie down."

There was that smile again, and though it might have transmitted *self-satisfied male*, she really didn't give a damn.

Then they were on the bed, aroused bodies on cool, crisp sheets, candlelight flickering like magic in the dark. And his hands, his mouth, went to work on her.

He runs a bowling alley, she thought as he simply saturated her with pleasure. How did he get hands like this? Where did he learn to . . . Oh my God.

She came in a long, rolling wave that seemed to curl up from her toes, ride over her legs, burst in her center then wash over heart and mind. She clung to it, greedily wringing every drop of shock and delight until she was both limp and breathless.

Okay, okay, was all her brain could manage. Okay, wow.

Her body was a feast of curves and quivers. He could have lingered over those lovely breasts, the strong line of torso, that feminine flare of hip for days. Then there were her legs, smooth and strong and . . . sensitive. So many places to touch, so much to taste, and all the endless night to savor.

She rose to him, wrapped around him, arched and flowed and answered. He felt her heart thundering under his lips, heard her moan as he used his tongue to torment. Her fingers dug into his shoulders, his hips, her hands squeezing then gliding to fray the taut line of his control.

Kisses became more urgent. The cool air of the room went hot, went thick as smoke. When the need became a blur, he slipped inside her. And yes, watched her eyes go blind.

He gripped her hands to anchor himself, to stop himself from simply plunging, from bulleting by the aching pleasure to release. Her fingers tightened on his, and that pleasure glowed on her face with each long, slow thrust. Stay with me, he thought, and she did, beat for beat. Until it built and built in her ragged breaths, in the shivering of her body. She made a helpless sound as she closed her eyes, turned her head on the pillow. When her body melted under him, he pressed his face to that exposed curve of her neck. And let himself go.

HE LAY QUIET, THINKING SHE MIGHT HAVE FALLEN asleep. She'd rolled so that her head was on his shoulder, her arm tossed across his chest, and her leg hooked around his. It was, he thought, a little like being tied up with a Quinn bow. And he couldn't find anything not to like about it.

"I was going to say something."

Not asleep, he realized, though her words were drunk and slurry.

"About what?"

"Mmm. I was going to say, when we first came into the room. I was going to say something." She curled closer, and he realized the heat sex had generated had ebbed, and she was cold.

"Hold on." He had to unwind her, to which she gave a couple of halfhearted mutters of protest. But when he pulled up the blanket, she snuggled right in. "Better?"

"Couldn't be any. I was going to say that I've been—more or less—thinking about getting you naked since I met you."

"That's funny. I've been more or less thinking the same about you. You've got an amazing body there, Quinn."

"Lifestyle change, for which I could now preach like an evangelist. However." She levered up so she could look down into his face. "Had I known what it would be like, I would've had you naked in five minutes flat."

He grinned. "Once again, our thoughts run on parallel lines. Do that thing again. No," he said with a laugh when her eyebrows wiggled. "This thing."

He tugged her head down again until it rested on his shoulder, then drew her arm over his chest. "And the leg. That's it," he said when she obliged. "That's perfect."

The fact that it was gave her a nice warm glow under her

heart. Quinn closed her eyes, and without a worry in the world, drifted off to sleep.

IN THE DARK, SHE WOKE WHEN SOMETHING FELL on her. She managed a breathless squeal, shoved herself to sitting, balled her hands into fists.

"Sorry, sorry."

She recognized Cal's whisper, but it was too late to stop the punch. Her fist jabbed into something hard enough to sting her knuckles. "Ow! Ow! Shit."

"I'll say," Cal muttered.

"What the hell are you doing?"

"Tripping, falling down, and getting punched in the head."

"Why?"

"Because it's pitch-dark." He shifted, rubbed his sore temple. "And I was trying not to wake you up, and you hit me. In the head."

"Well, I'm sorry," she hissed right back. "For all I knew you could've been a mad rapist, or more likely, given the location, a demon from hell. What are you doing milling around in the dark?"

"Trying to find my shoes, which I think is what I tripped over."

"You're leaving?"

"It's morning, and I've got a breakfast meeting in a couple hours."

"It's dark."

"It's February, and you've got those curtain deals over the windows. It's about six thirty."

"Oh God." She plopped back down. "Six thirty isn't morning, even in February. Or maybe especially."

"Which is why I was trying not to wake you up."

She shifted. She could make him out now, a little, as her eyes adjusted. "Well, I'm awake, so why are you still whispering?"

"I don't know. Maybe I have brain damage from getting punched in the head."

Something about the baffled irritation in his voice stirred her juices. "Aw. Why don't you crawl back in here with me where it's all nice and warm? I'll kiss it and make it better."

"That's a cruel thing to suggest when I have a breakfast meeting with the mayor, the town manager, and the town council."

"Sex and politics go together like peanut butter and jelly."

"That may be, but I've got to go home, feed Lump, drag Fox out of bed as he's in on this meeting. Shower, shave, and change so it doesn't look like I've been having hot sex."

As he dragged on his shoes, she roused herself to push up again, then slither around him. "You could do all that after."

Her breasts, warm and full, pressed against his back as she nibbled on the side of his throat. And her hand snuck down to where he'd already gone rock hard.

"You've got a mean streak, Blondie."

"Maybe you ought to teach me a lesson." She let out a choked laugh when he swiveled and grabbed her.

This time when he fell on her, it was on purpose.

HE WAS LATE FOR THE MEETING, BUT HE WAS feeling too damn good to care. He ordered an enormous breakfast—eggs, bacon, hash browns, two biscuits. He worked his way through it while Fox gulped down Coke as if it were the antidote to some rare and fatal poison in his bloodstream, and the others engaged in small talk.

Small talk edged into town business. It may have been February, but plans for the annual Memorial Day parade had to be finalized. Then there was the debate about installing new benches in the park. Most of it washed over Cal as he ate, as he thought about Quinn.

He tuned back in, primarily because Fox kicked him under the table.

"The Branson place is only a couple doors down from the Bowl-a-Rama," Mayor Watson continued. "Misty said it looked like the house on either side went dark, too, but across the street, the lights were on. Phones went out, too. Spooked her pretty good, she said when Wendy and I picked her up after the dance. Only lasted a few minutes."

"Maybe a breaker," Jim Hawkins suggested, but he looked at his son.

"Maybe, but Misty said it all flickered and snapped for a few seconds. Power surge maybe. But I think I'm going to urge Mike Branson to get his wiring checked out. Could be something's shorting out. We don't want an electrical fire."

How did they manage to forget? Cal wondered. Was it a defense mechanism, amnesia, or simply part of the whole ugly situation?

Not all of them. He could see the question, the concern in his father's eyes, in one or two of the others. But the mayor and most of the council were moving on to a discussion of painting the bleachers in the ballpark before Little League season began.

There had been other odd power surges, other strange power outages. But never until June, never before that final countdown to the Seven.

When the meeting was over, Fox walked to the bowling center with Cal and his father. They didn't speak until they were inside, and the door closed behind them.

"It's too early for this to happen," Jim said immediately. "It's more likely a power surge, or faulty wiring."

"It's not. Things have been happening already," Cal told him. "And it's not just Fox and I who've seen them. Not this time."

"Well." Jim sat down heavily at one of the tables in the grill section. "What can I do?"

Take care of yourself, Cal thought. Take care of Mom. But it would never be enough. "Anything feels off, you tell me. Tell Fox, or Gage when he gets here. There are more of us this time. Quinn and Layla, they're part of it. We need to figure out how and why."

His great-grandmother had known Quinn was connected, Cal thought. She'd sensed something. "I need to talk to Gran."

"Cal, she's ninety-seven. I don't care how spry she is, she's still ninety-seven."

"I'll be careful."

"You know, I'm going to talk to Mrs. H again." Fox shook his head. "She's jumpy, nervous. Making noises about leaving next month instead of April. I figured it was just restlessness now that she's decided to move. Maybe it's more."

"All right." Jim blew out a breath. "You two go do what you need to do. I'll handle things here. I know how to run the center," he said before Cal could protest. "Been doing it awhile now."

"Okay. I'll run Gran to the library if she wants to go today. I'll be back after, and we can switch off. You can pick her up, take her home."

CAL WALKED TO ESSIE'S HOUSE. SHE ONLY LIVED a block away in the pretty little house she shared with his cousin Ginger. Essie's concession to her age was to have Ginger live in, take care of the house, the grocery shopping, most of the cooking, and be her chauffeur for duties like doctor and dentist appointments.

Cal knew Ginger to be a sturdy, practical sort who stayed out of his gran's way—and her business—unless she needed to do otherwise. Ginger preferred TV to books, and lived for a trio of afternoon soaps. Her disastrous and childless marriage had turned her off men, except television beefcake or those within the covers of *People* magazine.

As far as Cal could tell, his gran and his cousin bumped along well enough in the little dollhouse with its trim front yard and cheerful blue porch.

When he arrived he didn't see Ginger's car at the curb, and wondered if his gran had an early medical appointment. His father kept Essie's schedule in his head, as he kept so much else, but he'd been upset that morning.

Still, it was more likely that Ginger had taken a run to the grocery store.

He crossed the porch and knocked. It didn't surprise him when the door opened. Even upset, his father rarely forgot anything.

But it did surprise him to see Quinn at the threshold.

"Hi. Come on in. Essie and I are just having some tea in the parlor."

He gripped her arm. "Why are you here?"

The greeting smile faded at the sharp tone. "I have a job to do. And Essie called me."

"Why?"

"Maybe if you come in instead of scowling at me, we'll both find out."

Seeing no other choice, Cal walked into his great-grandmother's lovely living room where African violets bloomed in purple profusion in the windows, where built-in shelves Fox's father had crafted were filled with books, family pictures, little bits and bobs of memories. Where the company tea set was laid out on the low table in front of the high-backed sofa his mother had reupholstered only the previous spring.

Where his beloved gran sat like a queen in her favored wingback chair. "Cal." She lifted her hand for his, and her cheek for his kiss. "I thought you'd be tied up all morning between the meeting and center business."

"Meeting's over, and Dad's at the center. I didn't see Ginger's car."

"She's off running some errands since I had company. Quinn's just pouring the tea. Go get yourself a cup out of the cupboard."

"No, thanks. I'm fine. Just had breakfast."

"I would've called you, too, if I'd realized you'd have time this morning."

"I've always got time for you, Gran."

"He's my boy," she said to Quinn, squeezing Cal's hand

before she released it to take the tea Quinn offered. "Thank you. Please, sit down, both of you. I might as well get right to it. I need to ask you if there was an incident last night, during the dance. An incident just before ten."

She looked hard at Cal's face as she asked, and what she saw had her closing her eyes. "So there was." Her thin voice quivered. "I don't know whether to be relieved or afraid. Relieved because I thought I might be losing my mind. Afraid because I'm not. It was real then," she said quietly. "What I saw."

"What did you see?"

"It was as if I were behind a curtain. As if a curtain had dropped, or a shroud, and I had to look through it. I thought it was blood, but no one seemed to notice. No one noticed all the blood, or the things that crawled and clattered over the floor, over the tables." Her hand lifted to rub at her throat. "I couldn't see clearly, but I saw a shape, a black shape. It seemed to float in the air on the other side of the curtain. I thought it was death."

She smiled a little as she lifted her tea with a steady hand. "You prepare for death at my age, or you damn well should. But I was afraid of that shape. Then it was gone, the curtain lifted again, and everything was exactly as it should be."

"Gran—"

"Why didn't I tell you last night?" she interrupted. "I can read your face like a book, Caleb. Pride, fear. I simply wanted to get out, to be home, and your father drove me. I needed to sleep, and I did. This morning, I needed to know if it was true."

"Mrs. Hawkins—"

"You'll call me Essie now," she said to Quinn.

"Essie, have you ever had an experience like this before?"

"Yes. I didn't tell you," she said when Cal cursed. "Or anyone. It was the summer you were ten. That first summer. I saw terrible things outside the house, things that couldn't be. That black shape that was sometimes a man, sometimes a dog. Or a hideous combination of both. Your grandfather didn't see, or wouldn't. I always thought he simply wouldn't see. There were horrible things that week."

She closed her eyes a moment, then took another soothing sip of tea. "Neighbors, friends. Things they did to themselves and each other. After the second night, you came to the door. Do you remember, Cal?"

"Yes, ma'am, I remember."

"Ten years old." She smiled at Quinn. "He was only a little boy, with his two young friends. They were so afraid. You could see and feel the fear and the, valor, I want to say, coming off them like light. You told me we had to pack up, your grandfather and I. We had to come stay at your house. That it wasn't safe in town. Didn't you ever wonder why I didn't argue, or pat you on the head and shoo you on home?"

"No. I guess there was too much else going on. I just wanted you and Pop safe."

"And every seven years, I packed for your grandfather and me, then when he died, just for me, now this year it'll be Ginger and me. But it's coming sooner and stronger this time."

"I'll pack for you, Gran, for you and Ginger right now."

"Oh, I think we're safe enough for now," she said to Cal. "When it's time, Ginger and I can put what we'll need together. I want you to take the books. I know I've read them, you've read them. It seems countless times. But we've missed something, somehow. And now, we have fresh eyes."

Quinn turned toward Cal, narrowed her eyes. "Books?"

Thirteen

FOX MADE A RUN TO THE BANK. IT WAS COMpletely unnecessary since the papers in his briefcase could have been dropped off at any time—or more efficiently, the client could have come into his office to ink them.

But he'd wanted to get out, get some air, walk off his frustration.

It was time to admit that he'd still held on to the hope that Alice Hawbaker would change her mind, or that he could change it for her. Maybe it was selfish, and so what? He depended on her, he was used to her. And he loved her.

The love meant he had no choice but to let her go. The love meant if he could take back the last twenty minutes he'd spent with her, he would.

She'd nearly broken down, he remembered as he strode along in his worn-down hiking boots (no court today). She never broke. She never even cracked, but he'd pushed her hard enough to cause fissures. He'd always regret it.

If we stay, we'll die. She'd said that with tears in her voice, with tears glimmering in her eyes.

He'd only wanted to know why she was so set to leave, why she was jumpier every day to the point she wanted to go sooner than originally planned.

So he'd pushed. And finally, she'd told him.

She'd seen their deaths, over and over, every time she closed her eyes. She'd seen herself getting her husband's deer rifle out of the locked case in his basement workroom. Seen herself calmly loading it. She'd watched herself walk upstairs, through the kitchen where the dinner dishes were loaded into the dishwasher, the counters wiped clean. Into the den where the man she'd loved for thirty-six years, had made three children with, was watching the Orioles battle the Red Sox. The O's were up two-zip, but the Sox were at the plate, with a man on second, one out. Top of the sixth. The count was one and two.

When the pitcher wound up, she pumped a bullet through the back of her husband's head as he sat in his favorite recliner.

Then she'd put the barrel under her own chin.

So, yes, he had to let her go, just as he'd had to make an excuse to leave the office because he knew her well enough to understand she didn't want him around until she was composed again.

Knowing he'd given her what she wanted and needed didn't stop him from feeling guilty, frustrated, and inadequate.

He ducked in to buy flowers. She'd accept them as a peace offering, he knew. She liked flowers in the office, and often picked them up herself as he tended to forget.

He came out with an armload of mixed blooms, and nearly ran over Layla.

She stumbled back, even took a couple extra steps in retreat. He saw upset and unhappiness on her face, and wondered if it was his current lot to make women nervous and miserable.

"Sorry. Wasn't looking."

She didn't smile, just started fiddling with the buttons of her coat. "It's okay. Neither was I."

He should just go. He didn't have to tap in to her mind to feel the jangle of nerves and misery surrounding her. It seemed to him she never relaxed around him, was always making that little move away. Or maybe she never relaxed ever. Could be a New York thing, he mused. He sure as hell hadn't been able to relax there.

But there was too much of the how-can-I-fix-this in him. "Problem?"

Now *her* eyes glimmered with tears, and Fox quite simply wanted to step into the street into the path of a passing truck.

"Problem? How could there possibly be a problem? I'm living in a strange house in a strange town, seeing things that aren't there—or worse, *are* there and want me dead. Nearly everything I own is sitting in my apartment in New York. An apartment I have to pay for, and my very understanding and patient boss called this morning to tell me, regretfully, that if I couldn't come back to work next week, she'll have to replace me. So do you know what I did?"

"No."

"I started to pack. Sorry, really, sorry, but I've got a *life* here. I have responsibilities and bills and a goddamn routine." She gripped her elbows in opposite hands as if to hold herself in place. "I need to get back to them. And I couldn't. I just couldn't do it. I don't even know why, not on any reasonable level, but I couldn't. So now I'm going to be out of a job, which means I won't be able to afford my apartment. And I'm probably going to end up dead or institutionalized, and that's after my landlord sues me for back rent. So problems? No, not me."

He listened all the way through without interruption, then just nodded. "Stupid question. Here." He shoved the flowers at her.

"What?"

"You look like you could use them."

Flummoxed, she stared at him, stared at the colorful blooms in her arms. And felt the sharpest edge of what might have been hysteria dulling into perplexity. "But . . . you bought them for someone."

"I can buy more." He waved a thumb at the door of the flower shop. "And I can help with the landlord if you get me the information. The rest, well, we're working on it. Maybe something pushed you to come here, and maybe something's pushing you to stay, but at the bottom of it, Layla, it's your choice. If you decide you have to leave . . ." He thought of Alice again, and some of his own frustration ebbed. "Nobody's going to blame you for it. But if you stay, you need to commit."

"I've—"

"No, you haven't." Absently, he reached out to secure the strap of her bag, which had slipped down to the crook of her elbow, back on her shoulder. "You're still looking for the way out, the loophole in the deal that means you can pack your bags and go without consequences. Just go back to the way things were. Can't blame you for it. But choose, then stick. That's all. I've got to finish up and get back. Talk to you later."

He stepped back into the florist and left her standing speechless on the sidewalk.

QUINN SHOUTED DOWN FROM THE SECOND FLOOR when Layla came in.

"It's me," Layla called up, and still conflicted, walked back to the kitchen with the flowers and the bottles and pots she'd bought in a gift shop on the walk home.

"Coffee." Quinn bustled in a few moments later. "Going to need lots and lots of . . . Hey, pretty," she said when she saw the flowers Layla was clipping to size and arranging in various bottles.

"They really are. Quinn, I need to talk to you."

"Need to talk to you, too. You go first."

"I was going to leave this morning."

Quinn stopped on the way to fill the coffeepot. "Oh."

"And I was going to do my best to get out before you came back, and talked me out of it. I'm sorry."

"Okay. It's okay." Quinn busied herself making the coffee. "I'd avoid me, too, if I wanted to do something I didn't want me to do. If you get me."

"Oddly enough, I do."

"Why aren't you gone?"

"Let me backtrack." While she finished fussing with the flowers, Layla related the telephone conversation she'd had with her boss.

"I'm sorry. It's so unfair. I don't mean your boss is unfair. She's got a business to run. But that this whole thing is unfair." Quinn watched Layla arrange multicolored daisies in an oversized teacup. "On a practical level I'm okay, because this is my job, or the job I picked. I can afford to take the time to be here and supplement that with articles. I could help—"

"That's not what I'm looking for. I don't want you to loan me money, or to carry my share of the expenses. If I stay, it's because I've chosen to stay." Layla looked at the flowers, thought of what Fox had said. "I think, until today, I didn't accept that, or want to accept it. Easier to think I'd been driven to come here, and that I was being pressured to stay. I wanted to go because I didn't want any of this to be happening. But it is. So I'm staying because I've decided to stay. I'll just have to figure out the practicalities."

"I've got a couple of ideas on that, maybe just a thumb in the dike. Let me think about them. The flowers were a nice idea. Cheer up a bad news day."

"Not my idea. Fox gave them to me when I ran into him outside the florist. I cut loose on him." Layla shrugged, then gathered up the bits of stems she'd cut off, the florist wrappings. "He's basically, 'How are you doing,' and I'm 'How am I doing? I'll tell you how I'm doing.' " She tossed the leavings in the trash, then leaned back and laughed. "God, I just blasted him. So he gives me the flowers he'd just bought, thrust them at me, really, and gave me a short, pithy lecture. I guess I deserved it."

"Hmm." Quinn added the information to the think-pot she was stirring. "And you feel better?"

"Better?" Layla walked into the little dining room to arrange a trio of flowers on the old, drop-leaf table they'd picked up at the flea market. "I feel more resolved. I don't know if that's better."

"I've got something to keep you busy."

"Thank God. I'm used to working, and all this time on my hands makes me bitchy."

"Come with me. Don't leave all the flowers; you should have some of them in your room."

"I thought they'd be for the house. He didn't buy them for me or—"

"He gave them to you. Take some of them up. You made me take the tulips up to mine." To solve the matter, Quinn picked up one of the little pots and a slender bottle herself. "Oh, coffee."

"I'll get it." Layla poured one of the mugs for Quinn, doctored it, then got a bottle of water for herself. "What's the project that's going to keep me busy?"

"Books."

"We already have the books from the library."

"Now we have some from Estelle Hawkins's personal store. Some of them are journals. I haven't really scratched the surface yet," Quinn explained as they headed up. "I'd barely gotten home ahead of you. But there are three of them written by Ann Hawkins. After her children were born. Her children with Giles Dent."

"But Mrs. Hawkins must have read them before, shown them to Cal."

"Right, and right. They've all been read, studied, pondered over. But not by us, Layla. Fresh eyes, different angle." She detoured to Layla's room to set the flowers down, then took the coffee mug on her way to the office. "And I've already got the first question on my notes: Where are the others?"

"Other journals?"

"Ann's other journals, because I'm betting there are

more, or were. Where's the journal she kept when she lived with Dent, when she was carrying her triplets? That's one of the new angles I hope our fresh eyes can find. Where would they be, and why aren't they with the others?"

"If she did write others, they might have been lost or destroyed."

"Let's hope not." Quinn's eyes were sharp as she sat, lifted a small book bound in brown leather. "Because I think she had some of the answers we need."

CAL COULDN'T REASONABLY BREAK AWAY FROM the center until after seven. Even then he felt guilty leaving his father to handle the rest of the night. He'd called Quinn in the late afternoon to let her know he'd be by when he could. And her absent response had been for him to bring food with him.

She'd have to settle for pizza, he thought as he carried the takeout boxes up the steps. He hadn't had the time or inclination to figure out what her lifestyle-change option might be.

As he knocked, the wind whistled across the back of his neck, had him glancing uneasily behind him. Something coming, he thought. Something's in the wind.

Fox answered the door. "Thank God, pizza and a testosterone carrier. I'm outnumbered here, buddy."

"Where's the estrogen?"

"Up. Buried in books and notes. Charts. Layla makes charts. I made the mistake of telling them I had a dry-wipe board down at the office. They made me go get it, haul it in here, haul it upstairs." The minute Cal set the pizza down on the kitchen counter, Fox shoved up the lid and took out a slice. "There's been talk of index cards. Colored index cards. Don't leave me here alone again."

Cal grunted, opened the fridge, and found, as he'd hoped and dreamed, Fox had stocked beer. "Maybe we were never organized enough, so we missed some detail. Maybe—"

He broke off as Quinn rushed in. "Hi! Pizza. Oh-oh. Well, I'll work it off with the power of my mind and with a session in the gym tomorrow morning."

She got down plates, passed one to Fox, who was already halfway through with his first slice. Then she smiled that smile at Cal. "Got anything else for me?"

He leaned right in, laid his mouth on hers. "Got that."

"Coincidentally, exactly what I wanted. So how about some more." She got a fistful of his shirt and tugged him down for another, longer kiss.

"You guys want me to leave? Can I take the pizza with me?"

"As a matter of fact," Cal began.

"Now, now." Quinn patted Cal's chest to ease him back. "Mommy and Daddy were just saying hello," she told Fox. "Why don't we eat in the dining room like the civilized. Layla's coming right down."

"How come I can't say hello to Mommy?" Fox complained as Quinn sailed off with the plates.

"Because then I'd have to beat you unconscious."

"As if." Amused, Fox grabbed the pizza boxes and started after Quinn. "Beverages on you, bro."

Shortly after they were seated, drinks, plates, napkins, pizza passed around, Layla came in with a large bowl and a stack of smaller ones. "I put this together earlier. I wasn't sure what you might bring," she said to Cal.

"You made salad?" Quinn asked.

"My specialty. Chop, shred, mix. No cooking."

"Now, I'm forced to be good." Quinn gave up the dream of two slices of pizza, settled on one and a bowl of Layla's salad. "We made progress," she began as she forked up the first bite.

"Yeah, ask the ladies here how to make tallow candles or black raspberry preserves," Fox suggested. "They've got it down."

"So, some of the information contained in the books we're going through may not currently apply to our situation." Quinn raised her eyebrows at Fox. "But one day I may be called on in some blackout emergency to make a tallow candle. By progress, however, I mean that there's a lot of interesting information in Ann's journals."

"We've read them," Cal pointed out. "Multiple times."

"You're not women." She held up a finger. "And, yes, Essie is. But Essie's a woman who's a descendent, who's part of this town and its history. And however objective she might try to be, she may have missed some nuances. First question, where are the others?"

"There aren't any others."

"I disagree. There aren't any others that were found. Essie said these books were passed to her by her father, because she loved books. I called her to be sure, but he never said if there were more."

"If there'd been more," Cal insisted, "he'd have given them to her."

"If he had them. There's a long span between the sixteen hundreds and the nineteen hundreds," Quinn pointed out. "Things get misplaced, lost, tossed out. According to the records and your own family's oral history, Ann Hawkins lived most of her life in what's now the community center on Main Street, which was previously the library. Books, library. Interesting."

"A library Gran knew inside and out," Cal returned. "There couldn't have been a book in there she didn't know about. And something like this?" He shook his head. "She'd have it if it was to be had."

"Unless she never saw it. Maybe it was hidden, or maybe, for the sake of argument, she wasn't *meant* to find it. It wasn't meant to be found, not by her, not then."

"Debatable," Fox commented.

"And something to look into. Meanwhile, she didn't date her journals, so Layla and I are dating them, more or less, by how she writes about her sons. In what we're judging to be the first, her sons are about two to three. In the next they're five because she writes about their fifth birthday very specifically, and about seven, we think, when that one ends. The third it seems that they're young men. We think about sixteen."

"A lot of years between," Layla said.

"Maybe she didn't have anything worth writing about during those years."

"Could be," Quinn said to Cal. "But I'm betting she did, even if it was just about blackberry jam and a trio of active sons. More important now, at least I think so, is where is the journal or journals that cover her time with Dent, to the birth of her sons through to the first two years of their lives? Because you can just bet your ass those were interesting times."

"She writes of him," Layla said quietly. "Of Giles Dent. Again and again, in all the journals we have. She writes about him, of her feelings for him, her dreams about him."

"And always in the present tense," Quinn added.

"It's hard to lose someone you love." Fox turned his beer bottle in his hand.

"It is, but she writes of him, consistently, as if he were alive." Quinn looked at Cal. "It is not death. We talked about this, how Dent found the way to exist, with this thing. To hold it down or through or inside. Whatever the term. Obviously he couldn't—or didn't—kill or destroy it, but neither could it kill or destroy him. He found a way to keep it under, and to continue to exist. Maybe only for that single purpose. She knew it. Ann knew what he did, and I'm betting she knew how he did it."

"You're not taking into account love and grief," Cal pointed out.

"I'm not discounting them, but when I read her journals, I get the sense of a strong-minded woman. And one who shared a very deep love with a strong-minded man. She defied convention for him, risked shunning and censure. Shared his bed, but I believe, shared his obligations, too. Whatever he planned to do, attempted to do, felt bound to do, he would have shared it with her. They were a unit.

Isn't that what you felt, what we both felt, when we were in the clearing?"

"Yeah." He couldn't deny it, Cal thought. "That's what I felt."

"Going off that, Ann knew, and while she may have told her sons when they were old enough, that part of the Hawkins's oral history could have been lost or bastardized. It happens. I think she would have written it out, too. And put the record somewhere she believed would be safe and protected, until it was needed."

"It's been needed for twenty-one years."

"Cal, that's your responsibility talking, not logic. At least not the line of logic that follows this route. She told you this was the time. That it was always to be this time. Nothing you had, nothing you could have done would have stopped it before this time."

"We let it out," Fox said. "Nothing would have been needed if we hadn't let it out."

"I don't think that's true." Layla shifted toward him, just a little. "And maybe, if we find the other journals, we'll understand. But, we noticed something else."

"Layla caught it right off the bat," Quinn put in.

"Because it was in front of me first. But in any case, it's the names. The names of Ann's sons. Caleb, Fletcher, and Gideon."

"Pretty common for back then." Cal gave a shrug as he pushed his plate away. "Caleb stuck in the Hawkins line more than the other two did. But I've got a cousin Fletch and an uncle Gideon."

"No, first initials," Quinn said impatiently. "I told you they'd missed it," she added to Layla. "C, F, G. Caleb, Fox, Gage."

"Reaching," Fox decided. "Especially when you consider I'm Fox because my mother saw a pack of red foxes running across the field and into the woods about the time she was going into labor with me. My sister Sage? Mom smelled the sage from her herb garden right after Sage was born. It was like that with all four of us."

"You were named after an actual fox? Like a . . . release-the-hounds fox?" Layla wanted to know.

"Well, not a specific one. It was more a . . . You have to meet my mother."

"However Fox got his famous name, I don't think we discount coincidences." Quinn studied Cal's face, saw he was considering it. "And I think there's more than one of Ann Hawkins's descendents at this table."

"Quinn, my father's people came over from Ireland, four generations back," Fox told her. "They weren't here in Ann Hawkins's time because they were plowing fields in Kerry."

"What about your mother's?" Layla asked.

"Wider mix. English, Irish. I think some French. Nobody ever bothered with a genealogy, but I've never heard of any Hawkins on the family tree."

"You may want to take a closer look. How about Gage?" Quinn wondered.

"No idea." And Cal was more than considering it now. "I doubt he does either. I can ask Bill, Gage's father. If it's true, if we're direct descendents, it could explain one of the things we've never understood."

"Why it was you," Quinn said quietly. "You three, the mix of blood from you, Fox, and Gage that opened the door."

"I ALWAYS THOUGHT IT WAS ME."

With the house quiet, and night deep, Cal lay on Quinn's bed with her body curled warm to his. "Just you?"

"They helped trigger it maybe, but yes, me. Because it was my blood—not just that night, but my heritage, you could say. I was the Hawkins. They weren't from here, not the same way I was. Not forever, like I was. Generations back. But if this is true . . . I still don't know how to feel about it."

"You could give yourself a tiny break." She stroked her hand over his heart. "I wish you would."

"Why did he let it happen? Dent? If he'd found a way to stop it, why did he let it come to this?"

"Another question." She pushed herself up until they were eye-to-eye. "We'll figure it out, Cal. We're supposed to. I believe that."

"I'm closer to believing it, with you." He touched her cheek. "Quinn, I can't stay again tonight. Lump may be lazy, but he depends on me."

"Got another hour to spare?"

"Yeah." He smiled as she lowered to him. "I think he'll hold out another hour."

LATER, WHEN HE WALKED OUT TO HIS CAR, THE air shivered so that the trees rattled their empty branches. Cal searched the street for any sign, anything he needed to defend against. But there was nothing but empty road.

Something's in the wind, he thought again, and got in his car to drive home.

IT WAS AFTER MIDNIGHT WHEN THE LOW-GRADE urge for a cigarette buzzed through Gage's brain. He'd given them up two years, three months, and one week before, a fact that could still piss him off.

He turned up the radio to take his mind off it, but the urge was working its way up to craving. He could ignore that, too; he did so all the time. To do otherwise was to believe there was solid truth in the old adage: like father, like son.

He was nothing like his father.

He drank when he wanted a drink, but he never got drunk. Or hadn't since he'd been seventeen, and then the drunkenness had been with absolute purpose. He didn't blame others for his shortcomings, or lash out with his fists on something smaller and weaker so he could feel bigger and stronger.

He didn't even blame the old man, not particularly. You

played the cards you were dealt, to Gage's mind. Or you folded and walked away with your pockets empty.

Luck of the draw.

So he was fully prepared to ignore this sudden, and surprisingly intense desire for a cigarette. But when he considered he was within miles of Hawkins Hollow, a place where he was very likely to die an ugly and painful death, the surgeon general's warnings seemed pretty goddamn puny, and his own self-denial absolutely useless.

When he saw the sign for the Sheetz, he decided what the hell. He didn't want to live forever. He swung into the twenty-four-hour mart, picked up coffee, black, and a pack of Marlboros.

He strode back to the car he'd bought that very evening in D.C. after his plane had landed, and before he'd paid off a small debt. The wind whipped through his hair. The hair was dark as the night, a little longer than he usually wore it, a little shaggy, as he hadn't trusted the barbers in Prague.

There was stubble on his face since he hadn't bothered to shave. It added to the dark, dangerous look that had had the young female clerk who rung up the coffee and cigarettes shivering inwardly with lust.

He'd topped off at six feet, and the skinny build of his youth had filled out. Since his profession was usually sedentary, he kept his muscles toned and his build rangy with regular, often punishing workouts.

He didn't pick fights, but he rarely walked away from one. And he liked to win. His body, his face, his mind, were all tools of his trade. As were his eyes, his voice, and the control he rarely let off the leash.

He was a gambler, and a smart gambler kept all of his tools well honed.

Swinging back onto the road, Gage let the Ferrari rip. Maybe it had been foolish to toss so much of his winnings into a car, but Jesus, it *moved*. And fucking A, he'd ridden his thumb out of the Hollow all those years ago. It felt damn good to ride back in in style.

Funny, now that he'd bought the damn cigarettes, the urge for one had passed. He didn't even want the coffee, the speed was kick enough.

He flew down the last miles of the interstate, whipped onto the exit that would take him to the Hollow. The dark rural road was empty—no surprise to him, not this time of night. There were shadows and shapes—houses, hills, fields, trees. There was a twisting in his gut that he was heading back instead of away, and yet that pull—it never quite left him—that pull toward home was strong.

He reached toward his coffee more out of habit than desire, then was forced to whip the wheel, slam the brakes as headlights cut across the road directly into his path. He blasted the horn, saw the other car swerve.

He thought: Fuck, fuck, *fuck!* I just bought this sucker.

When he caught his breath, and the Ferrari sat sideways in the middle of the road, he thought it was a miracle the crash hadn't come. Inches, he realized. Less than inches.

His lucky goddamn day.

He reversed, pulled to the shoulder, then got out to check on the other driver he assumed was stinking drunk.

She wasn't. What she was, was hopping mad.

"Where the hell did you come from?" she demanded. She slammed out of her car, currently tipped into the shallow ditch along the shoulder, in a blur of motion. He saw a mass of dark gypsy curls wild around a face pale with shock.

Great face, he decided in one corner of his brain. Huge eyes that looked black against her white skin, a sharp nose, a wide mouth, sexily full that may have owned its sensuality to collagen injections.

She wasn't shaking, and he didn't sense any fear along with the fury as she stood on a dark road facing down a complete stranger.

"Lady," he said with what he felt was admirable calm, "where the hell did *you* come from?"

"From that stupid road that looks like all the other stupid roads around here. I looked both damn ways, and you weren't there. Then. How did you . . . Oh never mind. We didn't die."

"Yay."

With her hands on her hips she turned around to study her car. "I can get out of there, right?"

"Yeah. Then there's the flat tire."

"What flat . . . Oh for God's sake! You have to change it." She gave the flat tire on the rear of her car an annoyed kick. "It's the least you can do."

Actually, it wasn't. The least he could do was stroll back to his car and wave good-bye. But he appreciated her bitchiness, and preferred it over quivering. "Pop the trunk. I need the spare and the jack."

When she had, and he'd lifted a suitcase out, set it on the ground, he took one look at her spare. And shook his head. "Not your day. Your spare's toast."

"It can't be. What the hell are you talking about?" She shoved him aside, peered in herself by the glow of the trunk light. "Damn her, damn her, damn her. My sister." She whirled away, paced down the shoulder a few feet, then back. "I loaned her my car for a couple of weeks. This is so typical. She ruins a tire, but does she get it fixed, does she even bother to mention it? No."

She pushed her hair back from her face. "I'm not calling a tow truck at this time of night, then sitting in the middle of nowhere. You're just going to have to give me a ride."

"Am I?"

"It's your fault. At least part of it is."

"Which part?"

"I don't know, and I'm too tired, I'm too mad, I'm too lost in this foreign wilderness to give a damn. I need a ride."

"At your service. Where to?"

"Hawkins Hollow."

He smiled, and there was something dark in it. "Handy. I'm heading there myself." He gestured toward his car. "Gage Turner," he added.

She gestured in turn, rather regally, toward her suitcase. "Cybil Kinski." She lifted her eyebrows when she got her first good look at his car. "You have very nice wheels, Mr. Turner."

"Yeah, and they all work."

Fourteen

CAL WASN'T PARTICULARLY SURPRISED TO SEE Fox's truck in his driveway, despite the hour. Nor was he particularly surprised when he walked in to see Fox blinking sleepily on the couch in front of the TV, with Lump stretched out and snoring beside him.

On the coffee table were a can of Coke, the last of Cal's barbecue potato chips, and a box of Milk Bones. The remains, he assumed, of a guy-dog party.

"Whatcha doing here?" Fox asked groggily.

"I live here."

"She kick you out?"

"No, she didn't kick me out. I came home." Because they were there, Cal dug into the bag of chips and managed to pull out a handful of crumbs. "How many of those did you give him?"

Fox glanced at the box of dog biscuits. "A couple. Maybe five. What're you so edgy about?"

Cal picked up the Coke and gulped down the couple of

warm, flat swallows that were left. "I got a feeling, a . . . thing. You haven't felt anything tonight?"

"I've had feelings and things pretty much steady the last couple weeks." Fox scrubbed his hands over his face, back into his hair. "But yeah, I got something just before you drove up. I was half asleep, maybe all the way. It was like the wind whooshing down the flue."

"Yeah." Cal walked over to stare out the window. "Have you checked in with your parents lately?"

"I talked to my father today. It's all good with them. Why?"

"If all three of us are direct descendents, then one of your parents is in the line," Cal pointed out.

"I figured that out on my own."

"None of our family was ever affected during the Seven. We were always relieved by that." He turned back. "Maybe relieved enough we didn't really ask why."

"Because we figured it, at least partly, was because they lived outside of town. Except for Bill Turner, and who the hell could tell what was going on with him?"

"My parents and yours, they came into town during the Seven. And there were people, you remember what happened out at the Poffenberger place last time?"

"Yeah. Yeah, I remember." Fox rubbed at his eyes. "Being five miles out of town didn't stop Poffenberger from strangling his wife while she hacked at him with a butcher knife."

"Now we know Gran felt things, saw things that first summer, and she saw things the other night. Why is that?"

"Maybe it picks and chooses, Cal." Rising, Fox walked over to toss another log on the fire. "There have always been people who weren't affected, and there have always been degrees with those who were."

"Quinn and Layla are the first outsiders. We figured a connection, but what if that connection is as simple as blood ties?"

Fox sat again, leaned back, stroked a hand over Lump's head as the dog twitched in his sleep. "Good theory. It shouldn't weird you out if you happen to be rolling naked with your cousin a couple hundred times removed."

"Huh." That was a thought. "If they're descendents, the next point to figure is if having them here gives us more muscle, or makes us more vulnerable. Because it's pretty clear this one's it. This one's going to be the all or nothing. So . . . Someone's coming."

Fox pushed off the couch, strode quickly over to stand by Cal. "I don't think the Big Evil's going to drive up to your house, and in a . . ." He peered closer as the car set off Cal's motion lights. "Holy Jesus, is that a Ferrari?" He shot a grin at Cal.

"Gage," they said together.

They went on the front porch, in shirtsleeves, leaving the door open behind them. Gage climbed out of the car, his eyes skimming over them both as he walked back to get his bag out of the trunk. He slung its strap over his shoulder, started up the steps. "You girls having a slumber party?"

"Strippers just left," Fox told him. "Sorry you missed them." Then he rushed forward, flung his arms around Gage in a hard hug. "Man, it's good to see you. When can I drive your car?"

"I was thinking never. Cal."

"Took your goddamn time." The relief, the love, the sheer pleasure pushed him forward to grip Gage just as Fox had.

"Had some business here and there. Want a drink. Need a room."

"Come on in."

In the kitchen, Cal poured whiskey. All of them understood it was a welcome-home toast for Gage, and very likely a drink before war.

"So," Cal began, "I take it you came back flush."

"Oh yeah."

"How much you up?"

Gage turned the glass around in his hand. "Considering expenses, and my new toy out there, about fifty."

"Nice work if you can get it," Fox commented.

"And I can."

"Look a little worn there, brother."

Gage shrugged at Cal. "Long couple of days. Which nearly ended with me in a fiery crash right out on Sixty-seven."

"Toy get away from you?" Fox asked.

"Please." Gage smirked at the idea. "Some ditz, of the female and very hot variety, pulled out in front of me. Not another car on the road, and she pulls out in this ancient Karmann Ghia—nice wheels, actually—then she jumps out and goes at me like it was my fault."

"Women," Fox said, "are an endless source of every damn thing."

"And then some. So she's tipped down in the little runoff," Gage went on, gesturing with his free hand. "No big deal, but she's popped a flat. No big deal either, except her spare's a pancake. Turns out she's heading into the Hollow, so I manage to load her two-ton suitcase into my car. Then she's rattling off an address and asking me, like I'm MapQuest, how long it'll take to get there."

He took a slow sip of whiskey. "Lucky for her I grew up here and could tell her I'd have her there in five. She snaps out her phone, calls somebody she calls Q, like James freaking Bond, tells her, as it turns out from the look I got of Q in the doorway—very nice, by the way—to wake up, she'll be there in five minutes. Then—"

Cal rattled off an address. "That the one?"

Gage lowered his glass. "As a matter of fact."

"Something in the wind," Cal murmured. "I guess it was you, and Quinn's Cybil."

"Cybil Kinski," Gage confirmed. "Looks like a gypsy by way of Park Avenue. Well, well." He downed the rest of the whiskey in his glass. "Isn't this a kick in the ass?"

"HE CAME OUT OF NOWHERE." THERE WAS A glass of red wine on the dresser Quinn had picked up in anticipation of Cybil's arrival.

As that arrival had woken Layla, Quinn sat beside her on what would be Cybil's bed while the woman in question swirled around the room, hanging clothes, tucking them in drawers, taking the occasional sip of wine.

"I thought that was it, just it, even though I've never seen any death by car in my future. I swear, I don't know how we missed being bloody pulps tangled in burning metal. I'm a good driver," Cybil said to Quinn.

"You are."

"But I must be better than I thought, and so—fortunately—was he. I know I'm lucky all I got was a scare and a flat tire out of it, but damn Rissa for, well, being Rissa."

"Rissa?" Layla looked blank.

"Cyb's sister, Marissa," Quinn explained. "You loaned her your car again."

"I know, I know. I *know*," she said, puffing out a breath that blew curls off her forehead. "I don't know how she manages to talk me into these things. My spare was flat, thanks to Rissa."

"Which explains why you were dropped off from a really sexy sports car."

"He could hardly leave me there, though he looked like the type who'd consider it. All scruffy, gorgeous, and dangerous looking."

"Last time I had a flat," Quinn remembered, "the very nice guy who stopped to help had a paunch over his belt the size of a sack of cement, and ass crack reveal."

"No paunch on this one, and though his coat prevented me from a good look, I'm betting Gage Turner has a superior ass."

"Gage Turner." Layla put a hand on Quinn's thigh. "Quinn."

"Yeah." Quinn let out a breath. "Okay, I guess it's hail, hail, the gang's all here."

IN THE MORNING, QUINN LEFT HER HOUSEMATES sleeping while she jogged over to the community center.

She already knew she'd regret jogging over, because that meant she'd have to jog back—after her workout. But it seemed a cheat on the lifestyle change to drive three blocks to the gym.

And she wanted the thinking time.

There was no buying, for any price, Cybil and Gage Turner had run into each other—almost literally—in the middle of the night just outside of town as a coincidence.

One more thing to add to the list of oddities, Quinn thought as she puffed out air in frosty vapors.

Another addition would be the fact that Cybil had a very sharp sense of direction, but had apparently made wrong turn after wrong turn to end up on that side road at the exact moment Gage was coming up the main.

One more, Quinn decided as she approached the back entrance of the community center, would be Cybil saying "he came out of nowhere." Quinn was willing to take that literally. If Cybil didn't see him, then maybe—in her reality, for just those vital moments—he *hadn't* been there.

So why had it been important for them to meet separately, outside the group? Wasn't it strange enough that they'd both arrived on the same night, at the same time?

She dug out her membership key—thanks, Cal—to open the door to the fitness area, pressed her guest pass number on the keypad.

The lights were still off, which was a surprise. Normally when she arrived, they were already on, and at least one of the trio of swivel TVs was tuned to CNN or ESPN or one of the morning talk shows. Very often there was somebody on one of the treadmills or bikes, or pumping weights.

She flipped on the lights, called out. And her voice echoed hollowly. Curious, she walked through, pushed open the door, and saw the lights were also off in the tiny attendant's office, and in the locker room.

Maybe somebody had a late date the night before, she decided. She helped herself to a locker key, stripped down to her workout gear, then grabbed a towel. Opting to start her session with cardio, she switched on the *Today* show before climbing onto the single elliptical trainer the club boasted.

She programmed it, resisting the urge to cheat a few pounds off her weight. As if it mattered, Quinn reminded herself. (Of course, it mattered.)

She started her warm-up pleased with her discipline, and her solitude. Still, she expected the door to slam open any minute, for Matt or Tina, who switched off as attendants, to rush in. By the time she was ten minutes in, she'd kicked up the resistance and was focused on the TV screen to help her get through the workout.

When she hit the first mile, Quinn took a long gulp of water from the sports bottle she'd brought with her. As she started on mile two, she let her mind drift to what she hoped to accomplish that day. Research, the foundation of any project. And she wanted to draft what she thought would be the opening of her book. Writing it out might spark some idea. At some point, she wanted to walk around the town again, with Cybil—and Layla if she was up for it.

A visit to the cemetery was in order with Cybil in tow. Time to pay a call on Ann Hawkins.

Maybe Cal would have time to go with them. Needed to talk to him anyway, discuss how he felt, what he thought, about Gage—whom she wanted to get a look at—and Cybil's arrival. Mostly, she admitted, she just wanted to see him again. Show him off to Cybil.

Look! Isn't he cute? Maybe it was completely high school, but it didn't seem to matter. She wanted to touch him again, even if it was just a quick squeeze of hands. And she was looking forward to a hello kiss, and finding a way to turn that worried look in his eyes into a glint of amusement. She *loved* the way his eyes laughed before the rest of him did, and the way he . . .

Well. Well, well, well. She was absolutely gone over him, she realized. Seriously hooked on the hometown boy. That was kind of cute, too, she decided, except it made her stomach jitter. Still, the jitter wasn't altogether a bad thing.

It was a combination of *oh-oh* and *oh boy!*, and wasn't that interesting?

Quinn's falling in love, she thought, and hit mile two with a dopey smile on her face. She might've been puffing, sweat might have been dribbling down her temples, but she felt just as fresh and cheerful as a spring daisy.

Then the lights went out.

The machine stopped; the TV went blank and silent.

"Oh, shit." Her first reaction wasn't alarm as much as, what now? The dark was absolute, and though she could draw a reasonable picture in her mind where she was in relation to the outside door—and what was between her and the door—she was wary about making her way to it blind.

And then what? she wondered as she waited for her breathing to level. She couldn't possibly fumble her way to the locker room, to her locker and retrieve her clothes. So she'd have to go out in a damn sports bra and bike pants.

She heard the first thud; the chill washed over her skin. And she understood she had much bigger problems than skimpy attire.

She wasn't alone. As her pulse began to bang, she hoped desperately whatever was in the dark with her was human. But the sounds, that unholy thudding that shook the walls, the floor, the awful *scuttling* sounds creeping under it weren't those of a man. Gooseflesh pricked her skin, partly from fear, partly from the sudden and intense cold.

Keep your head, she ordered herself. For God's sake, keep your head. She gripped the water bottle—pitiful weapon, but all she had—and started to ease off the foot pads on the machine to the floor.

She went flying blindly in the black. She hit the floor, her shoulder and hip taking the brunt. Everything shook and rolled as she fought to scramble up. Disoriented, she had no idea which direction to run. There was a voice behind her, in front of her, inside her head—she couldn't tell—and it whispered gleefully of death.

She knew she screamed as she clawed her way across the quaking floor. Teeth chattering against terror and cold, she rapped her shoulder against another machine. Think, think, think! she told herself, because something was coming, something was coming in the dark. She ran her shaking hands over the machine—recumbent bike—and with every prayer she knew ringing in her head, used its placement in the room to angle toward the door.

There was a crash behind her, and something thudded against her foot. She jerked up, tripped, jerked up again. No longer caring what might stand between herself and the door, she flung herself toward where she hoped it would be. With her breath tearing out of her lungs, she ran her hands over the wall.

"Find it, goddamn it, Quinn. Find the goddamn door!"

Her hand bumped the hinges, and on a sob she found the knob. Turned, pulled.

The light burst in front of her eyes, and Cal's body—already in motion—rammed hers. If she'd had any breath left, she'd have lost it. Her knees didn't get a chance to buckle as he wrapped his arms around her, swung her around to use his body as a shield between hers and the room beyond.

"Hold on, now. Can you hold on to me?" His voice was eerily calm as he reached behind him and pulled the door closed. "Are you hurt? Tell me if you're hurt." His hands were already skimming over her, before they came up to her face, gripped it.

Before his mouth crushed down on hers.

"You're all right," he managed, propping her against the stone of the building as he dragged off his coat. "You're okay. Here, get into this. You're freezing."

"You were there." She stared up into his face. "You were there."

"Couldn't get the door open. Key wouldn't work." He took her hands, rubbed them warm between his. "My truck's right up there, okay. I want you to go up, sit in my truck. I left the keys in it. Turn on the heat. Sit in my truck and turn on the heat. Can you do that?"

She wanted to say yes. There was something in her that

wanted to say yes to anything he asked. But she saw, in his eyes, what he meant to do.

"You're going in there."

"That's what I have to do. What you have to do is go sit in the truck for a few minutes."

"If you go in, I go in."

"Quinn."

How, she wondered, did he manage to sound patient and annoyed at the same time? "I need to as much as you, and I'd hate myself if I huddled in your truck while you went in there. I don't want to hate myself. Besides, it's better if there's two of us. It's better. Let's just do it. Just do it, and argue later."

"Stay behind me, and if I say get out, you get out. That's the deal."

"Done. Believe me, I'm not ashamed to hide behind you."

She saw it then, just the faintest glimmer of a smile in his eyes. Seeing it settled her nerves better than a quick shot of brandy.

He turned his key again, keyed in the touch pad. Quinn held her breath. When Cal opened the door, the lights were on. Al Roker's voice cheerily announced the national weather forecast. The only sign anything had happened was her sports bottle under the rack of free weights.

"Cal, I swear, the power went out, then the room—"

"I saw it. It was pitch-black in here when you came through the door. Those weights were all over the floor. I could see them rolling around from the light coming in the door. The floor was heaving. I saw it, Quinn. And I heard it from outside the door."

He'd rammed that door twice, he remembered, put his full weight into it, because he'd heard her screaming, and it had sounded like the roof was caving in.

"Okay. My things are in the locker room. I really want to get my things out of the locker."

"Give me the key, and I'll—"

"Together." She gripped his hand. "There's a scent, can

you smell it? Over and above my workout and panic sweat."

"Yeah. I always thought it must be what brimstone smells like. It's fading." He smiled, just a little, as she stopped to pick up a ten-pound free weight, gripped it like a weapon.

He pushed open the door of the women's locker room. It was as ordered and normal as the gym. Still, he took her key, nudged her behind him before he opened her locker. Moving quickly, she dragged on her sweats, exchanged coats. "Let's get out of here."

He had her hand as they walked back out and Matt walked in.

He was young, the college-jock type, doing the part-time attendant, occasional personal trainer gig. A quick, inoffensive smirk curved on his lips as he saw them come out of the women's locker room together. Then he cleared his throat.

"Hey, sorry I'm late. Damnedest thing. First my alarm didn't go off, and I know how that sounds. Then my car wouldn't start. One of those mornings."

"Yeah," Quinn agreed as she put back the weight, retrieved her water bottle. "One of those. I'm done for the day." She tossed him the locker key. "See you later."

"Sure."

She waited until they were out of the building. "He thought we'd been—"

"Yeah, yeah."

"Ever do it in a locker room?"

"As that was actually my first foray into a girl's locker room, I have to say no."

"Me, either. Cal, have you got time to come over, have coffee—God, I'll even cook breakfast—and talk about this?"

"I'm making time."

SHE TOLD HIM EVERYTHING THAT HAD HAPPENED while she scrambled eggs. "I was scared out of my mind," she finished as she carried the coffee into the little dining room.

"No, you weren't." Cal set the plates of eggs and whole-wheat toast on the table. "You found the door, in the pitch-black, and with all that going on, you kept your head and found the door."

"Thanks." She sat. She wasn't shaking any longer, but the inside of her knees still felt like half-set Jell-O. "Thanks for saying that."

"It's the truth."

"You were there when I opened the door, and that was one of the best moments of my life. How did you know to be there?"

"I came in early because I wanted to swing by here, see how you were. Talk to you. Gage—"

"I know about that. Tell me the rest of this first."

"Okay. I turned off Main to come around the back way, come here, and I saw Ann Hawkins. I saw her standing in front of the door. I heard you screaming."

"From inside your truck, on the street. That far away—through stone walls, you heard me?"

"I heard you." It hadn't been one of the best moments of his life. "When I jumped out, ran toward the door, I heard crashing, thumping, God knows what from inside. I couldn't get the goddamn door open."

She heard it now, the emotion in his voice, the fear he hadn't let show while they were doing what needed doing. She rose, did them both a favor and crawled right into his lap.

She was still there, cradled in his arms, when Cybil strolled in.

"Hi. Don't get up." She took Quinn's chair. "Anyone eating this?" Studying them, Cybil took a forkful of eggs. "You must be Cal."

"Cybil Kinski, Caleb Hawkins. We had a rough morning."

Layla stepped in with a coffee mug and sleepy eyes that clouded with concern the minute she saw Quinn. "What happened?"

"Have a seat, and we'll run it through for both of you."

"I need to see the place," Cybil said as soon as the story was told. "And the room in the bowling alley, anyplace there's been an incident."

"Try the whole town," Quinn said dryly.

"And I need to see the clearing, this stone, as soon as possible."

"She's bossy," Quinn told Cal.

"I thought you were, but I think she beats you out. You can come into the bowling center anytime you like. Quinn can get you into the fitness center, but if I can't be there, I'll make sure either Fox or Gage is. Better, both of them. As far as the Pagan Stone goes, I talked with Fox and Gage about that last night. We're agreed that the next time we go, we all go. All of us. I can't make it today and neither can Fox. Sunday's going to be best."

"He's organized and take-charge," Cybil said to Quinn.

"Yes." She pressed a kiss to Cal's cheek. "Yes, he is. And I've made you let your eggs get cold."

"It was a worthwhile trade-off. I'd better get going."

"We still have a lot to talk about. Listen, maybe the three of you should come to dinner."

"Is someone cooking?" Cal asked.

"Cyb is."

"Hey!"

"You ate my breakfast. Plus you actually cook. But in the meantime, just one thing." She slid out of his lap so he could stand. "Would Fox hire Layla?"

"What? Who? Why?" Layla sputtered.

"Because you need a job," Quinn reminded her. "And he needs an office manager."

"I don't know anything about—you just can't—"

"You managed a boutique," Quinn reminded her, "so that's half the job. Managing. You're on the anal side of organized, Miss Colored Index Cards and Charts, so I say you can file, keep a calendar, and whatever with the best of them. Anything else, you'll pick up as you go. Ask Fox, okay, Cal?"

"Sure. No problem."

"She calls me bossy," Cybil commented as she finished Quinn's coffee.

"I call it creative thinking and leadership. Now, go fill that mug up again while I walk Cal to the door so I can give him a big, sloppy you're-my-hero kiss."

Cybil smiled after them as Quinn pulled Cal out of the room. "She's in love."

"Really?"

Now Cybil turned her smile on Layla. "That got your mind off taking a bite out of her for pushing that job in your face."

"I'll get back to that. Do you think she's in love with Cal—the uppercase *L*?"

"About to be all caps, in bold letters." She picked up the mug and rose. "Q likes to direct people," she said, "but she's careful to try to direct them toward something helpful, or at least interesting. She wouldn't push this job business if she didn't think you could handle it."

She blew out a breath as she walked back toward the kitchen. "What the hell am I supposed to fix for dinner?"

Fifteen

IT WAS HARD FOR CAL TO SEE BILL TURNER AND say nothing about Gage being in town. But Cal knew his friend. When and if Gage wanted his father to know, Gage would tell him. So Cal did his best to avoid Bill by closing himself in his office.

He dealt with orders, bills, reservations, contacted their arcade guy to discuss changing out one of their pinball machines for something jazzier.

Checking the time, he judged if Gage wasn't awake by now, he should be. And so picked up the phone.

Not awake, Cal decided, hearing the irritation in Gage's voice, hasn't had coffee. Ignoring all that, Cal launched into an explanation of what happened that morning, relayed the dinner plans, and hung up.

Now, rolling his eyes, Cal called Fox to run over the same information, and to tell Fox that Layla needed a job and he should hire her to replace Mrs. Hawbaker.

Fox said, "Huh?"

Cal said, "Gotta go," and hung up.

There, duty done, he considered. Satisfied, he turned to his computer and brought up the information on the automatic scoring systems he wanted to talk his father into installing.

It was past time for the center to do the upgrade. Maybe it was foolish to think about that kind of investment if everything was going to hell in a few months. But, if everything was going to hell in a few months, the investment wouldn't hurt a thing.

His father would say some of the old-timers would object, but Cal didn't think so. If they wanted to keep score by hand, the center would provide the paper score sheets and markers. But he thought if someone showed them how it worked, gave them a few free games to get used to the new system, they'd jump on.

They could get them used and reconditioned, which was part of the argument he was prepared to make. They had Bill onboard, and he could fix damn near anything.

It was one thing to be a little kitschy and traditional, another to be old-fashioned.

No, no, that wasn't the tack to take with his father. His father liked old-fashioned. Better to use figures. Bowling accounted for more than half, closer to sixty percent, of their revenue, so—

He broke off at the knock on his door and inwardly winced, thinking it was Bill Turner.

But it was Cal's mother who popped her head in. "Too busy for me?"

"Never. Here to bowl a few games before the morning league?"

"Absolutely not." Frannie loved her husband, but she liked to say she hadn't taken a vow to love, honor, and bowl. She came in to sit down, then angled her head so she could see his computer screen. Her lips twitched. "Good luck with that."

"Don't say anything to Dad, okay?"

"My lips are sealed."

"Who are you having lunch with?"

"How do you know I'm having lunch with anyone?"

He gestured to her pretty fitted jacket, trim pants, heeled boots. "Too fancy for shopping."

"Aren't you smart? I do have a few errands, then I'm meeting a friend for lunch. Joanne Barry."

Fox's mother, Cal thought, and just nodded.

"We have lunch now and then, but she called me yesterday, specifically to see if I could meet her today. She's worried. So I'm here to ask you if there's anything I should know, anything you want to tell me before I see her."

"Things are as under control as I can make them, Mom. I don't have the answers yet. But I have more questions, and I think that's progress. In fact, I have one you could ask Fox's mom for me."

"All right."

"You could ask if there's a way she could find out if any of her ancestors were Hawkins."

"You think we might be related somehow? Would it help if we are?"

"It would be good to know the answer."

"Then I'll ask the question. Now answer one for me. Are you all right? Just a yes or no is good enough."

"Yes."

"Okay then." She rose. "I have half a dozen things on my list before I meet Jo." She started for the door, said, *"Damn it"* very quietly under her breath, and turned back. "I wasn't going to ask, but I have no willpower over something like this. Are you and Quinn Black serious?"

"About what?"

"Caleb James Hawkins, don't be dense."

He would've laughed, but that tone brought on the Pavlovian response of hunched shoulders. "I don't exactly know the answer. And I'm not sure it's smart to get serious, in that way, with so much going on. With so much at stake."

"What better time?" Frannie replied. "My levelheaded

Cal." She put her hand on the knob, smiled at him. "Oh, and those fancy scoring systems? Try reminding your father how much his father resisted going to projection-screen scoreboards thirty-five years ago, give or take."

"I'll keep that in mind."

Alone, Cal printed out the information on the automatic systems, new and reconditioned, then shut down long enough to go downstairs and check in with the front desk, the grill, the play area during the morning leagues games.

The scents from the grill reminded him he'd missed breakfast, so he snagged a hot pretzel and a Coke before he headed back up to his office.

So armed, he decided since everything was running smoothly, he could afford to take a late-morning break. He wanted to dig a little deeper into Ann Hawkins.

She'd appeared to him twice in three days. Both times, Cal mused, had been a kind of warning. He'd seen her before, but only in dreams. He'd wanted her in dreams, Cal admitted—or Giles Dent had, working through him.

These incidents had been different, and his feelings different.

Still, that wasn't the purpose, that wasn't the point, he reminded himself as he gnawed off a bite of pretzel.

He was trusting Quinn's instincts about the journals. Somewhere, at some time, there had been more. Maybe they were in the old library. He certainly intended to get in there and search the place inch by inch. If, God, they'd somehow gotten transferred into the new space and mis-shelved or put in storage, the search could be a nightmare.

So he wanted to know more about Ann, to help lead him to the answers.

Where had she been for nearly two years? All the information, all the stories he'd heard or read indicated she'd vanished the night of the fire in the clearing and hadn't returned to the Hollow until her sons were almost two.

"Where did you go, Ann?"

Where would a woman, pregnant with triplets, go during the last weeks before their births? Traveling had to have been extremely difficult. Even for a woman without the pregnancy to weigh her down.

There had been other settlements, but nothing as far as he remembered for a woman in her condition to have walked or even ridden to. So logically, she'd had somewhere to go close by, and someone had taken her in.

Who was most likely to take a young, unmarried woman in? A relative would be his first guess.

Maybe a friend, maybe some kindly old widow, but odds were on family.

"That's where you went first, when there was trouble, wasn't it?"

While it wasn't easy to find specifics on Ann Hawkins, there was plenty of it on her father—the founder of the Hollow.

He'd read it, of course. He'd studied it, but he'd never read or studied it from this angle. Now, he brought up all the information he'd previously downloaded on his office computer relating to James Hawkins.

He took side trips, made notes on any mention of relatives, in-laws. The pickings were slim, but at least there was something to pick from. Cal was rolling with it when someone knocked on his door. He surfaced as Quinn poked her head in just as his mother had that morning.

"Working. I bet you hate to be interrupted. But . . ."

"It's okay." He glanced at the clock, saw with a twinge of guilt his break had lasted more than an hour. "I've been at it longer than I meant to."

"It's dog-eat-dog in the bowling business." She said it with a smile as she came in. "I just wanted you to know we were here. We took Cyb on a quick tour of the town. Do you know there's no place to buy shoes in Hawkins Hollow? Cyb's saddened by that, as she's always on the hunt. Now she's making noises about bowling. She has a vicious competitive streak. So I escaped up here before she drags me into that. The hope was to grab a quick bite at your grill—maybe you could join us—before Cyb . . ."

She trailed off. Not only hadn't he said a word, but he was staring at her. Just staring. "What?" She brushed a hand over her nose, then up over her hair. "Is it my hair?"

"That's part of it. Probably part of it."

He got up, came around the desk. He kept his eyes on her face as he moved past her. As he shut and locked the door.

"Oh. *Oh*. Really? Seriously? Here? Now?"

"Really, seriously. Here and now." She looked flustered, and that was a rare little treat. She looked, every inch of her, amazing. He couldn't say why he'd gone from pleased to see her to aroused in the snap of a finger, and he didn't much care. What he knew, without question, was he wanted to touch her, to draw in her scent, to feel her body go tight, go loose. Just go.

"You're not nearly as predictable as you should be." Watching him now, she pulled off her sweater, unbuttoned the shirt beneath it.

"I should be predictable?" Without bothering with buttons, he pulled his shirt over his head.

"Hometown boy from a nice, stable family, who runs a third-generation family business. You should be predictable, Caleb," she said as she unbuttoned her jeans. "I like that you're not. I don't mean just the sex, though major points there."

She bent down to pull off her boots, tossing her hair out of her eyes so she could look up at him. "You should be married," she decided, "or on your way to it with your college sweetheart. Thinking about 401(k)s."

"I think about 401(k)s. Just not right now. Right now, Quinn, all I can think about is you."

That gave her heart a bounce, even before he reached out, ran his hands down her bare arms. Even before he drew her to him and seduced her mouth with his.

She may have laughed when they lowered to the floor,

but her pulse was pounding. There was a different tone from when they were in bed. More urgency, a sense of recklessness as they tangled together in a giddy heap on the office floor. He tugged her bra down so he could use his lips, his teeth, his tongue on her breasts until her hips began to pump. She closed her hand around him, found him hard, made him groan.

He couldn't wait, not this time. He couldn't savor; needed to take. He rolled, dragging her over so she could straddle him. Even as he gripped her hips, she was rising. She was taking him in. When she leaned forward for a greedy kiss, her hair fell to curtain their faces. Surrounded by her, he thought. Her body, her scent, her energy. He stroked the line of her back, the curve of her hips as she rocked and rocked and rocked him through pleasure toward desperation.

Even when she arched back, even with his vision blurred, the shape of her, the tones of her enthralled him.

She let herself go, simply steeped herself in sensation. Hammering pulses and speed, slick bodies and dazzling friction. She felt him come, that sudden, sharp jerk of his hips, and was thrilled. She had driven him to lose control first, she had taken him over. And now she used that power, that thrill, to drive herself over that same edgy peak.

She slid down from it, and onto him so they could lie there, heated, a little stunned, until they got their breath back. And she began to laugh.

"God, we're like a couple of teenagers. Or rabbits."

"Teenage rabbits."

Amused, she levered up. "Do you often multitask in your office like this?"

"Ah . . ."

She gave him a little poke as she tugged her bra back in place. "See, unpredictable."

He held out her shirt. "It's the first time I've multitasked in this way during working hours."

Her lips curved as she buttoned her shirt. "That's nice."

"And I haven't felt like a teenage rabbit since I was."

She leaned over to give him a quick peck on the lips. "Even nicer." Still on the floor, she scooted into her pants as he did the same. "I should tell you something." She reached for her boots, pulled one on. "I think . . . No, saying 'I think' is a cop-out, it's the coward's way."

She took a deep breath, yanked on the other boot, then looked him dead in the eye. "I'm in love with you."

The shock came first—fast, arrow-point shock straight to the gut. Then the concern wrapped in a slippery fist of fear. "Quinn—"

"Don't waste your breath with the 'we've only known each other a couple of weeks' gambit. And I really don't want to hear the 'I'm flattered, but,' either. I didn't tell you so you could say anything. I told you because you should know. So first, it doesn't matter how long we've known each other. I've known me a long time, and I know me very well. I know what I feel when I feel it. Second, you should be flattered, goes without saying. And there's no need to freak out. You're not obligated or expected to feel what I feel."

"Quinn, we're—all of us—are under a lot of pressure. We don't even know if we'll make it through to August. We can't—"

"Exactly so. Nobody ever knows that, but we have more reason to worry about it. So, Cal." She framed his face with her hands. "The moment's important. The right-this-minute matters a whole hell of a lot. I doubt I'd have told you otherwise, though I can be impulsive. But I think, under other circumstances, I'd have waited for you to catch up. I hope you do, but in the meantime, things are just fine the way they are."

"You have to know I—"

"Don't, absolutely don't tell me you care about me." The first hint of anger stung her voice. "Your instinct is to say all the cliches people babble out in cases like this. They'll only piss me off."

"Okay, all right, let me just ask this, without you getting pissed off. Have you considered what you're feeling might be something like what happened in the clearing? That it's, say, a reflection of what Ann felt for Dent?"

"Yes, and it's not." She pushed to her feet, drew on her sweater. "Good question though. Good questions don't piss me off. What she felt, and I felt through that, was intense and consuming. I'm not going to say some of what I feel for you isn't like that. But it was also painful, and wrenching. Under the joy was grief. That's not this, Cal. This isn't painful. I don't feel sad. So . . . do you have time to come down and grab some lunch before Cyb and Layla and I head out?"

"Ah . . . sure."

"Great. Meet you down there. I'm going to pop in the bathroom and fix myself up a little."

"Quinn." He hesitated as she opened the door, turned back. "I've never felt like this about anyone before."

"Now that is a very acceptable thing to say."

She smiled as she strolled away. If he'd said it, he meant it, because that was the way he was. Poor guy, she thought. Didn't even know he was caught.

A THICK GROVE OF TREES SHIELDED THE OLD cemetery on the north side. It fanned out over bumpy ground, with hills rolling west, at the end of a dirt road barely wide enough for two cars to pass. A historical marker faded by weather stated the First Church of the Godly had once stood on the site, but had been destroyed when it had been struck by lightning and razed by fire on July 7, 1652.

Quinn had read that fact in her research, but it was different to stand here now, in the wind, in the chill, and imagine it. She'd read, too, as the plaque stated, that a small chapel had stood as a replacement until it was damaged during the Civil War, and gone to ruin.

Now, there were only the markers here, the stones, the winter-hardy weeds. Beyond a low stone wall were the graves of the newer dead. Here and there she saw bright blots of color from flowers that stood out like grief against the dull grays and winter browns.

"We should've brought flowers," Layla said quietly as she looked down at the simple and small stone that read only:

ANN HAWKINS

"She doesn't need them," Cybil told her. "Stones and flowers, they're for the living. The dead have other things to do."

"Cheery thought."

Cybil only shrugged at Quinn. "I think so, actually. No point in being dead *and* bored. It's interesting, don't you think, that there are no dates. Birth or death. No sentiment. She had three sons, but they didn't have anything but her name carved in her gravestone. Even though they're buried here, too, with their wives, and I imagine at least some of their children. Wherever they went in life, they came home to be buried with Ann."

"Maybe they knew, or believed, she'd be back. Maybe she told them death isn't the end." Quinn frowned at the stone. "Maybe they just wanted to keep it simple, but I wonder, now that you mention it, if it was deliberate. No beginning, no end. At least not until . . ."

"This July," Layla finished. "Another cheery thought."

"Well, while we're all getting cheered up, I'm going to get some pictures." Quinn pulled out her camera. "Maybe you two could write down some of the names here. We may want to check on them, see if any have any direct bearing on—"

She tripped while backing up to get a shot, fell hard on her ass. "Ouch, goddamn it! Shit. Right on the bruise I got this morning. Perfect."

Layla rushed over to help her up. Cybil did the same, even as she struggled with laughter.

"Just shut up," Quinn grumbled. "The ground's all bumpy here, and you can hardly see some of these stones popping out." She rubbed her hip, scowled down at the stone that had tripped her up. "Ha. That's funny. Joseph Black, died eighteen forty-three." The color annoyance brought to her face faded. "Same last name as mine. Common name Black, really. Until you consider it's here, and that I just happened to trip over his grave."

"Odds are he's one of yours," Cybil agreed.

"And one of Ann's?"

Quinn shook her head at Layla's suggestion. "I don't know. Cal's researched the Hawkins's family tree, and I've done a quick overview. I know some of the older records are lost, or just buried deeper than we've dug, but I don't see how we'd both have missed branches with my surname. So. I think we'd better see what we can find out about Joe."

HER FATHER WAS NO HELP, AND THE CALL HOME kept her on the phone for forty minutes, catching up on family gossip. She tried her grandmother next, who had a vague recollection about her mother-in-law mentioning an uncle, possibly a great-uncle, maybe a cousin, who'd been born in the hills of Maryland. Or it might've been Virginia. His claim to fame, family-wise, had been running off with a saloon singer, deserting his wife and four children and taking the family savings held inside a cookie tin with him.

"Nice guy, Joe," Quinn decided. "Should you be my Joe."

She decided, since it would get her out of any type of food preparation, she had enough time to make a trip to Town Hall, and start digging on Joseph Black. If he'd died here, maybe he'd been born here.

WHEN QUINN GOT HOME SHE WAS GLAD TO FIND the house full of people, sound, the scents of food. Cybil, being Cybil, had music on, candles lit, and wine poured. She had everyone piled in the kitchen, whetting appetites with marinated olives. Quinn popped one, took Cal's wine and washed it down.

"Are my eyes bleeding?" she asked.

"Not so far."

"I've been searching records for nearly three hours. I think I bruised my brain."

"Joseph Black." Fox got her a glass of wine for her own. "We've been filled in."

"Good, saves me. I could only trace him back to his grandfather—Quinton Black, born sixteen seventy-six. Nothing on record before that, not here anyway. And nothing after Joe, either. I went on side trips, looking for siblings or other relatives. He had three sisters, but I've got nothing on them but birth records. He had aunts, uncles, and so on, and not much more there. It appears the Blacks weren't a big presence in Hawkins Hollow."

"Name would've rung for me," Cal told her.

"Yeah. Still, I got my grandmother's curiosity up, and she's now on a hunt to track down the old family Bible. She called me on my cell. She thinks it went to her brother-in-law when his parents died. Maybe. Anyway, it's a line."

She focused on the man leaning back against the counter toying with a glass of wine. "Sorry? Gage, right?"

"That's right. Roadside service a specialty."

Quinn grinned as Cybil rolled her eyes and took a loaf of herbed bread out of the oven.

"So I hear, and that looks like dinner's ready. I'm starved. Nothing like searching through the births and deaths of Blacks, Robbits, Clarks to stir up the appetite."

"Clark." Layla lowered the plate she'd taken out to offer Cybil for the bread. "There were Clarks in the records?"

"Yeah, an Alma and a Richard Clark in there, as I remember. Need to check my notes. Why?"

"My grandmother's maiden name was Clark." Layla managed a wan smile. "That's probably not a coincidence either."

"Is she still living?" Quinn asked immediately. "Can you get in touch and—"

"We're going to eat while it's hot," Cybil interrupted. "Time enough to give family trees a good shake later. But when I cook—" She pushed the plate of hot bread into Gage's hand. "We eat."

Sixteen

IT HAD TO BE IMPORTANT. IT HAD TO MATTER. Cal rolled it over and over and over, carving time out of his workday and his off time to research the Hawkins-Black lineage himself. Here was something new, he thought, some door they hadn't known existed, much less tried to break down.

He told himself it was vital, and time-consuming work, and that was why he and Quinn hadn't managed to really connect for the last couple of days. He was busy; she was busy. Couldn't be helped.

Besides, it was probably a good time for them to have this break from each other. Let things just simmer down a little. As he'd told his mother, this wasn't the time to get serious, to think about falling in love. Because big, life-altering things were supposed to happen after people fell seriously in love. And he had enough, big, life-altering things to worry about.

He dumped food in Lump's bowl as his dog waited for breakfast with his usual unruffled patience. Because it was

Thursday, he'd tossed a load of laundry in the washer when he'd let Lump out for his morning plod and pee. He continued his habitual weekday morning routine, nursing his first cup of coffee while he got out a box of Chex.

But when he reached for the milk it made him think of Quinn. Two percent milk, he thought with a shake of his head. Maybe she was fixing her version of a bowl of cereal right now. Maybe she was standing in her kitchen with the smell of coffee in the air, thinking of him.

Because the idea of that held such appeal, he reached for the phone to call her, when he heard the sound behind him and turned.

Gage got the coffee mug out of the cupboard he opened. "Jumpy."

"No. I didn't hear you come in."

"You were mooning over a woman."

"I have a lot of things on my mind."

"Especially the woman. You've got tells, Hawkins. Starting with the wistful, cocker spaniel eyes."

"Up yours, Turner."

Gage merely grinned and poured coffee. "Then there's that fish hook in the corner of your mouth." He hooked his finger in his own, gave a tug. "Unmistakable."

"You're jealous because you're not getting laid regular."

"No question about that." Gage sipped his black coffee, used one bare foot to rub Lump's flank as the dog concentrated his entire being on his kibble. "She's not your usual type."

"Oh?" Irritation crawled up Cal's back like a lizard. "What's my usual type?"

"Pretty much same as mine. Keep it light, no deep thinking, no strings, no worries. Who could blame us, considering?" He picked up the cereal, dug right into the box. "But she breaks your mold. She's smart, she's steady, and she's got a big, fat ball of string in her back pocket. She's already started wrapping you in it."

"Does that cynicism you carry around everywhere ever get heavy?"

"Realism," Gage corrected as he munched on cereal. "And it keeps me light on my feet. I like her."

"I do, too." Cal forgot the milk and just took a handful of cereal out of the bowl he'd poured. "She . . . she told me she's in love with me."

"Fast work. And now she's suddenly pretty damn busy, and you're sleeping alone, pal. I said she was smart."

"Jesus, Gage." Insult bloomed on two stalks—one for himself, one for Quinn. "She's not like that. She doesn't use people like that."

"And you know this because you know her so well."

"I do." Any sign of irritation faded as that simple truth struck home. "That's just it. I do know her. There may be dozens, hell, hundreds of things I don't know, but I know who—how—she is. I don't know if some of that's because of this connection, because of what we're all tied to, but I know it's true. The first time I met her, things changed. I don't know. Something changed for me. So you can make cracks, but that's the way it is."

"I'm going to say you're lucky," Gage said after a moment. "That I hope it works out the way you want. I never figured any of us had a decent shot at normal." He shrugged. "Wouldn't mind being wrong. Besides, you look real cute with that hook in your mouth."

Cal lifted his middle finger off the bowl and into the air.

"Right back atcha," Fox said as he strolled in. He went straight to the refrigerator for a Coke. "What's up?"

"What's up is you're mooching my Cokes again, and you never bring any to replace them."

"I brought beer last week. Besides, Gage told me to come over this morning, and when I come over in the morning, I expect a damn Coke."

"You told him to come over?"

"Yeah. So, O'Dell, Cal's in love with the blonde."

"I didn't say I—"

"Tell me something I don't know." Fox popped the top on the can of Coke and gulped.

"I never said I was in love with anyone."

Fox merely shifted his gaze to Cal. "I've known you my whole life. I know what those shiny little hearts in your eyes mean. It's cool. She was, like, made for you."

"He says she's not my usual type, you say she's made for me."

"We're both right. She's not the type you usually fish for." Fox gulped down more soda, then took the box of cereal from Gage. "Because you didn't want to find the one who fit. She fits, but she was sort of a surprise. Practically an ambush. Did I get up an hour early to come over here before work so we could talk about Cal's love life?"

"No, it was just an interesting sidebar. I got some information when I was in the Czech Republic. Rumors, lore, mostly, which I followed up when I had time. I got a call from an expert last night, which is why I told you to come over this morning. I might have ID'd our Big Evil Bastard."

They sat down at the kitchen table with coffee and dry cereal—Fox in one of his lawyer suits, Gage in a black T-shirt and loose pants, Cal in jeans and a flannel shirt.

And spoke of demons.

"I toured some of the smaller and outlying villages," Gage began. "I always figure I might as well pick up some local color, maybe a local skirt while I'm stacking up poker chips and markers."

He'd been doing the same for years, Cal knew. Following any whiff of information about devils, demons, unexplained phenomenon. He always came back with stories, but nothing that had ever fit the, well, the profile, Cal supposed, of their particular problem.

"There was talk about this old demon who could take other forms. You get werewolf stuff over there, and initially, I figured that was this deal. But this wasn't about biting throats out and silver bullets. The talk was about how this thing hunted humans to enslave them, and feed off their . . . the translation was kind of vague, and the best I got was essence, or humanity."

"Feed how?"

"That's vague, too—or colorful as lore tends to be. Not on flesh and bone, not with fang and claw—that kind of thing. The legend is this demon, or creature, could take people's minds as well as their souls, and cause them to go mad, cause them to kill."

"Could be the root of ours," Fox decided.

"It rang close enough that I followed it up. It was a lot to wade through; that area's ripe with stories like this. But in this place in the hills, with this thick forest that reminded me of home, I hit something. Its name is *Tmavy*. Translates to Dark. The Dark."

He thought, they all thought of what had come out of the ground at the Pagan Stone. "It came like a man who wasn't a man, hunted like a wolf that wasn't a wolf. And sometimes it was a boy, a boy who lured women and children in particular into the forest. Most never came back, and those who did were mad. The families of those who did went mad, too. Killed each other, or themselves, their neighbors."

Gage paused, rose to get the coffeepot. "I got some of this when I was there, but I found a priest who gave me the name of a guy, a professor, who studied and publishes on Eastern European demonology. He got in touch last night. He claims this particular demon—and he isn't afraid to use the word—roamed Europe for centuries. He, in turn, was hunted by a man—some say another demon, or a wizard, or just a man with a mission. Legend has it that they battled in the forest, and the wizard was mortally wounded, left for dead. And that, according to Professor Linz, was its mistake. Someone came, a young boy, and the wizard passed the boy his power before he died."

"What happened?" Fox demanded.

"No one, including Linz, is sure. The stories claim the thing vanished, or moved on, or died, somewhere in the early- to mid-seventeenth century."

"When he hopped a goddamn boat for the New World," Cal added.

"Maybe. That may be."

"So did the boy," Cal continued, "or the man he'd become, or his descendent. But he nearly had him over there, nearly did at some point in time—that's something I've seen. I think. Him and the woman, a cabin. Him holding a bloody sword, and knowing nearly all were dead. He couldn't stop it there, so he passed what he had to Dent, and Dent tried again. Here."

"What did he pass to us?" Fox demanded. "What power? Not getting a freaking head cold, having a broken arm knit itself? What good does that do?"

"Keeps us healthy and whole when we face it down. And there's the glimmers I see, that we all see in different ways." Cal shoved at his hair. "I don't know. But it has to be something that matters. The three parts of the stone. They have to be. We've just never figured it out."

"And time's almost up."

Cal nodded at Gage. "We need to show the stones to the others. We took an oath, we all have to agree to that. If we hadn't, I'd have—"

"Shown yours to Quinn already," Fox finished. "And yeah, maybe you're right. It's worth a shot. It could be it needs all six of us to put it back together."

"Or it could be that when whatever happened at the Pagan Stone happened, the bloodstone split because its power was damaged. Destroyed."

"Your glass is always half empty, Turner," Fox commented. "Either way, it's worth the try. Agreed?"

"Agreed." Cal looked at Gage, who shrugged.

"What the hell."

CAL DEBATED WITH HIMSELF ALL THE WAY INTO town. He didn't need an excuse to stop by to see Quinn. For God's sake, they were sleeping together. It wasn't as if he needed an appointment or clearance or a specific reason to knock on her door, to see how she was doing. To ask what the hell was going on.

There was no question she'd been distracted every time he'd managed to reach her by phone the last couple of days. She hadn't dropped into the center since they'd rolled around his office floor.

And she'd told him she was in love with him.

That was the problem. The oil on the water, the sand in the shoe, or whatever goddamn analogy made the most sense. She'd told him she loved him, he hadn't said "me, too," which she claimed she didn't expect. But any guy who actually believed a woman always meant exactly what she said was deep in dangerous delusion.

Now, she was avoiding him.

They didn't have *time* for games, for bruised feelings and sulks. There were more important things at stake. Which, he was forced to admit, was why he shouldn't have touched her in the first place. By adding sex to the mix, they'd clouded and complicated the issue, and the issue was already clouded and complicated enough. They had to be practical; they had to be smart. Objective, he added as he pulled up in front of the rental house. Cold-blooded, clear-minded.

Nobody was any of those things when they were having sex. Not if they were having really good sex.

He jammed his hands in his pockets as he walked up to her door, then dragged one out to knock. The fact that he'd worked himself up to a mad might not have been objective or practical, but it felt absolutely right.

Until she opened the door.

Her hair was damp. She'd pulled it back from her face in a sleek tail, and he could see it wasn't quite dry. He could smell the girly shampoo and soap, and the scents wound their way into him until the muscle in his gut tightened in response.

She wore fuzzy purple socks, black flannel pants, and a hot pink sweatshirt that announced: T.G.I.F. THANK GOD I'M FEMALE.

He could add his own thanks.

"Hi!"

The idea she was sulking was hard to hang on to when he was blasted by her sunbeam smile and buzzing energy.

"I was just thinking about you. Come inside. Jesus, it's cold. I've so had it with winter. I was about to treat myself to a low-fat mug of hot chocolate. Want in on that?"

"Ah—I really don't."

"Well, come on back, because I've got the yen." She rose up on her toes to give him a long, solid kiss, then grabbed his hand to pull him back to the kitchen. "I nagged Cyb and Layla into going to the gym with me this morning. Took some doing with Cyb, but I figured safety in numbers. Nothing weird happened, unless you count watching Cyb twist herself into some advanced yoga positions. Which Matt did, let me tell you. Things have been quiet in the otherworldly sense the last couple days."

She got out a packet of powdered mix, slapped it against her hand a couple of times to settle it before ripping it open to pour it into a mug. "Sure you don't want some?"

"Yeah, go ahead."

"We've been a busy hive around here," she went on as she filled the mug, half with water, half with two percent milk. "I'm waiting to hear something about the family Bible, or whatever else my grandmother might dig up. Today, maybe, hopefully by tomorrow. Meanwhile, we've got charts of family trees as we know them, and Layla's trying to shake some ancestry out of her relatives."

She stirred up the liquid and mix, stuck it in the microwave. "I had to leave a lot of the research up to my partners in crime and finish an article for the magazine. Gotta pay the doorman, after all. So?" She turned back as the microwave hummed. "How about you?"

"I missed you." He hadn't planned to say it, certainly hadn't expected it to be the first thing out of his mouth. Then he realized, it was obviously the first thing on his mind.

Her eyes went soft; that sexy mouth curved up. "That's nice to hear. I missed you, too, especially last night when I crawled into bed about one in the morning. My cold, empty bed."

"I didn't just mean the sex, Quinn." And where had *that* come from?

"Neither did I." She angled her head, ignoring the beep of the microwave. "I missed having you around at the end of the day, when I could finally come down from having to hammer out that article, when I wanted to stop thinking about what I had to do, and what was going to happen. You're irritated about something. Why don't you tell me what it is?"

She turned toward the microwave as she spoke to get her mug out. Cal saw immediately she'd made the move as Cybil was stepping through the kitchen doorway. Quinn merely shook her head, and Cybil stepped back and retreated without a word.

"I don't know, exactly." He pulled off his coat now, tossed it over one of the chairs around a little cafe table that hadn't been there on his last visit. "I guess I thought, after the other day, after . . . what you said—"

"I said I was in love with you. That makes you quiver inside," she noted. "Men."

"I didn't start avoiding you."

"You think—" She took a deep inhale through her nose, exhaled in a huff. "Well, you have a really high opinion of yourself, and a crappy one of me."

"No, it's just—"

"I had things to do, I had work. I am not at your beck any more than you're at mine."

"That's not what I meant."

"You think I'd play games like that? Especially now?"

"Especially now's the point. This isn't the time for big personal issues."

"If not now, when?" she demanded. "Do you really, do you honestly think we can label and file all our personal business and close it in a drawer until it's *convenient*? I like things in their place, too. I want to know where things are, so I put them where I want or need them to be. But feelings and thoughts are different from the goddamn car keys, Cal."

"No argument, but—"

"And my feelings and thoughts are as cluttered and messy as Grandma's attic," she snapped out, far from winding down. "That's just the way I like it. If things were normal every day, bopping right along, I probably wouldn't have told you. Do you think this is my first cannonball into the Dating and Relationship Pool? I was engaged, for God's sake. I told you because—because I think, maybe *especially* now, that feelings are what matter most. If that screws you up, too damn bad."

"I wish you'd shut up for five damn minutes."

Her eyes went to slits. "Oh, really?"

"Yeah. The fact is I don't know how to react to all of this, because I never let myself consider being in this position. How could I, with this hanging over my head? Can't risk falling for someone. How much could I tell her? How much is too much? We're—Fox and Gage and I—we're used to holding back, to keeping big pieces of this to ourselves."

"Keeping secrets."

"That's right," he said equably. "That's exactly right. Because it's safer that way. How could I ever think about falling in love, getting married, having kids? Bringing a kid into this nightmare's out of the question."

Those slitted blue eyes went cold as winter. "I don't believe I've yet expressed the wish to bear your young."

"Remember who you're talking to," he said quietly. "You take this situation out of the equation you've got a normal guy from a normal family. The kind who gets married, raises a family, has a mortgage and a big sloppy dog. If I let myself fall in love with a woman, that's how it's going to work."

"I guess you told me."

"And it's irresponsible to even consider any of that."

"We disagree. I happen to think considering that, moving toward that, is shooting the bird at the dark. In the end, we're each entitled to our own take on it. But understand me, get this crystal, telling you I love you didn't mean I expected you to pop a ring on my finger."

"Because you've been there."

She nodded. "Yes, I have. And you're wondering about that."

"None of my business." Screw it. "Yes."

"Okay, it's simple enough. I was seeing Dirk—"

"Dirk—"

"Shut up." But her lips twitched. "I was seeing him exclusively for about six months. We enjoyed each other. I thought I was ready for the next stage in my life, so I said yes when he asked me to marry him. We were engaged for two months when I realized I'd made a mistake. I didn't love him. Liked him just fine. He didn't love me, either. He didn't really get me—not the whole of me, which was why he figured the ring on my finger meant he could begin to advise me on my work, on my wardrobe, habits, and career options. There were a lot of little things, and they're not really important. The fact was we weren't going to make it work, so I broke it off."

She blew out another breath because it wasn't pleasant to remember she'd made that big a mistake. That she'd failed at something she knew she'd be good at. "He was more annoyed than brokenhearted, which told me I'd done the right thing. And the truth is, it stung to know I'd done the right thing, because it meant I'd done the wrong thing first. When I suggested he tell his friends he'd been the one to end it, he felt better about it. I gave him back the ring, we each boxed up things we'd kept in each other's apartments, and we walked away."

"He didn't hurt you."

"Oh, Cal." She took a step closer so she could touch his face. "No, he didn't. The situation hurt me, but he didn't. Which is only one of the reasons I knew he wasn't the one. If you want me to reassure you that you can't, that you won't break my heart, I just can't do it. Because you can, you might, and that's how I know you are. The one." She slipped her arms around him, laid her lips on his. "That must be scary for you."

"Terrifying." He pulled her against him, held her hard. "I've never had another woman in my life who's given me as many bad moments as you."

"I'm delighted to hear it."

"I thought you would be." He laid his cheek on top of her head. "I'd like to stay here, just like this, for an hour or two." He replaced his cheek with his lips, then eased back. "But I've things I have to do, and so do you. Which I knew before I walked in here and used it as an excuse to pick a fight."

"I don't mind a fight. Not when the air's clear afterward."

He framed her face with his hands, kissed her softly. "Your hot chocolate's getting cold."

"Chocolate's never the wrong temperature."

"The one thing I said before? Absolute truth. I missed you."

"I believe I can arrange some free time in my busy schedule."

"I have to work tonight. Maybe you could stop in. I'll give you another bowling lesson."

"All right."

"Quinn, we—all of us—have to talk. About a lot of things. As soon as we can."

"Yes, we do. One thing before you go. Is Fox going to offer Layla a job?"

"I said something to him." Cal swore under his breath at her expression. "I'll give him another push on it."

"Thanks."

Alone, Quinn picked up her mug, thoughtfully sipped at her lukewarm chocolate. Men, she thought, were such interesting beings.

Cybil came in. "All clear?"

"Yeah, thanks."

"No problem." She opened a cupboard and chose a small tin of loose jasmine tea from her supply. "Discuss or mind my own?"

"Discuss. He was worked up because I told him I love him."

"Annoyed or panicked?"

"Some of both, I think. More worried because we've all got scary things to deal with, and this is another kind of scary thing."

"The scariest, when you come down to it." Cybil filled the teakettle with water. "How are you handling it?"

"It feels . . . great," she decided. "Energizing and bouncy and bright, then sort of rich and glimmering. You know, with Dirk it was all . . ." Quinn held out a hand, drawing it level through the air. "This was—" She shot her hand up, down, then up again. "Here's a thing. When he's telling me why this is crazy, he says how he's never been in a position—or so he thinks—to let himself think about love, marriage, family."

"Whoa, point A to Z in ten words or less."

"Exactly." Quinn gestured with her mug. "And he was rolling too fast to see that the *M* word gave me a serious jolt. I practically just jumped off that path, and whoops, there it is again, under my feet."

"Hence the jolt." Cybil measured out her tea. "But I don't see you jumping off."

"Because you know me. I like where my feet are, as it turns out. I like the idea of heading down that path with Cal, toward wherever it ends up. He's in trouble now," she murmured and took another sip.

"So are you, Q. But then trouble's always looked good on you."

"Better than a makeover at the Mac counter at Saks." Quinn answered the kitchen phone on its first ring. "Hello. Hello, Essie. Oh. Really? No, it's great. It's perfect. Thanks so much. I absolutely will. Thanks again. Bye." She hung up, grinned. "Essie Hawkins got us into the community center. No business there today on the main level. We can go in, poke around to our hearts' content."

"Won't that be fun?" Cybil said it dryly as she poured boiling water for her tea.

ARMED WITH THE KEY, CYBIL OPENED THE MAIN door of the old library. "We're here, on the surface, for research. One of the oldest buildings in town, home of the Hawkins family. But . . ." She switched on the lights. "Primarily we're looking for hidey-holes. A hiding place that was overlooked."

"For three and a half centuries," Cybil commented.

"If something's overlooked for five minutes, it can be overlooked forever." Quinn pursed her lips as she looked around. "They modernized it, so to speak, when they turned it into a library, but when they built the new one, they stripped out some of the newfangled details. It's not the way it was, but it's closer."

There were some tables and chairs set up, and someone had made an attempt at some old-timey decor in the antique old lamps, old pottery, and wood carvings on shelves. Quinn had been told groups like the Historical Society or the Garden Club could hold meetings or functions here. At election times it was a voting center.

"Stone fireplace," she said. "See, that's an excellent place to hide something." After crossing to it, she began to poke at the stones. "Plus there's an attic. Essie said they used it for storage. Still do. They keep the folding tables and chairs up there, and that kind of thing. Attics are treasure troves."

"Why is it buildings like this are so cold and creepy when no one's in them?" Layla wondered.

"We're in this one. Let's start at the top," Quinn suggested, "work our way down."

"ATTICS ARE TREASURE TROVES," CYBIL SAID twenty minutes later, "of dust and spiders."

"It's not that bad." Quinn crawled along, hoping for a loose floorboard.

"Not that good either." Courageously, Layla stood on a folding chair, checking rafters. "I don't understand why people don't think storage spaces shouldn't be cleaned as regularly as anyplace else."

"It was clean once. She kept it clean."

"Who—" Layla began, but Cybil waved a hand at her, frowned at Quinn.

"Ann Hawkins?"

"Ann and her boys. She brought them home, and shared the attic with them. Her three sons. Until they were old enough to have a room downstairs. But she stayed here. She wanted to be high, to be able to look out of her window. Even though she knew he wouldn't come, she wanted to look out for him. She was happy here, happy enough. And when she died here, she was ready to go."

Abruptly, Quinn sat back on her heels. "Holy shit, was that me?"

Cybil crouched down to study Quinn's face. "You tell us."

"I guess it was." She pressed her fingers to her forehead. "Damn, got one of those I-drank-my-frozen-margarita-too-fast-and-now-have-an-ice pick-through-my-brain headaches. I saw it, her, them, in my head. Just as clear. Everything moving, like a time-action camera. Years in seconds. But more, I felt it. That's the way it is for you, isn't it—going the other way?"

"Often," Cybil agreed.

"I saw her writing in her journal, and washing her sons' faces. I saw her laughing, or weeping. I saw her standing at the window looking into the dark. I felt . . ." Quinn laid a hand on her heart. "I felt her longing. It was . . . brutal."

"You don't look well." Layla touched her shoulder. "We should go downstairs, get you some water."

"Probably. Yeah." She took the hand Layla offered to help her up. "Maybe I should try it again. Try to bring it back, get more."

"You're awfully pale," Layla told her. "And, honey, your hand's like ice."

"Plenty for one day," Cybil agreed. "You don't want to push it."

"I didn't see where she put the journals. If she put anything here, I didn't see."

Seventeen

IT WASN'T THE TIME, CAL DETERMINED, TO TALK about a broken stone or property searches when Quinn was buzzed about her trip to the past with Ann Hawkins. In any case, the bowling center wasn't the place for that kind of exchange of information.

He considered bringing it up after closing when she dragged him into her home office to show him the new chart Layla had generated that listed the time, place, approximate duration, and involved parties in all known incidents since Quinn's arrival.

He forgot about it when he was in bed with her, when she was moving with him, when everything felt right again.

Then he told himself it was too late to bring it up, to give the topics the proper time when she was curled up warm with him.

Maybe it was avoidance, but he opted for the likelihood it was just his tendency to prefer things at the right time, in the right place. He'd arranged to take Sunday off so the entire group could hike to the Pagan Stone. That, to his mind, was the right time and place.

Then Nature screwed with his plans.

When forecasters began to predict an oncoming blizzard, he kept a jaundiced eye on the reports. They were, in his experience, wrong at least as often as they were right. Even when the first flakes began to fall midmorning, he remained unconvinced. It was the third blizzard hype of the year, and so far the biggest storm had dumped a reasonable eight inches.

He shrugged it off when the afternoon leagues canceled. It had gotten so people canceled everything at the first half inch, then went to war over bread and toilet paper in the supermarket. And since the powers-that-be canceled school before noon, the arcade and the grill were buzzing.

But when his father came in about two in the afternoon, looking like Sasquatch, Cal paid more attention.

"I think we're going to close up shop," Jim said in his easy way.

"It's not that bad. The arcade's drawing the usual suspects, the grill's been busy. We've had some lanes booked. A lot of towners will come in later in the afternoon, looking for something to do."

"It's bad enough, and it's getting worse." Jim shoved his gloves in the pocket of his parka. "We'll have a foot by sundown the way it's going. We need to send these kids home, haul them there if they don't live within easy walking distance. We'll close up, then you go on home, too. Or you get your dog and Gage and come on over and stay with us. Your mother'll worry sick if she thinks you're out driving in this at night."

He started to remind his father that he was thirty, had four-wheel drive, and had been driving nearly half his life. Knowing it was pointless, Cal just nodded. "We'll be fine. I've got plenty of supplies. I'll clear out the customers, close up, Dad. You go on home. She'll worry about you, too."

"There's time enough to close down and lock up." Jim glanced over at the lanes where a six-pack of teenagers sent off energy and hormones in equal measure. "Had a hell of a storm when I was a kid. Your grandfather kept her open. We stayed here for three days. Time of my life."

"I bet." Cal grinned. "Want to call Mom, say we're stuck? You and me can ride it out. Have a bowling marathon."

"Damned if I wouldn't." The lines around Jim's eyes crinkled at the idea. "Of course, she'll kick my ass for it and it'd be the last time I bowled."

"Better shut down then."

Though there were protests and moans, they moved customers along, arranging for rides when necessary with some of the staff. In the silence, Cal shut down the grill himself. He knew his father had gone back to check with Bill Turner. Not just to give instructions, he thought, but to make sure Bill had whatever he needed, to slip him a little extra cash if he didn't.

As he shut down, Cal pulled out his phone and called Fox's office. "Hey. Wondered if I'd catch you."

"Just. I'm closing. Already sent Mrs. H home. It's getting bad out there."

"Head over to my place. If this comes in like they're whining about, it might be a couple days before the roads are clear. No point wasting them. And maybe you should stop, pick up, you know, toilet paper, bread."

"Toilet . . . You're bringing the women?"

"Yeah." He'd made up his mind on that when he'd taken a look outside. "Get . . . stuff. Figure it out. I'll be home as soon as I can."

He clicked off, then shut down the alley lights as his father came out.

"Everything set?" Cal asked.

"Yep."

The way his father looked around the darkened alley told Cal he was thinking they weren't just going to lose their big Friday night, but likely the entire weekend.

"We'll make it up, Dad."

"That's right. We always do." He gave Cal a slap on the shoulder. "Let's get home."

QUINN WAS LAUGHING WHEN SHE OPENED THE door. "Isn't this great! They say we could get three feet, maybe more! Cyb's making goulash, and Layla went out and picked up extra batteries and candles in case we lose power."

"Good. Great." Cal stomped snow off his boots. "Pack it up and whatever else you all need. We're going to my place."

"Don't be silly. We're fine. You can stay, and we'll—"

As clear of snow as he could manage, he stepped in, shut the door behind him. "I have a small gas generator that'll run little things—such as the well, which means water to flush the toilets."

"Oh. Toilets. I hadn't thought of that one. But how are we all going to fit in your truck?"

"We'll manage. Get your stuff."

It took them half an hour, but he'd expected that. In the end, the bed of his truck was loaded with enough for a week's trek through the wilderness. And three women were jammed with him in the cab.

He should've had Fox swing by, get one of them, he realized. Then Fox could've hauled half the contents of their house in *his* truck. And it was too late now.

"It's gorgeous." Layla perched on Quinn's lap, bracing a hand on the dash while the Chevy's windshield wipers worked overtime to clear the snow from the glass. "I know it's going to be a big mess, but it's so beautiful, so different than it is in the city."

"Remember that when we're competing for bathroom time with three men," Cybil warned her. "And let me say right now, I refuse to be responsible for all meals just because I know how to turn on the stove."

"So noted," Cal muttered.

"It *is* gorgeous," Quinn agreed, shifting her head from side to side to see around Layla. "Oh, I forgot. I heard from my grandmother. She tracked down the Bible. She's having her sister-in-law's granddaughter copy and scan the appropriate pages, and e-mail them to me." Quinn wiggled to try for more room. "At least that's the plan, as the granddaughter's the only one of them who understands how to scan and attach files. E-mail and online poker's as far as Grandma goes on the Internet. I hope to have the information by tomorrow. Isn't this great?"

Wedged between Quinn's butt and the door, Cybil dug in to protect her corner of the seat. "It'd be better if you'd move your ass over."

"I've got Layla's space, too, so I get more room. I want popcorn," Quinn decided. "Doesn't all this snow make everyone want popcorn? Did we pack any? Do you have any?" she asked Cal. "Maybe we could stop and buy some Orville's."

He kept his mouth shut, and concentrated on surviving what he thought might be the longest drive of his life.

He plowed his way down the side roads, and though he trusted the truck and his own driving, was relieved when he turned onto his lane. As he'd been outvoted about the heat setting, the cab of the truck was like a sauna.

Even under the circumstances, Cal had to admit his place, his woods, did look like a picture. The snow-banked terraces, the white-decked trees and huddles of shrubs framed the house where smoke was pumping from the chimney, and the lights were already gleaming against the windows.

He followed the tracks of Fox's tires across the little bridge over his snow- and ice-crusted curve of the creek.

Lump padded toward the house from the direction of the winter-postcard woods, leaving deep prints behind him. His tail swished once as he let out a single, hollow bark.

"Wow, look at Lump." Quinn managed to poke Cal with her elbow as the truck shoved its way along the lane. "He's positively frisky."

"Snow gets him going." Cal pulled behind Fox's truck, smirked at the Ferrari, slowly being buried, then laid on the horn. He'd be damned if he was going to haul the bulk of what three women deemed impossible to live without for a night or two.

He dragged bags out of the bed.

"It's a beautiful spot, Cal." Layla took the first out of his hands. "Currier and Ives for the twenty-first century. Is it all right if I go right in?"

"Sure."

"Pretty as a picture." Cybil scanned the bags and boxes, chose one for herself. "Especially if you don't mind being isolated."

"I don't."

She glanced over as Gage and Fox came out of the house. "I hope you don't mind crowds either."

They got everything inside, trailing snow everywhere. Cal decided it must have been some sort of female telepathy that divided them all into chores without discussion. Layla asked him for rags or old towels and proceeded to mop up the wet, Cybil took over the kitchen with her stew pot and bag of kitchen ingredients. And Quinn dug into his linen closet, such as it was, and began assigning beds, and ordering various bags carried to various rooms.

There wasn't anything for him to do, really, but have a beer.

Gage strode in as Cal poked at the fire. "There are bottles of girl stuff all over both bathrooms up there." Gage jerked a thumb at the ceiling. "What have you done?"

"What had to be done. I couldn't leave them. They could've been cut off for a couple of days."

"And what, turned into the next Donner Party? Your woman has Fox making my bed, which is now the pullout in your office. And which I'm apparently supposed to share with him. You know that son of a bitch is a bed hog."

"Can't be helped."

"Easy for you to say, seeing as you'll be sharing yours with the blonde."

This time Cal grinned, smugly. "Can't be helped."

"Esmerelda's brewing up something in the kitchen."

"Goulash—and it's Cybil."

"Whatever, it smells good, I'll give her that. She smells better. But the point is I got the heave-ho when I tried to get a damn bag of chips to go with the beer."

"You want to cook for six people?"

Gage only grunted, sat, propped his feet on the coffee table. "How much are they calling for?"

"About three feet." Cal dropped down beside him, mirrored his pose. "Used to be we liked nothing better. No school, haul out the sleds. Snowball wars."

"Those were the days, my friend."

"Now we're priming the generator, loading in firewood, buying extra batteries and toilet paper."

"Sucks to be grown up."

Still, it was warm, and while the snow fell in sheets outside, there was light, and there was food. It was hard to complain, Cal decided, when he was digging into a bowl of hot, spicy stew he had nothing to do with preparing. Plus, there were dumplings, and he was weak when it came to dumplings.

"I was in Budapest not that long ago." Gage spooned up goulash as he studied Cybil. "This is as good as any I got there."

"Actually, this isn't Hungarian goulash. It's a Serbo-Croatian base."

"Damn good stew," Fox commented, "wherever it's based."

"Cybil's an Eastern European stew herself." Quinn savored the half dumpling she'd allowed herself. "Croatian, Ukrainian, Polish—with a dash of French for fashion sense and snottiness."

"When did your family come over?" Cal wondered.

"As early as the seventeen hundreds, as late as just before World War Two, depending on the line." But she understood the reason for the question. "I don't know if there is a connection to Quinn or Layla, or any of this, where it might root from. I'm looking into it."

"We had a connection," Quinn said, "straight off."

"We did."

Cal understood that kind of friendship, the kind he saw when the two women looked at each other. It had little to do with blood, and everything to do with the heart.

"We hooked up the first day—evening really—of college." Quinn spooned off another minuscule piece of dumpling with the stew. "Met in the hall of the dorm. We were across from each other. Within two days, we'd switched. Our respective roommates didn't care. We bunked together right through college."

"And apparently still are," Cybil commented.

"Remember you read my palm that first night?"

"You read palms?" Fox asked.

"When the mood strikes. My gypsy heritage," Cybil added with a flourishing gesture of her hands.

And Cal felt a knot form in his belly. "There were gypsies in the Hollow."

"Really?" Carefully, Cybil lifted her wineglass, sipped. "When?"

"I'd have to check to be sure. This is from stories my gran told me that her grandmother told her. Like that. About how gypsies came one summer and set up camp."

"Interesting. Potentially," Quinn mused, "someone local could get cozy with one of those dark-eyed beauties or hunks, and nine months later, oops. Could lead right to you, Cyb."

"Just one big, happy family," Cybil muttered.

After the meal, chores were divvied up again. Wood needed to be brought in, the dog let out, the table cleared, dishes dealt with.

"Who else cooks?" Cybil demanded.

"Gage does," Cal and Fox said together.

"Hey."

"Good." Cybil sized him up. "If there's a group breakfast on the slate, you're in charge. Now—"

"Before we . . . whatever," Cal decided, "there's something we have to go over. Might as well stick to the dining room. We have to get something," he added, looking at Fox and Gage. "You might want to open another bottle of wine."

"What's all this?" Quinn frowned as the men retreated. "What are they up to?"

"It's more what haven't they told us," Layla said. "Guilt and reluctance, that's what I'm picking up. Not that I know any of them that well."

"You know what you know," Cybil told her. "Get another bottle, Q." She gave a little shudder. "Maybe we should light a couple more candles while we're at it, just in case. It already feels . . . dark."

THEY LEFT IT TO HIM, CAL SUPPOSED, BECAUSE IT was his house. When they were all back around the table, he tried to find the best way to begin.

"We've gone over what happened that night in the clearing when we were kids, and what started happening after. Quinn, you got some of it yourself when we hiked there a couple weeks ago."

"Yeah. Cyb and Layla need to see it, as soon as the snow's cleared enough for us to make the hike."

He hesitated only a beat. "Agreed."

"It ain't a stroll down the Champs Élysées," Gage commented, and Cybil cocked an eyebrow at him.

"We'll manage."

"There was another element that night, another aspect we haven't talked about with you."

"With anyone," Fox added.

"It's hard to explain why. We were ten, everything went

to hell, and . . . Well." Cal set his part of the stone on the table.

"A piece of rock?" Layla said.

"Bloodstone." Cybil pursed her lips, started to reach for it, stopped. "May I?"

Gage and Fox set theirs down beside Cal's. "Take your pick," Gage invited.

"Three parts of one." Quinn picked up the one closest to her. "Isn't that right? These are three parts of one stone."

"One that had been rounded, tumbled, polished," Cybil continued. "Where did you get the pieces?"

"We were holding them," Cal told her. "After the light, after the dark, when the ground stopped shaking, each one of us was holding his part of this stone." He studied his own hand, remembering how his fist had clenched around the stone as if his life depended on it.

"We didn't know what they were. Fox looked it up. His mother had books on rocks and crystals, and he looked it up. Bloodstone," Cal repeated. "It fit."

"It needs to be put back together," Layla said. "Doesn't it? It needs to be whole again."

"We've tried. The breaks are clean," Fox explained. "They fit together like a puzzle." He gestured, and Cal took the pieces, fit them into a round.

"But it doesn't do anything."

"Because you're holding them together?" Curious, Quinn held out her hand until Cal put the three pieces into it. "They're not . . . fused would be the word, I guess."

"Tried that, too. MacGyver over there tried superglue."

Cal sent Gage a bland stare. "Which should've worked—at least as far as holding the pieces together. But I might as well have used water. No stick. We've tried banding them, heating them, freezing them. No dice. In fact, they don't even change temperature."

"Except—" Fox broke off, got the go-ahead nod. "During the Seven, they heat up. Not too hot to hold, but right on the edge."

"Have you tried putting them back together during that week?" Quinn demanded.

"Yeah. No luck. The one thing we know is that Giles Dent was wearing this, like an amulet around his neck, the night Lazarus Twisse led that mob into the clearing. I saw it. Now we have it."

"Have you tried magickal means?" Cybil asked.

Cal squirmed a little, cleared his throat.

"Jesus, Cal, loosen up." Fox shook his head. "Sure. I got some books on spells, and we gave that a try. Down the road, Gage has talked to some practicing witches, and we've tried other rites and so on."

"But you never showed them to anyone." Quinn set the pieces down carefully before picking up her wine. "Anyone who might have been able to work with them, or understand the purpose. Maybe the history."

"We weren't meant to." Fox lifted his shoulders. "I know how it sounds, but I knew we weren't supposed to take it to, what, a geologist or some Wiccan high priestess, or the damn Pentagon. I just . . . Cal voted for the science angle right off."

"MacGyver," Gage repeated.

"Fox was sure that was off-limits, and that was good enough. That was good enough for the three of us." Cal looked at his friends. "It's been the way we've handled it, up till now. If Fox felt we shouldn't show you, we wouldn't be."

"Because you feel it the strongest?" Layla asked Fox.

"I don't know. Maybe. I know I believed—I believe—we survived that night, that we came out of it the way we came out of it because we each had a piece of that stone. And as long as we do, we've got a chance. It's just something I know, the same way Cal saw it, that he recognized it as the amulet Dent wore."

"How about you?" Cybil asked Gage. "What do you know? What do you see?"

His eyes met hers. "I see it whole, on top of the Pagan

Stone. The stone on the stone. And the flames flick up from it, kindling in the blood spots. Then they consume it, ride over the flat, down the pedestal like a sheath of fire. I see the fire race across the ground, fly into the trees until they burst from the heat. And the clearing's a holocaust even the devil himself couldn't survive."

He took a drink of wine. "That's what I see when it's whole again, so I'm in no big hurry to get there."

"Maybe that's how it was formed," Layla began.

"I don't see back. That's Cal's gig. I see what might be coming."

"That'd be handy in your profession."

Gage shifted his gaze back to Cybil, smiled slowly. "It doesn't hurt." He picked up his stone, tossed it lightly in his hand. "Anyone interested in a little five-card draw?"

As soon as he spoke, the light snapped off.

Rather than romance or charm, the flickering candles they'd lit as backup lent an eeriness to the room. "I'll go fire up the generator." Cal pushed up. "Water, refrigerator, and stove for now."

"Don't go out alone." Layla blinked as if surprised the words had come out of her mouth. "I mean—"

"I'm going with you."

As Fox rose, something howled in the dark.

"Lump." Cal was out of the room, through the kitchen, and out the back door like a bullet. He barely broke stride to grab the flashlight off the wall, punch it on.

He swept it toward the sound. The beam struggled against the thick, moving curtain of snow, did little but bounce the light back at him.

The blanket had become a wall that rose past his knees. Calling his dog, Cal pushed through it, trying to pinpoint the direction of the howling. It seemed to come from everywhere, from nowhere.

As he heard sounds behind him, he whirled, gripping the flashlight like a weapon.

"Don't clock the reinforcements," Fox shouted. "Christ,

it's insane out here." He gripped Cal's arm as Gage moved to Cal's other side. "Hey, Lump! Come on, Lump! I've never heard him like that."

"How do you know it's the dog?" Gage asked quietly.

"Get back inside," Cal said grimly. "We can't leave the women alone. I'm going to find my dog."

"Oh yeah, we'll just leave you out here, stumbling around in a fucking blizzard." Gage jammed his freezing hands in his pockets, glanced back. "Besides."

They came, arms linked and gripping flashlights. Which showed sense, Cal was forced to admit. And they'd taken the time to put on coats, probably boots as well, which is more than he or his friends had done.

"Go back in." He had to shout now, over the rising wind. "We're just going to round up Lump. Be right there."

"We all go in or nobody does." Quinn unhooked her arm from Layla's, hooked it to Cal's. "That includes Lump. Don't waste time," she said before he could argue. "We should spread out, shouldn't we?"

"In pairs. Fox, you and Layla try that way, Quinn and I'll take this way. Gage and Cybil toward the back. He's got to be close. He never goes far."

He sounded scared, that's what Cal didn't want to say out loud. His stupid, lazy dog sounded scared. "Hook your hand in my pants—the waistband. Keep a good hold."

He hissed against the cold as her gloves hit his skin, then began to trudge forward. He'd barely made it two feet when he heard something under the howls.

"You catch that?"

"Yes. Laughing. The way a nasty little boy might laugh."

"Go—"

"I'm not leaving that dog out here any more than you are."

A vicious gush of wind rose up like a tidal wave, spewing huge clumps of snow, and what felt like pellets of ice. Cal heard branches cracking, like gunfire in the dark. Behind him, Quinn lost her footing in the force of the wind and nearly took them both down.

He'd get Quinn back into the house, he decided. Get her the hell in, lock her in a damn closet if necessary, then come back out and find his dog.

Even as he turned to get a grip on her arm, he saw them.

His dog sat on his haunches, half buried in the snow, his head lifted as those long, desperate howls worked his throat.

The boy floated an inch above the surface of the snow. Chortling, Cal thought. There was a word you didn't use every day, but it sure as hell fit the filthy sound it made.

It grinned as the wind blasted again. Now Lump was buried to his shoulders.

"Get the fuck away from my dog."

Cal lurched forward; the wind knocked him back so that both he and Quinn went sprawling.

"Call him," Quinn shouted. "Call him, make him come!" She dragged off her gloves as she spoke. Using her fingers to form a circle between her lips, she whistled shrilly as Cal yelled at Lump.

Lump quivered; the thing laughed.

Cal continued to call, to curse now, to crawl while the snow flew into his eyes, numbed his hands. He heard shouting behind him, but he focused everything he had on pushing ahead, on getting there before the next gust of wind put the dog under.

He'd drown, Cal thought as he pushed, shoved, slid forward. If he didn't get to Lump, his dog would drown in that ocean of snow.

He felt a hand lock on his ankle, but kept dragging himself forward.

Gritting his teeth, he flailed out, got a slippery hold on Lump's collar. Braced, he looked up into eyes that glittered an unholy green rimmed with red. "You can't have him."

Cal yanked. Ignoring Lump's yelp, he yanked again, viciously, desperately. Though Lump howled, whimpered, it was as if his body was sunk in hardened cement.

And Quinn was beside him, belly down, digging at the snow with her hands.

Fox skidded down, shooting snow like shrapnel. Cal gathered everything he had, looked once more into those monstrous eyes in the face of a young boy. "I said you can't have him."

With the next pull, Cal's arms were full of quivering, whimpering dog.

"It's okay, it's okay." He pressed his face against cold, wet fur. "Let's get the hell out of here."

"Get him in by the fire." Layla struggled to help Quinn up as Cybil pushed up from her knees. Shoving the butt of a flashlight in his back pocket, Gage pulled Cybil to her feet, then plucked Quinn out of the snow.

"Can you walk?" he asked her.

"Yeah, yeah. Let's get in, let's get inside, before somebody ends up with frostbite."

Towels and blankets, dry clothes, hot coffee. Brandy—even for Lump—warmed chilled bones and numbed flesh. Fresh logs had the fire blazing.

"It was holding him. He couldn't get away." Cal sat on the floor, the dog's head in his lap. "He couldn't get away. It was going to bury him in the snow. A stupid, harmless dog."

"Has this happened before?" Quinn asked him. "Has it gone after animals this way?"

"A few weeks before the Seven, animals might drown, or there's more roadkill. Sometimes pets turn mean. But not like this. This was—"

"A demonstration." Cybil tucked the blanket more securely around Quinn's feet. "He wanted us to see what he could do."

"Maybe wanted to see what we could do," Gage countered, and earned a speculative glance from Cybil.

"That may be more accurate. That may be more to the point. Could we break the hold? A dog's not a person, has to be easier to control. No offense, Cal, but your dog's brainpower isn't as high as most toddlers'."

Gently, affectionately, Cal pulled on one of Lump's floppy ears. "He's thick as a brick."

"So it was showing off. It hurt this poor dog for sport." Layla knelt down and stroked Lump's side. "That deserves some payback."

Intrigued, Quinn cocked her head. "What do you have in mind?"

"I don't know yet, but it's something to think about."

Eighteen

CAL DIDN'T KNOW WHAT TIME THEY'D FALLEN into bed. But when he opened his eyes the thin winter light eked through the window. Through it, he saw the snow was still falling in the perfect, fat, white flakes of a Hollywood Christmas movie.

In the hush only a snowfall could create was steady and somehow satisfied snoring. It came from Lump, who was stretched over the foot of the bed like a canine blanket. That was something Cal generally discouraged, but right now, the sound, the weight, the warmth were exactly right.

From now on, he determined, the damn dog was going everywhere with him.

Because his foot and ankle were currently under the bulk of the dog, Cal shifted to pull free. The movement had Quinn stirring, giving a little sigh as she wiggled closer and managed to wedge her leg between his. She wore flannel, which shouldn't have been remotely sexy, and she'd managed to pin his arm during the night so it was now alive with needles and pins. And that should've been, at least mildly, annoying.

Instead, it was exactly right, too.

Since it was, since they were cuddled up together in bed with Hollywood snow falling outside the window, he couldn't think of a single reason not to take advantage of it.

Smiling, he slid a hand under her T-shirt, over warm, smooth flesh. When he cupped her breast he felt her heart beat under his palm, slow and steady as Lump's snoring. He stroked, a lazy play of fingertips as he watched her face. Lightly, gently, he teased her nipple, arousing himself as he imagined taking it into his mouth, sliding his tongue over her.

She sighed again.

He trailed his hand down, tracing those fingertips over her belly, under the flannel to skim down her thigh. Up again. Down, then up, a whispering touch that eased closer, closer to her center.

And the sound she made in sleep was soft and helpless.

She was wet when he brushed over her, hot when he dipped inside her. When he pressed, he lowered his mouth to hers to take her gasp.

She came as she woke, her body simply erupting as her mind leaped out of sleep and into shock and pleasure.

"Oh God!"

"Shh." He laughed against her lips. "You'll wake the dog."

He tugged down her pants as he rolled. Before she could clear her mind, he pinned her, and he filled her.

"Oh. Well. Jesus." The words hitched and shook. "Good morning."

He laughed again, and bracing himself, set a slow and torturous pace. She fought to match it, to hold back and take that slow climb with him, but it flashed through her again, and flung her up.

"God. God. God. I don't think I can—"

"Shh, shh," he repeated, and brought his mouth down to toy with hers. "I'll go slow," he whispered. "You just go."

She could do nothing else. Her system was already wrecked, her body already his. Utterly his. When he took her up again, she was too breathless to cry out.

THOROUGHLY PLEASURED, THOROUGHLY USED, Quinn lay under Cal's weight. He'd eased down so that his head rested between her breasts, and she could play with his hair. She imagined it was some faraway Sunday morning where they had nothing more pressing to worry about than if they'd make love again before breakfast, or make love after.

"Do you take some kind of special vitamin?" she wondered.

"Hmm?"

"I mean, you've got some pretty impressive stamina going for you."

She felt his lips curve against her. "Just clean living, Blondie."

"Maybe it's the bowling. Maybe bowling . . . Where's Lump?"

"He got embarrassed about halfway through the show." Cal turned his head, gestured. "Over there."

Quinn looked, saw the dog on the floor, his face wedged in the corner. She laughed till her sides ached. "We embarrassed the dog. That's a first for me. God! I feel good. How can I feel so good after last night?" Then she shook her head, stretched up her arms before wrapping them around Cal. "I guess that's the point, isn't it? Even in a world gone to hell, there's still this."

"Yeah." He sat up then, reached down to brush her tumbled hair as he studied her. "Quinn." He took her hand now, played with her fingers.

"Cal," she said, imitating his serious tone.

"You crawled through a blizzard to help save my dog."

"He's a good dog. Anyone would have done the same."

"No. You're not naive enough to think that. Fox and Gage, yeah. For the dog, and for me. Layla and Cybil, maybe. Maybe it was being caught in the moment, or maybe they're built that way."

She touched his face, skimmed her fingers under those patient gray eyes. "No one was going to leave that dog out there, Cal."

"Then I'd say that dog is pretty lucky to have people like you around. So am I. You crawled through the snow, toward that thing. You dug in the snow with your bare hands."

"If you're trying to make a hero out of me . . . Go ahead," she decided. "I think I like the fit."

"You whistled with your fingers."

Now she grinned. "Just a little something I picked up along the way. I can actually whistle a lot louder than that, when I'm not out of breath, freezing, and quivering with terror."

"I love you."

"I'll demonstrate sometime when . . . What?"

"I never thought to say those words to any woman I wasn't related to. I was just never going to go there."

If she'd been given a hard, direct jolt of electricity to her heart, it couldn't have leaped any higher. "Would you mind saying them again, while I'm paying better attention?"

"I love you."

There it went again, she thought. Leaps and bounds. "Because I can whistle with my fingers?"

"That might've been the money shot."

"God." She shut her eyes. "I want you to love me, and I really like to get what I want. But." She took a breath. "Cal, if this is because of last night, because I helped get Lump, then—"

"This is because you think if you eat half my slice of pizza it doesn't count."

"Well, it doesn't, technically."

"Because you always know where your keys are, and you can think about ten things at the same time. Because you don't back down, and your hair's like sunlight. Because you tell the truth and you know how to be a friend. And for dozens of reasons I haven't figured out yet. Dozens more I may never figure out. But I know I can say to you what I never thought to say to anyone."

She hooked her arms around his neck, rested her forehead on his. She had to just breathe for a moment, just breathe her way through the beauty of it as she often did with a great work of art or a song that brought tears to her throat.

"This is a really good day." She touched her lips to his. "This is a truly excellent day."

They sat for a while, holding each other while the dog snored in the corner, and the snow fell outside the windows.

When Cal went downstairs, he followed the scent of coffee into the kitchen, and found Gage scowling as he slapped a skillet onto the stove. They grunted at each other as Cal got a clean mug out of the dishwasher.

"Looks like close to three out there already, and it's still coming."

"I got eyes." Gage ripped open a pound of bacon. "You sound chipper about it."

"It's a really good day."

"I'd probably think so, too, if I started it off with some morning nookie."

"God, men are crude." Cybil strolled in, her dark eyes bleary.

"Then you ought to plug your ears when you're around our kind. Bacon gets fried, eggs get scrambled," Gage told them. "Anybody doesn't like the options should try another restaurant."

Cybil poured her coffee, stood studying him over the rim as she took the first sip. He hadn't shaved or combed that dark mass of hair. He was obviously morning irritable, and none of that, she mused, made him any less attractive.

Too bad.

"You know what I've noticed about you, Gage?"

"What's that?"

"You've got a great ass, and a crappy attitude. Let me

know when breakfast is ready," she added as she strolled out of the kitchen.

"She's right. I've often said that about your ass and attitude."

"Phones are out," Fox announced as he came in, yanked open the refrigerator and pounced on a Coke. "Got ahold of my mother by cell. They're okay over there."

"Knowing your parents, they probably just had sex," Gage commented.

"Hey! True," Fox said after a moment, "but, hey."

"He's got sex on the brain."

"Why wouldn't he? He's not sick or watching sports, the only two circumstances men don't necessarily have sex on the brain."

Gage laid bacon in the heated skillet. "Somebody make some toast or something. And we're going to need another pot of coffee."

"I've got to take Lump out. I'm not just letting him out on his own."

"I'll take him." Fox leaned down to scratch Lump's head. "I want to walk around anyway." He turned, nearly walked into Layla. "Hi, sorry. Ah . . . I'm going to take Lump out. Why don't you come along?"

"Oh. I guess. Sure. I'll just get my things."

"Smooth," Gage commented when Layla left. "You're a smooth one, Fox."

"What?"

"Good morning, really attractive woman. How would you like to trudge around with me in three feet of snow and watch a dog piss on a few trees? Before you've even had your coffee?"

"It was just a suggestion. She could've said no."

"I'm sure she would have if she'd had a hit of caffeine so her brain was in gear."

"That must be why you only get lucky with women without brains."

"You're just spreading sunshine," Cal commented when Fox steamed out.

"Make another damn pot of coffee."

"I need to bring in some wood, feed the generator, and start shoveling three feet of snow off the decks. Let me know when breakfast is ready."

Alone, Gage snarled, and turned the bacon. He still had the snarl when Quinn came in.

"I thought I'd find everyone in here, but they're all scattered." She got out a mug. "Looks like we need another pot of coffee."

Because she got the coffee down, Gage didn't have time to snap at her.

"I'll take care of that. Anything else I can do to help?"

He turned his head to look at her. "Why?"

"Because I figure if I help you with breakfast, it takes us both off the cooking rotation for the next couple of meals."

He nodded, appreciating the logic. "Smart. You're the toast and additional coffee."

"Check."

He beat a dozen eggs while she got to work. She had a quick, efficient way about her, Gage noted. The quick wouldn't matter so much to Cal, but the efficient would be a serious plus. She was built, she was bright, and as he'd seen for himself last night, she had a wide streak of brave.

"You're making him happy."

Quinn stopped, looked over. "Good, because he's making me happy."

"One thing, if you haven't figured it out by now. He's rooted here. This is his place. Whatever happens, the Hollow's always going to be Cal's place."

"I figured that out." She plucked toast when it popped, dropped more bread in. "All things considered, it's a nice town."

"All things considered," Gage agreed, then poured the eggs into the second skillet.

OUTSIDE, AS GAGE PREDICTED, FOX WATCHED Lump piss on trees. More entertaining, he supposed, had been watching the dog wade, trudge, and occasionally leap through the waist-high snow. It was the waist-high factor that had Fox and Layla stopping on the front deck, and Fox going to work with the shovel Cal had shoved into his hands on their way out.

Still, it was great to be out in the snow globe of the morning, tossing the white stuff around while more of it pumped out of the sky.

"Maybe I should go down, knock the snow off some of Cal's shrubs."

Fox glanced over at her. She had a ski cap pulled over her head, a scarf wrapped around her neck. Both had already picked up a layer of white. "You'll sink, then we'll be tossing you a lifeline to get you back. We'll dig out a path eventually."

"He doesn't seem to be spooked." She kept an eagle eye on Lump. "I thought, after last night, he'd be skittish about going out."

"Short-term doggie memory. Probably for the best."

"I won't forget it."

"No." He shouldn't have asked her to come out, Fox realized. Especially since he couldn't quite figure out how to broach the whole job deal, which had been part of the idea for having her tag along.

He was usually better at this stuff, dealing with people. Dealing with women. Now, he worked on carving down a shovel-width path across the deck to the steps, and just jumped in.

"So, Cal said you're looking for a job."

"Not exactly. I mean I'm going to have to find some work, but I haven't been looking."

"My secretary—office manager—assistant." He dumped snow, dug the shovel back down. "We never settled on a title, now that I think about it. Anyway, she's moving to Minneapolis. I need somebody to do the stuff she does."

Damn Quinn, she thought. "The stuff."

It occurred to Fox that he was considered fairly articulate in court. "Filing, billing, answering phones, keeping the calendar, rescheduling when necessary, handling clients, typing documents and correspondence. She's a notary, too, but that's not a necessity right off."

"What software does she use?"

"I don't know. I'd have to ask her." Did she use any software? How was he supposed to know?

"I don't know anything about secretarial work, or office management. I don't know anything about the law."

Fox knew tones, and hers was defensive. He kept shoveling. "Do you know the alphabet?"

"Of course I know the alphabet, but the point—"

"Would be," he interrupted, "if you know the alphabet you can probably figure out how to file. And you know how to use a phone, which means you can answer one and make calls from one. Those would be essential job skills for this position. Can you use a keyboard?"

"Yes, but it depends on—"

"She can show you whatever the hell she does in that area."

"It doesn't sound as if you know a lot about what she does."

He also knew disapproval when he heard it. "Okay." He straightened, leaned on the shovel, and looked dead into her eyes. "She's been with me since I set up. I'm going to miss her like I'd miss my arm. But people move on, and the rest of us have to deal. I need somebody to put papers where they belong and find them when I need to have them, to send out bills so I can pay mine, to tell me when I'm due in court, to answer the phone we hope rings so I'll have somebody to bill, and basically maintain some kind of order so I can practice law. You need a job and a paycheck. I think we could help each other out."

"Cal asked you to offer me a job because Quinn asked him to ask you."

"That would be right. Doesn't change the bottom line."

No, it didn't, she supposed. But it still griped. "It wouldn't be permanent. I'm only looking for something to fill in until . . ."

"You move on." Fox nodded. "Works for me. That way, neither of us are stuck. We're just helping each other out for a while." He shoveled off two more blades of snow, then stopped just to lean on it with his eyes on hers.

"Besides, you knew I was going to offer you the job because you pick up that sort of thing."

"Quinn asked Cal to ask you to offer it to me right in front of me."

"You pick up on that sort of thing," he repeated. "That's your part in this, or part of your part. You get a sense of people, of situations."

"I'm not psychic, if that's what you're saying." The defensive was back in her tone.

"You drove to the Hollow, when you'd never been here before. You knew where to go, what roads to take."

"I don't know what that was." She crossed her arms, and the move wasn't just defensive, Fox thought. It was stubborn.

"Sure you do, it just freaks you. You took off with Quinn that first night, went with her, a woman you'd never met."

"She was a sane alternative to a big, evil slug," Layla said dryly.

"You didn't just run, didn't haul ass to your room and lock the door. You got in her car with her, came with her out here—where you'd also never been, and walked into a house with two strange men in it."

"*Strange* might be the operative word. I was scared, confused, and running on adrenaline." She looked away from him, toward where Lump was rolling in the snow as if it were a meadow of daisies. "I trusted my instincts."

"Instincts is one word for it. I bet when you were working in that clothes shop you had really good instincts about what your customers wanted, what they'd buy. Bet you're damn good at that."

He went back to shoveling when she said nothing. "Bet you've always been good at that sort of thing. Quinn gets flashes from the past, like Cal. Apparently Cybil gets them of possible future events. I'd say you're stuck with me, Layla, in the now."

"I can't read minds, and I don't want anyone reading mine."

"It's not like that, exactly." He was going to have to work with her, he decided. Help her figure out what she had and how to use it. And he was going to have to give her some time and some space to get used to the idea.

"Anyway, we're probably going to be snowed in here for the weekend. I've got stuff next week, but when we can get back to town, you could come in when it suits you, let Mrs. H show you the ropes. We'll see how you feel about the job then."

"Look, I'm grateful you'd offer—"

"No, you're not." Now he smiled and tossed another shovel of snow off the deck. "Not so much. I've got instincts, too."

It wasn't just humor, but understanding. The stiffness went out of her as she kicked at the snow. "There's gratitude, it's just buried under the annoyance."

Cocking his head, he held out the shovel. "Want to dig it out?"

And she laughed. "Let's try this. If I do come in, and do decide to take the job, it's with the stipulation that if either of us decides it's not working, we just say so. No hard feelings."

"That's a deal." He held out a hand, took hers to seal it. Then just held it while the snow swirled around them.

She had to feel it, he thought, had to feel that immediate and tangible link. That recognition.

Cybil cracked the door an inch. "Breakfast is ready."

Fox released Layla's hand, turned. He let out a quiet breath before calling the dog home.

PRACTICAL MATTERS HAD TO BE SEEN TO. SNOW needed to be shoveled, firewood hauled and stacked. Dishes had to be washed and food prepared. Cal might have felt like the house, which had always seemed roomy, grew increasingly tight with six people and one dog stuck inside it. But he knew they were safer together.

"Not just safer." Quinn took her turn plying the shovel. She considered digging out a path to Cal's storage shed solid exercise in lieu of a formal workout. "I think all this is meant. This enforced community. It's giving us time to get used to each other, to learn how to function as a group."

"Here, let me take over there." Cal set aside the gas can he'd used to top off the generator.

"No, see, that's not working as a group. You guys have to learn to trust the females to carry their load. Gage being drafted to make breakfast today is an example of the basics in non-gender-specific teamwork."

Non-gender-specific teamwork, he thought. How could he not love a woman who'd use a term like that?

"We can all cook," she went on. "We can all shovel snow, haul firewood, make beds. We can all do what we have to do—play to our strengths, okay, but so far it's pretty much been like a middle school dance."

"How?"

"Boys on one side, girls on the other, and nobody quite sure how to get everyone together. Now we are." She stopped, rolled her shoulders. "And we have to figure it out. Even with us, Cal, even with how we feel about each other, we're still figuring each other out, learning how to trust each other."

"If this is about the stone, I understand you might bc annoyed I didn't tell you sooner."

"No, I'm really not." She shoveled a bit more, but it was mostly for form now. Her arms were *killing* her. "I started to be, even wanted to be, but I couldn't stir it up. Because I get that the three of you have been a unit all your lives. I don't imagine you remember a time when you weren't. Added to that you went through together—I don't think it's an exaggeration to say an earth-shattering experience. The three of you are like a . . . a body with three heads isn't right," she said and passed off the shovel.

"We're not the damn Borg."

"No, but that's closer. You're a fist, tight, even closed off to a certain extent, but—" She wiggled her gloved fingers. "Individual. You work together, it's instinctive. And now." She held up her other hand. "This other part comes along. So we're figuring out how to make them mesh." She brought her hands together, fingers linked.

"That actually makes sense." And brought on a slight twinge of guilt. "I've been doing a little digging on my own."

"You don't mean in the snow. And on your own equals you've told Fox and Gage."

"I probably mentioned it. We don't know where Ann Hawkins was for a couple of years, where she gave birth to her sons, where she stayed before she came back to the Hollow—to her parents' house. So I was thinking about extended family. Cousins, aunts, uncles. And figuring a woman that pregnant might not be able to travel very far, not back then. So maybe she'd have been in the general area. Ten, twenty miles in the sixteen hundreds was a hell of a lot farther than ten or twenty miles is today."

"That's a good idea. I should have had it."

"And I should've brought it up before."

"Yeah. Now that you have, you should give it to Cyb, give her whatever information you have. She's the research queen. I'm good, she's better."

"And I'm a rank amateur."

"Nothing rank about you." Grinning, she took a leap, bounced up into his arms. The momentum had him skidding. She squealed, as much with laughter as alarm as he tipped backward. He flopped; she landed face-first.

Breathless, she dug in, got two handfuls of snow to mash into his face before she tried to roll away. He caught her at the waist, dragged her back while she screamed with helpless laughter.

"I'm a champion snow wrestler," he warned her. "You're out of your league, Blondie. So—"

She managed to get a hand between his legs for a nice,

firm stroke. Then taking advantage of the sudden and dramatic dip of his IQ, shoved a messy ball of snow down the back of his neck.

"Those moves are against the rules of the SWF."

"Check the book, buddy. This is intergender play."

She tried to scramble up, fell, then whooshed out a breath when his weight pinned her. "And still champion," he announced, and was about to lower his mouth to hers when the door opened.

"Kids," Cybil told them, "there's a nice warm bed upstairs if you want to play. And FYI? The power just came back on." She glanced back over her shoulder. "Apparently the phones are up, too."

"Phones, electricity. Computer." Quinn wiggled out from under Cal. "I have to check my e-mail."

CYBIL LEANED ON THE DRYER AS LAYLA LOADED towels into the washing machine in Cal's laundry room. "They looked like a couple of horny snow people. Covered, crusted, pink-cheeked, and groping."

"Young love is immune to climatic conditions."

Cybil chuckled. "You know, you don't have to take on the laundry detail."

"Clean towels are a memory at this point, and the power may not stay on. Besides, I'd rather be warm and dry in here washing towels than cold and wet out there shoveling snow." She tossed back her hair. "Especially since no one's groping me."

"Good point. But I was bringing that up as, by my calculations, you and Fox are going to have to flip for cooking detail tonight."

"Quinn hasn't cooked yet, or Cal."

"Quinn helped with breakfast. It's Cal's house."

Defeated, Layla stared at the machine. "Hell. I'll take dinner."

"You can dump it on Fox, using laundry detail as leverage."

"No, we don't know if he can cook, and I can."

Cybil narrowed her eyes. "You can cook? This hasn't been mentioned before."

"If I'd mentioned it, I'd have had to cook."

Lips pursed, Cybil nodded slowly. "Diabolical and self-serving logic. I like it."

"I'll check the supplies, see what I can come up with. Something—" She broke off, stepped forward. "Quinn? What is it?"

"We have to talk. All of us." So pale her eyes looked bruised, Quinn stood in the doorway.

"Q? Honey." Cybil reached out in support. "What's happened?" She remembered Quinn's dash to the computer for e-mail. "Is everyone all right? Your parents?"

"Yes. Yes. I want to tell it all at once, to everyone. We need to get everyone."

She sat in the living room with Cybil perched on the arm of her chair for comfort. Quinn wanted to curl up in Cal's lap as she'd done once before. But it seemed wrong.

It all seemed wrong now.

She wished the power had stayed off forever. She wished she hadn't contacted her grandmother and prodded her into seeking out family history.

She didn't want to know what she knew now.

No going back, she reminded herself. And what she had to say could change everything that was to come.

She glanced at Cal. She knew she had him worried. It wasn't fair to drag it out. How would he look at her afterward? she wondered.

Yank off the bandage, Quinn told herself, and get it over with.

"My grandmother got the information I'd asked her about. Pages from the family Bible. There were even some records put together by a family historian in the late eighteen hundreds. I, ah, have some information on the Clark branch, Layla, that may help you. No one ever pursued that end very far, but you may be able to track back, or out from what I have now."

"Okay."

"The thing is, it looks like the family was, we'll say, pretty religious about their own tracking back. My grandfather, not so much, but his sister, a couple of cousins, they were more into it. They, apparently, get a lot of play out of the fact their ancestors were among the early Pilgrims who settled in the New World. So there isn't just the Bible, and the pages added to that over time. They've had genealogies done tracing roots back to England and Ireland in the fifteen hundreds. But what applies to us, to this, is the branch that came over here. Here to Hawkins Hollow," she said to Cal.

She braced herself. "Sebastian Deale brought his wife and three daughters to the settlement here in sixteen fifty-one. His eldest daughter's name was Hester. Hester Deale."

"Hester's Pool," Fox murmured. "She's yours."

"That's right. Hester Deale, who according to town lore denounced Giles Dent as a witch on the night of July seventh, sixteen fifty-two. Who eight months later delivered a daughter, and when that daughter was two weeks old, drowned herself in the pond in Hawkins Wood. There's no father documented, nothing on record. But we know who fathered her child. We know what fathered her child."

"We can't be sure of that."

"We know it, Caleb." However much it tore inside her, Quinn knew it. "We've seen it, you and I. And Layla, Layla experienced it. He raped her. She was barely sixteen. He lured her, he overpowered her—mind and body, and he got her with child. One that carried his blood." To keep them still, Quinn gripped her hands together. "A half-demon child. She couldn't live with it, with what had been done to her, with what she'd brought into the world. So she filled her pockets with stones and went into the water to drown."

"What happened to her daughter?" Layla asked.

"She died at twenty, after having two daughters of her own. One of them died before her third birthday, the other went on to marry a man named Duncan Clark. They had three sons and a daughter. Both she, her husband, and her youngest son were killed when their house burned down. The other children escaped."

"Duncan Clark must be where I come in," Layla said.

"And somewhere along the line, one of them hooked up with a gypsy from the Old World," Cybil finished. "Hardly seems fair. They get to descend from a heroic white witch, and we get the demon seed."

"It's not a joke," Quinn snapped.

"No, and it's not a tragedy. It just is."

"Damn it, Cybil, don't you see what this means? That *thing* out there is my—probably our—great-grandfather times a dozen generations. It means we're carrying some part of that in us."

"And if I start to sprout horns and a tail in the next few weeks, I'm going to be very pissed off."

"Oh, fuck that!" Quinn pushed up, rounded on her friend. "Fuck the Cybilese. He raped that girl to get to us, three and a half centuries ago, but what he planted led to this. What if we're not here to stop it, not here to help this end? What if we're here to see that it doesn't stop? To play some part in hurting them?"

"If your brain wasn't mushy with love you'd see that's a bullshit theory. Panic reaction with a heavy dose of self-pity to spice it up." Cybil's voice was brutally cool. "We're not under some demon's thumb. We're not going to suddenly jump sides and put on the uniform of some *dark entity* who tries to kill a dog to get his rocks off. We're exactly who we were five minutes ago, so stop being stupid, and pull yourself together."

"She's right. Not about being stupid," Layla qualified. "But about being who we are. If all this is part of it, then we have to find a way to use it."

"Fine. I'll practice getting my head to do three-sixties."

"Lame," Cybil decided. "You'd do better with the sarcasm, Q, if you weren't so worried Cal's going to dump you because of the big *D* for demon on your forehead."

"Cut it out," Layla commanded, and Cybil only shrugged.

"If he does," Cybil continued equably, "he's not worth your time anyway."

In the sudden, thundering silence a log fell in the grate and shot sparks.

"Did you print out the attachment?" Cal asked.

"No, I . . ." Quinn trailed off, shook her head.

"Let's go do that now, then we can take a look." He rose, put a hand on Quinn's arm, and drew her from the room.

"Nice job," Gage commented to Cybil. Before she could snarl, he angled his head. "That wasn't sarcasm. It was either literally or verbally give her a slap across the face. Verbally's trickier, but a lot less messy."

"Both are painful." Cybil pushed to her feet. "If he hurts her, I'll twist off his dick and feed it to his dog." With that, she stormed out of the room.

"She's a little scary," Fox decided.

"She's not the only one. I'm the one who'll be roasting his balls for dessert." Layla headed out behind Cybil. "I have to find something to make for dinner."

"Oddly, I don't have much of an appetite right now." Fox glanced at Gage. "How about you?"

Upstairs, Cal waited until they'd stepped into the office currently serving as the men's dorm. He pushed Quinn's back to the door. The first kiss was hard, with sharp edges of anger. The second frustrated. And the last soft.

"Whatever's in your head about you and me, because of this, get it out. Now. Understand?"

"Cal—"

"It's taken me my whole life to say what I said to you this morning. I love you. This doesn't change that. So pitch that out, Quinn, or you're going to piss me off."

"It wasn't—that isn't . . ." She closed her eyes as a storm of emotions blew through her. "All right, that was in there, part of it, but it's all of it, the whole. When I read the file she sent, it just . . ."

"It kicked your feet out from under you. I get that. But you know what? I'm right here to help you up." He lifted a hand, made a fist, then opened it.

Understanding, she fought back tears. Understanding, she put her palm to his, interlaced fingers.

"Okay?"

"Not okay," she corrected. "Thank God about covers it."

"Let's print it out, see what we've got."

"Yeah." Steadier, she glanced at the room. The messy, unmade pullout, the piles of clothes. "Your friends are slobs."

"Yes. Yes, they are."

Together, they picked their way through the mess to the computer.

Nineteen

IN THE DINING ROOM, QUINN SET COPIES OF THE printouts in front of everyone. There were bowls of popcorn on the table, she noted, a bottle of wine, glasses, and paper towels folded into triangles. Which would all be Cybil's doing, she knew.

Just as she knew Cybil had made the popcorn for her. Not a peace offering; they didn't need peace offerings between them. It was just because.

She touched a hand to Cybil's shoulder before she took her seat.

"Apologies for big drama," Quinn began.

"If you think that was drama, you need to come over to my parents' house during one of the family gatherings." Fox gave her a smile as he took a handful of popcorn. "The Barry-O'Dells don't need demon blood to raise hell."

"We'll all accept the demon thing is going to be a running gag from now on." Quinn poured a glass of wine. "I don't know how much all this will tell everyone, but it's more than we had before. It shows a direct line from the other side."

"Are you sure Twisse is the one who raped Hester Deale?" Gage asked. "Certain he's the one who knocked her up?"

Quinn nodded. "Believe me."

"I experienced it." Layla twisted the paper towel in her hands as she spoke. "It wasn't like the flashes Cal and Quinn get, but . . . Maybe the blood tie explains it. I don't know. But I know what he did to her. And I know she was a virgin before he—it—raped her."

Gently, Fox took the pieces of the paper towel she'd torn, gave her his.

"Okay," Gage continued, "are we sure Twisse is what we're calling the demon for lack of better?"

"He never liked that term," Cal put in. "I think we can go affirmative on that."

"So, Twisse uses Hester to sire a child, to extend his line. If he's been around as long as we think—going off some of the stuff Cal's seen and related, it's likely he'd done the same before."

"Right," Cybil acknowledged. "Maybe that's where we get people like Hitler or Osama bin Laden, Jack the Ripper, child abusers, serial killers."

"If you look at the lineage, you'll see there were a lot of suicides and violent deaths, especially in the first hundred, hundred and twenty years after Hester. I think," Quinn said slowly, "if we're able to dig a little deeper on individuals, we might find more than the average family share of murder, insanity."

"Anything that stands out in recent memory?" Fox asked. "Major family skeletons?"

"Not that I know of. I have the usual share of kooky or annoying relatives, but nobody's been incarcerated or institutionalized."

"It dilutes." Fox narrowed his eyes as he paged through the printouts. "This wasn't his plan, wasn't his strategy. I know strategy. Consider. Twisse doesn't know what Dent's got cooking that night. He's got Hester—got her mind under control, got the demon bun in the oven, but he doesn't know that's going to be it."

"That Dent's ready for him, and has his own plans," Layla continued. "I see where you're going. He thought—planned—to destroy Dent that night, or at least damage him, drive him away."

"Then he gets the town," Fox continued, "uses it up, moves on. Leaves progeny, before he finds the next spot that suits him to do the same."

"Instead Dent takes him down, holds him down until . . ." Cal turned over his hand, exposed the thin scar on his wrist. "Until Dent's progeny let him out. Why would he want that? Why would he allow it?"

"Could be Dent figured keeping a demon in a headlock for three centuries was long enough." Gage helped himself to popcorn. "Or that's as long as he could hold him, and he called out some reinforcements."

"Ten-year-old boys," Cal said in disgust.

"Children are more likely to believe, to accept what adults can't. Or won't," Cybil added. "And hell, nobody said any of this was fair. He gave you what he could. Your ability to heal quickly, your insights into what was, is, will be. He gave you the stone, in three parts."

"And time to grow up," Layla added. "Twenty-one years. Maybe he found the way to bring us here. Quinn, Cybil, and me. Because I can't see the logic, the purpose of having me compelled to come here, then trying to scare me away."

"Good point." And it loosened something inside Quinn's belly. "That's a damn good point. Why scare if he could seduce? Really good point."

"I can look deeper into the family tree for you, Q. And I'll see what I can find on Layla's and my own. But that's just busywork at this point. We know the root."

Cybil turned one of the pages over, used a pencil on the back. She drew two horizontal lines at the bottom. "Giles Dent and Ann Hawkins here, Lazarus Twisse and the doomed Hester here. Each root sends up a tree, and the trees their branches." She drew quickly, simply. "And at the right point, branches from each tree cross each other. In palmistry the crossing of lines is a sign of power."

She completed the sketch, three branches, crossing three branches. "So we have to find the power, and use it."

THAT EVENING, LAYLA DID SOMETHING FAIRLY tasty with chicken breasts, stewed tomatoes, and white beans. By mutual agreement they channeled the conversation into other areas. Normal, Quinn thought as it ranged from dissecting recent movies to bad jokes to travel. They all needed a good dose of normal.

"Gage is the one with itchy feet," Cal commented. "He's been traveling that long, lonesome highway since he hit eighteen."

"It's not always lonesome."

"Cal said you were in Prague." Quinn considered. "I think I'd like to see Prague."

"I thought it was Budapest."

Gage glanced at Cybil. "There, too. Prague was the last stop before heading back."

"Is it fabulous?" Layla wondered. "The art, the architecture, the food?"

"It's got all that. The palace, the river, the opera. I got a taste of it, but mostly I was working. Flew in from Budapest for a poker game."

"You spent your time in—what do they call it—the Paris of Eastern Europe playing poker?" Quinn demanded.

"Not all of it, just the lion's share. The game went for just over seventy-three hours."

"Three days, playing poker?" Cybil's eyebrow winged up. "Wouldn't that be a little obsessive?"

"Depends on where you stand, doesn't it?"

"But don't you need to sleep, eat? Pee?" Layla wondered.

"Breaks are worked in. The seventy-three hours was

actual game time. This was a private game, private home. Serious money, serious security."

"Win or lose?" Quinn asked him with a grin.

"I did okay."

"Do you use your precognition to help you do okay?" Cybil asked.

"That would be cheating."

"Yes, it would, but that didn't answer the question."

He picked up his wine, kept his eyes on hers. "If I had to cheat to win at poker, I should be selling insurance. I don't have to cheat."

"We took an oath." Fox held up his hands when Gage scowled at him. "We're in this together now. They should understand how it works for us. We took an oath when we realized we all had something extra. We wouldn't use it against anyone, or to hurt anyone, or, well, to screw anyone. We don't break our word to each other."

"In that case," Cybil said to Gage, "you ought to be playing the ponies instead of cards."

He flashed a grin. "Been known to, but I like cards. Wanna play?"

"Maybe later."

When Cybil glanced at Quinn with a look of apology, Quinn knew what was coming. "I guess we should get back to it," Cybil began. "I have a question, a place I'd like to start."

"Let's take fifteen." Quinn pushed to her feet. "Get the table cleared off, take the dog out. Just move a little. Fifteen."

Cal brushed a hand over her arm as he rose with her. "I need to check the fire anyway, probably bring in more wood. Let's do this in the living room when we're finished up."

THEY LOOKED LIKE ORDINARY PEOPLE, CAL thought. Just a group of friends hanging out on a winter night. Gage had switched to coffee, and that was usual. Cal hadn't known Gage to indulge in more than a couple drinks at a time since the summer they'd been seventeen. Fox was back on Coke, and he himself had opted for water.

Clear heads, he mused. They wanted clear heads if there were questions to be answered.

They'd gone back to gender groups. Had that been automatic, even intrinsic? he wondered. The three women on the couch, Fox on the floor with Lump. He'd taken a chair, and Gage stood by the fire as if he might just walk out if the topic didn't suit his mood.

"So." Cybil tucked her legs under her, let her dark eyes scan the room. "I'm wondering what was the first thing, event, instance, the first happening, we'll say, that alerted you something was wrong in town. After your night in the clearing, after you went home."

"Mr. Guthrie and the fork." Fox stretched out, propped his head on Lump's belly. "That was a big clue."

"Sounds like the title of a kid's book." Quinn made a note on her pad. "Why don't you fill us in?"

"You take it, Cal," Fox suggested.

"It would've been our birthday—the night, or really the evening of it. We were all pretty spooked. It was worse being separated, each of us in our own place. I talked my mother into letting me go in to the bowling center, so I'd have something to do, and Gage would be there. She couldn't figure out whether to ground me or not," he said with a half smile. "First and last time I remember her being undecided on that kind of issue. So she let me go in with my father. Gage?"

"I was working. Mr. Hawkins let me earn some spending money at the center, mopping up spills or carrying grill orders out to tables. I know I felt a hell of a lot better when Cal came in. Then Fox."

"I nagged my parents brainless to let me go in. My father finally caved, took me. I think he wanted to have a confab with Cal's dad, and Gage's if he could."

"So, Brian—Mr. O'Dell—and my dad sat down at the

end of the counter, having coffee. They didn't bring Bill, Gage's father, into it at that point."

"Because he didn't know I'd been gone in the first place," Gage said. "No point getting me in trouble until they'd decided what to do."

"Where was your father?" Cybil asked.

"Around. Behind the pins. He was having a few sober hours, so Mr. Hawkins had him working on something."

"Ball return, lane two," Cal murmured. "I remember. It seemed like an ordinary summer night. Teenagers, some college types on the pinballs and video games. Grill smoking, pins crashing. There was a kid—two or three years old, I guess—with a family in the four lane. Major tantrum. The mother hauled him outside right before it happened."

He took a swig of water. He could see it, bell clear. "Mr. Guthrie was at the counter, drinking a beer, eating a dog and fries. He came in once a week. Nice enough guy. Sold flooring, had a couple of kids in high school. Once a week, he came in when his wife went to the movies with girlfriends. It was clockwork. And Mr. Guthrie would order a dog and fries, and get steadily trashed. My dad used to say he did his drinking there because he could tell himself it wasn't real drinking if he wasn't in a bar."

"Troublemaker?" Quinn asked as she made another note.

"Anything but. He was what my dad called an affable drunk. He never got mean, or even sloppy. Tuesday nights, Mr. Guthrie came in, got a dog and fries, drank four or five beers, watched some games, talked to whoever was around. Somewhere around eleven, he'd leave a five-dollar tip on the grill and walk home. Far as I know he didn't so much as crack a Bud otherwise. It was a Tuesday night deal."

"He used to buy eggs from us," Fox remembered. "A dozen brown eggs, every Saturday morning. Anyway."

"It was nearly ten, and Mr. Guthrie was having another beer. He was walking by the tables with it," Cal said.

"Probably going to take it and stand behind the lanes, watch some of the action. Some guys were having burgers. Frank Dibbs was one of them—held his league's record for high game, coached Little League. We were sitting at the next table, eating pizza. Dad told us to take a break, so we were splitting a pizza. Dibbs said, 'Hey, Guth, the wife wants new vinyl in the kitchen. What kind of deal can you give me?'

"And Guthrie, he just smiles. One of those tight-lipped smiles that don't show any teeth. He picks up one of the forks sitting on the table. He jammed it into Dibbs's cheek, just stabbed it into his face, and kept walking. People are screaming and running, and, Christ, that fork is just sticking out of Mr. Dibbs's cheek, and blood's sliding down his face. And Mr. Guthrie strolls over behind lane two, and drinks his beer."

To give himself a moment, Cal took a long drink. "My dad wanted us out. Everything was going crazy, except Guthrie, who apparently *was* crazy. Your dad took care of Dibbs," Cal said to Fox. "I remember how he kept his head. Dibbs had already yanked the fork out, and your father grabbed this stack of napkins and got the bleeding stopped. There was blood on his hands when he drove us home."

Cal shook his head. "Not the point. Fox's dad took us home. Gage came with me—my father took care of that. He didn't get home until it was light out. I heard him come home; my mother had waited for him. I heard him tell her they had Guthrie locked up, and he was just sitting in his cell laughing. Laughing like it was all a big joke. Later, when it was all over, he didn't even remember. Nobody remembered much of what went on that week, or if they did, they put it away. He never came in the center again. They moved away the next winter."

"Was that the only thing that happened that night?" Cybil asked after a moment.

"Girl was raped." Gage set his empty mug on the mantel. "Making out with her boyfriend out on Dog Street. He didn't stop when she said stop, didn't stop when she started to cry, to scream. He raped her in the backseat of his secondhand Buick, then shoved her out on the side of the road and drove off. Wrapped his car around a tree a couple hours later. Ended up in the same hospital as she did. Only he didn't make it."

"Family mutt attacked an eight-year-old boy," Fox added. "Middle of that night. The dog had slept with the kid every night for three years. The parents woke up hearing the kid screaming, and when they got to the bedroom, the dog went for them, too. The father had to beat it off with the kid's baseball bat."

"It just got worse from there. That night, the next night." Cal took a long breath. "Then it didn't always wait for night. Not always."

"There's a pattern to it." Quinn spoke quietly, then glanced up when Cal's voice cut through her thoughts.

"Where? Other than ordinary people turn violent or psychotic?"

"We saw what happened with Lump. You've just told us about another family pet. There have been other incidents like that. Now you've said the first overt incident all of you witnessed involved a man who'd had several beers. His alcohol level was probably over the legal limit, meaning he was impaired. Mind's not sharp after drinking like that. You're more susceptible."

"So Guthrie was easier to influence or infect because he was drunk or well on the way?" Fox pushed up to sitting. "That's good. That makes good sense."

"The boy who raped his girlfriend of three months then drove into a tree hadn't been drinking." Gage shook his head. "Where's that in the pattern?"

"Sexual arousal and frustration tend to impair the brain." Quinn tapped her pencil on her pad. "Put those into a teenage boy, and that says susceptible to me."

"It's a valid point." Cal shoved his hand through his hair. Why hadn't they seen it themselves? "The dead crows. There were a couple dozen dead crows all over Main Street the morning of our birthday that year. Some broken windows where they'd repeatedly flown into the glass. We always figured that was part of it. But nobody got hurt."

"Does it always start that way?" Layla asked. "Can you pinpoint it?"

"The first I remember from the next time was when the Myerses found their neighbor's dog drowned in a backyard swimming pool. There was the woman who left her kid locked in the car and went into the beauty salon, got a manicure and so on. It was in the nineties that day," Fox added. "Somebody heard the kid crying, called the cops. They got the kid out, but when they went in to get the woman, she said she didn't have a baby. Didn't know what they were talking about. It came out she'd been up two nights running because the baby had colic."

"Sleep deprivation." Quinn wrote it down.

"But we knew it was happening again," Cal said slowly, "we knew for sure on the night of our seventeenth when Lisa Hodges walked out of the bar at Main and Battlefield, stripped down naked, and started shooting at passing cars with the twenty-two she had in her purse."

"We were one of the cars," Gage added. "Good thing for all concerned her aim was lousy."

"She caught your shoulder," Fox reminded him.

"She *shot* you?"

Gage smiled easily at Cybil. "Grazed me, and we heal fast. We managed to get the gun from her before she shot anyone else, or got hit by a car as she was standing buck naked in the middle of the street. Then she offered us blow jobs. Rumor was she gave a doozy, but we weren't much in the mood to find out."

"All right, from pattern to theory." Quinn rose to her feet to work it out. "The thing we'll call Twisse, because it's better to have a name for it, requires energy. We're all made up of energy, and Twisse needs it to manifest, to work. When he's out, during this time Dent is unable to hold him, he seeks out the easiest sources of energy first.

Birds and animals, people who are most vulnerable. As he gets stronger, he's able to move up the chain."

"I don't think the way to stop him is to clear out all the pets," Gage began, "ban alcohol, drugs, and sex and make sure everyone gets a good night's sleep."

"Too bad," Cybil tossed back, "because it might buy us some time. Keep going, Q."

"Next question would be, how does he generate the energy he needs?"

"Fear, hate, violence." Cal nodded. "We've got that. We can't cut off his supply because you can't block those emotions out of the population. They exist."

"So do their counterparts, so we can hypothesize that those are weapons or countermeasures against him. You've all gotten stronger over time, and so has he. Maybe he's able to store some of this energy he pulls in during the dormant period."

"And so he's able to start sooner, start stronger the next time. Okay," Cal decided. "Okay, it makes sense."

"He's using some of that store now," Layla put in, "because he doesn't want all six of us to stick this out. He wants to fracture the group before July."

"He must be disappointed." Cybil picked up the wine she'd nursed throughout the discussion. "Knowledge is power and all that, and it's good to have logical theories, more areas to research. But it seems to be we need to move. We need a strategy. Got any, Mr. Strategy?"

From his spot on the floor, Fox grinned. "Yeah. I say as soon as the snow melts enough for us to get through it, we go to the clearing. We go to the Pagan Stone, all of us together. And we double-dog dare the son of a bitch."

IT SOUNDED GOOD IN THEORY. IT WAS A DIFFERENT matter, in Cal's mind, when you added the human factor. When you added Quinn. He'd taken her there once before, and he'd zoned out, leaving her alone and vulnerable.

And he hadn't loved her then.

He knew there was no choice, that there were bigger stakes involved. But the idea of putting her at risk, at deliberately putting her at the center of it with him, kept him awake and restless.

He wandered the house, checking locks, staring out windows for any glimpse of the thing that stalked them. The moon was out, and the snow tinted blue under it. They'd be able to shovel their way out the next day, he thought, dig out the cars. Get back to what passed for normal within a day or two.

He already knew if he asked her to stay, just stay, she'd tell him she couldn't leave Layla and Cybil on their own. He already knew he'd have to let her go.

He couldn't protect her every hour of every day, and if he tried, they'd end up smothering each other.

As he moved through the living room, he saw the glow of the kitchen lights. He headed back to turn them off and check locks. And there was Gage, sitting at the counter playing solitaire with a mug of coffee steaming beside the discard pile.

"A guy who drinks black coffee at one a.m. is going to be awake all night."

"It never keeps me up." Gage flipped a card, made his play. "When I want to sleep, I sleep. You know that. What's your excuse?"

"I'm thinking it's going to be a long, hard, messy hike into the woods even if we wait a month. Which we probably should."

"No. Red six on black seven. You're trying to come up with a way to go in without Quinn. Without any of them, really, but especially the blonde."

"I told you how it was when we went in before."

"And she walked out again on her own two sexy legs. Jack of clubs on queen of diamonds. I'm not worried about her. I'm worried about you."

Cal's back went up. "Is there a time I didn't handle myself?"

"Not up until now. But you've got it bad, Hawkins. You've got it bad for the blonde, and being you, your first and last instinct is going to be to cover her ass if anything goes down."

"Shouldn't it be?" He didn't want any damn coffee, but since he doubted he'd sleep anyway, he poured some. "Why wouldn't it be?"

"I'd lay money that your blonde can handle herself. Doesn't mean you're wrong, Cal. I imagine if I had a woman inside me the way she's inside you, I wouldn't want to put how she handled herself to the test. The trouble is, you're going to have to."

"I never wanted to feel this way," Cal said after a moment. "This is a good part of the reason why. We're good together, Gage."

"I can see that for myself. Don't know what she sees in a loser like you, but it's working for her."

"We could get better. I can feel we'd just get better, make something real and solid. If we had the chance, if we had the time, we'd make something together."

Casually, Gage gathered up the cards, shuffled them with a blur of speed. "You think we're going down this time."

"Yeah." Cal looked out the window at the cold, blue moonlight. "I think we're going down. Don't you?"

"Odds are." Gage dealt them both a hand of blackjack. "But hell, who wants to live forever?"

"That's the problem. Now that I've found Quinn, forever sounds pretty damn good." Cal glanced at his hole card, noted the king to go with his three. "Hit me."

With a grin, Gage flipped over a nine. "Sucker."

Twenty

CAL HOPED FOR A WEEK, TWO IF HE COULD MANage it. And got three days. Nature screwed his plans again, this time shooting temperatures up into the fifties. Mountains of snow melted into hills while the February thaw brought the fun of flash flooding, swollen creeks, and black ice when the thermometer dropped to freezing each night.

But three days after he'd had his lane plowed and the women were back in the house on High Street, the weather stabilized. Creeks ran high, but the ground sucked up most of the runoff. And he was coming up short on excuses to put off the hike to the Pagan Stone.

At his desk, with Lump contentedly sprawled on his back in the doorway, feet in the air, Cal put his mind into work. The winter leagues were winding up, and the spring groups would go into gear shortly. He knew he was on the edge of convincing his father the center would profit from the automatic scoring systems, and wanted to give it one more solid push. If they moved on it soon, they could have the systems up and running for the spring leagues.

They'd want to advertise, run a few specials. They'd have to train the staff, which meant training themselves.

He brought up the spreadsheet for February, noted that the month so far had been solid, even up a bit from last year. He'd use that as more ammunition. Which, of course, his father could and would counter that if they were up the way things were, why change it?

As he was holding the conversation in his head, Cal heard the click that meant a new e-mail had come in. He toggled over, saw Quinn's address.

Hi, Love of My Life,

I didn't want to call in case you were knee-deep in whatever requires you to be knee-deep. Let me know when you're not.

Meanwhile, this is Black's Local Weather Service reporting: Temperatures today should reach a high of forty-eight under partly sunny skies. Lows in the upper thirties. No precipitation is expected. Tomorrow's forecast is for sunny with a high of fifty.

Adding the visual, I can see widening patches of grass in both the front and backyard. Realistically, there's probably more snow, more mud in the woods, but, baby, it's time to saddle up and move out.

My team can be ready bright and early tomorrow and will bring suitable provisions.

Also, Cyb's confirmed the Clark branch connection, and is currently climbing out on some Kinski limbs to verify that. She thinks she may have a line on a couple of possibilities where Ann Hawkins stayed, or at least where she might have gone to give birth. I'll fill you in when I see you.

Let me know, soon as you can, if tomorrow works.

XXOO Quinn.

(I know that whole XXOO thing is dopey, but it seemed more refined than signing off with: I wish you could come over and do me. Even though I do.)

The last part made him smile even though the text of the post had a headache sneaking up the back of his skull.

He could put her off a day or two, and put her off honestly. He couldn't expect Fox to dump his scheduled clients or any court appearances at the snap of a finger, and she'd understand that. But if he were to use that, and his own schedule, he had to do it straight.

With some annoyance, he shot an e-mail to Fox, asking when he could clear time for the trip to the clearing. The annoyance increased when Fox answered back immediately.

Fri's good. Morning's clear, can clear full day if nec.

"Well, fuck." Cal pushed on the ache at the back of his head. Since e-mail wasn't bringing him any luck, he'd go see Quinn in person when he broke for lunch.

AS CAL PREPARED TO CLOSE OUT FOR THE MORNing, Bill Turner stopped in the office doorway.

"Ah, got that toilet fixed in the ladies' room downstairs, and the leak in the freezer was just a hose needed replacing."

"Thanks, Bill." He swung his coat on as he spoke. "I've got a couple of things to do in town. Shouldn't be above an hour."

"Okay, then. I was wondering if, ah . . ." Bill rubbed a hand over his chin, let it drop. "I was wondering if you think Gage'll be coming in, maybe the next day or two. Or if maybe I could, maybe I could run over to your place to have a word with him."

Rock and a hard place, Cal thought, and bought himself some time by adjusting his jacket. "I don't know if he's thinking about dropping by, Bill. He hasn't mentioned it. I think . . . Okay, look, I'd give him some time. I'd just give it some time before you made that first move. I know you want—"

"It's okay. That's okay. Appreciate it."

"Shit," Cal said under his breath as Bill walked away. Then, "Shit, shit, shit," as he headed out himself.

He had to take Gage's side in this, how could he not? He'd seen firsthand what Bill's belt had done to Gage when they'd been kids. And yet, he'd also witnessed, firsthand, the dozens of ways Bill had turned himself around in the last few years.

And, hadn't he just seen the pain, guilt, even the grief on Bill's face just now? So either way he went, Cal knew he was going to feel guilty and annoyed.

He walked straight out and over to Quinn's.

She pulled open the door, yanked him in. Before he could say a word her arms were locked around his neck and her mouth was very busy on his. "I was hoping that was you."

"Good thing it was, because Greg, the UPS guy on this route, might get the wrong idea if you greeted him that way."

"He is kind of cute. Come on back to the kitchen. I'd just come down to do a coffee run. We're all working on various projects upstairs. Did you get my e-mail?"

"Yeah."

"So, we're all set for tomorrow?" She glanced back as she reached up for the coffee.

"No, tomorrow's no good. Fox can't clear his slate until Friday."

"Oh." Her lips moved into a pout, quickly gone. "Okay then, Friday it is. Meanwhile we'll keep reading, researching, working. Cyb thinks she's got a couple of good possibilities on . . . What?" she asked when she got a good look at his face. "What's going on?"

"Okay." He took a couple paces away, then back. "Okay, I'm just going to say it. I don't want you going back in there. Just be quiet a minute, will you?" he said when he saw the retort forming. "I wish there was a way I could stop you from going, that there was a way I could ignore the fact that we all need to go. I know you're a part of this, and I know you have to go back to the Pagan Stone. I know there's going to be more you have to be a part of than I'd wish otherwise. But I can wish you weren't part of this, Quinn, and that you were somewhere safe until this is over. I can want that, just as I know I can't have what I want.

"If you want to be pissed off about that, you'll have to be pissed off."

She waited a beat. "Have you had lunch?"

"No. What does that have to do with anything?"

"I'm going to make you a sandwich—an offer I never make lightly."

"Why are you making it now?"

"Because I love you. Take off your coat. I love that you'd say all that to me," she began as she opened the refrigerator for fixings. "That you'd need to let me know how you felt about it. Now if you'd tried ordering me to stay out of it, if you'd lied or tried to do some sort of end-run around me, I'd feel different. I'd still love you, because that sort of thing sticks with me, but I'd be mad, and more, I'd be disappointed in you. As it is, Cal, I'm finding myself pretty damn pleased and a hell of a lot smug that my head and heart worked so well together and picked the perfect guy. The perfect guy for me."

She cut the sandwich into two tidy triangles, offered it. "Do you want coffee or milk?"

"You don't have milk, you have white water. Coffee'd be fine, thanks." He took a bite of the turkey and Swiss with alfalfa on whole wheat. "Pretty good sandwich."

"Don't get used to the service." She glanced over as she poured out coffee. "We should get an early start on Friday, don't you think? Like dawn?"

"Yeah." He touched her cheek with his free hand. "We'll head in at first light."

SINCE HE'D HAD GOOD LUCK WITH QUINN, AND gotten lunch out of it, Cal decided he was going to speak his mind to Gage next. The minute he and Lump stepped into the house, he smelled food. And when they wandered back, Cal found Gage in the kitchen, taking a pull off a beer as he stirred something in a pot.

"You made food."

"Chili. I was hungry. Fox called. He tells me we're taking the ladies for a hike Friday."

"Yeah. First light."

"Should be interesting."

"Has to be done." Cal dumped out food for Lump before getting a beer of his own. And so, he thought, did this have to be done. "I need to talk to you about your father."

Cal saw Gage close off. Like a switch flipped, a finger snapped, his face simply blanked out. "He works for you; that's your business. I've got nothing to say."

"You've got every right to shut him out. I'm not saying different. I'm letting you know he asks about you. He wants to see you. Look, he's been sober five years now, and if he'd been sober fifty it wouldn't change the way he treated you. But this is a small town, Gage, and you can't dodge him forever. My sense is he's got things to say to you, and you may want to get it done, put it behind you. That's it."

There was a reason Gage made his living at poker. It showed now in a face, a voice, completely devoid of expression. "My sense is you should take yourself out of the middle. I haven't asked you to stand there."

Cal held up a hand for peace. "Fine."

"Sounds like the old man's stuck on Steps Eight and Nine with me. He can't make amends on this, Cal. I don't give a damn about his amends."

"Okay. I'm not trying to convince you otherwise. Just letting you know."

"Now I know."

IT OCCURRED TO CAL WHEN HE STOOD AT THE window on Friday morning, watching the headlights cut through the dim predawn, that it had been almost a month exactly since Quinn had first driven up to his house.

How could so much have happened? How could so much have changed in such a short time?

It had been slightly less than that month since he'd led her into the woods the first time. When he'd led her to the Pagan Stone.

In those short weeks of the shortest month he'd learned it wasn't only himself and his two blood brothers who were destined to face this threat. There were three women now, equally involved.

And he was completely in love with one of them.

He stood just as he was to watch her climb out of Fox's truck. Her bright hair spilled out from under the dark watch cap. She wore a bold red jacket and scarred hiking boots. He could see the laugh on her face as she said something to Cybil, and her breath whisked out in clouds in the early morning chill.

She knew enough to be afraid, he understood that. But she refused to allow fear to dictate her moves. He hoped he could say the same as he had more to risk now. He had her.

He stood watch until he heard Fox use his key to unlock the front door, then Cal went down to join them, and to gather his things for the day.

Fog smoked the ground that the cold had hardened like stone overnight. By midday, Cal knew the path would be sloppy again, but for now it was quick and easy going.

There were still pockets and lumpy hills of snow, and he identified the hoofprints of the deer that roamed the woods, to Layla's delight. If any of them were nervous, they hid it well, at least on this first leg of the hike.

It was so different from that long-ago day in July when he and Fox and Gage had made this trip. No boom box pumping out rap or heavy metal, no snacks of Little Debbies, no innocent, youthful excitement of a stolen day, and the night to come.

None of them had ever been so innocent again.

He caught himself lifting a hand to his face, where his glasses used to slide down the bridge of his nose.

"How you doing, Captain?" Quinn stepped up to match her pace to his, gave him a light arm bump.

"Okay. I was just thinking about that day. Everything hot and green, Fox hauling that stupid boom box. My mother's lemonade, snack cakes."

"Sweat rolling," Fox continued from just behind him.

"We're coming up on Hester's Pool," Gage said, breaking the memory.

The water made Cal think of quicksand rather than the cool and forbidden pool he and his friends had leaped into so long ago. He could imagine going in now, being sucked in, deeper and deeper until he never saw light again.

They stopped as they had before, but now it was coffee instead of lemonade.

"There's been deer here, too." Layla pointed at the ground. "Those are deer prints, right?"

"Some deer," Fox confirmed. "Raccoon." He took her arm to turn her, pointed to the prints on the ground.

"Raccoons?" Grinning, she bent to take a closer look. "What else might be in here?"

"Some of my namesakes, wild turkey, now and then—though mostly north of here—you might see bear."

She straightened quickly. "Bear."

"Mostly north," he repeated, but found it as good an excuse as any to take her hand.

Cybil crouched by the edge of the pool, stared at the water.

"A little cold to think about taking a dip," Gage told her.

"Hester drowned herself here." She glanced up, then looked over at Cal. "And when you went in that day, you saw her."

"Yeah. Yeah, I saw her."

"And you and Quinn have both seen her in your heads. Layla's dreamed of her, vividly. So . . . maybe I can get something."

"I thought yours was precog, not the past," Cal began.

"It is, but I still get vibes from people, from places that

are strong enough to send them out. How about you?" She looked back at Gage. "We might stir up more in tandem. Are you up for that?"

Saying nothing, he held out a hand. She took it, rose to her feet. Together, they stared at that still, brown surface.

The water began to beat and froth. It began to spin, to spew up white-tipped waves. It roared like a sea mating with a wild and vicious storm.

And a hand shot out to claw at the ground.

Hester pulled herself out of that churning water—bone white skin, a mass of wet, tangled hair, dark, glassy eyes. The effort, or her madness, peeled her lips back from her teeth.

Cybil heard herself scream as Hester Deale's arms opened, as they locked around her and dragged her toward that swirling brown pool.

"Cyb! Cyb! Cybil!"

She came back struggling, and found herself locked not in Hester's arms, but Gage's. "What the hell was that?"

"You were going in."

She stayed where she was, feeling her heart hammer against his as Quinn gripped her shoulder. Cybil took another look at the still surface of the pool. "That would've been really unpleasant."

She was trembling, one hard jolt after the next, but Gage had to give her points for keeping her voice even.

"Did you get anything?" she asked him.

"Water kicked up; she came up. You started to tip."

"She grabbed me. She . . . embraced me. That's what I think, but I wasn't focused enough to feel or sense what she felt. Maybe if we tried it again—"

"We've got to get moving now," Cal interrupted.

"It only took a minute."

"Try nearly fifteen," Fox corrected.

"But . . ." Cybil eased back from Gage when she realized she was still in his arms. "Did it seem that long to you?"

"No. It was immediate."

"It wasn't." Layla held out another thermos lid of coffee. "We were arguing about whether we should pull you back, and how we should if we did. Quinn said to leave you be for another few minutes, that sometimes it took you a while to warm up."

"Well, it felt like a minute, no more than, for the whole deal. And it didn't feel like something from before." Again, Cybil looked at Gage.

"No, it didn't. So if I were you, I wouldn't think about taking a dip anytime soon."

"I prefer a nice blue pool, with a swim-up bar."

"Bikini margaritas." Quinn rubbed her hand up and down Cybil's arm.

"Spring break, two thousand." Cybil caught Quinn's hand, squeezed. "I'm fine, Q."

"I'll buy the first round of those margaritas when this is done. Ready to move on?" Cal asked.

He hitched up his pack, turned. Then shook his head. "This isn't right."

"We're leaving the haunted pool to walk through the demonic woods." Quinn worked up a smile. "What could be wrong?"

"That's not the path." He gestured toward the thawing track. "That's not the direction." He squinted up at the sun as he pulled his old Boy Scout compass out of his pocket.

"Ever thought about upgrading to a GPS?" Gage asked him.

"This does the job. See, we need to head west from here. That trail's leading north. That trail shouldn't even be there."

"It's not there." Fox's eyes narrowed, darkened. "There's no trail, just underbrush, a thicket of wild blackberries. It's not real." He shifted, angled himself. "It's that way." He gestured west. "It's hard to see, it's like looking through mud, but . . ."

Layla stepped forward, took his hand.

"Okay, yeah. That's better."

"You're pointing at a really big-ass tree," Cybil told him.

"That isn't there." Still holding Layla's hand, Fox walked forward. The image of the large oak broke apart as he walked through it.

"Nice trick." Quinn let out a breath. "So, Twisse doesn't want us to go to the clearing. I'll take point."

"I'll take point." Cal took her arm to tug her behind him. "I've got the compass." He had only to glance back at his friends to have them falling in line. Fox taking center, Gage the rear with the women between.

As soon as the track widened enough to allow it, Quinn moved up beside Cal. "This is the way it has to work." She glanced back to see the other women had followed her lead, and now walked abreast with their partners. "We're linked up this way, Cal. Two-by-two, trios, the group of six. Whatever the reasons are, that's the way it is."

"We're walking into something. I can't see what it is, but I'm walking you and the others right into it."

"We're all on our own two feet, Cal." She passed him the bottle of water she carried in her coat pocket. "I don't know if I love you because you're Mr. Responsibility or in spite of it."

"As long as you do. And since you do, maybe we should think about the idea of getting married."

"I like the idea," she said after a moment. "If you want my thoughts on it."

"I do." Stupid, he thought, stupid way to propose, and a ridiculous place for it, too. Then again, when they couldn't be sure what was around the bend, it made sense to grab what you did now, tight and quick. "As it happens, I agree with you. More thoughts on the idea would be that my mother, especially, will want the splash—big deal, big party, bells and whistles."

"I happen to agree with that, too. How is she with communication by phone and/or e-mail?"

"She's all about that."

"Great. I'll hook her up with my mother and they can go for it. How's your September schedule?"

"September?"

She studied the winter woods, watched a squirrel scamper up a tree and across a thick branch. "I bet the Hollow's beautiful in September. Still green, but with just a hint of the color to come."

"I was thinking sooner. Like April, or May." Before, Cal thought. Before July, and what might be the end of everything he knew and loved.

"It takes a while to organize those bells and whistles." When she looked at him he understood she read him clearly. "After, Cal, after we've won. One more thing to celebrate. When we're—"

She broke off when he touched a finger to her lips.

The sound came clearly now as all movement and conversation stopped. The wet and throaty snarl rolled across the air, and shot cold down the spine. Lump curled down on his haunches and whined.

"He hears it, too, this time." Cal shifted, and though the movement was slight, it put Quinn between him and Fox.

"I don't guess we could be lucky, and that's just a bear." Layla cleared her throat. "Either way, I think we should keep moving. Whatever it is doesn't want us to, so . . ."

"We're here to flip it the bird," Fox finished.

"Come on, Lump, come on with me."

The dog shivered at Cal's command, but rose, and with its side pressed to Cal's legs, walked down the trail toward the Pagan Stone.

The wolf—Cal would never have referred to the thing as a dog—stood at the mouth of the clearing. It was huge and black, with eyes that were somehow human. Lump tried a halfhearted snarl in answer to the low, warning growl, then cowered against Cal.

"Are we going to walk through that, too?" Gage asked from the rear.

"It's not like the false trail." Fox shook his head. "It's not real, but it's there."

"Okay." Gage started to pull off his pack.

And the thing leaped.

It seemed to fly, Cal thought, a mass of muscle and teeth. He fisted his hands to defend, but there was nothing to fight.

"I felt . . ." Slowly, Quinn lowered the arms she'd thrown up to protect her face.

"Yeah. Not just the cold, not that time." Cal gripped her arm to keep her close. "There was weight, just for a second, and there was substance."

"We never had that before, not even during the Seven." Fox scanned the woods on both sides. "Whatever form Twisse took, whatever we saw, it wasn't really *there*. It's always been mind games."

"If it can solidify, it can hurt us directly," Layla pointed out.

"And be hurt." From behind her Gage pulled a 9mm Glock out of his pack.

"Good thinking," was Cybil's cool opinion.

"Jesus Christ, Gage, where the hell did you get that?"

Gage lifted his eyebrows at Fox. "Guy I know down in D.C. Are we going to stand here in a huddle, or are we going in?"

"Don't point that at anybody," Fox demanded.

"Safety's on."

"That's what they always say before they accidentally blow a hole in the best friend."

They stepped into the clearing, and the stone.

"My God, it's beautiful." Cybil breathed the words reverently as she moved toward it. "It can't possibly be a natural formation, it's too perfect. It's designed, and for worship, I'd think. And it's warm. Feel it. The stone's warm." She circled it. "Anyone with any sensitivity has to feel, has to know this is sacred ground."

"Sacred to who?" Gage countered. "Because what came up out of here twenty-one years ago wasn't all bright and friendly."

"It wasn't all dark either. We felt both." Cal looked at Fox. "We saw both."

"Yeah. It's just the big, black scary mass got most of our attention while we were being blasted off our feet."

"But the other gave us most of his, that's what I think. I walked out of here not only without a scratch, but with twenty-twenty vision and a hell of an immune system."

"The scratches on my arms had healed up, and the bruiscs from my most recent tussle with Napper." Fox shrugged. "Never been sick a day since."

"How about you?" Cybil asked Gage. "Any miraculous healing?"

"None of us had a mark on him after the blast," Cal began.

"It's no deal, Cal. No secrets from the team. My old man used his belt on me the night before we were heading in here. A habit of his when he'd get a drunk on. I was carrying the welts when I came in, but not when I walked out."

"I see." Cybil held Gage's eyes for several beats. "The fact that you were given protection, and your specific abilities, enabled you to defend your ground, so to speak. Otherwise, you'd have been three helpless little boys."

"It's clean." Layla's comment had everyone turning to where she stood by the stone. "That's what comes to my mind. I don't think it was ever used for sacrifice. Not blood and death, not for the dark. It feels clean."

"I've seen the blood on it," Gage said. "I've seen it burn. I've heard the screams."

"That's not its purpose. Maybe that's what Twisse wants." Quinn laid her palm on the stone. "To defile it, to twist its power. If he can, well, he'll own it, won't he? Cal?"

"Okay." His hand hovered over hers. "Ready?" At her nod, he joined his hand to hers on the stone.

At first there was only her, only Quinn. Only the courage in her eyes. Then the world tumbled back, five years, twenty, so that he saw the boy he'd been with his friends, scoring his knife over their wrists to bind them together. Then rushing back, decades, centuries, to the blaze and the screams while the stone stood cool and white in the midst of hell.

Back to another waning winter where Giles Dent stood with Ann Hawkins as he stood with Quinn now. Dent's words came from his lips.

"We have only until summer. This I cannot change, even for you. Duty outstrips even my love for you, and for the lives we have made." He touched a hand to her belly. "I wish, above all, that I could be with you when they come into the world."

"Let me stay. Beloved."

"I am the guardian. You are the hope. I cannot destroy the beast, only chain it for a time. Still, I do not leave you. It is not death, but an endless struggle, a war only I can wage. Until what comes from us makes the end. They will have all I can give, this I swear to you. If they are victorious in their time, I will be with you again."

"What will I tell them of their father?"

"That he loved their mother, and them, with the whole of his heart."

"Giles, it has a man's form. A man can bleed, a man can die."

"It is not a man, and it is not in my power to destroy it. That will be for those who come after us both. It, too, will make its own. Not through love. They will not be what it intends. It cannot own them if they are beyond its reach, even its ken. This is for me to do. I am not the first, Ann, only the last. What comes from us is the future."

She pressed a hand to her side. "They quicken," she whispered. "When, Giles, when will it end? All the lives we have lived before, all the joy and the pain we have known? When will there be peace for us?"

"Be my heart." He lifted her hands to his lips. "I will be your courage. And we will find each other once more."

Tears slid down Quinn's cheeks even as she felt the images fade. "We're all they have. If we don't find the way, they're lost to each other. I felt her heart breaking inside me."

"He believed in what he'd done, what he had to do. He believed in us, though he couldn't see it clearly. I don't think he could see us, all of us," Cal said as he looked around. "Not clearly. He took it on faith."

"Fine for him." Gage shifted his weight. "But I put a little more of mine in this Glock."

It wasn't the wolf, but the boy that stood on the edge of the clearing. Grinning, grinning. He lifted his hands, showed fingernails that were sharpened to claws.

The sun dimmed from midday to twilight; the air from cool to frigid. And thunder rumbled in the late winter sky.

In a lightning move so unexpected Cal couldn't prevent it, Lump sprang. The thing who masked as a boy squealed with laughter, shinnied up a tree like a monkey.

But Cal had seen it, in a flash of an instant. He'd seen the shock, and what might have been fear.

"Shoot it," Cal shouted to Gage, even as he dashed forward to grab Lump's collar. "Shoot the son of a bitch."

"Jesus, you don't actually think a bullet's going to—"

Over Fox's objection, Gage fired. Without hesitation, he aimed for the boy's heart.

The bullet cracked the air, struck the tree. This time no one could miss the look of shock on the boy's face. His howl of pain and fury gushed across the clearing and shook the ground.

With ruthless purpose, Gage emptied the clip into it.

It changed. It grew. It twisted itself into something massive and black and sinuous that rose over Cal as he stood his ground, fighting to hold back his dog, who strained and barked like a mad thing.

The stench of it, the *cold* of it hammered down on him like stones. "We're still here," Cal shouted. "This is our place, and you can go to hell."

He staggered against a blast of sound and slapping air.

"Better reload, Deadeye," Cybil commanded.

"Knew I should've bought a howitzer." But Gage slapped in a full clip.

"This isn't your place," Cal shouted again. The wind threatened to knock him off his feet, seemed to tear at his clothes and his skin like a thousand knives. Through the scream of it, he heard the crack of gunfire, and the rage it spewed out clamped on his throat like claws.

Then Quinn braced against his side. And Fox shouldered in at his other. They formed a line, all six.

"This," Cal called out, "is ours. Our place and our time. You couldn't have my dog, and you can't have my town."

"So fuck off," Fox suggested, and bending picked up a rock. He hurled it, a straightaway fast ball.

"Hello, got a gun here."

Fox's grin at Gage was wild and wide as the feral wind battered them. "Throwing rocks is an insult. It'll undermine its confidence."

Die here!

It wasn't a voice, but a tidal wave of sound and wind that knocked them to the ground, scattered them like bowling pins.

"Undermine, my ass." Gage shoved to his knees and began firing again.

"You'll die here." Cal spoke coolly as the others took Fox's tack and began to hurl stones and sticks.

Fire swept across the clearing, its flames like shards of ice. Smoke belched up in fetid clouds as it roared its outrage.

"You'll die here," Cal repeated. Pulling his knife from its sheath, he rushed foward to plunge it into the boiling black mass.

It screamed. He thought it screamed, thought the sound held something of pain as well as fury. The shock of power sang up his arm, stabbed through him like a blade, twin edges of scorching heat and impossible cold. It flung him away, sent him flying through the smoke like a pebble from a sling. Breathless, bones jarred from the fall, Cal scrambled to his feet.

"You'll die here!" This time he shouted it as he gripped the knife, as he charged forward.

The thing that was a wolf, a boy, a man, a demon looked at him with eyes of hate.

And vanished.

"But not today." The fire died, the smoke cleared as he bent over to suck in air. "Anybody hurt? Is everybody okay? Quinn. Hey, Lump, hey." He nearly toppled backward when Lump leaped up, paws on shoulders to lap his face.

"Your nose is bleeding." Scurrying over on her hands and knees, Quinn gripped his arm to pull herself to her feet. "Cal." Her hands rushed over his face, his body. "Oh God, Cal. I've never seen anything so brave, or so goddamn stupid."

"Yeah, well." In a defiant move, he swiped at the blood. "It pissed me off. If that was its best shot, it fell way short."

"It didn't dish out anything a really big drink and a long hot bath won't cure," Cybil decided. "Layla? Okay?"

"Okay." Face fierce, Layla brushed at her stinging cheeks. "Okay." She took Fox's outstretched hand and got to her feet. "We scared it. We scared it, and it ran away."

"Even better. We hurt it." Quinn took a couple shuddering breaths, then much as Lump had, leaped at Cal. "We're all right. We're all okay. You were amazing. You were beyond belief. Oh God, God, give me a really big kiss."

As she laughed and wept, he took her mouth. He held her close, understanding that of all the answers they needed, for him she was the first.

They weren't going down this time, he realized.

"We're going to win this." He drew her away so he could look into her eyes. His were calm, steady, and clear. "I never believed it before, not really. But I do now. I know it now. Quinn." He pressed his lips to her forehead. "We're going to win this, and we're getting married in September."

"Damn straight."

When she wrapped around him again, it was victory enough for now. It was enough to stand on until the next time. And the next time, he determined, they'd be better armed.

"Let's go home. It's a long walk back, and we've got a hell of a lot to do."

She held on another moment, held tight while he looked over her head into the eyes of his brothers. Gage nodded, then shoved the gun back in his pack. Swinging it on, he crossed the clearing to the path beyond.

The sun bloomed overhead, and the wind died. They walked out of the clearing, through the winter woods, three men, three women, and a dog.

On its ground the Pagan Stone stood silent, waiting for their return.

Hawkins Hollow
June 1994

ON A BRIGHT SUMMER MORNING, A TEACUP poodle drowned in the Bestlers' backyard swimming pool. At first, Lynne Bestler, who'd gone out to sneak in a solitary swim before her kids woke, thought it was a dead squirrel. Which would've been bad enough. But when she steeled herself to scoop out the tangle of fur with the net, she recognized her neighbor's beloved Marcell.

Squirrels generally didn't wear rhinestone collars.

Her shouts, and the splash as Lynne tossed the hapless dog, net and all, back into the pool, brought Lynne's husband rushing out in his boxers. Their mother's sobs and their father's curses as he jumped in to grab the pole and tow the body to the side, woke the Bestler twins, who stood screaming in their matching My Little Pony nightgowns. Within moments, the backyard hysteria had neighbors hurrying to fences just as Bestler dragged himself and his burden out of the water. As, like many men, Bestler had developed an attachment to ancient underwear, the weight of the water was too much for the worn elastic.

So Bestler came out of his pool with a dead dog, and no boxers.

The bright summer morning in the little town of Hawkins Hollow began with shock, grief, farce, and drama.

Fox learned of Marcell's untimely death minutes after he stepped into Ma's Pantry to pick up a sixteen-ounce bottle of Coke and a couple of Slim Jims.

He'd copped a quick break from working with his father on a kitchen remodel down Main Street. Mrs. Larson wanted new countertops, cabinet doors, new floors, new paint. She called it freshening things up, and Fox called it a way to earn enough money to take Allyson Brendon out for pizza and the movies on Saturday night. He hoped to use that gateway to talk her into the backseat of his ancient VW Bug.

He didn't mind working with his dad. He hoped to hell he wouldn't spend the rest of his life swinging a hammer or running a power saw, but he didn't mind it. His father's company was always easy, and the job got Fox out of gardening and animal duty on their little farm. It also provided easy access to Cokes and Slim Jims—two items which would never, never be found in the O'Dell-Barry household.

His mother ruled there.

So he heard about the dog from Susan Keefaffer, who rang up his purchases while a few people with nothing better to do on a June afternoon sat at the counter over coffee and gossip.

He didn't know Marcell, but Fox had a soft spot for animals, so he suffered a twist of grief for the unfortunate poodle. That was leavened somewhat by the idea of Mr. Bestler, whom he *did* know, standing "naked as a jaybird," in Susan Keefaffer's words, beside his backyard pool.

While it made Fox sad to imagine some poor dog drowning in a swimming pool, he didn't connect it—not then—to the nightmare he and his two closest friends had lived through seven years before.

He'd had a dream the night before, a dream of blood

and fire, of voices chanting in a language he didn't understand. But then he'd watched a double feature of videos—*The Night of the Living Dead* and *The Texas Chainsaw Massacre*—with his friends Cal and Gage.

He didn't connect a dead French poodle with the dream, or with what had burned through Hawkins Hollow for a week after his tenth birthday. After the night he and Cal and Gage had spent at the Pagan Stone in Hawkins Wood—and everything had changed for them, and for the Hollow.

In a few weeks he and Cal and Gage would all turn seventeen—and that was on his mind. Baltimore had a damn good chance at a pennant this year, so that was on his mind. He'd be going back to high school as a senior, which meant top of the food chain at last, and planning for college.

What occupied a sixteen-year-old boy was considerably different than what occupied a ten-year-old. Including rounding third and heading for home with Allyson Brendon.

So when he walked back down the street, a lean boy not quite beyond the gangly stage of adolescence, his dense brown hair tied back in a stubby tail, golden brown eyes shaded with Oakleys, it was, for him, just another ordinary day.

The town looked as it always did. Tidy, a little old-timey, with the old stone townhouses or shops, the painted porches, the high curbs. He glanced back over his shoulder toward the Bowl-a-Rama on the square. It was the biggest building in town, and where Cal and Gage were both working.

When he and his father knocked off for the day, he thought, he'd head on up, see what was happening.

He crossed over to the Larson place, walked into the unlocked house where Bonnie Raitt's smooth Delta blues slid smoothly out of the kitchen. His father sang along with her in his clear and easy voice as he checked the level on the shelves Mrs. Larson wanted in her utility closet. Though the windows and back door were open to their screens, the room smelled of sawdust, sweat, and the glue they'd used that morning to lay the new Formica.

His father worked in old Levi's and his Give Peace a Chance T-shirt. His hair was six inches longer than Fox's, worn in a tail under a blue bandanna. He'd shaved off the beard and mustache he'd had as long as Fox remembered. Fox still wasn't quite used to seeing so much of his father's face—or so much of himself in it.

"A dog drowned in the Bestlers' swimming pool over on Laurel Lane," Fox told him, and Brian stopped working to turn.

"That's a damn shame. Anybody know how it happened?"

"Not really. It was one of those little poodles, so think it must've fallen in, then it couldn't get out again."

"You'd think somebody would've heard it barking. That's a lousy way to go." Brian set down his tools, smiled at his boy. "Gimme one of those Slim Jims."

"What Slim Jims?"

"The ones you've got in your back pocket. You're not carrying a bag, and you weren't gone long enough to scarf down Hostess Pies or Twinkies. I'm betting you're packing the Jims. I get one, and your mom never has to know we ate chemicals and meat by-products. It's called blackmail, kid of mine."

Fox snorted, pulled them out. He'd bought two for just this purpose. Father and son unwrapped, bit off, chewed in perfect harmony. "The counter looks good, Dad."

"Yeah, it does." Brian ran a hand over the smooth, eggshell surface. "Mrs. Larson's not much for color, but it's good work. I don't know who I'm going to get to be my lapdog when you head off to college."

"Ridge is next in line," Fox said, thinking of his younger brother.

"Ridge wouldn't keep measurements in his head for two minutes running, and he'd probably cut off a finger dreaming while he was using a band saw. No." Brian smiled, shrugged. "This kind of work isn't for Ridge, or for you, for that matter. Or either of your sisters. I guess I'm going to have to rent a kid to get one who wants to work with wood."

"I never said I didn't want to." Not out loud.

His father looked at him the way he sometimes did, as if he saw more than what was there. "You've got a good eye, you've got good hands. You'll be handy around your own house once you get one. But you won't be strapping on a tool belt to make a living. Until you figure out just what it is you want, you can haul these scraps on out to the Dumpster."

"Sure." Fox gathered up scraps, trash, began to cart them out the back, across the narrow yard to the Dumpster the Larsons had rented for the duration of the remodel.

He glanced toward the adjoining yard and the sound of kids playing. And the armload he carried thumped and bounced on the ground as his body went numb.

The little boys played with trucks and shovels and pails in a bright blue sandbox. But it wasn't filled with sand. Blood covered their bare arms as they pushed their Tonka trucks through the muck inside the box. He stumbled back as the boys made engine sounds, as red lapped over the bright blue sides and dripped onto the green grass.

On the fence between the yards, where hydrangeas headed up toward bloom, crouched a boy that wasn't a boy. He bared its teeth in a grin as Fox backed toward the house.

"Dad! Dad!"

The tone, the breathless fear had Brian rushing outside. "What? What is it?"

"Don't you—can't you see?" But even as he said it, as he pointed, something inside Fox knew. It wasn't real.

"What?" Firmly now, Brian took his son's shoulders. "What do you see?"

The boy that wasn't a boy danced along the top of the chain-link fence while flames spurted up below and burned the hydrangeas to cinders.

"I have to go. I have to go see Cal and Gage. Right now, Dad. I have to—"

"Go." Brian released his hold on Fox, stepped back. He didn't question. "Go."

He all but flew through the house and out again, up the sidewalk to the square. The town no longer looked as it usually did to him. In his mind's eye Fox could see it as it had been that horrible week in July seven years before.

Fire and blood, he remembered, thinking of the dream.

He burst into the Bowl-a-Rama, where the summer afternoon leagues were in full swing. The thunder of balls, the crash of pins pounded in his head as he ran straight to the front desk where Cal worked.

"Where's Gage?" Fox demanded.

"Jesus, what's up with you?"

"Where's Gage?" Fox repeated, and Cal's amused gray eyes sobered. "Working the arcade. He's . . . he's coming out now."

At Cal's quick signal, Gage sauntered over. "Hello, ladies. What . . ." The smirk died after one look at Fox's face. "What happened?"

"It's back," Fox said. "It's come back."